FIC
Hose
Win.2
W9-BFV-340
39098082293019
Hungry ghosts : a novel

HUNGRY GHOSTS

ALSO BY KEVIN JARED HOSEIN

The Repenters

The Beast of Kukuyo

HUNGRY GHOSTS

A Novel

KEVIN JARED HOSEIN

ecco

An Imprint of HarperCollins*Publishers*

This is a work of fiction. Names, characters, places, and incidents are products of the author's imagination or are used fictitiously and are not to be construed as real. Any resemblance to actual events, locales, organizations, or persons, living or dead, is entirely coincidental.

HUNGRY GHOSTS. Copyright © 2022 by Kevin Jared Hosein. All rights reserved. Printed in the United States of America. No part of this book may be used or reproduced in any manner whatsoever without written permission except in the case of brief quotations embodied in critical articles and reviews. For information, address HarperCollins Publishers, 195 Broadway, New York, NY 10007.

HarperCollins books may be purchased for educational, business, or sales promotional use. For information, please email the Special Markets Department at SPsales@harpercollins.com.

Ecco® and HarperCollins® are trademarks of HarperCollins Publishers.

Originally published in Great Britain in 2022 by Bloomsbury Publishing.

FIRST U.S. EDITION

Frontispiece © Aleksandr Matveev/stock.adobe.com

Library of Congress Cataloging-in-Publication Data has been applied for.

ISBN 978-0-06-321338-8

23 24 25 26 27 LBC 5 4 3 2 1

For the ancestors
and everything they grew.

'Without doubt, all kings, O son,
must once behold hell.'

The Mahābhārata

Main Players

Hansraj Saroop (Hans).
Shweta – His wife.
Krishna – Their son.
Tarak – Their nephew.
Dalton Changoor – A prosperous man.
Marlee Changoor – His wife.

Dolly – Neighbour to Hansraj and Shweta.
Umesh – Her husband, deceased.
Lata – Their daughter.
Mandeep – Tarak's father. Hansraj's older brother.
Tansi – His wife, deceased.
Kalawatie & Teeluck – An older couple in the barracks.
Rookmin & Murali – Another older couple.
Niala – Their pregnant daughter.
Sachin – Their son.
White Lady – The barrack dog.

Rudra & Rustam Lakhan – Twins with a bloodstained past.
Bhagran Lakhan – Their father, deceased.

Baig & Robinson – Men under Changoor's employ.
DSP Badree – A lawman from Bell Village.
Mikey & Dylan – His sons.

I

A Gate to Hell

Sometime in the 1940s, Trinidad

Four boys ventured to the river to perform a blood oath. Two brothers and two cousins. The brothers were twins, both fifteen; the cousins, fourteen and thirteen. They passed around a boning knife, making clean cuts across their palms. The blood bubbled to the surface like their veins were boiling. They let the blood drip into a stolen bottle of cow's milk. They drank, passing the bottle around until all was gone. Then they hugged each other, a minute at a time, holding on tight as if the world were ending. When it was over, the rains came down so hard that the four boys thought the clouds would fall as well. The force of the water stung the wounds and washed them clean.

'Gonna have nothin more important than this,' the twins told the cousins.

The older brother christened their union with a name: *Corbeau*, for the large vulture, a carrion feeder, a bird that stays alive by seeking the dead.

Why not an ibis? Or a kingfisher? Or a peacock?

Because a corbeau will always be a corbeau, even if it trades its black feathers for a peacock's. It must eat corpses for breakfast, knowing to savour bowels and maggoty flesh, realising those too are meals fit for kings. For what is a king but one who is nourished by his kingdom? One that circles overhead, making his presence known. A corbeau will always be a corbeau – hated by the world that it will eventually eat.

The youngest boy was reluctant to identify with the scavenger bird until hearing it put like that. He was an only child, frail but uncommonly precocious. Large intelligent eyes. His nose deep in old, crumpled magazines. The frown of an old holy man in these troubling times. Skin so fair that the elders had said it was touched by the goddess Radha. He once had hair like a wild child, a haven of lice. Never wanted it combed. Ruffled it and teased it back out if anyone did.

This boy's name was Krishna Saroop.

Krishna was from a family of three.

The father, Hans, was in his early thirties. Sunkissed skin. Palms like pressed leather. He had eyes that smiled. The remnants of his marasmic childhood still perceptible. Sometimes his limbs seemed more spindly than they really were. But when he laboured in the canefields, he was as handsome and strong and spirited as the war god Subrahmanya. Worked hard his whole life for a pittance. Enough for a dust of flour from the Chinese merchants, some *Bermudez* biscuits and a scoop of ghee. And made do with it. For the past year, he'd worked on the Changoor estate, where he built fences and repaired doors and maintained the land. His job description changed every week because he could do everything.

The mother, Shweta, had sunken eyes that made her look as if she were always fighting slumber. A sturdy backbone and skin dark as the tilled earth. A stud on her left nostril to keep her from outside seduction. Always wore simple white cotton dresses that stopped midcalf, her muslin dupatta slung like a sash. When she saw her son in the morning, the flex in her cheeks became prominent. She kept a bandhania garden in a barrel trough. A few tulsi sprouts had inveigled their way in there over time. She let them be – things pushed themselves into life whether you liked them or not. It'd still be dark when she woke up to cook roti at the clay chulha using the firewood that her husband gathered on the weekends. On a good day, she would make pumpkin tarkari. Nothing was ever wasted. All left behind was used as fish bait. Life sprung from detritus. Bright pink lotuses in night soil.

The three lived in a sugarcane estate barrack. These barracks were scattered like half-buried bones across the plain, strewn from their colonial corpse. In their marrow, the ghosts of the indentured. And the offspring of those ghosts. This particular barrack sat by its lonesome, raw and jagged as a yanked tooth in the paragrass-spangled stretch of meadow, beyond the canefield, beyond the rice paddies, the village proper and the sugar mill – in a corner where God had to squint to see. Neighbour to nothing. One donkey-cart ride away from the closest dry goods store.

This, a place of lesser lives. A tangle of wood and iron that seemed to slightly shift shape every time a strong wind galloped over it. There was a communal yard for cooking and drinking and fighting. Inside, five families and five rooms, ten-by-ten-feet. Between each were cracked wooden partitions that didn't go all the way up. The cold earthen ground. Clothes stitched from old flour bags. Coconut fibre mattresses, permanently depressed, topped with pillows stuffed with sugarcane tassels. The macadam roads here had no names. Only distinguished by the frequency of their fractures.

Here, the snakes' calls blurred with the primeval hiss of wind through the plants. Picture *en plein air*, all shades of green soaked with vermilion and red and purple and ochre. Picture what the good people call fever grass, wild caraille, shining bush, timaries, tecomarias, bois gris, bois canot, christophene, chenet, moko, moringa, pommerac, pommecythere, barbadine, barhar. Humanity as ants on the savannah. Picture curry leaves springing into helices; mangroves cross-legged in the decanted swamp; bastions of sugarcane bowing and sprawled even and remote; the spoiled smell of sulphate of ammonia somewhere in there; pink hearts of caladium that beat and bounce between burnt thatches of bird cucumber – all lain like tufts and bristles and pelages upon the back of some buried colossus. The Churchill–Roosevelt Highway sliced that colossus in half. On one side, the belief of bush and burlap and sohari and jute and rattan and thatch and tapia. On the other was Bell Village, the dogma of a new world, howling and preaching steel and diesel and rayon and vinyl and gypsum and triple-glazed glass.

Trinidad had been killed, and now it was to be resurrected.

In Bell, the Presbyterian church stood broad as a gunslinger in a silent face-off with the temple's kaleidoscope of jhandi flags. A slow, evangelic takeover. Every week, one fewer bamboo pole and one more shilling on the offering plate, brass stained with the blood of Christ. The crucifix and the steeple so dappled in birdshit that they had merged with the mortar. The shadow of the sugar mill black like molasses. Chipped millhouses like firebombed rubble. The silos visible in the distance – tall, domed, phallic. The love children of industrialists and missionaries. England, Canada, Holland, Courland, wherever – you made sure to call them *sahib* or *sir.* Though most of them knew now that their time was almost up. Elephants marching to the graveyard.

The schoolhouse was modelled after the church.

Krishna was the only child in the barrack enrolled there. Despised it. They cut his hair. His classmates were all from Bell. Despised them all. Some were Hindu at home but Presbyterian at school. Not him. One cannot be both, is what he thought. You must choose one. Only a fool would spread his soul thin. For Christmas, the Nova Scotia missionaries and their wives brought gifts. To the boy on his right, a toy locomotive. The girl to his left, a Little Traveler's sewing kit. Her little brother, a Mother Goose colouring book and a packet of jumbo crayons. And for Krishna, a chewed pencil and a Bible, which found good use as wrapping paper for fish.

The teachers wore thick jackets in the hot sun and seemed to become aroused when they put their tamarind whips to use – each one ascribed a Biblical moniker. Gomorrah. Rapture. Revelations. A few children were whipped harder than others, Krishna among them. The boy didn't know what 'Elegy Written in a Country Churchyard' had to do with him, yet knew the first three stanzas by heart.

He had no friends at school. He was the oldest in his class because of his late start. A small group of his classmates turned the others against him when he gave the girls lice. He was pestered incessantly, the taunting maddening, like a heightening tinnitus. They spread the word that he still lived in a barrack because his grandpa loved rum more than his children. Because nobody in his family could spell their own names. Because none of them could add without using their fingers and toes. They told the class that he drank the same pondwater that the goats squatted in. That spiders nested in his food and cockroaches crawled into his nostrils at night. That he stank of his father's semen, because his father took his mother in front of him – and that he daydreamed of joining in. It was hard for him to hear those things – as some of them were true.

After school one evening, those same boys from his class kicked him down and took turns spitting on his head. It hadn't been the first time. But this time, he would not stand for it. He had the bold blood of his companions running through him. Something had gotten into him since then. The promise of a blood oath. Corbeau blood. He pictured himself as the scorned bird. Enough was enough.

And later that evening, while these classmates bathed in the river, he and his companions put dogshit in their shoes. Things escalated from there. They hurled rocks at each other. Skirmished, fists to cheeks, hands to throats. Fought like they had been rivals since the beginning of time.

Krishna enlisted his cousin, Tarak, to get revenge. A tall boy made even taller as he kept his long hair bundled high and bristly, like the crown of a pineapple. He was thin, but a diet of dasheen and cod had lined his body with a tight fibrousness. He had a distinct way of twitching his shoulders like a hound trying to shake its fleas. Krishna was one year younger, but Tarak admired him like he was an elder sibling. They spiked the bullies' water with Glauber salts. Exploded their bowels. The twins put scorpions in the latrine. Inevitably, someone got stung. Anaphylactic shock.

Tarak was willing to take the fall, but Krishna wanted them to know it was him.

'That poor boy could've died,' was all the sahib schoolmaster said to Krishna after being told about the bullying.

Even though his father got on his knees and begged the schoolmaster, Krishna was suspended for the rest of the school year. But the schoolmaster, taking pity on the grovelling man, agreed to consider allowing the boy to repeat the standard in September.

Krishna's mother, after hearing the news, crafted a mala from ixora flowers, lit a wick in a deya and circled it over her son three times while chanting a holy mantra. Made him wear an aranjanam string around his waist for a week in case the boys' mothers paid a demon to put a hex on him.

Krishna ate dinner by flambeau light, trying to bat away the mosquitoes from his bhaji rice. After sunset, his mother put out the flambeau. The plains were so dark now that he could barely see his own hands. The egrets flew overhead. When the toads quieted, the world outside vanished. There was nothing left to do now but sleep. As he drifted off, he reminded himself:

Don't let the dreams fool you.
This is your place in this world.
And there is no other world out there but this one.
There is no other body than the one the gods have paired you with.
And there is no other life but the one to which you are bound.

I
A Lost Prayer

Late July

The music was still playing when Dalton Changoor vanished into thin air.

Marlee, Dalton's young wife, had only realised he was gone when the winds swept up the yellow tarp that usually covered his red Chevrolet pickup. The tarp now thrashed, flabellate, between two coconut palms. Against the lightning, it looked like a giant long-winged harrier in descent. The study, where Dalton had left a record of Roaring Lion's 'Ugly Woman' playing, was vacant. As was the porte cochère where he usually kept his pickup parked. Though his sudden absence concerned Marlee, she didn't let it weigh on her thoughts. That was until she found a note on the kitchen table, written in a hasty scrawl:

> Leave the doors locked. I have the spare key with me.
> Tell my mother I love her.
> P.S. Go to the cherries and untie Brahma.

Dalton owned three German shepherds. Vishnu, Shiva and Brahma. He bought them from a breeder who lived in Sangre Grande. The breeder, a wiry man who looked canine himself, told him to starve the dogs in their early days. It's for the best, the man said, keeps them hungry, keeps them vicious. Dalton ended up spoiling them fat instead. They were only efficient as sirens. Never gave chase, never dared to bite. But they looked like they would – that's what mattered. There had been no shortage of prowlers and larceners from the various barracks and settlements lain radial across the plain. Some of them Dalton believed to be kith and kin of past groundsmen.

Whenever he heard the dogs at night, he retrieved a red biscuit tin from under the bed. Inside were firecrackers he purchased whenever he attended a fair. Using a tinderbox, he'd light them and toss them from the window, the bursts of sound like cracks of gunshots. Sent the prowlers scampering and the dogs howling. Despite having a loaded Smith & Wesson revolver in his nightstand drawer, two Colts in the dresser and a Winchester shotgun hidden behind the bedroom closet, the firecrackers remained his preference. Saved bullets that way.

Marlee had never been fond of the dogs. They'd been there longer than she had, and they were keenly aware of it. On the day she arrived, five years ago, the German shepherds lay bundled as a trio of necks on the foot of the porch, watching as Dalton pulled up to the porte cochère that extended from the side of the house. They snarled and barked until their nostrils expelled mucus. One of them made a move to snap at her. After all this, they had never warmed to her. And never would.

It was strange how much life could change in five years. Five days. Five seconds. How they had met was a secret to the world. All was past and prologue – and she was thankful that Dalton never reminded her of it. She gathered that a man so nonchalant about his spouse's past was a man who wished others could feel the same about his. Back then, her hair was a long, braided rope. Her skin light brown as the throat of a forest flood. Eyes bright and soft as misted stars. The misery of ethnicity did not seem to concern her – not even she knew exactly which ancestral spotlight to stand beneath. She was no older than seventeen when she met Dalton, who was more than twenty years her senior.

He thought she was the most beautiful girl he'd ever seen. Something classical and gothic about her as a Botticelli belle. Darkly angelic, as if her presence should be accompanied by a canticle. He, on the other hand, had a face that looked like a wine bottle had been smashed into it. A gangly, greasy man.

Sharp, cutting features. Aquiline nose. Sinuses always stuffed. A small brown naevus in his left eye, as if his iris had splintered. If you saw his silhouette in the twilight, you might have mistaken him for a scarecrow come to life. Children would've snickered at his appearance if they weren't aware of his money. Fiend money. Was easy to think of him as a fiend if it weren't for his fair skin, almost Kashmiri. People thought twice before swindling a sahib.

Marlee decided that she'd wait until morning to check on Brahma. Dalton usually carried a leash with him if he ever went down the hill to the Surinam cherry orchard. The area was fenced so the dogs couldn't venture there on their own. Surinam cherries were poisonous to dogs, and so Dalton tied them to a wooden stake when he was down there with one. He must have forgotten to undo Brahma that night. As eccentric as her husband was, he took sedulous care of those dogs. To relinquish such a chief responsibility to her was unheard of. And if he expected her to venture out into a storm just to unleash a hound, then he must have truly lost it.

When Dalton first brought her here, she was surprised at how far removed it was from the village. For at least a mile and a half in each direction, there was nothing but road and woodland and the odd shack filled with rumours. The row of electrical poles leading up the undulating roadside seemed only to supply this house. The house, a cage locked in a vault of boscage.

Before they were married, she had questioned his business. His answers always came in the form of gifts – linens, sandals, bangles, skirts, rouge. His business was his business. There were very few people that he trusted. He told her that he'd fired all of the house staff two years before she'd met him. The chef, the chauffeur, the housekeeper, everybody. They weren't to be trusted, he said. He hired three new men to tend to the grounds and to the crops, but they were to never set foot inside his house.

He told her that he'd inherited the land from his father. And his father from his. He imported crates of furniture, artwork, ornaments and tapestries from India and England. The arable land and crops yielded profits – Marlee was certain. But the kind of money that Dalton brought in seemed flecked with blood.

He was involved in criminality; it was the only explanation. His secrets insidious, his soul scripted to perdition. The principles of the underworld shift all the time. That is its nature. Every faction sets up its own morals. Every god breaks its own rules. A spinning wheel, where everything comes back to the beginning, sooner or later. If he was willing to be a spoke in that wheel, Dalton had to know that he was going to have to pay for his sins one day.

She let the record play again, made Ceylon tea and listened to the storm. There was something scary and fantastic and exciting as the lightning seemed to creep through the window. As if God was reaching out to her. As if to answer some lost prayer.

★

The morning after the note, Marlee went downstairs to prepare breakfast. Dalton wasn't there – usually, he would be at the kitchen table with his bifocals, skimming the newspaper. He brewed his own coffee and drank until his nerves were shot. Preferred imported arabica to the locally grown robusta. Marlee maintained the house, did the washing, the folding, the sweeping, the dusting, the chopping, the cooking, the baking. Did it for her own sake, at least. There were never any guests, soirees, coffee klatches, birthday parties. The living room, kitchen, bedrooms, the wainscotted staircase only held memories of them both. Because of this, the house always felt like some concealed shrine.

The wordless stillness of the house now made the gloom of the air more apparent. Its silence holy and eerie. For most of the day, she was a ghost roaming a haunted manor. If he wasn't in the kitchen, perhaps he was in the outhouse – a single-roomed shed that he had fashioned into some sort of strange sanctum.

A nymphaeum that held nothing but a giant oil painting of a Chinese goddess.

He made it clear – she was never to enter unless he was there too. As if she were too profane for it. The goddess, like the dogs, had been there before her. The goddess, draped in lavender and topped with a phoenix crown, was surrounded by four jade maidens and giant messenger bluebirds.

Marlee very slowly turned the knob, tipping the door open. Dust wafted like snowfall within the dim, tomblike room. Dalton was not there. The goddess and her maidens glared at her sternly as if she had interrupted some invocation. It was only recently that Dalton had shared the goddess's name with Marlee.

Xi Wang Mu, Queen Mother of the West.

One day, he admitted that his mother's soul had been absorbed by the painting and spoke to him through the canvas. She also learnt that the apparition had once been impressed with her and even suggested his marriage to her. But no more. His mother now saw Marlee as a liar and a charlatan. *That woman simply isn't devoted, Dalton.* He confessed that there was little he could do to change his mother's mind. All of this he had divulged unprovoked.

Marlee married Dalton, knowing he was unsound of mind – but his condition had significantly worsened over the past five years. Paranoia, dementia, monomania – she wasn't sure how to describe it. He had rooms with towers of newspapers and magazines and boxes and all sorts of ephemera. Flew into rages at the slightest mention of tidying those rooms. The house itself was a hodgepodge of things foreign and colonial and postcolonial and antebellum and pretty and gold and red and scintillating. It was ungainly and disgusting, just like him.

The note about the spare key was still on the table.

It was only then Marlee remembered Brahma.

Still in her cotton nightgown, she slipped on her outdoor shoes. The tarp now hung flaccidly in a yellow grin from the coconut boughs. The land was wet but up on the hill, flooding was never a problem. Downhill, where the cherry orchard was located, a rivulet fed a pond a short distance away. The rivulet had gotten hungry over the years and each time it rained, it engorged. Ate the land around it. It was bad for the cherries, and so Dalton grew them only for personal enjoyment.

A small stone stairway was cut into the hill. Only two steps down and Marlee could see how damaged the land had become.

The river had indeed widened, the soil scarred with muddy rills. Her hand went straight to her mouth when she noticed the wooden stake. The attached leash, taut, led downward into the still-rumbling river. She took slow steps until she came to the edge, where she could see the dog attached to the other end.

A bloated ball of sinew and fur.

Brahma must have slipped down the embankment. The river was climbing to meet him, growling like some predatory animal.

Marlee turned around to see Vishnu and Shiva behind her. Their faces didn't show it, but she could hear their growls. *Wasn't me who killed your brother*, she wanted to tell them. She went to the steps and whistled for them to follow, but neither obeyed.

On her way back to the house, she pondered her own feelings about the dead dog. There was no sadness. Surely, this was not her doing. It was not her who forgot to untie the dog, and certainly, she was not to be expected to brave a late-night thunderstorm to make up for its owner's carelessness.

She returned to the house, where the crapaudback pumpkin patch and avocado trees came into view. She called his name. No response. At the empty homestead, she called again. Again, nothing. With that, she returned to the kitchen, made Ceylon tea. She would usually sit on the porch to drink but that morning, she took it to Dalton's shrine. Left the door open, sat cross-legged on the dusty floor and sipped, staring Xi Wang Mu right in the eyes. The goddess stared back. Both in silent judgement of each other.

When she was done, she went to the stairs of the porch, arms outstretched to the sun. Ahead was a fenced patch of land, once used as a paddock and recently converted into a small playing field. Dalton had prepared it for the children of Bell Village. Didn't make much sense to her – him opening his gates to a bunch of little strangers. During the last county fair, after much deliberation, he stepped onto the podium and announced it to the village. All under the guise of giving back – though Marlee was suspicious. From the end of the school year to the beginning of the next, all children were welcome. He wanted them to use the paddock for sport.

He set up a radio he'd bought from the Rediffusion company. Then toys, which he packed into a chest. Miniature dollhouses, plastic soldiers, slinky springs, dimestore comic books. He had his three main workers prepare the dusty course of a cricket pitch in the middle of the paddock, bought willow-wood cricket bats, smoothed with linseed oil, and a crate of cork balls. Now there was no longer the need to forage for a coconut branch and baby shaddocks to play the game.

The children arrived in droves. Wild shadows dancing under the afternoon sun. To them, the house stood as tall as the range, the front topped with three steep eaves, an ethereal sunburst atop the middle spire. The sides were of simple fenestration with the exception of two Demerara windows that always made it appear as if the house were peeking out with half-opened eyes. They were only allowed to enter the first room to the left of the foyer. They were, under no circumstances, to venture past the staircase. Upon entrance, greeting them was a triptych portrait. Paradise, earthliness and, finally, apocalypse. In the details were creatures and expressions cryptic and wonderful. It lay open like some mystical book, a butterfly in an abandoned church. Despite its ornate fretwork and fanlights and craftsmanship that teetered between Mughal and Art Deco, there was something intangible and sad about the Changoor house – as if it solely existed to recall greater times of heritage. Like a general of the vanguard, felled in battle, still adorned in his military emblems.

The room to the left was bright, immediately visible. Inside were goose-feather cushions strewn across a floral velveteen rug. A small, round table set up with a centrepiece of poinsettias flanked by two carnival glass bowls. One with cut guavas, the other with carambolas. The mahogany stand at the end of the room like a king before its loyal subjects. Its crown, the box radio prattling the words of Abbott and Costello.

Vinyls were stacked on a stand. A royal flush of big band and jazz and calypso. Glenn Miller and Benny Goodman. The crooning of Vera Lynn and Dorothy Lamour. The brass of Atilla the Hun, Roaring Lion and Lord Invader. Songs about the poor, the heartbroken, the departed. About the American soldiers stationed in north Trinidad. And about all the local girls who loved them.

Marlee had no part to play in this invitation, though she was aware that many believed Dalton had done all of this for her. It rattled him how she couldn't bear children for him – and he had once called her *as dry as the Atacama*. But she believed it was the opposite – it was he who couldn't accomplish the deed. If he couldn't have his own children, he would treat others' children as his own, he'd said to her. Said that his mother told him it was the right thing to do. Marlee was greatly worried by this sentiment. If his sense of the right thing to do came from a possessed painting – then in actuality, there was no sense of the right thing to do. There was no sense at all! Recently, she'd wondered if the painting had commanded him to fire all of the house staff. Now she knew. Then again, had Dalton ever done anything to suggest he was sane?

She had begun to notice an odd habit he'd taken up with the children. He would come into the recreation room in the middle of the radio shows, hay sprouting from his boots, tracking mud on the herringbone tiles. Asked children their names, their parents' names, their birth dates. His face uncomfortably close to theirs, grinning and staring unblinkingly into their eyes. As if searching for their soul.

As if waiting for a sign.

Two weeks later, he told Marlee that he had looked into a boy's eyes and seen the devil. No firecrackers and tinderbox this time. He opened the nightstand drawer, got the Smith & Wesson. Came outside to the grounds, held the gun up to the sky, fired two bullets and screamed, *Back to Hades with you!* The children scattered, carrying the horror and confusion back to the village. *A gate to hell has opened up*, were his words while the gun was still smoking.

This singular act of psychosis was eventually chalked up to be a product of *stress.* That was the word many used to describe it. A few claimed that he fired the gun because a damn barrack child must've stolen something – and good for him! You give an inch, and they take a mile! But everyone could agree on one thing – the Changoors had a different type of blood running through their veins. Blue blood. They weren't like everyone else. The people of Bell had always questioned Dalton's wealth, though only in the form of idle gossip. The theories never ending. His money soaked and baptised in pure evil. Which evil – the dockyard drug lords, the contrabandistas beyond the Gulf, a *bacoo* spirit from the Burro Burro River down in Guyana – no one could say for sure. Two weeks back, his business was his business, nobody wanted to know.

But people always hummed a different tune when children were involved. Now, the villagers stood fastidious. United like a council. All faiths condemned the man. The Christians likened him to Judas Iscariot, who stole from the money box, long apostate before betraying Jesus. And the Hindus compared him to the Ayodhyan Prince that shot Shravan Kumar, a poor boy who he'd mistaken for an animal. Shravan had forgiven the prince before he died. They were told: Men like Dalton Changoor, in their hearts, believed that all those below him were animals. Dalton was no prince. He was just a man. And so, the devotees were asked: would *you* forgive a man for mistaking your child for an animal?

After that week, nobody wanted their children to have anything more to do with the Changoors. They would still nod at him. Still welcome him to hand out prizes at the Maypole. But his reputation was forever tarnished. Marlee felt deep shame to be the wife of a lunatic – to have his instability cast into the public eye. The nights of the week before he disappeared, he took long walks into the forest, lost himself gazing at the night sky. In the hours surrounding midnight, he sometimes walked to the front gate and into the road as if expecting visitors.

Dalton's accelerated flightiness since that day made her nervous. He no longer took to the bed – instead he slept on the floor and moaned at phantoms in his head. Slept with a dagger. Not just any dagger, but an SS honour dagger, scabbard burnished with black, some quote in German along the axis of the blade. He was the kind of man who could get such a thing. Usually kept it in a glass case, but now it was under his pillow. He said the blade was infused with the demon magic of the Third Reich. Now the dagger was missing as well – wherever he'd vanished, he'd taken it with him.

Marlee eavesdropped on his final conversation with the painting – blubbering to his mother that the village still held him in disdain. That the devil was coming to get him. And that it might already be too late. That he would no longer be able to buy her a *flower-eyed grandchild* from Bell – a child who would have become the true heir to the Changoor estate.

2

A Creature as Dumb as This

The three workers arrived at 8 a.m.: Baig, Robinson and Hans. Baig was part-time. Worked in the boilers at the sugar factory and was only scheduled to be at the farm three times a week. His hair sparse with growth, tucked under a tweed scally cap. He worked the crops. Weeding, pruning, taking care of the fungus and fruit flies. A boisterous man with no filter.

Robinson did the tilling, irrigation, mulching. He'd retired from his old job as a machinist and enjoyed the solace of the farm. He had a pickup of his own and often ran the errands. Seedlings, fertilisers, iron nails, plywood, dry goods, haberdashery, he knew where to get them. A wide-brimmed sun hat shaded his eyes, crimped his wavy, ash-hued hair. He was tall, his features sharp like a stray cat's. Spoke with a samaan tree baritone. Always had his sleeves rolled up to his elbows, his forearms rippling with muscle. Baig frequently remarked on his neat manner of dress and that more Black men should take as much pride in their appearance as he did. Robinson never entertained such remarks.

Hans was the most visible worker of the three. Marlee often lost herself gawking at him. He was fit. Rugged in all the right places. She was infatuated. That he'd spent his entire life in a barrack was a shame – but he never had that aura of filth like the other people from such a life. She had no person she considered to be a real friend and, in Hans, sensed something kindred. Something beyond lifestyle and customs.

She told the workers that Dalton had urgent business to attend to. Wasn't a lie, according to his note. It seemed simpler to say this than mention the note. Despite him being their boss, she didn't want them thinking too hard about Dalton. Telling people anything before knowing the full story herself wasn't smart. At the same time, she thought to let them discover Brahma on their own – but ultimately decided against it. She directed Hans to the coconut trees to remove the tarp. Then told Baig and Robinson about the dog. When she led them down to the cherry orchard, the wind had already started to whiff the smell of decomposition into the humid air.

'A damn shame,' said Baig, arms akimbo. 'Aint that right, pardner? A damn shame.'

'Which one that be?' asked Robinson, going for the rope.

'Like you could tell which damn dog is which.' Baig laughed.

'Look like Brahma to me.'

Marlee took a step back from the rope, giving a nod.

'How you could tell?' asked Baig, genuinely curious.

'Brahma is the only one that have that ring of black round the neck.'

Baig nodded. 'What the hell happen here anyhow? The boss forget to untie the dog? Had to be for it to end up in a state like this.'

Robinson's veins surfaced as he pulled the dog up.

'It was an accident,' was all Marlee could muster, her attention on the rope.

'A damn unlucky accident. A sin, almost.'

Marlee to Baig, 'I'd appreciate you not saying anything about it. Mr Changoor doesn't know about it yet, and I want to be the one to inform him.'

'Yes, ma'am.' Baig to Robinson now, 'Hear that, Robinson? Don't go runnin your mouth.'

Marlee tipped her chin. 'Help him, Baig.'

Baig, nonchalantly, 'Need help there, pardner?'

'No, sir.' With one final tug, Robinson pulled the dog's body onto land with the vigour of a bluejacket bringing up an anchor. The rigor mortis long set in. Mouth wide open, tongue lolling out the side. The stench unbearable now. Muck water osmosed into rancid flesh. The dog's face had drooped to the point where its features had lost their symmetry. The three pinched their noses.

'You want me to bury him, Mrs Changoor?' asked Robinson.

'Yes, please do that.' Marlee pointed to a spot of earth far from the cherry trees. 'You are a saint, Robinson.'

Robinson hesitated. 'A foot too close to the water. Mind if I go further up?'

'Whatever is best.' The smell, now close to making her eyes water, overpowered everything else. She couldn't look at the dog any more.

'I gon head up, grab a shovel,' said Baig, eager to escape the stench as well.

'A bag too. A big one, you hear?' Robinson said. When Baig went up, Robinson turned to Marlee. 'You want to say something for the hound, Mrs Changoor?'

She squinted. 'Something? Like what?'

'Just some words. A prayer would be appropriate.' He paused, looking at the dog's deformed face. 'Seem only right.'

Marlee, at a loss for words, shook her head.

An awkward silence before he felt compelled to ask, 'Mind if I say something then, ma'am?'

Marlee's eyes fluttered. 'By all means.'

He bowed his head. 'All things bright and beautiful. All creatures great and small. All things wise and wonderful. Jesus, thank you for them all. Rest in peace.'

'Rest in peace,' repeated Marlee.

Baig returned with the shovel and bag and helped Robinson slip the dog in. As Robinson began digging, Marlee asked, 'Mind if I leave? The smell, I can't...'

'I'll take care of it, ma'am.'

Halfway up the steps, she noticed Baig following her. She turned around. 'Stay down there with him in case he needs help.'

Baig twisted his mouth. 'Right.'

Back at the field, Hans was done taking down the tarp. He rolled a spare tyre over it to keep it in place. Wiped his hands on his trousers as he walked up to Marlee. 'Baig was tellin me about the dog.'

Marlee rubbed her forehead. 'I hope that idiot doesn't go tattling.' Then with clasped hands, 'Would you mind keeping this to yourself, Hans? At least until I have the chance to tell Mr Changoor about it. You know he's been under a lot of stress lately, and how much he treasures those dogs.'

Hans nodded. 'I understand, Mrs Changoor.' Had to keep his eyes from straying to the swell of flesh exposed at her collar. 'And what bout you? Any stress? I mean, any stress aside from this mornin. The way Baig was talking, he make it sound like a bad dream. Aint nothin a lady should lay her eyes on.'

'It's only you who asks me these things, Hans.' She smiled, bit her lower lip and gave him a playful shove on the shoulder. 'Even bad dreams come to an end.'

With a twinkle in his eye, 'Good dreams too.'

'Unfortunately.' She stood closer to him. He was tall enough for his collar to cradle her chin. 'I expect it to cast a shadow on the rest of my day, to tell you the truth. I may go inside to take a nap.'

Hans gazing at the sky. 'Don't worry bout them dogs. We gon see bout the other two.'

'You're a godsend.' Her eyes lingering on the sweat beading at his collar.

'Should we keep a lookout for Mr Changoor?'

She nodded several times. 'Yes, yes. Please do. He wasn't clear on whether he was returning by midday or this evening.'

'That there is a busy man.'

'Quite,' she said, feigning a smile.

★

Night fell. The crescent moon like a shimmering sickle above the land. Dalton still hadn't returned. Marlee reflected on his last conversation with the painting – what did he mean when he said that the devil had returned? Who was the devil? An underworld rival? An old nemesis? The Ghost of Christmas Past? She paced the kitchen, feeling gradually more and more weightless. Turned to the clock. A whole day had passed since Dalton's departure and still no word. The questions in a frenetic dance in her head.

Where the hell was he? Why had he left in such a hurry? Was he with another woman? It wasn't her first time entertaining the latter thought, but it had always seemed improbable. Something was off with him when it came to women. He spoke of alcohol and contraband tobacco and exotic wild meats and other earthly delights, but never of former lovers. She suspected him of being a virgin when they had met – even though he was close to his forties. He had the habit of picking his skin, so he had scabs on his shoulders and chest, and because of this, he always kept his shirt on during the act. Maybe if he had talked to her about this habit then she would've had historical context. Without conversation, it could never be anything more than grotesquerie.

The most important question now: was Dalton Changoor dead?

It filled her with dread to think about it. Not for his sake, but hers. If something had come for him, it was only a matter of time before it would get to her as well. The shadows never discriminate.

Behind that dread was the nascent sense of a silver lining, like this same slivered moon in the dark night. Was she free of him now? She once tried to love him but ended up only loving what he owned – and what she hoped would be hers as well. The thought made her anxious and feverish and giddy. But what if he wasn't dead? What if he were out there bleeding, waiting for a rescue team? She wondered, how would a wife's actions be construed were she to not report her husband's absence? He did leave a note. She'd have to report it, just not now. But then what? Return to a life governed by a painting? If he was indeed in trouble, he'd know how to get out of it. Or maybe not. Who knew what would be his fate? Only God could tell. And maybe it was best to wait until God was willing to tell.

She climbed into bed and pulled the blanket over her feet.

★

The howling woke her up. She reached for the red biscuit tin and tinderbox, set them on the nightstand. Parted the drapes, looked outside. The grounds illuminated with phantasmal moonlight. Something odd and anomalous in the distance, sticking out from the branches of an old mango tree. At first, she believed it to be an owl. But it was too big to be an owl.

Whatever it was – it was moving upwards now. A strange feeling budded in her. A humming in the flesh, like a thousand cicadas were trilling inside her bones. Slow, deliberate movements like a wolf spider as it crept up the tree. Kept moving until it reached the very top. She couldn't make out the figure – it was all shadow – but whatever it was, it was balancing on the topmost branch, like an angel atop a Christmas tree. The dogs still howling, hidden in the shadows of the boughs.

She lit a firecracker and tossed it out of the window. The sharp burst sent the dogs running. Sent the bats flying. But the figure did not budge. The Smith & Wesson was in the nightstand drawer, already loaded in case of a last resort. Because a last resort rarely gives you the courage to hold a bullet without dropping it. She made sure the safety was off before stuffing it under her pillow, but she needed another weapon. One that she could swing. She went into the kitchen and found an empty wine bottle below the sink. With one great arc, the thick base could brain a bodybuilder.

When she returned to the window, the figure was gone.

But whatever silver lining there may have been was obscured now. Surfacing now was a grave feeling of melancholy, like some dark zone had begun to swallow up the Northern Range. And it was slowly making its way to her, where she lived, where she slept. If Dalton was dead, who killed him? For what reason – or did it even matter? Money? He kept a large sum in a padlocked iron box. He had even more with Western Union and Barclays. Revenge? Revenge is inherited, and she was the heiress to it all.

Every half hour until sunrise, she got up to check the window. Nothing each time. She began to wonder if she'd seen anything in the first place. Maybe she was just paranoid. In the daylight, there was nothing there. She made Ceylon tea, went to the porch.

Vishnu trotted up to her. She could see Shiva in the middle of the grounds, on his side. Nervous, she whistled for the dog's attention.

But there was no reply.

Snapped her fingers and called its name. Nothing.

There is usually the moment at the betokening of horror, where one simultaneously accepts and rejects it. Where two worlds blend into one. The gradient of the shadow where light and dark meet, where time slows and hope cowers. A closing slit in the deep promise of pessimism. Where a long-sick child on a bed has croaked and wheezed themself to sleep – or something deeper than sleep. The long silence that follows. That silence came for Marlee, and in that silence was the promise of coming darkness.

She set the tea down on the white rattan table, sat upright for a pensive half minute, knowing better than to snap her fingers once more. Forced herself to get up and walked to the lying dog, its brother trailing behind. Before she could see its face, that same smell of decomposition hit her.

The dog had ejected the watery contents of its entire gut. The fur on its rear and tail were matted with it. A long, broken trail of it on the grass. Somebody had poisoned this dog.

She ran into the house and locked the door before realising that the workmen were soon scheduled to arrive. Kept a lookout from the bedroom window. Thankfully, it took only a matter of minutes until a pickup pulled up at the gate. Robinson and Hans. When Marlee came up to them, they looked at her with aged weariness in their eyes. She led them to the dead dog.

Hans knelt beside it to inspect it. 'What happen here?'

Marlee kept her distance because of the smell. 'I woke up, found him like this.'

He stroked its ears as if it were his own. A long pause before Marlee uttered, 'I think somebody—'

'Christ in heaven, my brain jump out my head,' Robinson muttered suddenly.

She paused. 'What do you mean?'

'When I bury Brahma, I didn't think to whistle them damn dogs back up. I left them there. Them dogs aint accustom going down there like that.'

Hans covered his mouth, in shock.

Marlee narrowed her eyes, overwhelmed. 'What are you talking about, Robinson?'

'Apologies, ma'am. I'm saying I shoulda clear that area up before leaving. Now look and what gone and happen.'

Hans got up. 'He sayin that the dog probably eat the cherries.'

Robinson turned to Vishnu and then uttered in a worrisome tone, 'I wonder if this other fella was foolish enough to do the same thing. God have mercy!'

Marlee's eyes fluttered. 'The Surinam cherries did this?'

Robinson explained, 'Them cherries does kill dogs. One or two, no. But a handful is serious problems. The dog bowels done blow up there. Is like senna tea for them, but worse. Much worse. I know a fella from church. Drink a whole case of senna tea. Dead on the floor, you know!' He got on his feet. 'Mrs Changoor, if you don't mind me sayin so, I think you need to watch yourself. Bad luck is one thing. But it look like somebody put the *maljeaux* on you. We should ask Reverend Kissoon for a blessing.'

'Is nobody fault,' Hans said, scratching his head. 'Right?' As if he himself needed convincing.

Marlee pursed her lips, wary of the consolation that this was yet another accidental death. A mirage of hope in the quickly gathering darkness. She didn't want to fool herself. Or else she would be no different from this dog, having shat itself to death.

Robinson in a resigned tone, 'Suppose I gonna have to bury this one too then.'

'I'm sorry. I know it's early...'

'You should say a nice word for this one then,' he said sternly.

The smell was getting to Marlee now. It was worse this time. 'I'm sorry... That smell...'

'The Missus should get outta here,' Hans said. 'This aint no sight to see.'

Robinson kept up his tone. 'If something living with you suddenly departs from this earth, that's a piece of you that's gone. That's how I think bout it. So, I think is only right to give it the time and say something. Even for a creature as dumb as this.'

She held her breath. 'You're right. I'll give it the time, Robinson. Just not now.'

*

At the end of the week, there was still no word from Dalton. His absence caused concern among the workers as Friday was the day they received their week's wages. Usually, Dalton kept a tasksheet and based the stipend on the quantity and type of work done. Marlee had done no such thing. She felt embarrassed, almost betrayed, when Baig brought it up. Why didn't they inform her? Because it wasn't their job to inform her, she reminded herself. That would've been her husband's job. For a second, she contemplated telling the truth, that he had gone missing, disappeared with only a cryptic note. But the lie came to her at the same time.

Dalton had left for Georgetown, she said. He was seeking out investors in Guyana – investors for what? She wasn't sure. Those were *his* words – she was always careful to reiterate that. *His* words. He'd meant to return in the morning but was delayed. She couldn't come up with a reason why and so left it at that. She had no idea what the usual stipend was for each worker, and though she was ashamed to ask, she had no choice. She believed Robinson and Hans told the truth. However, the number that Baig claimed was greater than Robinson's and Hans's combined. Nevertheless, she paid him. His astonished smirk gave away the sham.

As he pocketed his pay, he asked her, 'The boss went by boat or by plane?'

'To Guyana?' A pause. 'Flight. Mr Changoor has his way of chartering flights.'

'He leave on the Tuesday, you say?'

'Tuesday night, yes,' she quickly replied, before steering the conversation elsewhere. 'I wanted to wire him about Brahma but changed my mind at the last minute. I thought it would be best for him to find out when he comes back. He doesn't need to have something like that on his mind while he's over there. He already has so much on his plate.'

'When you think he gonna be back?'

'In a week. Maybe… two?' She answered as if it were a question.

'Just be careful, ma'am.' Baig nodded, before meeting the others at the gate.

Overhead, a flock of birds flew past, followed by a cold updraught. 'Swifts,' Robinson said aloud, his eyes upturned to the clouds. 'When you see swifts flyin like that, you know the big rain comin.' Turned to Hans. 'Your place holdin down good in this season?'

Hans nodded. 'I doin some fixes. Goin to that new store to get some things.'

'Salloum's?' Robinson asked.

'Hans, while you down there,' said Baig, 'tell the damn bank to approve my loan. They treatin me like I livin in a barrack.'

'Ignore this fool, Hans,' Robinson said, getting into his pickup. 'Hop in. I could get you to Salloum's.'

Baig scoffed. 'Robbie, you know you gonna smash up your vehicle goin down that *buss-up* road that Hans livin down.'

Hans shook his head, looked at the sky. 'Me and my boy was gonna walk down there.'

'You sure?' Robinson turned the key and the engine rumbled.

'Don't worry bout we. Is a twenty-minute walk.'

'And a two-hour swim,' Baig quipped.

Hans laughed. 'The boy have to learn to swim sometime.'

Baig glanced at the house. 'You think the Missus could swim?'

'Get the Missus outta your mind,' Robinson said over the purr of the engine.

Baig laughed. 'Hans, you givin her swimmin lessons?'

Hans didn't pretend to smile. 'What you talkin bout?'

'You lyin if you say you aint want to see the Missus in a two-piece. I'd pay a pretty penny for that, I tellin you.' He whistled.

'Your mouth gonna get you in trouble, Baig,' Hans said, shaking his head.

'Only with Robbie. Robbie aint never covet another woman in he whole life—'

'Enjoy your weekend, Mr Baig!' Robinson cut him off. 'Be safe, Hans.' Then stepped on the gas.

★

In the night, a loud racket came from downstairs. Even through the clatter of rain, she heard it clear. A continuous rapping. Someone, or something, banging at the front door. She gripped onto the balustrade that shouldered the staircase, heart racing as the banging persisted. Then turned around and returned to the bedroom, making as little noise as possible. Lifted her pillow and rested her palm upon Dalton's gun.

Vishnu had a tendency to bump his head into things. The dog was going blind, which made Marlee a little nervous. She couldn't depend on Vishnu to sound the alarm. The damn dog was of no use to her bumbling about the porch and getting its head stuck between the wooden spindles. But this was too loud to be a dog.

There was someone out there.

At night, the lights of the house called attention to itself. Like the noctilucae of a secluded river. It all looked like something out of a dark fairy tale. Past a certain point on the grounds, there was a significant cleft between the light and dark. A point where the dark opened up like a whale's mouth. Where Marlee had come from, there was always something happening in the night. The echoes of a drunkard stumbling into the street. The distant washing of the sea. The echoes of affronted dogs. Cats leaping, knocking over garbage lids.

Dalton always had records playing at night. He never snapped his fingers, never danced to any of it. Marlee supposed he kept the music on for greater reasons than enjoyment. It made the house feel more populated than it was. Perhaps, she thought, he was also aware of how isolated they were. When the music came off, the silence that followed was jarring and immediate. There would be the toads and the crickets and the cicadas and the *tak tak tak tak* of anole lizards – all a reminder of how far they were from another human soul.

She peered out of the upstairs window. Through the blanket of rain, the porch, where he usually parked his pickup, was still in view. Still empty. She sat at her vanity, the banging downstairs getting louder and louder. The mirror showed a haggard face – eyes sunken, jaw heavy with worry. She combed her hair to calm herself. Then the banging stopped.

But there was something else now.

A light creaking. Even through the rain, she heard it.

The brush fell from her hand and the fear rose up, clutched her throat.

She paced downstairs, gun in hand. Nearly jumped out of her skin when she saw it – the door open, wavering slightly as if it had just been tampered with. Had it been open this whole time? The sound of the banging – was it the wind rattling it against its frame? Sometimes only a modicum of force can evaluate the difference between open and closed. In and out. Life and death.

She kept a cat's stare at it for a full minute, until she was suddenly reminded of the gothic allure of the night. The crickets in tandem with the toads. The stars and the clouds and the rain and the moon and all the secrets hidden in the darkness that the Northern Range overlooked. All seeming in harmony with itself. But step outside and the wolves were waiting.

She crept towards the door, each step feeling like the ground could give way. Like the very foundation that she stood on could betray her at any second. Even if that happened, she thought, she had to keep going forward. When she got to the porch, her heart jumped.

A figure in the corner.

Vishnu, his big panting mouth curved into a silly smile. The loud wind swept the rain onto the porch. Just as she half turned to the door, she noticed something on the white rattan mini-table.

A shoebox. She took it inside, locked the door. Set it on the table, hesitating to open it. Poured herself a glass of cherry brandy, downed it in one gulp. She opened the box and the blood rushed from her head.

She went pale. Nearly fainted when she saw it.

A dead rat, freshly killed. A dark depression on the side of its abdomen where it was struck. Mouth open like it had just released its final squeak. Below, a note. She gagged, pinched the end of the paper with trembling fingers. In capital letters in childish scrawl:

$3000. MONDAY. 4 A.M. NO. 4 BRIDGE.
TELL AND U DIE. WE R WATCHING!

That same betokening of horror came upon her then. That deep promise of pessimism. She had to reread the note three or four more times before the words could have any semblance of sense. Even when she could put them together, it took her a full minute to accept that it was real. When the questions came, she had to sit, her eyes flicking between the note and the dead rat. A warning of a coming plague. She was shaking – but strangely, the fear had seemed so distant. She now knew that whatever it was, it was coming.

It was already here – at her doorstep.

Now she had to stare it in the eye. Was the note meant for her or for Dalton? Was it a ransom note? Did this mean Dalton had been kidnapped? Were they really watching? Where were they watching from? Was he dead? Alive? Was the money in exchange for his release? In exchange for her life? Would they leave her alone once they got it? And most of all…

… what would happen if she didn't care to pay?

3
A Family Store

Krishna, Tarak and Hans made their way along the macadam road to the train tracks, where children usually teetered, picking daisies and feeding them to the cows. Where the tracks ran perpendicular to the river, they served as diving platforms. There was nobody there except two village boys who'd fashioned hibiscus branches into slingshots and aimed them at the birds perched on the boughs. As they crossed the boys' line of sight, the cousins, Krishna and Tarak, flinched as if they would train the slingshots on them. Hans just smiled and waved at the boys.

When they passed the railway yard, it was odd to see it so empty on a Friday afternoon. Usually then, there'd be top-spinning contests. Bets thrown down. One shilling down on the guavawood *dodo* sharpened with a broken bottle. Two on the orangewood spinner sleeked shiny with a British fighting knife. Both set dizzy with marling twine.

There was a cold tension in the air. At the pond, a gang of bison rustled beneath a samaan, deaf to the strikes of a distant plough. Thunderheads stood like turrets in a dark castle of cloud that presaged rain. Violent rain. By nightfall, the roads would become rivers. Fish would swivel through flowers. Tadpoles dancing on lingams. Strewn all the way up the ravine, toppled murtis of Lakshmi and Saraswati. Fiddler crabs latched to their panchaloha cheeks.

Krishna began to think that perhaps it wasn't smart of his father to run this errand on a blustery afternoon like this. And it wasn't smart for him and Tarak to accompany him to the store. His mother definitely did not think so. The boy recalled her exasperation as they left the barrack. She stood in silent judgement between the clothes lines, his merino shirts beating against her petite body like a flurry of giant silk moths. Pulled the clothes down in unspoken anger and slung them around her neck before going inside.

He knew they were close to the village when the roads became flatter and softer. The bitumen almost like keloids on the earth. In the backdrop, the Northern Range. A geometric sketch now delineated by molten eventide. Some of the houses on the periphery were stilted, assuming the posture of fancy ladies fording a flood with skirts hoisted. The missionary school Krishna attended lay here on the outskirts of the village, so he never had to venture here into its heart. The often-busy streets seemed near abandoned that funereal afternoon. No water wagons, no women with rattan baskets tending to gardens, no men smoking cigarettes, mixing concrete, playing draughts on the benches, no donkey-carts. Market vendors were already packing up. A sunburnt yard boy hurriedly scooped up some donkey ordure from the sidewalk.

Down one lane, rusty houses like old petrol can shacks stood as if on the firing line, ready to be taken down. In their place, some variety store, boutique, rec lodge, some pub masquerading as a calypso cabaret, some office filled with briefcases and filing cabinets and mortgages and chattel and accession and abuttals. In their place, the fated, the future.

Krishna was to be part of that future, was the hope of his parents – at least for his mother. Hans had shot a second glance at a small, lonely plot of land swathed in bushes. A FOR SALE sign jabbed into the dirt, slantways like a bookkeeper's pen. This could be his new home. It was a real possibility once his father talked to the right people. Krishna wanted no part of it. Not this place, not these people.

Hans stopped before a two-storey building with a wide blue awning, the front fitted with immaculate glass. On one of the panes was the name of the store fitted into a bold half-moon: SALLOUM'S BAZAAR. The store had opened only a week ago and was supposed to be the new cornerstone of imported goods.

Despite the boding of grim weather, there were some people mulling around inside. The unfamiliar ding of the cash register gave Tarak a small startle. Standing sleek behind the register was a pretty pearl-fleshed woman, hair fashioned into a neat ponytail. Displayed behind the glass were bath towels curled up like sugar-frosted cinnamon rolls, large jugs of polychromatic confectioneries, ladies' hats snug on faceless plastic heads, decorative boxes with little animals painted on the sides. A stack of magazines. Not the latest issues, but at least they weren't three years behind like the ones selling in the tumbledown kiosk in Tully Settlement. And at least they weren't kinked and rolled up like they'd once been used to swat insects.

Every month, heeding a suggestion from Robinson, Hans would buy one for his son. Whatever he could pick up that seemed suitable for a boy – *National Geographic*, *Picture Play*, *Life*, *Look*. Krishna's favourite was *Popular Mechanics*, but they rarely ever had that one at the kiosk. But there it was in this store, sitting proud and mint, top of the rack.

'We have money for *Popular Mechanics*, pa?'

'Your ma say you have enough books for now. She want you to finish the ones you have.'

'I read them out, pa. And read them over.'

Gave his son a smile. 'We gon get that *Popular Mechanics* then.' Hans turned to his nephew. 'What you want from in there, Tarak?'

Tarak chuckled. He wasn't expecting anything – he'd just come for the walk. He shyly pointed at the candy jars.

From the doorstep, Hans smiled at the pretty cashier, rubbing his hands together as if a hot meal had been placed before him. The woman's face fell as she signalled to a young lanky man in suspenders. A patchy beard but his hair slicked into a smooth dome. He'd been stacking tins of pomade into a tiny pyramid. The man came to the door, held up an authorial hand to the two and shook his head.

'Somethin wrong, mister?' Hans asked.

The man folded his scrawny arms, his eyes on Hans's tattered work boots, scrunching his nose as if he just smelled a fart. 'Only one of you.' He looked to be in his twenties, several years younger than Hans.

Hans thought about the sentence for a while. 'Only one of we could come in?'

'I only have one pair of eyes,' said the man with a nod.

Krishna craned his neck to observe the patrons inside. There were at least two mothers with their children. Scowling at the man, he asked, 'What you sayin here, mister?'

Tarak hunched over, stayed quiet.

The man kept eye contact with Hans. 'The boys stay outside.'

Hans nodded. 'Yessir.'

'So, what bout them in there?' Krishna pointed to the children in the store.

'Quiet,' said Hans, his palm on the boy's back.

The man kept his gaze on Hans. 'We've had bad experiences and I only have one pair of eyes.'

'Bad experiences with what? We have money. We aint stealin nothin from your stupid store,' Krishna said to the man. Turned to his father, 'Tell him somethin, pa. Call him a jackass.'

Hans covered the boy's mouth. Tarak gently pulled his cousin closer to him.

The man sneered. 'This is a family store. I'm afraid I'm going to have to ask you to—'

'Hold on, hold on, sir.' Hans held up his hand, put on a smile for the man. 'I come to get one thing from the hardware and that's it, sir. I have the money.' He pulled some bills out of his pocket. 'See?'

'But pa—!'

'Hush, I say!' He lightly smacked the boy on the back of his head.

The man thought about it for a few seconds. 'OK. Go ahead.' Then pointed to Krishna. 'But this one says another word, I'm phoning the police.'

'Yessir. In and out.' Gave Krishna a stern glance.

'Don't forget the *Popular Mechanics*, pa.' But he wasn't sure if his father had heard.

Tarak led Krishna to the sidewalk, where they both sat. Tarak slung his arm around his cousin's back. A whorled-up pothound sat on the other side of the street, quietly growling at them every time they made eye contact. Krishna kept his eyes upturned. The crosshatching of power lines sliced through the sky.

'They aint have no right,' said Krishna. 'This place should burn down.'

'It more likely to flood out with the rain comin tonight.' Tarak let out a small titter, rubbed his cousin's shoulders. 'Don't worry bout them, boy.'

Visible in the distance was the church, a monolith so tall that it was visible from any walk. The rictus of Christ more like an adjudicating scowl than a pained grimace. The chorus of some Friday evening rehearsal warming the still air like birdsong. Suddenly, the sound of a bell. A lady in the store commented to a clerk, *Hear that? Look like Miss Betsy finally pass on, God rest that old woman soul.* Krishna wondered if the bell tolled for all souls – or only for the ones that'd been baptised.

As Hans browsed the confectionery jars, the young man in suspenders loomed behind him. When he moved to reach his hand inside, the man nervously tapped his shoulder and asked him how many candies he was buying. 'Four,' said Hans, reaching in again. The clerk slapped his wrist like a nervous schoolteacher. Krishna felt ashamed to see his father go through this. The clerk then reached in himself and gave Hans a random four – the children inside got to choose which ones they wanted. When his father went up to the cashier, Tarak noticed that he'd forgotten to pick up the copy of *Popular Mechanics*. When he told Krishna about it, the boy told him to leave it be. He didn't want any damn thing from that damn store anyway. Even gave Tarak his share of the candy.

A single flick of rain slid down Krishna's brow. He remembered a story of a drowned child from Bell Village, about two years back. Drowned in a gully that was lucky to be fed a trickle of water. That season, the rains transformed that gully into a rapid. He heard that when they found the boy, he had worms in his mouth, chiggers crawling out of his feet. He didn't know the boy but perhaps he had it coming, was his thought. Most people from this village did. And a church bell can only toll so many times before it finally cracks.

4
A Difficult Wife

The swifts in the darkening sky were moving like a knife slitting the dusk. Shweta Saroop gazed into the distance, imagining that she could take off skyward like those birds to scan the shadowed plain. What she'd see: a scarlet ribbon of ibises flocking to the mangroves; agoutis squeezing into tree logs; the reeds cushioning toads and snails and prawns. Every creature of the land wary of nature's wrath, except for her husband.

Here, in this dingy barrack, the corrugated iron would clang with each raindrop. Open barrels positioned in rows dribbling like babies. Piles of wet ash and firewood slushing into black paste beside the cast iron pots and tavas and discarded trade bands. The wooden partitions within would become cages; each room a diving bell. Because when the rain fell during hurricane season, so did the sky.

Hans shouldn't encourage the boys to be reckless, Shweta thought. Krishna was sensitive. Gave time for thought. Took his time with things. Once, he listened to his mother. Not any more. She supposed that was the nature of things – sons look to their fathers when they are healthy and to their mothers when they are hurt. His eyes, once warm, had hollowed and refilled with this frightful determination to prove himself – especially to the two guttersnipes he and Tarak had recently grouped up with.

The Lakhan twins.

Hans believed the twins were harmless. Shweta had to ask him, *You know who their father was, right?*

To which Hans responded, *Them boys is not their father. It aint right to judge people like that.*

Made sense for him to say that. Hans's own father had subjected his family to a lifetime's worth of abuse. Hans was the antithesis. Loving, high-spirited, skittish to a fault. Though Shweta had long been witness to it, her husband could never find it in himself to speak of the pain the man had inflicted on him, his mother and his brother. But comparing Hans's father to the Lakhans' father was like comparing a termite to a tarantula. Bhagran Lakhan was a notorious man, a mass murderer, so begrimed, so reptile, that he might have been dredged from a bog.

The twins were ruffians for sure, her husband conceded. But Krishna and his friends were at that age, that ineluctable phase, where boys must be ruffians, even if just for a year or two. Even if it meant getting suspended from school. Krishna wasn't a baby any more, he reminded her. He was already thirteen. Boys will be boys, yes, but they must one day grow to be men. All boys must experience rivalry, he said. They must know what it feels like to become overpowered and bruised. He claimed Shweta wouldn't understand, her being a woman. Boys have to learn to wear their bruises like badges. For a bruise not worn as a badge only serves to invite more bruises. The world could sniff your blood and send all manners of beast to line up around the corner waiting to gulp. So lay the natural order of things.

Perhaps she was too doting, too concerned, she thought. Maybe what she wanted for the boy wasn't best for him. Maybe his father was right, and she was a difficult wife. At times, she believed she was missing some part that would make her a good mother. She supposed many mothers became afflicted with such an emotion after losing a child. There was little understood about malady and little consequence to violence in these parts, so it wasn't unusual for a mother to cremate her own child.

A section of river was black with the ashes of babies. Her daughter, Hema, among them. A bug in the water had killed the little girl. It swam into her, never came out. That's how it was told. But who told it like that? The nurses? A pundit? Rookmin, the elder who lived three doors over? Everything back then a fever dream. A hand shoved a bottle of desi daru into her mouth the day the body burned. Voices in her ear, *Don't worry, gal. Let that one sleep. Your husband gon give you another one just now, just now.* Shweta drank and wept and vomited and never spoke the child's name again. There was no memento, nothing left behind for this world but memories bedimmed by unspoken sorrow. But more than a decade later, her daughter's name still resounded. It resounded that very minute.

It was a name that neither she nor Hans had uttered, even to each other, since that day. And the fact that the rest of the barrack had seemed to forget her existence cemented that Krishna would never know that he once had a sister. Thoughts, years later, weren't prepared to be full thoughts. Only fragments of malady and mortality. That skin still looks as warm and brown as the final minute of life surges within it. That the eyes are the first to go. That death is more concerned with stillness than sleep. How the dead wilt in one's arms, angling downward to the ground as if impatient to melt into the earth. How old was she when she died? Ten months? Eleven? Nobody could remember.

Rookmin had made a mound of clay in the middle of Hans and Shweta's room and told Shweta that her daughter's spirit would dwell there, fluctuating between troubled sleep and terrified consciousness. Before Hema's passing, Shweta believed in the deities but not in rakshasas and djinns – not in the way the elders like Rookmin did. But the old lady was the only one she felt she could be sincere with about her grief. The others either gave her rum or told her to focus on having the next child. Krishna was there within the year. But the sorrow lingered.

Rookmin's skin was fair, almost diaphanous. Always a small woman, she'd shrunk a few inches since Shweta's time as a little girl. Was as if life had whittled down her bones over the years. She draped a yellow dupatta over her head to hide a balding spot. Spoke in resonant purrs, the words almost evaporating as they reached the ear. She communicated by touch, liked to caress the hands of those she held in serious conversation. Held a strange electricity in her fingertips, which she transferred to the spines of others. Refused to do so for men, out of respect for her husband, Murali. Despite her religious convictions, she listened without preaching, without interrupting. Her voice garnered a young confidence whenever she relayed her knowledge about spirits and gods.

She made a batch of rice balls for Shweta and told her that it was to feed her daughter's spirit, now a *preta* – a hungry ghost. Her daughter's belly had expanded to twice and thrice the size of her head. Ghosts always hunger for company and so bring other ghosts with them. Six rice balls were to be offered to these other ghosts; ten for the hungriest one, the preta. Shweta was to abstain from any form of pleasure or grooming. Rookmin was firm about this. No brush should touch her hair. No water should touch her face. No bed should touch her trunk. And finally, no man should touch her flesh. In her mourning, there was no room for reluctance. Shweta decided that she would adhere to the instructions. She slept outside in the cold night and came down with pneumonia.

Three days in, without saying a word, Hans kicked the clay mound and tossed the rice balls to the blackbirds. The only words he uttered that day were in great anger to Rookmin, *You tryin to kill my wife?*

He nursed his wife back to health. Boiled eucalyptus oil in a pot and let her breathe the steam. Rubbed her back as she hacked globs of orange phlegm onto the same spot where the clay mound had been. Laid her naked body on a blanket quilted of his merinos and cleaned her with a sponge. Anytime she thought back to it, she could only remember helplessness. Bitterness. She wanted to have the pneumonia. Wanted to stay sick – and he was robbing her of it. It felt right to deteriorate, even if just for a while. She could never say such a thing aloud, especially not to the other women. *What a difficult wife*, they would say. A deck of cards missing the queen of hearts. A punch board with no prize slips.

In that moment, the sickness felt like a prayer. Her health as an offertory to the Ashwini Kumaras – deities of medicine, bringing light on their chariot pulled by geese and buffalo. On that third day of sleeping outside in the cold – at dawn, she saw their chariot like a bright comet before passing out.

Only once had she asked Rookmin about restarting the ritual, to which the old woman just shook her head and said, *I gon pray that your daughter's mouth remain small.* In the following days, Shweta thought herself selfish. Ungrateful. Hansraj Saroop is a good man, she reminded herself with those exact words. A deliberate man not yet outgrown the haste and wonder of a child. But ultimately good. Hema's passing was of no consequence to his own shortcomings. He was there in the aftermath. Rubbed her back while she vomited, held onto her as she wailed and bucked backwards against him like an injured goat. A lesser man would have been lost in the rum shop.

That was where Mandeep, his older brother, was holed up when his wife, Tansi, succumbed to malaria in the clinic. They had to glue her eyes shut because she had haemorrhaged behind them. Looked like two bleeding cherries. Mandeep's only words to his son, Tarak, were, *What I coulda do? Bring the woman bark to chew? The clinic aint have no quinine. This world aint fair. Om shanti.*

And his words to Tansi's sister, Kalawatie, *God will it this way. Who is me to tell God to change such a thing? Om shanti.*

After her sister's death, Kalawatie couldn't go to the latrine by herself after sundown. Rookmin said she would hear Tansi in the wind, see her shadow behind the barhar tree. She had Kalawatie walking backwards into rooms, had her spreading circles of salt leading up to the door, so that the spirit wouldn't follow her inside. Her husband, Teeluck, took turns with Hans in accompanying her, a flambeau in hand, waiting for her to finish squatting. After a week, Teeluck left Hans to take on the sole burden. Shweta thought it inappropriate. Kalawatie was married to Teeluck, not Hans. A husband ought not to involve himself in another married woman's affairs – not like this. Taking a grown woman to pee and shit.

Shweta knew that what was wrong could never be made right, no matter how it was presented. Just as a lie could never be made truth. Truth is singular and simple. A man must devote himself to his family and to the world he knows, not to a world he is not a part of. In the end, she said nothing of it. *I married a man too good for his own good*, she conceded. Gripping the fire, standing out in the sodden mud in the midnight swelter, listening to another man's wife fart and blubber about rakshasas and pretas and ghosts. *Go wipe her ass too*, she wanted to tell him. And he might have.

Hans remained as hardy and cavalier as in his youth. His body firm-fleshed, his fey spirit always undefeated. The years of toil that had accrued in him made him flourish with even more life. Shweta was the polar opposite, feeling as if her body and mind were gradually perishing. She often thought she was sick. Whenever on her back, her lungs became congested, causing her to cough unremittingly. Her body radiated with dull aches, especially in her joints. Her eyes watered. The skin around her sockets looked as if ash had been rubbed into them. Perhaps there were many reasons for this. And all those reasons converged upon a singular locus – the barrack.

When Krishna came into the world, Shweta always felt like he was on borrowed time. She always reckoned this barrack would be the end of him – same as her daughter. Three months ago, she saw that she was right. A few years before Krishna was born, a gaping hole in the barrack roof had appeared over Hans and Shweta's room, expanded from a singular shilling of rust decades prior. Hans and some others had managed to haul a large sheet of iron and some bricks on the roof to seal the hole. For years, it held. Krishna wasn't in bed when the brick crashed through and landed right where his head would've been if he were.

The child is a blessed one, Rookmin had said to Shweta.

This was not a blessing, she rebutted. But a warning. A sign from Lord Rama. The barrack was a fossil embedded in quicksand. No longer attached to an estate. Attached to any higher purpose whatsoever. And anything without a higher purpose was destined to be eaten by time.

Two weeks ago, when Hans heard that a plot of land had gone up for sale in Bell, Shweta knew that Lord Rama and Mother Lakshmi had eyes on her family. Hans should have money saved for a down payment, she knew – but even his son's close brush with death hadn't seemed to strike him with the willpower to move until three days ago, following the last bout of rain.

Their room burbled ankle-high with rainwater. Seeped through the cracks in the walls. The coconut fibre mattresses stank the following morning. Tadpoles in their rice bags. Hans was fed up. Said he was going up to Bell Village to solve this problem right away. Her heart swelled as she mused of plumbing and vinyl floors and cupboards and bedframes and round-tables and any other appurtenances of modern living. Even a corner nook for her tiny shrine to Lakshmi. She didn't want to think about the possibility that someone else could snatch that plot from them. Couldn't happen. Hans could get things done. Yes, he could get this done.

Now in the barrack yard, she had a fire going with *baigan choka* – mashed eggplants and onions – roasting on a tava. The other women of the barrack were there as well. Kalawatie boiling rice to go with salted cod and tomatoes – she had Teeluck, Mandeep and Tarak to feed. Rookmin with tomatoes and spinach and sada roti; her daughter, Niala, was pregnant and always craved spinach. A smaller pot beside her boiling water for ginger tea. Goat-bearded Murali sometimes kept his wife company during cooking; he was useful for little else. He always wore a long white dhoti and, when he was there, a share of Rookmin's attention had to remain dedicated to keeping its pleat-ends away from the fires. Dolly, closest in age to Shweta, wore a displeased expression as she stood over her pot of callaloo, realising that the pumpkin had only halfway melted on the bhaji leaves. A viscous green slime that robbed her of all appetite. Dolly lived with her daughter, Lata. Her husband, Umesh, had died from the sprue a few years back.

None of the women conversed while cooking. Neither compliments nor criticisms. Neither gossip nor natter. It was a simple respect they paid to each other. A way of life, necessary in maintaining the mental illusion that this place was each wholly theirs – and the others were only passing through. That even though they never thought of this forsaken jumble of wood and zinc as a house – it could at least murmur the privacy of one during moments like these. The barrack, of course, was not one family but five.

The dog, White Lady, so named for her coat, sat among the women. She was born from a dozen breeds. Belonged to no one in particular but spent most of her time with Tarak when food wasn't being prepared or consumed. He had tied a yellow handkerchief around her neck, which she never gave fuss about. Not many of the dwellers were particularly affectionate to the dog but fed her and kept her around as she was rarely a nuisance.

The storm clouds were closing in, slow and sure as lava. Dolly extinguished the fire, toted her pot back inside. One by one, the others followed. Shweta lagged behind, lugging the clothes to her room before returning to the empty yard. White Lady had already taken shelter under a tentlike heap of corrugated iron. The baigan on the tava had burst open, seeds and innards spilling out onto the charred iron. At Shweta's feet was a wicker basket of peeled potatoes that would remain uncooked for now. She hugged herself, content for this moment of quietude. The Northern Range now obscured, the distant rain looking like grey marionette strings dangling from the sky.

She threw water on the fire and scooped the roasted baigan choka into an enamel bowl. Then spotted three figures coming up the road. A man and two boys. Hans, with Krishna and Tarak trailing some steps behind, their hand-scrubbed merinos tremulous in the wind. She reached her hand as far as she could to wave at them – as if to warn them. As if the shadow from the minaret of rain clouds could wash over them like a tidal wave.

The rain came down, loud as poured gravel, the moment they bolted the door. Shweta set the food down and fashioned a flambeau out of an empty cane rum bottle. Filled it with kerosene, topped it with a cloth soaked in pitch oil, struck a match and set the burning bottle down in the centre of the room. Tiny white sprays of water sibilated through the end wall. She positioned the flame away from them to keep it alive. Hans got up, a large white tube in his hand almost the size of a banana. He cut its tip with a paring knife.

'What the hell is that?' asked Shweta, pointing.

'Silicone caulk,' said Hans confidently. 'From Salloum's.'

Shweta steepled her fingers at her chin, unable to hide her disappointment. 'You aint never say you was gon buy that. This is what you went to Bell for?'

His eyes were to the door already. 'Holes need caulking up.'

A scoff of disbelief escaped her. 'Who doing that? You? Out in this rain? How much this damn thing cost, Hansraj?'

'It aint taking more than two minutes.' He ignored the last question with these words of determination. Straightened himself and set for the door. 'Just have to squeeze this tube here and the miracle come out.'

'You gon go out there and get yourself sick…'

'Two minutes. Wait and see.' Off went his shirt.

Shweta followed him to the narrow hallway. He was already outside. Even through the grating sound of the rain against the iron roof, she could hear Teeluck from the opposite end, quarrelling with Kalawatie about the cod being undercooked. Shweta returned to the room. Krishna sat facing the wall, quietly curious. In only a minute, the water spurts began to withdraw. Hans returned to the room, lethargic, as if he'd just woken up, water dripping from his trouser pockets.

'Out there, the whole place white with rain,' he said. He slicked his hair back and went to work on the interior side of the wall. When he finished, water was still coming in but only in weak seepages, equivalent to the rheum from a child's sleepy eyes. His eyes met his wife's, and he raised his eyebrows, impressed with his own handiwork.

He turned to Krishna. 'Quality product here.'

The boy was leafing through one of his old water-damaged magazines. He had nothing to offer but a solemn nod.

Shweta gestured for Hans to sit. Looking at the size of the tube, it was hard to hide her annoyance. The question burst out of her again, 'How much you pay for that?'

'Never mind the cost.'

'What size is that? Aint it have smaller sizes than that?'

'This here is for everybody,' he said, finally sitting. 'Have enough for all the rooms in here.' He paused, then added,

'A bucket with one hole just as useless as a bucket with five, you know.'

Shweta was still in disbelief. 'Krishna, tell me how much your father pay for that thing.'

Krishna finally spoke, 'I aint go in the store, ma. The man there was being a jackass.'

'You just have to learn how to talk to people,' said Hans, wiping his face.

A pout. 'I aint want to talk to them. I hate them people. All of them.'

Hans gave a dismissive wave. 'The caulk will last a very long time. Months. Years, probably.'

Shweta's face fell. 'Years,' she muttered.

She had a mind to bring up the plot but decided that they should eat first. She propped the flambeau on a small crate. She and Krishna on a flour bag bedding on the coconut fibre mattress, their backs to the partition. Hans on a rice bag. They finally ate the baigan choka and even though they realised they would still be hungry after it was done, they were grateful that the food was still warm.

When they finished, Shweta cleared the wares from the ground. She got up, feeling a slight sting of cold on her nose. Looked up and on her eyelid, a similar sting. Water was coming through the roof now. Each drop speckled black from how much black sage and zebapique had been boiled within these walls. Her head ached. She scooted to get out of the way.

Krishna sat close to a candle, flipping through a copy of *National Geographic*. He once had pasted a few pages on the walls using a flour paste that his father had mixed. A bright picture of a toucan. A photograph of a misty mountain in Japan. An article entitled 'How to STOP a Tank!' The leaking walls made sure that none of them stayed there for long.

'Krishna, you gon spoil your eyes,' she said.

'Aint readin. Just watchin the pictures.'

'Let the boy read his book,' said Hans.

Shweta narrowed her eyes. 'You know we aint have no money for glasses.'

The boy ignored her, kept flipping.

Hans reached out his hand. In it, a tightly wrapped set of pastel-coloured Smarties Candy Rockets. 'We eat we own on the way back. We decide to save the best one for you.'

She looked at it for a while. At first, she wondered if the candy was to somehow pacify her. She didn't want it – but how could she not take it? How would it look? She squeezed it in her palm. 'Them's the ones that turn into dust when you rub them together,' Hans said with a great smile.

She held back on calling him a child. In fact, the two had known each other as children – each one still calling back to vivid images of their juvenile selves. She remembered him as a boy, the same age as Krishna, when he'd go down to the station yard to beg the engineers for the train tokens – the circular metal tablets presented as proof of passage. And if he couldn't get one, he made his own. Coconut frond rib looped through a dried husk. He and the other boys pretended to be locomotives, dashing back and forth along the train tracks straddling the riverbank, from the catechist's house to the tall neem tree where people bathed. She thought he would grow up to work with the trains. Was this the same person? Did he really grow up to settle for scraps?

He eyed a dark band on the fibre mattress where decomposition had been settling in. Soon, the entire room would smell high of mildew, and he would have to see about restuffing it. She knew he didn't like that. He just learnt to shut his mouth about it. He once complained to his father when he was a child, only to have his teeth nearly kicked out. He understood not to be needy about such things.

'What you doin about that plot in Bell Village?' She needed to know. 'We have the money, right? You talk to the people, right?' Instantly, Hans's mouth kinked. She lowered her voice now to keep it from travelling over the partitions, 'You can't tell me you aint have enough, Hansraj. You aint fed up lend money to Mandeep? Every time, he lose it playing cards. He aint never pay you back a cent. Let Murali buy the vitamins for Niala. And you aint need to buy this expensive brand of flour every single time—'

'You aint want me to buy that flour?' he asked, eyes to the ground.

'Not if it holdin we back from somethin better! Rats live in them rafters up there.' She pointed. 'You don't hear them in the night?'

He kept his eyes on his feet, nodding slowly, then pulled his legs up to his belly. She knew he envied men from the village. Men who owned property, owned land. But discussion of finances always made Hans coil up tight as a spring. The money constantly evaporated, and he was always dumbfounded when it was all gone, as if a dust devil had come overnight and swept it up into the sky. She didn't feel like a nagging wife when he was so stupefied by reality. Felt more like his mother – a feeling she had much disdain for.

Hans was a good worker. And he worked for people who lived in a mansion. She told him straight, 'If we aint have the money, I tellin you so many times that you need to ask that Mr Changoor for a pay raise.'

He steadied his head as if resisting to shake it. 'I gon ask,' he replied meekly. 'Is just that lately, the bossman aint been himself. He keep talkin bout how he have things to sort out—'

'What you care bout what he have to sort out? Just ask the man for it. Tell him what the money is for.'

Krishna peered up from the magazine.

'It don't work like that,' Hans said.

'You just don't want to do it.' She got up, stamped her foot. 'You do *nothing* for this family!'

She left the room, slamming the door behind her. Down the damp hall, the four other rooms were probably aware of the squabble they were having. Beads of rat droppings stained the walls. She pulled her dupatta tight over her hair. The sound of the downpour couldn't fully drown the unholy retching that was coming from behind Rookmin's door. It was Niala. Six months into the worst pregnancy any of them had ever witnessed. The baby inside – everyone hoped it was a baby – was killing her. She vomited a dozen times a day, so much that the back of her teeth had begun to brown. She was always at risk of dying from dehydration and so had to drink water by the bucket. A nurse at the hospital said it had something to do with hormones. There was nothing else anybody could do.

Rookmin and Murali usually kept their door latched, as if to protect the world from the sight of their daughter. She on her side, sweaty hair slicked back, belly on a flour bag, her disoriented expression like a dying animal's. Two buckets within reach. One for drinking, one for vomit. Her pregnant belly looked like it held pus instead of life. She wouldn't say who the father was. They rarely talked about their daughter's difficult pregnancy now. And there was a point where everyone stopped asking. Shweta didn't expect the baby to live.

Only when she rubbed her eyes did she notice the other figure in the hall. It was Tarak, nestled into a corner on the ground, head on his flour bag pillow. He wasn't yet asleep. Raised his head. 'You good, auntie?' His voice, no longer croaky from puberty, had smoothed like a neatly folded sheet.

She gave a quick nod. 'You sleepin out here on this hard ground?'

'I put my blanket over the ground, so I good.' A pause. 'Pa drunk. He sleepin right now. But in case he wake up—'

'I understand.' She didn't need to hear the rest.

'Tell Krishna I say hello.'

She nodded, went back inside. As she did, her husband, doe-eyed, reached his hand out to her. She hadn't regretted her tone, nor the words that accompanied it. Hans needed to hear her like this – the more often the better. He needed to understand the urgency. Whenever anyone in this barrack was in need, Hans helped them out. Lent money. Ran errands for them. Repaired their doors, shelves, relationships. Helped mop up when Dolly peed herself after being belt-whipped by her husband. Tended to Tarak's wounds after his father slapped him around the yard. He was perhaps this way because of how helpless he was against his own father. His mother's skin had turned a completely different complexion from all the violence.

She took his hand. A long pause. 'I will go mad if someone else get that plot, Hans.'

He kissed her hand. 'We gettin the plot, Shweta.'

'We have enough money?' she asked, bracing for his response.

Like a whimper, 'I dunno.' Then, 'As soon as the boss come back, I gonna ask him for the raise.'

'Come back? He aint there?'

'He gone down to Guyana to fix up some business, the Missus say.'

'So, when he comin back?'

He shook his head. 'Maybe in a week.'

'A week is a long time.'

'We can't live somewhere else?' Krishna spoke, looking up from his magazine. 'I say already, I aint livin in no Bell.'

'So, where you want to live then?' Hans ruffled the boy's hair. 'You gon catch a horse and carriage up to Port of Spain?'

Shweta added, 'You gon learn to cook your own food? Scrub your own clothes?'

'I rather live with rats than live in Bell.'

Shweta looked at the boy now, all laughter abated. His face had lost some of its roundness. In a few years, his jaw would be as chiselled as his father's. He asked questions, laughed at jokes. His way of walking had morphed into an uneven trudge. He had lost his light, possibly from all the time spent with those Lakhan brothers.

Hans reaffirmed his promise, 'As soon as the Mister come back, I gon ask. Only the Missus is there now, and she don't come out the house much. So, we don't have eyes on we the whole time like when the Mister there. Baig does leave early, and she don't realise. Not me. God know I working.'

'And that's exactly why you deserve a pay raise, Hansraj. Is a year you workin for that man and you aint making much more than when you was in the canefields with a cutlass—'

'The workin conditions is better,' he cut in.

'That aint the point. Tell him straight what you need. You know he have the money.'

'He have worries. And now he gone all the way down to Guyana with them worries. I aint envy the man.'

Shweta shook her head. 'He shootin guns in front of children. He have more than worries.'

'That was cause a bunch of damn hooligans steal from him. You could never have nothin good in this place.'

'Speakin of hooligans, tell Krishna to stop seein them Lakhan boys.'

'Leave the boy alone. Let him have friends. Boys need a lil action sometimes. Like when I used to wrestle down by the river.'

Shweta shook her head. 'Krishna aint that kinda boy. He gonna do things you and me coulda never do in this life.'

Krishna, eager to change the topic, put the magazine down. 'You really used to wrestle, pa?'

'Mmhmm. And I aint never lose a match neither. Every morn, you coulda find me down by that blacksmith, looking for iron to lift.'

Shweta nodded, the image of a teenaged Hans forming in her mind's eye. Though she didn't wish to glaze over her previous point, a warm wave of nostalgia washed over her, and she was reminded of the image of the man she had become so attracted to.

'You know your father coulda haul that grinding stone from the workshop to the preacher man's manse and back?' Shweta said to Krishna.

Krishna looked at his father. Hans nodded, proud. 'That's right. All the way and back.'

'Tell him bout the picture, Hans,' said Shweta with a pursed smile.

Hans ruminated on the statement for a while before giving up. 'What picture is that?'

Shweta, excited by the memory, explained, 'Up in the blacksmith's. Post up on the wall was a page rip clean from a magazine. The strongman from India. He had a mace like Hanuman.' Hans nodded slowly. Shweta added, 'You used to worship that man. That was your Lord.'

'*The Great Gama*.' His head bowed in chagrin, a dozen embarrassing memories flooding in. 'He had some features I never care bout. Belly like a turtle shell and a moustache like a big hairy caterpillar. Wasn't so much bout how he look but how he attach himself to the lifestyle—'

'Your father ever tell you bout the time he try to eat three buckets of mango?' Shweta cut him off.

Krishna's eyebrows shot up. '*Three* buckets?' He put the magazine down.

Shweta released a broad smile at the boy's awestruck expression. It was comforting to behold this childish glint in his eyes. A boy must be a boy. But just as important, a child must be a child.

'This aint no kinda story to be tellin the boy,' said Hans, shaking his head. He turned to Krishna. 'Don't listen to your mother. She trying to make me look like a fool in front of you.'

'You shouldn't be shame.'

He gave a shrug. 'I aint shame. Go ahead and tell him.'

'Your father wanted to be a strongman so bad. He hear that man in the picture used to eat three buckets of fruit a day. And he and the fellas get to drinking and quarrelling bout who have the most strength. A Negro man working with the coopers, name Cumberbatch, coulda match everything your father do. Then your father blurt out that he could eat three buckets of mango.'

Hans scratched the back of his head. A few more raindrops came through the roof. Thunder boomed outside. Hans continued, 'We had all kinda mango that day. Starch mango. *Doux-doux* mango. Julie mango. Me and some other fellas and their girlfriends spend the whole day plucking them trees bare. And we tote them in three big buckets all the way to the railway station.'

'Your father faint halfway into the second bucket,' Shweta said, stifling a laugh. 'Everybody thought he was dead.'

Hans let out a scoff. 'I was taking a nap.'

Shweta chuckled. 'So, you was gon wake up and finish the second and third bucket then?'

Hans snorted. 'I coulda damn well finish it after I finish my nap. But you all had to go snatch up the rest of them mangoes and eat them.'

'Nobody aint want to waste them ripe mangoes.'

'What happen to Cumberbatch?' asked Krishna.

'He was smart enough to walk away after seeing your father lying on the ground like a sick old dog,' Shweta answered.

Hans shook his head. 'He aint eat a single mango because he know he couldn't top me.'

When Krishna fell asleep, Shweta picked him up, laid him on the mattress on the opposite side of the room, folded the coverlet over him and pulled the curtain. She was careful not to let the cloth touch the flambeau. The curtain cut the room in half.

Outside, the rain was still heavy and would remain so throughout the night. Still, there was a skim of moonlight that let Shweta see the outline of Hans's defined body after she snuffed the flame. The shape of him was enough for her. The rest of the world disappeared. It was just them, ensnared in themselves, him inside her, and she had to remind herself that the others could still be awake, could hear them through the partitions. Maybe she could risk letting out a moan – the rattling of the zinc roof should drown it out. As soon as she did, his hand clamped her mouth with the speed of a frog's tongue snatching an insect from the air.

She contended with the sound of his breathing, and he with hers. His breath into her body. She heard a tussling from behind the curtain. Had the boy awakened? She turned her head on her cheek, squinting her eyes to make out any kind of silhouette. She couldn't tell. As they kept going, she could feel the warm sensation of a distant orgasm.

Maybe this time the gods would let her have it, she hoped.

She pleaded to them, *Please let me have this one.*

Please let me enjoy my husband.

The vague outlines of the dark room began taking the shapes of insects and worms and all manners of parasite and detritivore. *No, no, no*, she thought, as the orgasm fizzled. This had been a curse. A hex on her since her daughter's death. The phantasmagoria came like a train, claimed everything in her.

Hema's entire back covered in shit and flies.

That *ick ick* sound of her cough.

The crackle of her body inside the pyre's flame.

Hans apologising to the wardens after being scolded for his daughter's cremation. *The sickness dissolves into the water and kills the fish*, were their words. And Hans could just nod to these people who'd just equated his daughter to a dead guppy floating downriver.

Fragments of memories swirled like wasps over Shweta. Woodlice in her nose. Slugs in her lungs. She couldn't breathe. Her strumming fingers turned to violent flailing as the walls of the barrack burst like floodgates. She seized up and what had felt so good now felt like razor grass dragging along her vulva. Hans threw himself off her body and helped her sit up. Rubbed her back until the nightmare was over. His erection pressed against her waist.

She didn't say anything and neither did he. She thought to apologise but always decided against it. She had to endure this anguish to conceive Krishna. Her entire breathless body filled with pure and undiluted pain. That was thirteen years ago. The gods weren't ready for her to let this go. *Your pleasure from this day will forever be pain*, they proclaimed to her. She suspected that Hans dreaded doing this with her – but always went along with it. She wondered why. A husband's duty? Maybe, each time, he still held hope that the curse would be broken. The curse could be broken with a word. One word they could utter to each other. *Hema.* But she found herself unable to say it to him, even by force.

She thought of finishing him by hand, but she could barely make a fist.

He sat in a corner of the room, facing the wall, and did it himself. When he returned, he collapsed onto the mattress, looking the same as he did on that day he passed out with a bucket of mangoes in his stomach.

5
A Strange Proposal

Marlee went to the pantry to get flour, sugar and butter. She carried the ingredients to the kitchen and went to work, beating the fat and sugar together until they were white and creamy. Then worked the flour into the fat with her hands until it became a stiff paste. Sifted the rest of the flour on the table and rolled the mixture until it was a flat circle. Using a small knife, she cut the shape of the shortbread biscuits and put them in the oven. Took down the jar of guava jelly to serve with them. When the shortbread biscuits were done, she mixed a potspoon of sugar into a mug of lime juice. She could've just gone to the village and bought all of these things, of course – but the roads were flooded and all she had was her Raleigh bicycle. Regardless, it was a suitable distraction. Nobody cooked or baked better than her, in her opinion.

The night before, she steamed her hair over a pot of hot water, rubbing the oils off with a towel. In the bedroom, she worked her hair into pin curls with bobby pins. After she was done in the kitchen, she combed her hair with a boar-bristle brush. Changed into a red gingham dress with a white belt that cinched her waist. Decided against a neckerchief. With this outfit, a pair of red mules fitted pleasingly. A spot of mascara on her eyelashes complemented her gently coloured eyebrows. A dab of Vaseline to keep them slick. Painted her lips into a hunter's bow. A touch of petroleum jelly to keep it glossy. As she patted her neck and wrists with perfume water, she wondered what the point of doing all of this was. It had become so habitual. After the heavy night rains, she didn't expect Robinson and Baig to show up that morning. But even with a flood, she knew she could rely on Hans. He'd want to check on the damages, at least.

The morning ritual was Dalton's formulation, but Marlee gave it personality. The mascara, the perfume, the lipstick, the mules. He dictated whether he wanted her matte or glossy or smoky or soft. One day, she looked to be an elegant woman of equestrian pursuits. Another, of lagenlook antifashion. It wasn't only that he desired for her to look a certain way, but he also failed to recognise her without the maquillage. He clasped his heart in alarm if she went without it. Her natural self became a stranger to this house. She entered into the marriage knowing that she was to be his doll. A store mannequin to play dress up. As empowering as it felt at first to stroll through the village and have all eyes on her, it became exhausting when she had to do it every morning, every evening, just to sit down and have dinner with him. It was a hefty price to pay for privilege. She grew to hate doing it. But perhaps she only hated doing it for him.

Nevertheless, she completed her routine.

She tried to busy her mind, looking for tiny flaws and crinkles in the mirror, to calm herself. She hadn't slept well the night before – she'd woken up half a dozen times to reread the threatening letter. That she was being watched. That she had to pay up. She wondered if the dog had indeed poisoned itself by eating those Surinam cherries – or was it a warning? Seemed foolish now not to consider it. Despite the promise of danger, she wanted to keep the police out of it. Not to abide by the letter's instructions, no. She just preferred to keep matters in her own hands.

She waited for Hans on the porch, her legs crossed. She felt something untamed in her when looking at him – she'd always felt a physical attraction that she could corral, but now, with Dalton gone and the sense of peril sharp in her mind, temptations could gallop wild. Hans was physically strong, humble, obedient and seemed just the right amount of naïve. At a time like this, he could serve her well in many ways. He could keep her safe. He could comfort her.

She went to the deck, pulled up a chair and called over to him. Laid the tray of shortbread biscuits on the table. Poured the juice into a silver pannikin and swathed the metal with a napkin before handing it to him. He didn't sit until she insisted. She waited for him to take the first bite before helping herself. He seemed preoccupied, a distant look in his eyes.

'You didn't have to come out today, you know,' she said. 'I'm glad you did. Don't get me wrong – seeing your face always brightens my day. But you didn't have to. If only you had a telephone, I could've called. But I suppose barracks don't have telephones.' As she chuckled at her own joke, she realised such a thing wouldn't be funny to him.

Still, he let out a semi-amused grunt that sounded almost like a hiccup. Ate the shortbread biscuits slowly, almost lethargically.

Marlee asked, 'How do they taste? New recipe.'

'Good, Mrs Changoor.'

She was taken aback by his monotone. She fluffed her hair. 'Marlee. I prefer Marlee.'

'All right, Mrs Marlee.' Monotone again.

'Better than what you find in the bakery,' she said, giving him a smile. When he didn't reciprocate, she decided to pry a little. 'A penny for your thoughts, Hans. You have things on your mind. Talk to me. We're friends.'

The comment made him smile and his lips moved a little as if he were going to comply. But he said nothing. Like a sneeze that failed to come. Then, he mumbled, 'When Mr Changoor come back.' A pause. 'Is somethin I want to ask him.'

She leaned in. 'Tell me. Let me see what I can do, Hans.'

It took him a while, as if he was considering it for a second before shaking it off again. 'When he come back next week, I gon ask.'

She clutched her dress and made sure her voice lilted with the right amount of vulnerability. 'It seems like Mr Changoor's return to Trinidad has been postponed. I won't go into the details.' Took a breath. 'But he's decided to stay for much longer than anticipated.'

'How much longer?' His face sank.

'A few weeks.' Her eyes on a pair of bard antshrikes sitting on a balata tree bough. She asked, looking at his pannikin, 'Would you like more juice?'

He nodded, and she poured. Then she said to him, 'There's something I have to ask you, Hans. But first, you should tell me what's on your mind.'

He rubbed his palms together like a shy child. 'The pay aint enough,' he said flatly. After the words came out, his shoulders loosened as if they had been holding up a mountain. 'The work is good but the pay aint enough. And I think I been a good worker. If I get more pay, I gon be able to put down for a house in Bell. See, it have an empty lot on the street nearby the church. It aint gon be there forever. And me and the wife aint want to be in that barrack forever. And then it have the cost of materials and—'

'Consider it done.'

A pause to take it in. 'Done?'

'You need more money, you'll get more money.' She kept her eyes on him. 'You're a committed worker, Hans. Your presence today alone speaks of that. Mr Changoor isn't the one for words like that, but I know he'd be all the poorer without you. You're one of the only men he seems to trust.' A small smile. 'And you know I trust you as well.'

His palms together as if in prayer. 'Thank you so much, Mrs Marlee.'

'Are you ready to hear me out?'

'Yes, yes.' He nodded quickly. She could tell he had already forgotten. 'What's the question?'

'Hans,' she said his name as delicately as she could. 'It's not so much a question, but a proposal. And I know this proposal is going to come off as strange. But hear me out.' She clicked her tongue. 'You have a family, and this might be hard for them.'

'What is the proposal?'

She took a breath, like a schoolgirl reciting a poem before the class. 'I've never said anything of it and Mr Changoor wouldn't want anyone knowing, so I'm trusting you to keep this secret.

I would especially prefer the authorities not to get involved. News travels too quickly when it arrives at the Bell Village Police Station. You already know that prowlers are drawn to this farm, especially during night-time. Most of the time, it's just a couple of stupid young boys. Usually, they'll make off with a bag of avocados, not even ripe yet. Mr Changoor sometimes lets them be and doesn't bother reporting it. I've never agreed with this action because, in my opinion, mild transgressions eventually lead to more serious ones. Wouldn't you agree, Hans?'

He nodded. 'A small thief always grow up to be a big thief.'

'Exactly.' A brief smile before continuing, 'There's a particularly nasty bunch that's been skulking around for the past two nights. They rattle the doors, throw rocks at the house, make all sorts of hideous animal noises. It could just be their idea of a fun time, yes, but I'll be candid to admit that I'm quite frightened. I know I shouldn't feel that way and that it's probably nothing. But you never know the kind of things that could happen in the night. And me, being a woman and all—'

A wide-eyed look from Hans. Made her nervous to look at it, so she turned her eyes to the table. Her voice wavered a little as she went on, 'I know you have a family and I know it is intrusive to ask—'

'Forgive me,' he said, bowing his head. 'I dunno anyone who been comin round here. Can't be anyone in the barrack. Must be them Tully Settlement boys.'

Took Mrs Marlee a while to realise that Hans had the idea that she was pressing him for information. She let out a chuckle. 'Hans, no no no no.'

'If I hear anything, I'll be sure to let you know. And me and Robinson could give them a good scare once we find who they is.'

Cheeks flushed red, she turned to the balata tree once more, trying to rephrase the proposal in her head. Hans grabbed one of the biscuits, taking a wolfish bite out of it. A drizzle of crumbs fell on the table, some sticking to the corner of his mouth. He looked embarrassed when it happened. A downward glance as if he were in trouble. Marlee chuckled, grabbed a napkin.

'Don't be shy. It's OK.' She got up from her chair and swept the crumbs off the table. Took a handkerchief out of her pocket and leaned in close. She locked eyes with him as she gently wiped the sides of his mouth. Her fingers on his skin like a spirit's wings. Smooth as the stem of a young palm. Her body arcuate, a blessed melange of muscle and fat. Her scent warm, balsamic, holy. Felt as if lights were rising within his body. His posture almost phototropic as he angled towards her. When she was finished, they kept winsome gazes on each other. And he wasn't sure if she was getting closer, or he was. Or both. Almost nuzzling each other now. In that moment, he felt simultaneously ill and illumined.

Quickly, she pulled away.

Returned to her seat. A direct stare now, sitting up with her chest out as if asserting herself to an employer. 'My proposal is this: that you stay here. Until my husband's return.'

He wiped some sweat from his brow. 'Stay ... ? Here?'

'Yes, at nights. In the capacity of a watchman. I'll have you set up at the homestead.'

'Homestead?' Hans said it as if he'd never heard the word.

She pointed to a structure he already knew as the shed. The shed with the flaky walls and crooked roof. She told him, 'It's close enough to the house and you'll have a nice foam mattress in there to lay your head on in the morning.'

He kept his eyes on the shed, silent for about half a minute. Then, 'I don't know—'

'You were talking about money. I'll pay you a flat fee of two hundred dollars.'

His mouth half open. '*Two hundred dollars?*' His gaze returned to the shed. That was four months' salary for him. 'I have to talk to my wife first.'

'Talk to her, yes.'

'And this gon be for ... how many nights?'

'Until Mr Changoor returns. You'll only be needed from sundown. I don't mind you taking your own time and seeing about your family during the day. Baig and Robinson will be here. You won't have to worry about food. I'll cook dinner for you. It's felt strange cooking only for myself. It would feel like a return to normalcy if I knew I were cooking for another mouth as well.'

'Could I ask somethin, Mrs Marlee?'

'By all means.'

'Mr Changoor aware of this arrangement?'

A pause. 'I'll admit to you. I'll have to ask his permission.' As she spoke, she could see his face falling with doubt. 'But you'll have to trust me when I tell you that Dalton Changoor will pay any amount for his wife's safety and state of mind. You've always been our best man and we trust you. I, myself, think you are a very good man.'

'Thank you, Mrs Marlee.'

'Take the rest of the day for yourself, Hans. Talk to your wife. I'll make sure you're paid for today.'

Hans got up in a hurry and thanked her again. As he turned to leave, she asked, 'What's her name? Your wife?'

'Shweta.'

'Tell Shweta I won't take no for an answer.' She laughed.

6

A Hole in Everything

When Krishna was ten years old, his parents made an agreement with Dolly, who lived in the neighbouring room. They'd take Dolly's daughter, Lata, into their room from the hours of Saturday night to Sunday's sunrise. Lata was eleven at the time. This was when Dolly's husband, Umesh, was still alive. Was also when Hans was still taking on odd tasks at the canefield, being paid in sixpence by a rotund bookkeeper, before his employment under Mr Changoor. Dolly and Umesh worked alongside Hans. Umesh also took on tasks while Dolly made her pittance as a water carrier for the labourers. Hans usually brought his own water in a calabash, the drinking hole corked with a stiff wedge of caneroot, and so never required Dolly's service until late in the day.

Umesh had agreed to make the proposition to Hans, but days passed without him uttering a word of it. Dolly knew she would have to do it herself. Hans was easier to speak to than Shweta. He had a way that he made all of himself available to you, as if he'd been neglected all of his life and your presence was a welcomed respite. She stood before him as he sat against a bundle of harvested cane, his grass knife flat before his beaten boots. He was in the middle of lunch but put his food down and readied himself to stand to greet her. She gestured for him to remain as he was, and so he did. She kept conversation brief. Umesh knew their business, but that didn't stop the others from gossiping, especially when they had daru in them.

She kept the terms simple. They wanted privacy for one night a week, is all she said. Hans was already aware of their situation. Their room being positioned under a snapped rafter made it difficult to attach a curtain. They had tried. And they had asked Hans, who could hit a nail square on a ladybug, but not even he could get it to hold. She kept details out of it. Like the fact that Dolly and Umesh had done most of their copulation in the latrine, an affair that was hardly clandestine. The grunts and moans often sifted past the vent pipe and the wire mesh that acted as a fly screen. Only when Rookmin started spreading salt around the latrine to ward off ghosts that Murali told her what was actually happening in there.

There was no privacy in the barrack – only the injudicious illusion of it.

A few times, Dolly and Umesh ventured about a hundred steps into the tallest part of the canefield. The trysts were brief and clumsy, his chinos bundled at his ankles and her dress ruched over her tailbone. Drinking daru a half hour before the act made it less cumbrous, though only slightly. Once, midway into it, a flock of egrets fled from their presence, scattering overhead to signal their carnal arrangement to the rest of the labourers. With nothing to ballast them, their standing positions inelegantly became kneeling positions close to the finish.

Dolly always kept two orange peels in her pocket, one for her and one for Umesh. They chewed the peels to overpower the scent of daru on the breath, finding more contentment in this than the awkward, sexual balancing act preceding it. They sat on the grass, backs to each other. No words to be said. The damselflies dipping on the stalks. It was the denouement to a climax with no pleasure. Release without catharsis.

Talk to Shweta bout what I say, were her last words to Hans. Hans knew that Dolly wouldn't make such a request of the other barrack dwellers – and for the moment, felt honoured to oblige the couple. When he told Shweta of the request, she thought of it for a few minutes. She eventually agreed.

In return for the favour, Dolly brought Shweta some of her cooking ingredients – curry masala, onions, chives, hot peppers for buljol, whatever she had on hand. Whenever Lata was there, Krishna would sleep between his parents. He was small enough to fit on their mattress, snug and sandwiched between their trunks.

On the nights that Lata was there, Krishna awakened at midnight. Gazed at her in unabated wonder. He studied her. The way her roguish eyebrows valleyed gave her a look like she was always mid-smirk. She had a faint scar running down the left side of her jaw. Her right eyebrow was slightly longer than her left. The second digit on her right foot dwarfed her big toe. Her sleeping position was dependent on the temperature of the night. On a cold night, she assumed the foetal position, legs drawn up to her belly, a small strip of skin visible above her waist where her dress hiked up. Krishna thought of reaching out and running his fingers along that small section of spine, like caressing the notches of a canestalk. If the night got unpleasantly hot, she would be flat on her back, sweat pooled at the collar, her face uncomfortably tucked to the side the way a macaw would rest its sleepy head on its wing. She looked different with her eyes closed, her face not so puckish then. All of her facial muscles loosened. He thought of crawling in with her, perhaps sneaking five minutes of an embrace before returning to his parents. It wasn't so much sexual desire but a desire for closeness to the opposite sex. Lata had been the only girl around his age that he spoke to, and she was the only one he had ever felt that desire for.

One night, he woke up to find her gone.

Not wanting to wake his parents, it took him a full minute to squirm out from between their bodies. He managed to do this without rousing either of them. His father closed the gap quite naturally, like a timarie leaf gently folding into itself. His arm around his wife, his head pressed into the crook of her shoulder. Krishna went out in the hallway and with each step, waited for his eyes to adjust to the light.

No sign of Lata.

He went outside, careful to not step on the grass, listening for the slightest hiss that could be a scorpion. Scorpions were strangely more detectable at night, as moonlight made their bodies glisten. He started in the direction of the latrine but spotted Lata well before that. Found her crouched before the exterior wall of the barrack. Her forehead pressed against a plank of wood, one hand tilting a plank to the side while the other batted mosquitoes. The cold night air gave Krishna a runny nose.

He sniffed, causing the girl to jump. Grasped her chest in relief when she saw him. 'Shit. Is only you.'

'What you doin over here?' asked Krishna, craning his neck to look at the plank.

She got to her feet, wiped a bead of sweat from her brow, still recovering from alarm. 'I just come out to pee.' The lie went into a whisper.

His eyes returned to the plank. 'What it have over there?' he asked, similarly lowering his voice.

She took a few steps back from the wall, reached out her hand to Krishna as if coaxing him away from an angry bull. She was wound tight, surely hiding something.

He asked her straight, 'What you was peepin at there?'

Taken aback, he expected her to murmur a denial, but she admitted right away. 'Don't tell nobody nothin about this, you hear?' She slid the plank to reveal a hole.

'What's that?'

'What you think?'

'It always had that hole there?'

A shrug. 'It have a hole in everything.'

Krishna didn't question why she was spying on them. He kept his eye on the peephole, twitching his nose, suddenly feeling as if he could smell the musk of sweat emanating from it. Inching towards the wall without realising it. He turned to Lata, who was now anxiously gesturing for him to move away.

He ignored her, eventually kneeling before the peephole and gazing in.

At first, it had felt like he had thrust his entire head into the hole and for those few moments, forgot that Lata was behind him. Through it, the flicker of a flambeau and two naked bodies; man and woman. Umesh standing, Dolly spread eagle. The dimming light and restricted angle of vision made the two look suspended in dark waters. A halo of muted light radiating from their skin dissolved into a vignette of black. No matter how much Krishna strained his eyes, neither of their faces could become visible. The woman's skin golden brown in the light, the flesh over her thighs and bosom as soft and bleary as a guava's pericarp. Krishna traced his eyes over her imperfections. The purple marks around her nipples that he presumed were bruises. Her upper arms to her shoulders were darkly pocked with mosquito-bite scars. The cellulite made her legs look like they had been chewed and spat out. One of her hands rested on her forehead while the other was rooted between her thighs, the apron of her belly obscuring the fingers. Umesh was now faced away from the hole, the weight of his flesh sidling down his back into two drooping lumps.

He drew breath. Then the flambeau light went out.

Even when there was nothing to see, Krishna found it difficult to pull away from the peephole. He'd never lain eyes on such a thing before, though he had listened to his own parents in the act. The sounds of theirs were freakish. What would begin quietly, almost as any stir in the night, would eventually rise to a panicked crescendo. Enormous quaffs of air. Epiglottal wheezing. A nightmarish, snorting bull on the other side of the curtain instead of his parents.

Only when Lata put her hand on his shoulder did he realise how quickly his heart was beating. 'Someone comin,' she whispered. 'Get up. Get up now.'

The barrack entrance door suddenly opened. The two scampered, stooped behind a bush. The figure came into view. Rookmin. She left the door open, held the flambeau in front of her as if warding off evil. Slow steps towards the latrine. The two hurried into the barrack. Lata back on the mattress and Krishna into the nook of his parents' chests, the space between them reopening just as smoothly as it had closed.

★

The rain outside had stopped, but its apparition still flicked its idle fingers against the galvanised roof. A slow *tut tut tut* sound as the water dripped into the already overflowing barrels. Krishna rubbed his eyes. His parents asleep. A few nicks of light pinched through the slats in the upper part of the wall. Still, inside the barrack remained dimly lit in the dawn. The languid shuffling of dust like methane from a rice paddy. The ground mostly dry. The caulk had managed to hold, though rainwater was still dripping from the roof.

Krishna, careful not to wake his mother, unlatched the door. Before he could get to the barrack exit, a whisper came from behind him, 'Krishna. Krishna. Where you goin, Krishna?'

Sachin – Rookmin and Murali's idiot son. A twenty-four-year-old man child. His sharp face would be intimidating if it weren't for his slow eyes and quivering ratlike nostrils. His speech often so quick that it came off as incoherent, like his mouth was filled with something hot. He stuck his head out of his room and said, 'I come? I come, Krishna?'

'Go back to sleep.'

'Krishna? Krishna? I come, Krishna? Niala vomit on me.'

'Leave me alone. Go.'

Krishna made his way towards the barrack yard. From there, he could see the plains. Everywhere flooded. The rich petrichor smell. The wide expanse of water thick as dal, washing over the field. In the water, a vast reflection of the mauve sky. The morning wind chilly, drowsy. The first sight of the rising sun like a pinwheel through the wind-tilted paragrass.

A voice. 'Fish! Get your fresh fish! Tilapia, sardine, cascadura!'

Tarak stood at the other end of the yard, two flour bags in hand. His feet also wrapped in flour bags, tied with twine above the ankles.

'Where them fish at?'

Tarak gestured north, towards the rice paddies. 'The whole river wash up.' Whenever the plain flooded, the overflow from the ponds and rivers crept into the roads and paddies. The tilapia were easy to spot. Belts of red, floundering through the coppery haze of muckwater.

He added, 'Rudra and Rustam gon be out there too, I sure.' Though their usual haunt was at the riverside shack, it was a customary event that the twins Rudra and Rustam Lakhan crossed paths with them in the paddies. It was how their paths converged in the first place, catalysed by the weather, as if their fellowship had always been brewing in the skies. 'They wasn't at the river last week. Is like they gone into hiding. Think somethin happen?'

Krishna wondered as well. 'I aint worryin.'

Tarak let out a whistle. White Lady came crawling out from below her iron-sheet shelter. Her entire belly black and stringy with mud, though the rest of her had managed to stay clean. Tarak liked believing that White Lady was his dog. He ran a jagged fingernail through some matted hair on her ears. Her eyes limpid, tiny black splotches dotting the whiskers, a pucker of scar tissue at her left thigh where she had a hotspot. Her fur on a normal day smelled of the sugarcane she often galloped through. She was not a big dog. But she was able to reach Tarak's arms if she were to stand on her hind legs. Enough for them to lead each other into a slow dance. To Krishna, she was the single innocent creature to frequent this yard. She was an old dog, and she liked their company enough to spend the twilight of her life with them. In that way, he thought, White Lady was better than most people. A creature that worshipped those who loved her and begged no worship in return.

Tarak reached down to scratch the dog's scruff. In response, she angled her head upward and licked his ear. 'You need to stay your ass here,' he spoke to the dog as if she were a younger sibling. 'You go out there, you gon scare away all them fish.'

'Have a rope right there by that barrel. Why you don't tie she up?'

Tarak went solemn. 'Nah, I aint tyin up the dog.'

'Nothin you tell this dog gon stop she from runnin bout in that water.'

Tarak clicked his tongue, shook his head. 'I say I aint tyin she up.' He breathed a sigh. 'You know them three dogs they have there in that Changoor house?'

'Yeah. The big ones. German shepherds.'

'Some days ago, when the rain come down hard like this, seem they leave one of them tie up near the ravine. The dog slip down, the leash still on him. He tread water till he realise the rain wasn't stoppin. And I suppose he give up at a point.'

'What you sayin? The dog drown?'

'I aint never want to drown. Worst way to dead.'

Krishna shook his head. 'You sure this is the Changoor house you talkin bout?'

'Yeah.'

'My pa aint never say nothin bout no dog drownin.'

Tarak turned to the dog. 'He probably aint like thinkin bout it. Same way I aint like thinkin bout it.'

'How you find this out then?'

'My pa play cards with a man who work up there sometimes – Mr Baig. My pa was laughing when he was tellin it but it make my blood boil. That Mr Changoor probably just say is a dumb dog. Nothin worth going out in the rain for. Them people aint care bout nothin. Dogs smart, you know, but is only dumb animals to them. Just like we. So, I aint tyin up the dog, you hear?'

Krishna bit his lip. 'What you gon do when she scare away all the fish then?'

'Nothin. The fish live to see another day—'

'Your ma know you goin swimmin in shitwater, Krishna?' a voice behind them called out.

It was Lata. Her trousers catching the morning breeze. A white shawl over her hair. A colander of unshelled peas in her grip. She laid a large jute bag over a wooden crate and sat on it.

'You sound like you want to come,' Krishna said.

She pointed to her clean trousers. 'No thanks. I have to wash my own clothes when they get dirty. Boys aint have to do that.'

'We gon wash them for you, Lata,' Tarak said.

'Yeah,' Krishna added.

She shook her head. 'Damn liars.'

'You want we bring back a fish for you, Lata?' asked Krishna with a small grin.

'Unless you scaling and cookin that fish for me, don't bring back nothin for me, not even a tadpole.'

'We bringin back five for you then.' Krishna held up a splayed palm.

She laughed. 'You even gonna catch five?' She began shelling the peas. 'Also, you lookin to catch the *typhoon*? Gon grab them bags by that woodpile there and cover your feet.'

Krishna retrieved the two crocus bags and tied them around his feet.

'What you gon do without me, boy?' She feigned a wide smile before placing her focus back on the colander.

Krishna stood watching her, lost in thought until Tarak hit his shoulder. 'Stop daydreamin. Let's go.'

The two boys and the dog set off in the direction of the paddies. The rice plants were still young and looked more like weeds. The water opaque. Each step they took raised a plume of muck to the surface. When they stood still, tiny outlines of fishes swam in spirals. They ran the bag through the water and scooped up a catch of mostly tadpoles and guppies. They spent about half an hour doing this, hoping to get something juicy in there.

'The big ones round here somewhere,' Tarak mumbled.

Krishna spotted a pocket with a couple of larger outlines. 'I think they swimmin over there.'

Before they could get there, the dog bounded to the pocket and began splashing, spattering mud all over her back. 'White Lady!' Krishna called out. 'Why you gone and do that for?'

'Is because you was pointing with your hand,' said Tarak, wiping some mud from his chin. 'Point with your chin next time.'

The water so murky now that all the outlines were obscured. 'This paddy is a big waste of time,' said Krishna, shaking his head. 'All them fish swimmin right back into the river now.'

Tarak thought for a while. 'Is a long way and gonna be even longer walkin through this damn flood, but it have some catchments down by the old Hudswell. We could corner them easy there. If the dog start barkin, the fish just gon get scared and flop right onto land.'

They set out to find the catchments, first crossing the remains of the abandoned estate. In the distance, shadows of old buildings still standing flaked and weathered, a compound of warehouses lain like crumpled matchboxes. The two kept on the path where the land undulated until they came to a fractured track of wood and warped iron. The water had pooled in several spots in this area. Ten strides from there was a long mint-green locomotive sitting lopsided on the track. Briars of bagasse and straw protruded from its trolley like the carcass of a giant metal porcupine. On its side the name read in tarnished letters: *Hudswell Clarke*.

They waded into a shallow catchment, the water scaling their knees.

'Don't move!' Tarak exclaimed, pointing to Krishna's feet. He stooped, gripping the flour bag between his teeth, and plunged his hands down into the water. He moved them back and forth, his fingers splayed out and wiggling like starfish legs. Then swung his arms up, cleaving the water's crest and splashing Krishna in the face.

'*Ptuh!*' Krishna spat in disgust. 'Boy, watch it with that water!'

Tarak held his palms up, revealing two tomato-red tilapia nipping at his thumbs. With one quick motion, he slapped both of them into the bag. A wide grin. He pinched the top of the bag into a small hole to show Krishna. 'You see that? Two in one, brother!'

'You damn good at this,' said Krishna, impressed.

'Go ahead, give it a try,' said Tarak, still giddy.

Krishna retracted. 'I don't catch nothin. Them fish aint like me.'

'Make the fish like you then. So, think bout the things that the fish like.' He instructed Krishna to crane forward, only one hand in the water this time. 'Fish like to eat worms. So, you have to move your fingers like worms. The right amount of movement.

You have to believe each finger is a separate worm. Like they aint part of you no more.'

'I have to stop believing I have a hand?'

'Yeah. At least until you feel them. Is a soft kinda feeling. Like if you was holding a small hummingbird. You curl your finger like a hook and pull it up.'

A trio of tilapia approached Krishna's hand. 'And they don't bite your finger?' Krishna asked, leaning over to watch.

'The teeth too small for it to be any kinda bite. You just have to remain still. You hear?'

'Yeah.'

'You concentratin?'

'Yeah.' One of the fish kissed Krishna's finger.

'When you gonna marry Lata?' Tarak suddenly asked.

Krishna swooped his arm up, nearly losing his balance. '*What?*' All the fish dispersed.

Tarak burst into laughter, nearly dropping the bag into the water. 'You shoulda see your face! It gone red like a tomato!'

'That aint funny! I nearly fall in this water!'

'She gon make a good wife for you one day, that Lata. I can see it.'

Krishna splashed some water at Tarak. 'Stop sayin them things!'

'When you have children, they could call me Uncle Tarak.'

'*Hush!*' He splashed again.

'She like you too?'

'Nobody aint like nobody! I thought we come to catch fish?'

'Calm down, calm down,' he said, sucking his teeth, pointing to an adjacent pool. 'Some slow ones here.'

'We being serious now?' said Krishna, still flustered.

'Serious now.' Tarak gave a big nod, almost like a bow.

Krishna reached his hand into the water, his eyes closed in concentration. He tried to do as Tarak said – to release his hand from his own body.

But the stillness this time was interrupted by White Lady's barking.

Then a voice: 'What you doing squattin down there? You takin a shit in that water there?'

Krishna opened his eyes, looked to the top of the hill. Tarak and White Lady did too.

There, a group of three boys, figures silhouetted by the morning sun. Even though Krishna couldn't see their faces, he knew who they were. In the middle, Mikey Badree, bareback, the ringleader, and at his side, two toadies – Shane and Addy – the latter's name was actually Adhiraj but he couldn't stand how it sounded. Krishna's classmates and tormentors. The toadies holding empty crocus bags slowly filling with breeze. The trio were in raincoats and galoshes. At Mikey's left temple, sprawling over his cheek like brown tendrils was a bad scar that made him look like he had a lazy eye. Made the skin look like it was folded and doubled over itself.

'Looking like he trying to catch a crab up he asshole,' Addy blurted out with a laugh.

'Them's we fish,' said Shane.

Tarak twitched his shoulders. 'How them's your fish? Them fish have your father name on it?'

'How you would know, dumb-dumb?' asked Mikey. 'Bet you can't even spell your own name.'

Tarak's face immediately fell.

'We was here first!' shouted Krishna.

Mikey scooted down the hill, Shane and Addy following. The two groups came face to face.

Addy said with a chuckle, 'Go home and suck your mother breast, you hear?'

Shane added, 'Yeah, your balls aint even drop yet.'

'What bout *your* balls...' Tarak started but couldn't think of a comeback.

Shane asked Krishna, 'You start gettin hair on your prick yet, lice boy?' Before Krishna could say anything, 'Pull down your pants, lemme see. I bet it real small. Small like a canned sausage.'

'Don't worry, cockroach,' Mikey said, holding up a hand to quiet the two at his side. 'We gon leave the tadpoles for you and the pothound.' White Lady's tail pointed straight up now, a vigilant look in her eyes. She started barking. Mikey's palm shot up to his scarred eye. 'If that dog come near me, I gon dropkick it, you hear?'

'She aint want to come near you.' Tarak put a gentle hand on her and she stopped. 'And you aint want to come near we. Just be fair. We was here first.'

'First? Aint matter who first,' said Shane. 'The only thing that matter is that it have three of we. And two of you.'

'I gon say it louder for you. Go home and suck your mother breast,' said Addy. 'Or I will go there and suck it for you.'

Tarak narrowed his eyes at Addy, another spasm in his shoulders. Krishna put a hand on his shoulder, trying to calm the boy's laboured breathing. He remembered what his father had once told him – that you cannot let your enemies know you're angry. They'll know what's coming if you do that.

Mikey went over to the tail end of the locomotive and grabbed a wooden plank. He already knew that he had riled Tarak enough for him to consider taking a swing. Mikey was ready with the plank. Krishna thought it didn't make sense to challenge them here – not for two fish.

'Take it back,' Tarak grunted, eyes burning into Addy.

'Take what back?' said Addy, chuckling.

'Don't talk bout my mother, you hear me? My mother aint do nothin to you.'

'Leave him alone, *Adhiraj*,' Krishna said, emphasising the name in a subtle taunt.

Addy gritted his teeth a little.

'He's right,' said Mikey, taking note of Tarak's hands, now balled into fists. He turned to Addy. 'Tell the man you sorry, Addy.'

Addy approached Tarak with his hands out. 'Sorry. We gonna come to an agreement then.' He turned to the others and began walking back. Halfway there, he spun around, and his voice rose to a shout, 'You suck one breast, and I will suck the other!' In unison, the three village boys burst into laughter.

Tarak dropped the bag. Lunged at Addy. The two tilapia flopped out into the pangola grass. Shane rushed over. Yanked Tarak off. Tried to, anyway. Tarak was stronger than them both.

Pulled Shane into the grime. Their shirts soaked and heavy with grey mud.

Mikey, for a few seconds, gave a bewildered look at the muddle of bodies before him. Raised the plank high.

Brought it down sharp onto Tarak's shoulder.

Tarak let out a loud, pained grunt. Mikey raised the plank again. Was about to bring it down again when Krishna signalled to Tarak as a warning.

'*Go!*' Tarak yelled and White Lady went running. Pounced on Mikey, threw him down. The plank in the pool.

Two separate tussles now.

Mikey bawling, '*Get-it-off get-it-off get-it-off!*' then, '*Gon-kill-it gon-kill-it gon-kill-it!*'

A hot iron ball weighing down Krishna's stomach.

The dog bit down on Mikey's wrist. He screamed like he was dying.

Krishna ran to get the plank. Skated in the mud. Crashed face-first into the water. The two tilapia still flopping madly. Krishna scrambled for the wood. Reached his hand into the water. Finally got hold of it. Hoisted it into the air as if he'd already claimed victory. A shrill line of kingfishers fluttered over them.

Mikey yelled out, wrapped his arms around the dog's hind. Rotated her, turned her upside down. Her bottom half dangling like some unstable pendulum. The way she flailed – like a fowl at the cutting block. Mikey rushed over to another pool. Grip sturdy on her rear.

Submerged the dog face-forward into the turbid water.

The sound she made as she thrashed about, Krishna had never heard anything like it before. The gurgling and wheezing as bubbles of mud came up. Then high-pitched squealing. The second the dog managed to squirm upward for air, her head was thrust back down into the water.

Tarak cried out, 'Let she go! You gon kill she!'

Krishna made a fierce dash up to Mikey. Put his fists out to him. Too late. Came crashing to the ground again as Shane broke from his tussle and tackled him.

At the last moment, with all of his might, Krishna tossed the plank into the pile of bagasse sitting in the locomotive. Addy pressed his knee on Tarak's neck and told him to watch. Learn a lesson. Tarak stared morosely, hands shaking. Face mud-stained.

This was no longer a fight, Krishna realised. This was a point of no return.

The dog stopped jerking. Stopped moving. Legs gone limp.

'*Get im!*' Another voice.

Two figures of equal height sprinted down the hill.

Rudra and Rustam. Rustam and Rudra. Dirt worked into their flesh. Eyes like boiling tar. Unbuttoned shirt-jacks, creases like writing on parchment, hiding the scars on their backs. Hair long and wild, like tendrils of black smoke trailing behind them. Rudra brought Addy down with one left hook to the temple. Another to make sure. Rustam wrapped his fingers around Mikey's neck. Threw him to the ground. Stomped his heel on his sternum. Even with White Lady free of Mikey's grasp, her snout remained buried in the pool.

Tarak, now free as well, hurried to the dog. Pulled her out onto the grass.

Shane let loose of Krishna. And before Krishna could turn to look, Shane was gone. So was Addy. At the same time, he noticed the bloody bandage wrapped around Rudra's right palm.

There was still movement within the dog's thorax. Her breathing forced and irregular as if she were in her last throes of life. Tarak knelt beside her, desperate as a votary ready to self-flagellate. Pumped his hands on her belly. Did it again. And again. And again, until a squirt of water came out of her nose. Then pumped some more.

Still under Rustam's foot, Mikey to the twins, 'You gon pay for this. I tellin you.'

'Pay for what?' said Rustam. 'You's the one out here startin shit, asshole.'

'You gon be sorry. All of you, real sorry,' hissed Mikey.

Rudra flicked his hand, signalling for his brother to let him go. The dog was of greater concern right now. Rustam kicked Mikey in his ribs one last time. Then let him go. Mikey stumbled back, spoke like a weight was on his tongue, 'That dog give me rabies!'

'Listen to me, rabies boy,' Rustam said. 'If that dog die, you die.'

Mikey scurried to the hill. When he got to the top, he looked like he was about to yell something, but instead stole away from sight, the four boys now focused on keeping the dog from death.

7
A Prayer for the Dying

Down the hill from where the house stood, the land sat in the water, slowly crinkling. When Hans completed the descent, he came to a clear division between the foot of the hill and the water. As if the hill where the house stood became some kind of skerry. The Isle of Changoor. Up ahead was the Northern Range, looking like a distant country – a shallow ocean separating the two.

He stepped into the turbid water, his work boots feeling twice as heavy now. Floods always brought Hema to mind. Little Hema, not even a year old, dead before she could make a proper footprint on the earth. Dead before the world could hear anything she had to say. He didn't like being reminded of Hema. His memories of her all impaled with regret. It'd been raining that night and, as usual, water was coming through the walls. It felt strange to recall that he and Shweta weren't even twenty years old yet. It had been simple. A glimpse of her thighs. His breath on her ear. They had unlocked secrets within each other. Lovemaking was normal back then, uninterrupted by angry gods.

Shweta had her knees bent back, her gaze on her daughter, knowing that the water was rising. Every rhythm matched that night. Her flesh rose to meet his. She strummed her fingers on his back, a habit that he knew telegraphed her orgasms. After they were done, she held her husband. He was asleep within the minute. She knew she should've gotten up. Unintentionally, she fell asleep as well.

A few hours later, just before dawn. she woke up in a fright. Water had pooled into a sunken corner of the room. And little Hema wading in it. Skin filthy and pruned. They wiped her, set her on their bed, went back to sleep. It was the stench that woke them in the early morning. The bedding soaked in a watery mustard yellow, and it was still pouring out of Hema at that point. The only sound from her, a choked gurgle.

Shweta tried to say something, but no sound could escape. Her throat constricted from shock. Hans grabbed the baby, raced outside onto the muddy ground. Held her upside down and began patting her rear until she retched, let the sickness out. He filled a basin, and he and Shweta washed the filth off. But it could never get clean. The more they washed, the more came out. A carousel of voices revolved around them.

'Oh God! What happen there?' asked Kalawatie.

'Poor thing get the sprue, it look like,' said Murali.

'Get that child to the hospital right now, right now,' said Dolly.

'Everybody pray!' exclaimed Rookmin. 'Say a prayer for the dying!'

Hans put on his boots and ran two miles to the village clinic. That she was retching and soiling herself let him know she was still alive. After the doctors took her in, a nurse directed Hans to an outdoor shower. The stench was potent in the lobby, but she was polite about it. He washed himself with blue soap, scrubbed his arms until they bled. When he returned to the lobby, the nurse informed him that Hema had died. Confused by his initial lack of reaction, she had to repeat the horrible words. She took him into a dim room, where the baby was still lying in a hyper-flexed position in the middle of a metal table.

The nurse asked Hans if he wanted to hold her, and he despondently shook his head. Then asked if he wanted a quiet moment with her, to which he agreed. When the nurse left the room, he found himself looking at his daughter with the same morbid curiosity as his childhood self gazing upon a felled pigeon. The nurse hadn't said how she died. Still on the shelf were a red Ambu bag and laryngoscope. The way Hema was positioned, he couldn't see her face. Couldn't bear to.

When he left, he came to a room where someone else had just passed away. A woman, looked to be about thirty years old. A terrifying stillness to her body. A little girl, presumably her daughter, craned over the bedside. Hans couldn't be sure how long the woman had been dead and didn't want to ask. The girl sobbing and asking the woman why she had to die. Hans wasn't sure what compelled him, but he entered that room and put his arms around that girl. At first, she was detached, befuddled – her gaze focused forward as if she were walking down some unlit road in the middle of the night. She reciprocated the hug, nearly squeezing the breath out of Hans, this stranger. His eyes lit up electric as she did.

At the end of the embrace, he kissed her eyes. Then left. He never learnt her name and never saw her again. Never told anybody about her, not even his wife. Afterwards, he informed a nurse in the hallway of the dead woman. She had already known. The dead woman's features remained blurred in his memory. Hema's as well. But he always remembered that little girl's face.

*

As Hans came up the macadam road, he could already see the commotion up ahead. In the cacophony of voices, his brother, Mandeep's was the loudest. He was still too far away to make a count of the gathered crowd, but it didn't seem to be a fight. There was movement and shouting, but no tussling. He picked up the pace and as he got closer, he could see that the smallest figure there was his son. Two boys kneeling – Hans immediately recognised them as the Lakhan twins. Sachin jumping around, hollering like a monkey that had its food stolen. Lata stood frozen with both palms over her mouth. Rookmin was the only calm one, sitting on a crate, observing from afar as she smoked her kush.

'What trouble happen here?' asked Hans.

Mandeep said from the barrack door, a cigarette in his mouth, 'Look at what they gone and do.'

Sachin held his head, breathing like he was choking.

Old man Murali scolded him, 'Boy! Cut that out!'

At that point, Hans saw White Lady lying on her back. Her belly black like she had been dragged through pitch. The fur stiff like fresh broomstraw. Tiny bubbles popping out of her nose. Fighting to keep her eyes open. Sachin mimicked the dog's struggle to breathe. *Huh! Ack! Huh! Ack!* One of the twins kneeling at the dog's side, pumping his palm against the arch of her ribcage. The other wiped her nose with a leaf.

'They get themself into a fight,' said Shweta, pulling Krishna close.

Hans bit his lip. 'Tarak, what happen here?'

As soon as Tarak opened his mouth, Mandeep, his father, shouted at the twins, 'The two of you – go back to the swamp your mother lay you in! Couple of crocodiles!' They ignored him. Hans waved his hand at Mandeep, signalling for him to stop, before redirecting his attention to Tarak.

Tarak, his shoulders fluttering, said in a shaky voice, 'We was just fishin. And they come and start the shit.'

Hans looked him in the eye. 'Who come?'

Tarak wiped his nose. 'Some village fellas.'

One brother motioned to the other to pry the dog's mouth open. Then reached into the dog's throat and gave the tongue a good yank. Lay it to the side of her mouth like a wet pink ribbon. Took a deep breath before sealing her nose with his mouth and exhaling into it. The other one pressed down on the rib with the heel of his hand. And so, the twins repeated the actions while the others argued.

'Why them fellas hurt the dog like that?' asked Murali, leaning over to see.

'They take we fish,' Krishna said. 'We fight back, and this is what they do.'

'*Fish?*' asked Mandeep in disbelief.

Tarak nodded. 'They's thieves.'

'Is just fish! Nasty mudwater fish! It have fish for days. Let them take it!' said Mandeep, shaking his head. 'Where your brains gone? You two is damn fools invitin that kinda trouble into this place.'

Sachin called out, mocking, '*It have fish for days!*'

'How them boys is fools, Mandeep?' asked Rookmin, exhaling some smoke. 'Is fish today. Who know what it is tomorrow?'

Shweta turned to Rookmin, put her hands out in frustration. 'These boys could lose their good life over foolishness. Look at what happen to this dog.'

'Thank God is just the dog!' Mandeep said.

Rookmin sighed. 'The dog today. Who tomorrow?'

Shweta turned to Hans, 'Is your fault – I tell you he aint have no place bein friends with them twins!'

Hans gave a small guilty nod; had nothing to say in response. He suggested, 'I think we should make a report.'

Mandeep asked, 'Report to who?'

'The police.'

'*Police?*' Mandeep said defiantly. 'Sometimes I feel like you does forget who you is, Hans. You tell the police and I guarantee everybody in here gettin a bloody floggin with the *cat*. If police find out we associating with the Lakhans ...'

Sachin shouted, '*You tell the police! You tell the police!*'

Mandeep's words gave Hans pause.

'Report, my ass.' Mandeep walked up, grabbed the kneeling brother by the shoulders, flung him to the ground. The dog cried out. A pained, frightening shriek. The boy landed on his side.

Tarak shouted, 'Leave them!'

Mandeep moved to pick up the boy again, when Tarak leapt on his back. Mandeep spun in circles trying to shake him off.

Shweta could feel Krishna trying to break from her arms. Held him even tighter and shouted, 'All of you, *stop it*!'

Sachin followed, jumping up and down, '*Stoppit! Stoppit!*'

The standing brother just watched. Tarak threw a punch. Landed it on his father's temple. Sent him stumbling. Sachin still yelling. '*Stoppit! Stoppit! Stoppit!*'

Hans ran to the fracas, managed to pull the two boys off. As he did, he locked his arms around Mandeep's shoulders, shackling their bodies together. 'Mandeep, stop!' Hans bellowed. The others recoiled, as it was not often that Hans raised his voice.

Even Sachin went quiet. Rookmin raised her eyebrows with a grin.

In the newfound silence, Hans remained firm with Mandeep. 'Go inside and cool off,' he said. 'You makin everything worse out here.'

'You aint helpin at all!' Shweta added.

Rookmin blew some smoke. 'I have some kush inside, Mandeep.'

'Let me go, Hansraj,' Mandeep said, no longer struggling.

'Tell me you goin inside and cool down.'

'I goin, I goin.'

With that, he let him go. The twins hurried over to the dog. Continued the resuscitation. Mandeep cracked his knuckles, his neck. Told the gathered crowd, 'Come hell or high water, these Lakhan brothers gonna bring the whole of Bell down on we. Wait till anybody start talk of we allowin these crocodiles in here...'

Hans stamped his foot, pointed to the barrack door.

With that, Mandeep went inside. The crowd huddled around the dog as if mesmerised by how coordinated the Lakhan brothers were. One gave the dog breath while the other pumped her chest. In two minutes, the dog hocked up a ball of water from her throat. They continued the procedure and the dog brought up more and more water. When no more came up and it was evident that the dog would live, they let Tarak take over.

As they left the barrack yard, Tarak enveloped the dog with his body. His eyes still hot. Shoulders still tense and quivering.

The twins walked up the macadam road, back onto the flooded plain in the direction of the rice paddies. The dog still on her side but breathing well now. Her muscles still strained from the brush with death. Rookmin hopped off the crate, sauntered over to the dog and gently blew smoke in her face.

Hans looked at his son, pummelled and bruised, brimming with silent anger. In his son, saw the soul of his father. Not a protector, but a pugilist. He knew his father to be a fighting man who had been knocked down more times than he could count – and because of that, he made his family into his opponent. Because that was at least a fight he could win. The man was eventually found in a ravine somewhere off the highway, a cutlass having severed half of his neck. They never found who did it but everyone who knew him said it was coming. No loss, really. He was a gambler, adulterer and card cheat after all. Never had money. Didn't know what love was.

Hans stood in his room, arms folded, watching Shweta tend to Krishna's wounds. Lata had come to help as well. Both of them with tender looks, dewy with perspiration. In that moment, it was like the boy had two mothers. When they were done, Shweta pulled her dupatta over her scalp, held her palms open and asked Lata to pray with her. They prayed to Lord Vishnu for healing and to Devi Durga for peace.

He wondered what his wife would say to the proposition. Two hundred dollars for standing watch for a few nights. Two hundred dollars to scare away some meagre Tully Settlement rascals. Would she think him foolish for not immediately leaping at the proposition? Would she have doubts that they'd have to be apart? After all, this family had never before spent a single night apart.

He closed his eyes to join the prayer. A memory of Marlee manifested. Felt a warm jolt in his groin as it played out. Before they'd been formally introduced. He'd finished for the day, and she was tending to some tomato trellises. Suddenly, she began to itch. Lowered her dress on one side like she was about to breastfeed. Her creamy, half-exposed chest maculated by mites. One of her nipples winked at him, big and domed and puffy from the hot sun. Intentional or not, Hans was never sure. Since then, he'd kept that image of her filed away in his mind. That fair speckled chest. It was one he could go to, like a devotee's morning mantra.

The next time Hans laid Shweta down, he let it play and replay in his mind like a scrap of overexposed film in a picture show. Then he saw it in dreams. Now it had made its way into prayer. He kept aware that women like Marlee Changoor were unappeasable and were only meant to be kept in the imagination.

Roll out mackled fantasies of them like a printing press, excuse yourself, do what you have to do privately, and return to your daily tasks.

And so, before Shweta and Lata could finish their prayer, he silently excused himself to the latrine.

II

A Small Sacrifice

In 1941, the same year the Americans arrived on Trinidadian shores, a fisherman and his niece received notice that they would have to relocate. They weren't alone. Their entire village was to be demolished and all surrounding holiday facilities, henceforth, closed. The beaches that they had claimed as part of their identity would no longer be theirs.

The Americans' arrival was scheduled after Nazi U-boats were spotted in the Caribbean Sea, presumably to disrupt shipment lines. A naval base was to be set up on the northwest peninsula of Chaguaramas. There was some dispute, but the Americans won in the end. The villagers bade goodbye to their homes and to each other, their community forever fractured.

The fisherman and his niece were relocated into temporary housing at the nearby coastal village of Carenage. The niece was fourteen years old at the time, and one of the top students in her class, but decided to drop out of school when her uncle suffered a stroke and lost control of his left side. Against his wishes, she served as his caretaker. It was the least she could do for him after her father had abandoned her and fled to Venezuela. As she considered it, her mother had abandoned her as well. Never left a note. Never said a word of her plan to anyone. After her father left, her mother walked into the sea. A large portion of that sea was now delegated to a degaussing range.

The fisherman's niece admired the American officers, sometimes to the point of jealousy. The fact that they could break free from the land and be guided with the wind and the stars. She found herself gawking at them. Their shoulders broader than their uniforms, broad like the destroyers they sailed in on. Muscles lined their braced bodies, tensed from dragging giant snails of rope, hawsers with cables thicker than their bones. The muddle of whistles and instruments filled the town harbour. All of them victim to the tropical weather. Sunburnt skin rufescent like a bison's tongue had repeatedly brushed their flesh. The men were extensions of their vessels, wanderers of the seas. The wide ocean was their sky and to them, the stars fell into the sea every night.

The officers had a sort of composed chaos that exhilarated all the village children. Even though their presence had forever disrupted the course of their lives, the children often flocked to the shoreline to see them pull into the dockyard. They stood on the hulls on old dinghies, in awe of the destroyers – the four-stackers – as they docked in the distance. At sunset, the stacks like dark crowns of gold. Majestic, but there was something morose about them. Just their size in this small harbour made them into tragic giants. Anchored to the beach by huge crabs of black steel. A ship's horn like a heifer wailing in grief.

Once, an older woman from the village chided the niece for admiring the officers. Said that there was a Spanish name for these men: *encantado.* The encantado were river dolphins that turned into humans. Humans would fete with the dolphinmen, and the dolphinmen would bed them before sprouting fins and racing back to the river. You could know who was an encantado if you could see their blowhole. So, most of them hid their blowholes under their hats, she said.

They had good money. Their clothes were always clean and well fitted. They wore waterproof wristwatches. They had that laugh, that smooth accent – it was like the radio was talking to you. Women liked them. Sometimes they even went with them for free. Just for their own pleasure. But why do that when you could get paid for your pleasure?

There was a young woman in the fishing village named Celita. She constantly boasted of her escapades with the officers. Flashing a wad of bills, she said that the tip of an American penis looked like a tulip bud. If she could hook one of them, they would make sure her feet were properly stockinged. Her skin swaddled in silk and cashmere. Floating on a cloud of Shalimar Eau de Parfum. It wasn't likely, she knew. But it felt good to live in the American dream, even if just for a few minutes.

You couldn't have that with a mangy Trinidadian boy who had to bat mosquitoes from his girlfriend's neck while she was on her knees for him. Whose prized possession was a small burlap bag full of marbles collected from the periphery of some chalk circle sketched on a back-alley stretch. Even if the boy had more than that – even if he worked behind a louvred office in Port of Spain and put himself out to be the son of a rich upholsterer or fabric salesman in Woodbrook – there was nothing exhilarating about the Trinidadian male. The Trinidadian male was a barnacle upon the bow of a retired schooner.

Soon, the other women in the village tired of Celita's stories, collectively saying that Celita was trying hard to convince herself that she was more than a common whore. A whore who takes a preference to white American men is still a blasted whore. Maybe worse. Still, the tales she told were embedded in the niece's mind. Each time Celita went out on the wharf, the niece was curious to follow her. She wondered: some of these American officers had American girls back home and yet they paraded around with Trinidadian girls as well. Why was that?

Because they could.

Because they covered their blowholes with their hats.

*

The fisherman died penniless, the last of his savings squandered on hopeless medicine. His niece, sixteen at the time, was alone. He'd been her last trace of family. After his death, she was lost. The world seemed to move on without her. She approached

Celita and expressed interest in joining her. Celita was initially cautious but eventually took her to meet a man who called himself Lord Harris. There had been an actual Lord Harris, a governor, some time ago – but this Lord Harris was Lord of the Oyster House, where all the ladies were called *pearls*.

He sized up the niece, told her she looked too pretty to be doing something like this. Then asked her age. She claimed to be eighteen, prompting a guffaw from the vulpine man. Nevertheless, he agreed to take her under his wing. She was now under his employ at the Oyster House. Not as a pearl – not right now. It was too early for her. She had to ferment first.

He gave her two main tasks. Make sure the rooms were ready. And keep time for the customers.

The Oyster House looked like any other building. It was all white save for a strip of burgundy that lined the top like a bandana. No sign. Each window striped with black wrought iron. The showers curtainless. The bathroom stained with soap scum and the mirror's frame loose, splintered at the top into three frosty peaks, her empty gaze reflecting from each. The fisherman's niece imagined that proper women had a conurbation of bottles, serums, facial oils, essences, creams. But the bathroom vanity here was bare, bald except for a few incense sticks.

Outside, down the street, people gathered at the theatre and vendors emerged from oblivion with magazines and cotton candy and tutti frutti chewing gum. She bought a yo-yo and usually played with it to pass the time.

The first customer wasn't an American but the manager of a nearby haberdashery. A stocky, damp-looking French Creole man. He eyed the niece, told Lord Harris that he wanted her. Lord Harris shook his head, told him that she wasn't for sale. The man laughed, told him that he was missing out on good business. Eventually went in with a pearl that he insisted call herself Ginger. Grunted loudly during the act as if he were lifting heavy furniture. Outside, the street vendors in a loop, a litany of soft drink flavours: *cream soda, black, red, orange, banana!*

The next few customers were Americans. Two ensigns and three warrant officers. They all wanted the niece as well, and again,

Lord Harris had to turn them down. Even after one of them offered to pay double.

The fisherman's niece realised that each of the doors was fitted with a reverse peephole. She frequently observed the couples, especially when they got loud. Their naked bodies curved and distorted through the fisheye lens like figures dancing in a funhouse mirror. All of the officers were rough with the women. Pulled their hair, spat on them, bit their breasts. This included Celita. The only time the officers spoke to them was to ask them if they liked it or to tell them to beg for more. Never said a word after the act. What was done was done; the women no longer existed to them. They showered, put their uniforms on and left.

One morning, the fisherman's niece noticed a foul musty smell pervading the bathroom. At first, she thought it to be the general stench of muck and age, walls and pipes unscrubbed for years. But no, this was worse. The more she noticed it, the more unbearable it became. The smell was coming from under the vanity, she finally realised. When she opened the two doors outward, the reek might as well have been a fog for how thick it was. Inside, a pile of old blankets rolled up tight like Cuban cigars.

When she shifted them aside, she nearly fell backwards.

A rat. A dead rat.

Had been lodged in there for days, most likely dead from the heat before it could starve. Looked as dark and still as its own shadow. Usually, dead animals lie to their side. This one was still upright. And she only realised why when she accidentally brushed its body with the cloth. The fabric cut right through its fur, flesh, organs as if it were a dark grey marshmallow. The thing had melted in there and fused with the wood. Its feet came right off. The eyes stared straight at her. That look of resignation. It must have known it would die in there, crushed into a corner in the morbid heat.

There are images in life you never forget. This was one.

She couldn't imagine dying in this place.

One night a little later, a lieutenant came in. He said it was his birthday and from his breath and slur, she knew he'd been drinking. Maybe since morning. Strangely, he didn't want anything sexual with the pearl he chose. Removed his uniform but kept his vest and shorts on and climbed into bed with her. Embraced her, periodically taking deep whiffs at her neck. Caressed her belly and rested his head upon it. She stroked his hair until he fell asleep. His hour was up before she woke him. Groggily, the lieutenant rose from the bed, put his uniform on and stumbled out the door. When the fisherman's niece wished him happy birthday, he muttered a curse and left.

When changing the sheets, she noticed that the lieutenant had forgotten his wallet on the nightstand. Out of curiosity, she reached for it, peeked inside. Slotted between the few American bills was a photo of a pretty woman. She was sitting comfortably atop a magnificent white horse, looking as if she always belonged there. An accomplished pose. Large eyes. Long auburn hair styled into bumper bangs. A bright megawatt smile. The niece knew she would never meet this woman – and the woman would never know of the lieutenant's time here at the Oyster House. On the back of the photo read:

I love you to the end of the world and back.
—*Your Marlee*

That night, she felt like she had dreamt a year in another woman's life. Dreamt that she was in America, living in a townhouse surrounded by a white picket fence. Kept a row of basil and mint on her windowsill. Sat on a porch, sipping Ceylon tea, watching her children run in circles. Rode around her neighbourhood on a red Raleigh bicycle. Closet packed with sundresses and cotton tops. Danced naked in the privacy of her home. Music and carpet. When she woke up, she couldn't ascribe any other word to the feeling than *shattering*. She now pined for a life she never had, could never have. Not here, not like this.

She gave the wallet to Celita, who promptly pocketed the money from it. 'Finders keepers,' she said cheekily. She offered to take the fisherman's niece to the cinema. They made it to the night show. The line stretched around the corner. It was for a

Warner Bros production, *High Sierra*. Celita had seen it before, she admitted, but said that watching it with someone new would be like seeing it for the first time. The blood-red posters had been pasted all over town. The niece was electrified from start to finish – she had never seen anything like it. Humphrey Bogart and Ida Lupino were like colossi out of some fable. When the credits rolled, she was delirious. Though when Celita joked that they should thank the drunk lieutenant for sponsoring them, the niece became a little worried. She wondered if this had been a habitual thing – and what would happen if she were to be caught.

It was a Tuesday, which meant that she had to take the sheets to wash at 9 a.m. The launderette was one street over and made a tidy profit from the Oyster House. That day, the niece observed a man in the street, sitting on an ironwood bench with one leg folded over the other, reading a newspaper. Every once in a while, he glanced over at her. An older man, looking late into his thirties, nerved by coffee, hair crimped, not handsome in the slightest. Thin as Jesus on the cross. A rural sort, or at least looked the part.

She saw him each week after that. Suspected that he'd purposely synced his schedule with hers. His presence was exasperating, this stranger. It was clear that he was smitten, as if seeing her was the highlight of his week. She felt awkward, realising this. One morning, she noticed him holding a wooden case in his lap. While the laundry was going, for the sake of conversation, she asked him about it. He said that it was a rare treasure. A piece of history in the making. Her interest was piqued.

He opened the case. In it was a dagger, the handle's glossy black lacquer glinting in the sun. At first, she was a little disappointed. She didn't know what she had expected. He didn't take it out of the box, but pointed at an inscription in German. Said that it translated to 'My honour is loyalty'. It was an SS-Ehrendolch, he called it. Straight from the Nazi party, meant to be used against any soul that violated the honour of the SS. He'd paid a pretty penny for it and had to pick it up himself – something like this couldn't be trusted with a courier. The girl dared not ask the man his line of business. The average person, even the average entrepreneur, couldn't have gotten his hands on something like that. Still, he told her that his family owned an estate some miles off the Churchill–Roosevelt Highway. Said that he'd be glad to give her a tour.

The laundry was done by then. She didn't give him an answer.

A few days later, she returned to the Oyster House to find a naval officer trashing one of the rooms. Closet doors flung open, vanity ransacked, threats to cut open each mattress. Celita in the corner, cowering, her hands on her head. Lord Harris barged in and held the officer back. The officer explained that he had lost something very important in this room, and if he'd found out it had been stolen, he would have the place shut down and every whore thrown in jail. Lord Harris knew the man was bluffing but humoured him, telling him that he would interrogate each of his workers. The officer left with a threat – whomever had stolen his belongings had committed a crime. A crime against an American was a crime against God.

Later that night, the fisherman's niece discovered what it was. Celita took her to the bathroom, stood on a chair and removed a tile from the ceiling. Felt around for a few seconds before finding it. The fisherman's niece's eyes widened as she produced it. A Colt Government pistol, US standard issue. She grinned madly like she had all the power in the world. The niece asked Celita why she stole it, to which Celita replied, 'Because he call me a nigger. Wasn't enough to steal his money.'

A week later, on the most humid night of the month, three ensigns raided the Oyster House. It was not an official order. Didn't matter for crimes against God. After only ten minutes, they found the pistol stashed in the bathroom ceiling. To everyone's surprise, they took no action. No arrests, no shutdown, not even words being thrown. Lord Harris supposed that the whole incident was an embarrassment to the officers, and the less people that knew about it, the better. He let Celita go that night, told her to never return. Her face emotionless when he informed her, as if her remorse and relief had cancelled each other out.

Celita returned to Carenage. Only two days later, she was back on the dockyard. A free agent this time. Her hair loose in the night wind. The niece feared for her and so decided to follow. She hid behind a mount of crates and observed. Each breath of the damp air like a weight upon her lungs. The night itself slow, lazy. Even the tides that normally spilled over the timber stakes along the beach just seemed to sluggishly lap against the pier. There was a section of the dock that was poorly lit, behind a knoll of cargo containers where a dimmed sodium lamp went purposely neglected. A nightwalker hotspot.

She was there for about ten minutes before two shadows emerged. The niece didn't notice the bricks in their hands until Celita was on the ground. Her body like spilled milk. Her black hair covering her face like a tarpaulin sack. The niece was too stunned to move, taking breaths bigger than herself. Each one hit Celita one more time. Threw the bricks into the water. Then the body.

'Stupid nigger thief,' one of them muttered. The words went into the wind, blew away.

But the niece recognised the voice as one of the ensigns that raided the house.

The other officer's eyes met the niece's. All of his features blackened except his blue eyes. As she bolted off, she heard a cry, 'Come back here, bitch!'

She ran like she had never run before. Hid in a decommissioned bus. Never went to sleep that night. The next morning was Tuesday. At 9 a.m., showed up to work, took the sheets to the launderette. The rural man was there, as predicted. She recognised his red Chevrolet pickup. When he wasn't looking, she climbed into the tray. Hid under a tarp. Took only five seconds. Eventually fell asleep.

He got home later that night. It was raining. His three dogs alerted him to her presence. She was straightforward with him, explaining what had happened. All truth but her name. He seemed sensible and told her that she could stay with him until she was ready to be taken back. In that moment, he looked a little charming.

That time never came. Her stay would be indefinite. She became accustomed to the house, the life. One day, he took her to the outhouse. In it was a painting of a Chinese goddess. There, he told her that if she were to enter into this life with him, she had to become a proper woman fitting his wealth. So, it had to be. So, he bought books of etiquette and classical literature for her. He started her with the Royal Readers and then moved on to Swift and Stevenson and Brontë. He decided from then on, that she would speak only the Queen's English. She'd never spoken many words in her life, and so, with practice it came naturally to her. He had her prepare a new meal each week: stuffed caraille with roasted geera, pelau with coriander and caramelised fowl, curried muscovy in mother-in-law pepper and lime.

They had a small civil ceremony at the house, the only witnesses being two men under his employ. Paid a clerk to forge a few documents. No honeymoon – he was busy with his work the following day. She lost her virginity on the wedding night. Sex with him was difficult. It troubled her how much she was physically repulsed by the act with him.

Over time, he moulded her into somebody totally different – she did not recognise herself any more. She became the nose-pierced, neck-powdered, kohl-eyed Marlee Changoor, the jewel of the land. And no matter a person's appearance on these plains – dal-bellied, yellow-eyed, skin-tagged, wrinkled, rhino-scaled, cattle-boiled, pockmarked, spider-veined – she would always remember to give them a beautiful smile. So were her husband's demands. She foresaw that one day she would tire of the routine, but it was a small sacrifice to make for Shangri-La.

In the early morning, he left to meet a business partner. She sat on the porch, the grand house to herself. Every brick and tile and pipe and wire and drape. Every fleur-de-lis on the backsplash. Everything porcelain and mahogany and crosshatched glass. Sipped Ceylon tea. Suddenly, her heart began to race. She shot up from her chair, gripped the balustrade, remembering her dream.

What if this too were a dream?

No, she thought. *This is it.*

The hard times are over. The past is dead and long behind.

The dream has come true. The long and painful journey ends here.

8

A Husband's Absence

Early August

The clock struck midnight, bringing in Monday. In four hours, Marlee was supposed to have three thousand dollars delivered to the No. 4 bridge. And if Dalton really were being held for ransom, she was his last hope. It would be all up to her. She didn't have any plans to deliver the money. Being Dalton's last hope was as far as she was willing to go. He never asked her to be anything more than that. He wanted her to be the ballerina in the music box – but the tune was almost over. There were still four hours left. Then he'd be gone. Only then could she tell the police the truth. She wondered how many gleefully smoking wives stood over their husbands, watching them wrestle their own bodies and die of heart attacks. Or how many saw them choking at the dinner table only to continue eating their meals like nothing was happening. Just pleased that God listened for once in His life.

She needed a drink.

He had an inspired collection of liquors. All in a row like praying monks inside the temple of the mahogany cabinet. Bottles of Four Roses Whiskey, Carta de Oro, Daws Cherry Brandy, Fernet Branca, El Dorado, among others. It gave him the appearance of a connoisseur, one who could taste history in a drop of spirit. The fields of sugarcane, the rivers and the herons that waded in them. Who could wax poetic of all the souls who laboured to get it here. But that wasn't the reality. Dalton drank them all just the same. Didn't care for taste or flavour notes or viscosity. If it came in a pretty bottle and got him drunk, he bought it.

Marlee took a bottle of Demerara white rum from the cabinet and poured herself a glass. Drank the whole thing to ease her nerves. Then decided to take the whole bottle with her to the study. The study had been reassembled to accommodate the village children. Sitting cushions all over the floor. Toy chest in the corner like a scolded child. The real furniture in another corner. After the children stopped coming, Dalton hadn't bothered to return the room to its previous arrangement.

Marlee had spent most of her first year of marriage in this room. Devoured dozens of his books there, feeling a whiff of sadness with each one she completed, knowing she could never discuss it with anyone. Dalton had read almost none of the books he owned. This room brought only anger to her now. She recalled the last conversation he had with the painting. A *flower-eyed grandson*. The *true heir*. This entire room was a ruse fashioned from psychosis.

During that first year of marriage, she had deconstructed her entire self with the revered language of dead writers. Patched herself with ideas and metaphors until she wasn't sure where her former self died and this new self was born. Her mind its own Ship of Theseus. She often read aloud to train her voice, taking laborious care to commit each new word to memory. So many people in the county spoke like they had a mouthful of marbles or with such weakness that the wind destroyed their words – at the time, she understood why Dalton wanted her manner of speaking to be as unfaltering and as elegant as the text in these books. But just as this room, she was also a ruse fashioned from psychosis.

Dalton wasn't a social creature. He kept himself disconnected from everyone else. Never mingled unless he had something to gain from it. Had no real friends – no one who would come looking for him. Never learnt how to play any card games. When he drank, he never did so with company, not even with her. All drinking occurred in twilit solitude. Owned books for the sake of their jackets, not their words. Owned art that he neither admired nor analysed. Even this marriage, she wasn't sure he enjoyed. He took orders and counsel from an inanimate object, for Christ's sake – and then those orders were passed on to her. The more she thought she knew, the less she realised she did. Sometimes she imagined he was hosting some speakeasy beneath a hidden door in the floor. Or maybe there really was nothing behind his large vacant eyes. Nothing at all.

Did he even know who he was?

Dalton had no family, as far as she knew. No children, siblings, cousins, none that were alive anyway. His mother was trapped in a painting. His father was only relevant because of the inheritance. Marlee was his only family. She and the one remaining dog. He might as well be an *encantado*, come to fete with the humans before returning to the river.

She put on Roaring Lion's 'Ugly Woman'.

She closed the door of the study, started dancing. Began slow, twisted her body to the brass melody, put one foot before the other, careful not to entangle her stride. Took sporadic swigs of the liquor until it was empty. Danced with the empty bottle in her embrace. Returned to the cabinet, opened a bottle of whiskey. 'Mad Dogs and Englishmen' came on. Shifted her feet until her lower half was in jitters, her nightgown trying to catch up with her. 'Tea for Two', she dragged her feet at first. But soon enough was stomping the ground, echoing the tempo of the piano. Cab Calloway's 'Minnie the Moocher'. Sang along, its prolonged chant of laughter-like vowels. Warm energy filling her lungs. The hustle of brass kicked in again and she rapidly spun around with her arms out, the empty bottle of rum still in hand. Imagined a world full of people doing the same thing, everyone unsure of who was mimicking whom. At the end of the song, she collapsed to the ground in insane laughter. The merry-go-round of the world still spinning alongside her.

She remained there for the rest of the early morn, long after the clock struck four.

If they were to kill her, her ghost would still be dancing.

★

At noontime break, Hans went over to Robinson, hard at work in the pumpkin patch. Robinson often broke into soliloquy during his tasks. For the past hour, while he toiled on the fence, Hans listened to Robinson talk to the leaves and the stems and the flowers before him. He even spoke to the soil and the wind. When he wasn't conversing with nature, he prattled off the long roster of psalms he'd committed to memory. Just as his facial expressions often matched those of an old preacher's, so did his cadence.

When Robinson noticed Hans's shadow over him, he ceased his soliloquy. Tipped his hat. 'Workin hard over there, hero?'

'Not harder than you, sir,' said Hans, squinting as the sun bore down on him. The flood had receded over the past two days. Now, aside from some patches of mud and new rills around the paragrass, the plains looked as if they had never been disturbed. The froghoppers darted in and out of cloisters of cane. The low hum of Jack Spaniards returned to the barhar trees. Agoutis popped into the daylight and then out again. It gave Hans a respect for these plains, like no force of nature could hold lordship over it.

Robinson chucked a hoe into the soil, brought up clods of dirt. Had a bucket of water beside him, where he dipped the clumps and moulded them into thick patties. Then laid a patty over a runner, where the main leaves sprouted. One by one, he did this. Before Hans could think to ask, Robinson explained, 'This make the root grow. More root, so the plant could pull more food from the earth. If you aint have no root in the earth, you gon slowly perish.'

'The pumpkin don't have roots already?'

'That they do. But this bring more root. A father root, I like to call it. You have the mother root – that's the first one. And now the father root. See, even family values come into the garden.'

Hans broke into a grin. 'You have a church saying for that?'

Robinson looked up, dipping his hat to shade his eyes from the sun. Closing his eyes, he spoke like a spirit borrowed his tongue, 'If one does not provide for his own, he has denied the faith and is worse than an unbeliever.'

'You know everything, old man.' An amused laugh from Hans. Robinson gave him a look and shook his head before going back to his mud. 'Don't be mocking me, young boy.'

'Aint no mockery here, sir. I aint have room in my head for all them sayings.'

Robinson shrugged, stooped once again and went back to making patties. 'The Lord God is constant. Unlike the price of flour, it don't change. That's why I always make room for it in my head.' Turned to Hans. 'You talk to Harold Vaughan about that plot I tell you bout?'

Hans scratched his head. 'That Mr Vaughan ... he aint honest.'

Robinson, brow crinkled, 'What you mean?'

Hans folded his arms. 'That price he call, it aint seem right.'

'Land aint cheap, Hans. And it get more expensive by the minute. But is worth it.' A pause. 'What's the matter? You aint have the money?'

'I'm short bout three hundred.'

'He probably call a higher price for you, you being a Hindu and all. Harold Vaughan is a staunch Christian. He think Hinduism is a bunch of cow god, monkey god devil worship.'

'What I hafta do then? Convert? Get myself a baptism?'

'Aint a bad idea. A bunch of barrack coolies start moving in, it drives the property value down, I suppose. I don't mean you, of course. I know you one of the good ones.' A slight smirk as he dipped another clod into the bucket of water. 'Join the church, bring your wife and boy and all of you get baptised, is my advice. Make a decision, good and proper. Get your family outta that place. In the beginning, you mightn't have nothin in the house but God. But there's something about owning a home ... aint like no other feeling. Something to pass down and keep passing down. A man without a house, without a household, without land, is nothing, Hans.'

'But you know I's not nothing, Robinson.'

A shrug. 'Is not me who selling the land, Hans. Is not me you have to convince.'

Hans's gaze went blank after the last sentence. It took him a while to say something. 'I aint the most committed Hindu. But every morn, my wife wake up and pray to Mother Lakshmi, Robinson. She like the religion. How you think she gon feel when I tell she to convert?'

'I aint make the rules.' Robinson got up, struck the hoe against the earth.

'Baig is a Hindu. And he livin in Bell.'

'Baig is a Hindu, yes. His father wasn't. And his father snatch up that land years ago, when it was a fraction of the price it is today. Baig have to be pullin teeth to get a loan at the bank. I aint sayin bein Hindu is the wrong way to be, Hans. But bein Hindu gon disadvantage you in life, especially if you lookin to make a deal with a church man like Harold Vaughan. And not just him. A pundit marry you, right? Under the bamboo?'

'Yeah.'

'Well, the state would say you aint even a married man, Hans. Some would say your son is a bastard child.' Hans looked disoriented upon hearing this. Robinson hesitated to ask, 'Surely you know this? I aint sayin I agree with them. But I aint make the law. You aint considered wedded if you do it the old Hindu way.'

Hans didn't know it. And he didn't want to talk about it any more – Robinson's words had disturbed him to the core. He changed the topic. 'You workin here much longer than me, Robinson. I want to ask you somethin. There plenty bandits up this way?'

Robinson scratched his chin, went back to making patties. 'Well, the bandits is the reason them three dogs come here in the first place, I suppose. Wherever it have cheese, you gon attract rats. Maybe from Tully or Cheddi Settlement. It have bandits this way, that way, every way. But me – I wouldn't want to live here. Here, it aint have nowhere to run to if you get cornered in the middle of the night. Nothing but bush and road on either side. Me, I can't even imagine being the Missus at a time like this.'

'You seen the Missus for the day?'

He stopped to think. 'Early in the morn, when I come. Come to think of it, she aint look right. Kinda look like how you expect a woman to look when she childrens wander off. Aint you know that look? Sweaty and all over the place.'

'Friday gone, she tellin me bout some hooligans.' This was what he had really come to talk about. 'They come in the middle of the night, bangin up the door, making monkey noises. She say she aint been sleepin because of it.'

Robinson sucked his teeth, shook his head. 'Them boys aint got nothin better to do but trouble a good woman? These youth boys nowadays like to take things too far. Back in the day, we know when to stop. Times change. Aint that right? Poor lass must be frighten for her life.' He laid another patty down.

'I was thinkin about it. As you say, times change. We know we woulda do nothin to bring harm but who's to say bout these new ones? I aint want it on my conscience if one of them boys break down the door and – forgive me for sayin it out loud – have their way with the Missus.'

Robinson paused to look at him. 'Don't let the devil hear them words.'

A wary pause. 'See, the Missus ask me to keep up here for the next few nights to make sure nothin happen.'

Robinson squinted. 'You mean till the Mister come back?'

'To scare off them boys.'

'She payin you good?'

'Yeah.'

'And what you say to that?' Robinson asked, turning to the shed again.

'Nothin yet.'

'What your wife say?'

A pause. 'I aint ask her yet.'

Robinson shot a glance at him. 'Why?'

'I dunno if is right to take up an offer like that.'

'I hear a night shift usually spell trouble for a family in a barrack. Stories about women and daughters having to fight for their dignity in a husband's absence. The kinda things that could happen in the night.'

'I aint worryin bout that.' Hans had considered it. But he never felt like he had to worry about that. Mandeep, his brother, wouldn't dare. Sachin was an idiot. Teeluck was too lame. And Murali was too frail. 'You think is right to take up the offer, Robinson?'

'What bout it don't seem right? You gettin paid.'

'Yeah, but what you think going to happen if the Mister come home in the middle of the night to find another man here on his property? How you think his state of mind going to be? The man have guns and know how to shoot—'

Robinson gave a confused look. 'I assume this whole thing woulda be the Mister's idea. Is not?'

Hans fumbled, 'Yeah.'

'Then you talkin nonsense and worryin for nothin.'

'I suppose the job sound a little dangerous, is all.'

Robinson got up, dusted the dirt off his hands. 'You have to think about that too. If somethin happen to you, what your wife and son gon do? See, I'm not the one to talk to, Hans. Can't see why you wouldn't talk to your wife about this first. You know that your wife is suppose to be the first of friends—'

'*Hansraj! Oh Lord!*' a shout cut through the air. Robinson's ears lifted with eagerness while Hans tried to discern the direction of the voice. Only upon the second calling of his name did he determine that it was coming from the front gate. Hurried over to see Shweta clutching the front of her dress, legs bowed inward as if she were holding in a hot pee. Felt strange to see her here. He wasn't sure if she had even entertained the thought of visiting before.

Her voice in shuddering breaths, '*Is Krishna! Is Krishna!*' Her face red, pulsing with blood, looking like it was ready to pop.

'What happen to Krishna?'

'They take him and Tarak to the lockup!'

'Who?'

'They hit him, Hansraj!'

A confused pause. 'Why they hit him? What he do?'

'He aint do nothing!' She looked like she was about to fall to her knees. Took a deep breath and before she spoke again, made an audible swallow. Her voice steadied now. 'We have to go down to Bell right now.'

Robinson came up a distance behind Hans, enough for him to hear the exchange. His posture slowly wavered in the wind as he tried to keep still. His mouth furled into a frown as his eyes met Shweta's. 'Hans, get going. I'll hold the fort,' he muttered, removing his hat.

Hans was already out of the gate. Left it swinging open. Robinson closed it, put the latch back on.

9
A Crime Against Humanity

Hans and Shweta cut through the market square. Shoals of people through the stalls. A river of crocus bags and elbows. Tables jammed tight as teeth in a lion's mouth. From all directions, *Ochro! Tomato! Baigan! Chive! Bandhania!* Hans walked with his arms tucked in front of him. Shweta felt as if people were intentionally bumping into her. Every corner, every electrical pole, a sign. Cheap plywood and sorrel-red paint. Phone numbers scribbled across a wall. Stacks of fish lined the stalls at the end, some with their heads lopped off, some red like bauxite. Old brass scales hung up from iron rods.

A short, old man sat on the lid of an icebox, eyed Shweta, spoke with a half-smoked cigarette in his mouth, 'Come get a fish. I have a good one for you, lady.'

She began, 'I don't have any—'

'Not good enough to eat? Eat your damn dollar then, bitch!'

Hans didn't hear – he was already way ahead. Shweta hurried to catch up. At the other end of the market, two village men sang a song and clapped, doing an off-key rendition of 'Boogie Woogie Bugle Boy'. A middle-aged man in tattered clothes gyrated before them, drawing a small crowd who cheered and laughed at him. His raucous motion not matching the deadness of his eyes. People pitched coins into an old bean can. Shweta felt ashamed for the man.

The Bell Village Police Station was low-slung, wider than all the other buildings on the street. It sat at the crossroad, where all cardinal points converged. The reach of a sapodilla tree shaded the sidewalk to the station, where a wiry-looking officer stuck notices on a billboard. Shweta gave her husband an anxious look before they entered.

Inside, the ground was hard and the air sharp and thin. A temporary dizziness came over Shweta as her eyes adjusted to the dim interior. Dim, even though the walls were lined with large rectangular windows. A few officers at their desks piled with paperwork, cigarettes in mouth, the light from the windows diffusing through the smoke.

Shweta huddled in close to Hans and whispered, 'Hans, if they beat Krishna, I swear …'

He whispered back, 'Nothin gon happen to Krishna once we talk some sense.'

Before them, the front desk, a large open ledger as its centrepiece. Sitting at the desk was a man who, to Shweta, looked too bony to be a police officer. Writing something in a manner so sluggish that it had to be intentional. Hans stood before him, his shadow cast over the desk, awaiting acknowledgement. Shweta followed. Hans put his palm on Shweta's back to steady her jitters. After about ten seconds, Hans wished the man good afternoon, to which the man grunted something unintelligible.

Hans didn't say anything else for a while. Took the time to cautiously form the words in his head. He knew not to be brash with the officers, especially the bony ones like these. Officers like these overcompensated for their lack of build by having nasty attitudes that they thought made them tough. Hans spoke carefully, 'You bring two boys in here—'

'Your son?' the man cut him off, eyes still on his pen. 'The big one or the little one?'

'The little one,' said Hans. 'The other is my brother son.'

'Your nephew then.'

'Nephew, yeah.'

Shweta found herself taken aback by Hans's modest tone. Found herself smothering the impulse to rip that pen away. The man continued writing, saying nothing else. Her eyes drifted to the corkboard on the wall. On it, newspaper articles and snippets of descriptions of wanted criminals, most for burglary. One prominent poster pinned to the middle depicted a badly drawn sketch of a man. Written below, WANTED FOR THEFT. MALE. 20s. DARK. SCAR ON RIGHT CHEEK. BARRACK COOLIE. Behind her, near the doorway, a long wooden bench and beside it, a bare wooden coat rack.

'You better not aint do nothin to him,' said Shweta hastily, not in any manner to cause offence, though Hans must have thought so by the way he grabbed her wrist and gave it a squeeze. As if to tell her to shut her mouth. The desk officer didn't seem to take any offence by her tone, though it was hard to discern his thoughts.

'He's behaving,' said the man with a small chuckle.

Hans said, 'His name is Krishna Saroop. My name is Hansraj Saroop and this is his mother, Shweta Saroop. I know the boys had a run-in with a couple of the fellas yesterday mornin. Somethin happen during this incident that we dunno about? Because ...'

With each word, Shweta felt more and more like her insides were ready to fall out of her body. It was hard for her to keep everything in. Tapped her feet, rubbed her palms together like she had come down with pins and needles. Like a wild bird trapped in a cage. How could Hans reason with someone who wasn't even listening? Who pretended that he was invisible? Her eyes were on the officer's pen, drifting slowly over the paper. Another officer at the back, hands in his trouser pockets, moving as if he were jingling coins *clink, clink, clink*. He was so far away but she swore she could've heard it. *Clink, clink. Clink, clink.* And it was getting louder and louder, eventually drowning out Hans's voice.

Shweta stepped up. Cut in, 'Officer, my husband is speakin to you.'

The desk officer was still writing – she wasn't sure if he didn't hear or if he was ignoring her. Hans muttered to her, 'Quiet. Let me talk.'

'You talkin, but who listenin?' She approached the ledger and shifted it to the side. The man's pen made a long scrawl where he'd been writing.

He eyed her for a long time. Then hit the desk in a sudden rage. 'You know you could be charged for touching this book!'

An officer at the back drew his baton. From the corner hidden by a partition, a senior officer emerged in full khaki guayabera attire. He came to the lobby, cast a long stare at the couple. Hans took this time to read his nametag: *DSP BADREE*. He was a brooding man, towered over all others in the room. His shiny black hat pulled down so low that it shaded his eyes. Shoes shone as if they had never brushed the dusty ground. He faced Hans, then Shweta.

A tiny smile crept across the deputy's face, and he gave a sidelong glance at the desk officer. 'What's all this commotion?' A voice as deep as a bull.

'This woman touched the book! That's a charge!'

'Who the hell are these people?'

'They say they's the parents of the two boys.'

'Just the little one,' Hans corrected.

Shweta nodded, saying, 'Krishna.' Her tone more subdued this time. 'The other one is Tarak Saroop, our nephew. But we aint in charge of him.'

'Who is in charge of him?' asked the desk officer.

'My brother,' said Hans. 'Mandeep Saroop.'

'And where, pray tell, is Mandeep Saroop?' A slight smirk.

'He aint here,' said Shweta. 'But we right here.'

The deputy said, 'Ma'am, sir, do you know about Bhagran Lakhan?'

Hans answered, 'I know about him, but—'

'See them bullet holes?' The deputy pointed to a trio of imperfections in the wall behind him. Hans squinted to see, but the deputy made a note to point them out, counting them, 'One. Two. And this is three,' as he traced his fingers over the dents. 'Two good men get their life cut short in here that day. One of them married for only two months. This is not to speak of the countless other lives that was robbed because of Bhagran

Lakhan. But you know what is this station's crowning achievement? We killed Bhagran Lakhan. A man whose existence was a crime against humanity.'

Shweta said, 'Why you tellin we this? My son have *nothin* to do with any of this.'

'Ma'am, your son is in a gang led by the sons of Bhagran Lakhan.'

Hans and Shweta gave each other baffled looks. Hans scratched the back of his neck. 'A gang? My son aint part of no gang.'

'You know how much hell is going to raise in this place if we have two, three, four Bhagran Lakhans walking around? You know how much destruction—'

Shweta cut in, 'Officer, my son woulda never get into that fight if he wasn't with them other boys.' Hans noticed Shweta's balled fists and steely glare.

'They call their gang the *Corbeau*,' said the deputy sternly. This elicited a scoff from the desk officer.

'The *Corbeau*?' Shweta repeated, twisting her mouth. Hans gripped her wrist again, but she refused to be quiet. 'Them two brothers kill somebody? Rape somebody? If they do that, lock *them* up! My son aint do none of them things.'

Hans pleaded to the officers. 'Krishna and Tarak had nothin to do with whatever them Lakhan boys did.' A pause to think. 'What do you want we to do? What's the plan goin forward?'

'Plan?' the desk officer scoffed. 'You people make plans?'

Shweta rose to a shout, 'Let my son go!' Hans instinctively put his hand on her belly as if he thought she would lunge at the deputy. The deputy's expression remained stiff as it was.

Hans took Shweta's wrist between his palms into a caress. She knew what he was thinking, that her disposition wasn't helping matters. Certainly not with people like this, who believed that barrack dwellers were guilty until proven innocent. Who would sock a child in the eye and feel good about it.

Despite this, she turned to the deputy, 'Can I ask somethin?' Hans squeezed her wrist until it hurt. She tugged it away, 'What the hell you hit my child for?'

The deputy was more amused than anything by her rage. He turned to Hans, 'Control your wife, sir.'

'He try to take a swing at Corporal Edwards, ma'am,' said the desk officer.

'That what you write in your stupid book? I aint blind. I was right there, mister. That big, hardback man hit my son first. He come there to cause trouble. Only then Krishna make a move to defend heself!'

The deputy held up his hand to the desk officer. Narrowed his eyes into slits at Shweta. 'I want you to listen to me, miss. I'll tell you what happened. Corporal Edwards was acting on my orders. I told him to hit that rascal. Wind up his arm like Joe Louis and hit him right in the face,' he said, the vehemence dripping from his voice like bile. 'I said to hit him because your cockroach-gobbling son tried to drown mine.'

It took Hans a while to finally put the pieces of the picture together. Shweta's face was already tensed with rage. Couldn't contain it any longer. 'You aint no police. You's just a *dirty shithound*!' she shouted.

The desk officer shook his head. 'Put a damn muzzle on that woman!'

The deputy chuckled. Signalled to an officer at the back. Calmly, 'Officer, arrest this woman for obscene language.'

As the officer produced his handcuffs, the deputy had already begun walking away. 'Don't touch me,' Shweta hissed at him, eyes tearing up. Turned to her husband, resigned, his palm against his brow. 'Hans. Do something—'

The officer made a move to grab her wrist. She grabbed the coat rack in the corner and, with as much force she could muster, threw it at him.

It hit the ground with a thump and a crunch. A peg broke off from the top. Everything silent then, save for Shweta's quivering breathing.

The deputy returned, eyeing the broken coat rack in shock.

'That was a gift from Governor Young himself,' he said coldly. 'That's destruction of public property.'

She couldn't find any words except, 'You wasn't using that damn thing anyway.'

At the same time, the shrill ring of the wall telephone sounded. The desk officer got up to answer it, and he straightened his back when he heard the voice. Balanced the receiver on the top of its housing and went to get the deputy. The deputy didn't give a glance to Hans and Shweta on his return. Went to the phone and as the conversation proceeded, his mouth visibly fell. He fumbled a few words during the one-sided conversation, 'But... no, superintendent... sir... we have... but, sir they assaulted... yes, superintendent...'

Before he hung up, he banged the receiver against the housing. Rubbed his forehead like he had come down with a great headache. 'Let them go,' he murmured to the officer who was about to arrest Shweta. 'The boys. Take them out of holding.'

Turned to the Saroops. 'God smile on you today. Seem like somebody call in a favour for you.'

We must all answer to a God, Shweta had been told all through her childhood. Seemed that all deputy superintendents must answer to superintendents. She tittered at the thought. For a moment, she was curious where the favour had come from.

All these thoughts dissolved once she spotted Krishna and Tarak being escorted to them. Shweta saw the swollen eye before she saw her son. Held him tightly, not noticing that he didn't reciprocate. Hans kept his eye on Tarak, who was scanning the room for his own father. He ruffled the top of the boy's hair, still tied and jutting out like quills.

Shweta and Krishna were already on the road. Krishna turned around, spat on the steps. Tarak turned to Hans and thanked him, his voice as a hoarse whisper.

On their way back, Hans looked up at the church. He turned to the house catty-corner to it, where some Hindu devotees lived. He remembered just a few months back, the bamboo poles and jhandi flags that proudly fluttered in its yard. Those flags were gone now.

10
A Spoiled Child

That afternoon, Hans took Krishna for a walk along the train line. Just two years back, Hans remembered the lively way his son trod these tracks. The railway sleepers, cut from balata wood, lain equidistant from each other, were just far enough apart to match the little boy's stride. And so he used to hop and skip from sleeper to sleeper, trying his best not to let his feet touch the ground. Hans would emulate the boy and together they would make it all the way to the point where the tracks ran parallel to the river's embankment. There, they shed their merino shirts and Hans would take the boy into the water, holding him horizontal, plank-like, his buoyant body resting neatly along his forearms. Both their cheeks round and pouting with held breaths as they went under. Here, Hans taught him how to float, how to paddle, how to do a backstroke.

Nowadays, Krishna didn't care where his feet fell. Didn't look ahead. Instead, kept a downward gaze as if thorns were underfoot. Hans stopped to check on the boy's eye, still a raw watermelon pink where the officer had landed his fist. By tomorrow, it would be as purple as an open caimito. The boy's sullen bearing was indicative of any male after defeat. Even with an opponent double in size, a man cannot help but feel diminished after being taken down. There is no part of a true fighting man that allows him to rationalise a loss. Even in an unfair battle, there must be some way forward, some missed road to victory. Once one recognises that not all fights are won with square blows and that anything can go, there are no unwinnable fights.

Hans knew he had his own moments like this, his foremost rival being his own father. Not only could he not overpower the brutish man, but only one night after her beatings, his mother would give his father an embracing glance, and he and Mandeep would know to stay out of the room for the night. Sleep under the mango tree. There was no escape for the woman – until her life finally ended. Hans thought he finally beat his father when he married Shweta. Promised never to lay a heated hand on her.

He and Krishna were almost at the No. 11 bridge. Close by, a mangrove coppice, pocketing a nook of cloying, soft humidity. They hadn't made it all the way during that first visit two years ago. At the opposite end of the bridge, lain against the eroded banks, was a queue of spectacled caimans. Near-camouflaged against the pewter-grey mud. Krishna had overheard a story at school about a cow wandering into the colony of caimans only to be quickly ripped apart, limb by limb, chunk by chunk, until the entire river flowed red for half a day. Back then, Hans assured him that the story wasn't true, that his young imagination had gotten the best of him.

Now, Krishna stopped in his tracks as the caimans came into view. Snatched a fallen palm branch and kept it in hand, just as a sepoy would brandish a sword. One of the caimans half surfaced from the shallow ravine. Krishna approached the end of the bridge, keeping a cautious gaze on the bony ridge at the incline of the caiman's partially submerged mouth. When he saw that the caimans weren't budging, he picked up his pace and marched headstrong along the bank, Hans tagging behind him. Now he wondered if Krishna had realised it – that two years later, the boy had risen above those caimans. He was growing and becoming stronger. He had exerted such little effort to walk past those creatures. That's how it was supposed to be, Hans thought. One day, a test. The next day, a custom.

They ventured off another trail and made it to a secluded section of river, where water lazily sluiced over smooth semi-circular rocks that glimmered under the sun like a gemstone. Here, the land levelled and then dwindled into a delta-like taper. Shrubbery and bamboo mimicked the arch of a gateway. The air acerbic with stinkbugs. Hans cleared some stones and foliage to form a neat sitting area for him and the boy. Together, they sat with their knees pulled up against their chests. As they settled, there was uncomfortable quietness.

Hans turned to the boy. 'Still have a good hour to sundown. What you say we take a swim?'

The boy shook his head, put a hand over his bad eye. Hans asked again but got the same reply. He pulled his merino shirt over his head and hung it on a tree. Made it halfway into the water before beckoning once again for the boy to join him. 'The water good, boy.' Again, the boy refused.

Hans waded a few steps deeper into the river, cutting through a cordon of baby mullets swimming downstream. Hans had known this spot since he was a boy. It was difficult to find solace in the barrack, so he would often cut paths through brush and thorn in search of it. Whenever he found one of these natural enclaves, it was like a chamber ordained by God. When something bad happened to him, he came here. Washed himself clean. Bad feelings, bad memories flowing downstream with the ditch frogs. This river was one of the few still-accessible spots that had remained uninterrupted over the years. Now he could share it with his son. This virginal patch of earth undisturbed by man, with damselflies and agouti holes and baby caimans. Afternoon light shot in like divine spears.

Initially, it disappointed him that the boy refused to join him. Every few minutes, he called him, but the boy shook his head. Hans eventually forgot about it, doing backstrokes and breaststrokes from one end of the bank to the next. By the time he was done, an hour had passed. He got out of the water and peed into a bush before returning to the sitting area. The boy scooted to the side. Together they sat quietly, the cicadas and susurrating of leaves filling the lazy silence.

Krishna picked a twig off the ground, began digging into the dirt with it. Moved with steady deliberation like he was digging a grave.

'It aint fair,' he said. Sounded like he had been building himself up to say more than those words, but that was what came out.

Hans nodded. 'It aint fair, boy. What I could say?'

'You ever wanted to kill anybody, pa?' Krishna asked straight.

Despite Hans's astonishment at the question, his father immediately came to mind. 'That aint somethin to have in your head. I aint want you talkin that kinda talk.'

Krishna still digging. 'Mikey Badree. I wish he was dead.'

Hans, annoyed now, 'Your mouth big like your ma own, you know that? The two of you cause enough trouble for the day.' A pause to temper his tone. 'Have certain people you can't touch in this life. You still learnin that. Your ma too.'

Krishna got back to digging. 'But they could touch we?'

He rubbed the boy's back. 'They could touch you, but you have to learn not to feel it.'

The boy's eyes met his. 'You don't feel nothin, pa?'

Hesitation. 'No. I learn not to take it on.' As he said it, he knew it wasn't the truth. But what was the point of the truth at this time? The insults, the discriminatory remarks, all the jaundiced eyes locking onto him as he shuffled into a general store. It did bother him. But what was the point of fighting it? They were outnumbered.

He continued, 'You a strong boy. You come from me. One day, all of this that goin on today, you gon use it to build up yourself. Make yourself even stronger. All this that you think is so big, gon be like nothin. People move forward. How long you gon grieve for something? Your sis—' He stopped himself from mentioning Hema. His mother probably didn't want him knowing, he thought. Those who were old enough to remember her never brought her up – the boy didn't need that on his mind. Let the dead stay dead. Fortunately, the slip-up had gone over the boy's head. He carried on, 'Me and your mother want to see you become bigger than all this. You gon finish your education and become something big.'

Krishna, still digging. 'I aint want to go back to school, pa. I aint belong there.'

Hans had to let the words settle before replying, 'What you talkin bout? You goin to a proper school.'

'That school aint proper at all. I aint need to be there no more.'

'You soundin like a spoil child.'

A pout. 'I goin to burn that school down if I go back.'

'Stop with that kinda talk. Next time them boys come round, you just turn round and get outta there, you hear? We can't afford no more trouble if we is to live there. You will find your ass back in that schoolhouse in September and behave yourself this time, you hear me?'

Krishna, digging again. 'You aint never went to school.'

'That's cause I aint smart. Boy, I woulda pull you out long time if you wasn't smart. I woulda pull you out and put you to catch froghoppers in that there canefield. You tryin to tell me you stupid? That what you callin yourself now?'

A sigh. 'No, pa.'

'Good. So you gonna finish school.'

'It aint fair.'

'Stop diggin!' Hans snapped. He grabbed the stick from his son, flung it into the river. 'I get on my knees, and I *beg* that schoolmaster not to expel you! On my knees, Krishna! That is what I have to do for you. And you tellin me now you aint goin back? I aint know what else you and your ma want from me. You two is peas in a pod. And nothin I do is good enough. Stubborn, the two of you.'

He pictured the bullet holes in the station. The way the deputy pointed them out to him. Violence he so often wanted to forget existed. Men had become so enamoured by vengeance and cruelty. Begging for hell to take them.

Hans went on, 'I aint want you talkin to them Lakhan boys again.'

Krishna stared at the trees. 'You never had a problem with them before.'

'Not till you end up in a jail cell. If they was your true friends, they woulda be in that cell with you. They aint good for you. And they aint good for this family. Their pa throw all them people in the sea—'

'He aint throw them. They jump in.'

'*Stop being a jackass!*' Hans lashed out before taking a cool moment for himself. Muttered something under his breath. Krishna couldn't make it out. Sounded like *bat the child*.

Krishna looked at him in shock, no words. First time his father had spoken to him like this.

Hans continued, tempered, 'People in the village already think the lowest of we. That we cannot behave. That we have no control.' He looked at his son. 'You know your ma nearly get sheself lock up today?'

Krishna wasn't sure where this was coming from.

Hans went on, 'You have Mrs Marlee to thank for bailing you out, boy. Your ma too.'

'Who is Mrs Marlee?'

A pause. 'Mrs Changoor. You'd still be in that station if she aint step in. Your ma in there with you.' He gazed at the scintillating water. 'Mrs Marlee is somebody we need in we lives. She could get things done. I think I know what I have to do now.'

Krishna looked at him, waiting for his father to elaborate. What did he have to do?

But the man just got up and started on his way back without saying anything else. Was only when they had returned to the barrack that Krishna realised what his father had muttered. Not *bat the child*. It was *bastard child*.

11
An Act of Kindness

When Marlee woke from her nap that Monday evening, she wasn't sure if it were of her own accord or if something had rattled her out of slumber. The music was on downstairs. Ella Fitzgerald belting out 'What is This Thing Called Love?' Rubbed the sleep out of her eyes, trying hard to recall the dream she was having.

She'd been at the bridge with a large cloth bag – bulky and heavy as a laundry sack. There was night around her, but she could sense that a pallid sun made itself known to the other areas in the county. Toads and dragonflies and millipedes stirring in the circle of darkness surrounding her. She could hear the Ella Fitzgerald song as if it were coming from the sky. Even then, she didn't think it to be a dream. She knew she was waiting for something but wasn't sure what. When she awoke, she still didn't know.

She went downstairs to find the window at the foyer broken. Noticed the glints of glass below the star-shaped shatter. Among the shards was a stone that she assumed was the missile. A closer glance revealed something strange. An off-white and wrinkled texture. A piece of paper had been crumpled to fit over the stone. She peeled it off. A note.

4 A.M. WENSDAY. SAME PLACE. $3000.
TELL AND U DIE.

She made tea. Sat at the kitchen table, sliding her fingers over the words. *Wensday.* Traced her fingers along the zigzags of the *W*, the curl of the *e* and dithered over the rest, mumbling the word over and over as if hypnotised. It was a habit she'd developed with new words, new phrases. She traced the shapes of each. No other word she'd done this with more than *Marlee*. Repeating the syllables until she felt that pop of the disconnect between sound and meaning. But what did it really mean now? This persona, this poltergeist that had been created – who was this woman? She had escaped one life already. Why not this one?

An hour after receiving the note, Vishnu came barking. A knock on the door. Then a voice. It was Hans. She wasn't expecting him. She folded the note and placed it with the first in an elephant-shaped teapot that sat inside of an armoire. When she went to the door, Hans had already noticed the broken window. She told him to be mindful of his step as she led him into the parlour.

Even as he sat on the cushioned chair, his eyes couldn't leave the mess of glass on the floor. 'What happen there, Mrs Marlee?' he asked.

'We'll talk about it after, Hans. Do you want tea, coffee or juice?'

A pause to think. 'Tea?'

'Javanese, Ceylon or Assam?'

'I … not sure. Assam?'

'With lemon, milk or cream?'

'Mrs Marlee, anything.'

'A little bit of lemon then. Crackers or cake?'

'Crackers. Anything.'

'I'll get some for you.' She returned, a teacup with hand-painted monkeys in one hand, a small bowl of salt crackers in the other. She sat opposite to him, with another cup for herself. The tiny spoon clinked as she slowly stirred the sugar in her cup. 'I wasn't expecting you here today. Robinson told me you had an emergency concerning your son. Anyway, I hope you didn't mind me taking care of it.'

'I hope it wasn't trouble—'

'As I said, you're a good worker, a good man. And Dalton has sponsored the police's annual football tournament for the past three years. The man doesn't even like football or anything athletic on the whole, but now I can see why he bothers. I called in for an act of kindness, is all.'

'That was more than an act of kindness there, Mrs Marlee. Be kind to yourself too. Call in for them to find whoever that hooligan was that break your damn window there.'

They finished their tea. Marlee gave a long hesitant look at the kitchen, debating whether to show the note to him. Decided against it; too risky to divulge the details. There were villains afoot. Villains who terrorised women and broke windows. That was all he needed to know. Her main concern right now was of safety. She was set on not going down with Dalton.

Some deaths echo into the souls within earshot, spreading like a blighted cough. Some deaths weren't pleased with being solitary or sanitary. She couldn't underestimate that fact. She needed a loyal pair of eyes open in the dead of night to make sure safety wouldn't be breached. Needed a barrier to absorb the force of impact that was soon to come.

Leaning in closer to Hans. 'About the window. I think it was just to scare me. Nobody came in as far as I know. I checked everywhere. I didn't notice anything missing.'

Hans's frown prominent. 'You tell the police?'

'I'll file a report in the morning,' she lied. 'But then what? The police here are incompetent, Hans. You've seen that for yourself.'

'You can't call in another act of kindness?'

'An act of kindness isn't enough when it comes to things like this. I can't rely on them to act on time if something else happens. Things can change for the worst in a minute. In a second! By the time word gets to them, my brains would be all over this floor.'

He shifted in his chair. 'Don't say things like that.'

'The police aren't enough. I need someone here. Someone who will look out for me.' Marlee looked him in the eye. 'Hans, I'll offer double what I originally said.'

'Double?'

'Four hundred dollars.'

Hans's jaw dropped. '*Four hundred dollars?*'

'The offer's on the table, Hans. I want someone who is sure they can do it. If I can't get that from you, then I'll have to ask someone else.' She knew it was a risk making this bluff. There was no one else she wanted for the job but Hans.

'I'll take the offer. But I need to know how long I'm stayin.'

'Until Mr Changoor returns. Maybe in two weeks.'

With raised eyebrows, 'Weeks?'

'I'd like it if you could start from tonight.' She motioned for him to lean in as well, until they were close enough to hear each other's breaths. Her voice went into a whisper. 'I don't know why they're doing this. Whoever they are, they're quite determined. They know Dalton is gone. They know I'm here by myself.'

Hans drew back. 'Tonight then.' A pause. 'I gon head back and give Shweta word. That kinda money will be a blessing to us. But most of all, I want to make sure you safe.'

'Thank you, Hans.'

Hans got up, headed to the door. Caught a glance at the evening sky out of the broken window. 'I'll head out now.'

'Hans, dear.'

He turned around.

'I have to show you something very important when you get back. But we need the light. So, hurry back before sundown!'

12

A Man's Soul at Night

A patient fire burned in the centre of the room, an ashy saucepan of water with pawpaw leaves boiling over it. The sun setting outside. Dolly helped Shweta with the tea, set the cups on the enamel saucer. Krishna sat up on the coconut mattress. Shweta gave him a damp cloth, told him to keep it pressed over his bruised eye. Threw water over the fire when the tea was done. The two women sat cross-legged on the ground, their cups held over their laps. Tiny cinders still peeped out from the memory of the fire between them.

Hans returned to the barrack yard, out of breath. He'd been running. Outside, Shweta was getting ready to prepare pumpkin tarkari. Pimentos, geera and garlic already portioned off into tiny cups, the pumpkin already sliced and heaped into a larger bowl. Hans's favourite. The only meal he was ever impatient for. This time, he didn't even seem to notice it. He was distracted by something, barely able to stand still. The way an agouti's nose giddily twitches as it observes its surroundings. Or how a spider recoils after a lizard crosses its path.

He said to Shweta, almost in a whisper, that he had to speak with her. She reminded him that it was going to get dark soon and she wanted to start cooking. He insisted, and so she asked Kalawatie to keep an eye on her ingredients, as White Lady had a bad habit of dipping her snout into unattended receptacles.

He took Shweta to the barrack room, where Krishna was now asleep. Hastily explained to her the deal he'd struck with Marlee Changoor. Shweta was taken aback. For a moment, it seemed like manna from heaven. Then, without eating, he had left. Shweta explained the whole thing to Dolly, keeping her voice down so it wouldn't rise above the partitions.

Dolly raised her eyebrows and blinked repeatedly as Shweta went on, making mention of the significant stipend Hans would be paid for this job. Though hesitant to tell her the exact amount, she noted that it was enough for a down payment on the lot in Bell Village – the primary reason that she hadn't protested. But while relating the events, she realised she had never exactly agreed either.

Dolly bit her knuckle. 'You lettin your husband go ahead with this? For a whole two weeks?'

Shweta cocked her head. 'Only nights. He gon be here in the mornings.'

'Woman, you have me in shock. Your husband aint have no experience fighting off bandits. Bandits who might have guns.'

Shweta regretted saying anything to Dolly now. 'Is probably just a bunch of little boys with nothin better to do. I dunno. All I know is that he gon have the money to put down for the lot once he done.' She thought of the goddess Lakshmi, whom all women were supposed to be embodiments of. Lakshmi on the lotus, the deity of prosperity – the wish for wealth. All women yearned for the comfort of prosperity, didn't they? Rookmin had described the deity as such. Sprouting from a cosmic Ocean of Milk along with the moon and the stars as it churned. The celestial yearned to emerge from under, waiting to be born. This was a blessing.

'I know you say you aint want to be here the rest of your life.' Dolly said. 'But you never hear the rumours about Marlee Changoor?'

Shweta sighed. 'I aint want to know.'

'Before she come here, she use to lay down in a whorehouse. That's how Mr Changoor meet she.'

'Everybody know that aint true. That is rumshop talk you listenin to.'

'You have to be a certain kind of woman to work in a place like that. Someone pay a hundred dollars to watch she take a goat, I hear. You hear bout that one? God aint make the hole between your leg to—'

'*Stoppit, Dolly*,' Shweta snapped, closing her eyes tight for a few moments. When she reopened them, she downed her tea in one gulp, letting it burn her throat all the way down. She added, calm now, 'Why you tryin to stir up trouble?'

Dolly shook her head. 'I just lookin out for you.'

Shweta turned to Krishna. Looking at the boy now, she was reminded of the strange fact that Hans hadn't woken him up to say goodbye. Soured her to think about it. Felt like the man had been thrown off-balance, like a bird blundering in a violent headwind. In an attempt to prolong his stay, Shweta had told Hans she was making pumpkin tarkari and for him to at least eat before he left. He'd refused, said that he had to get going. Would be back at sunrise.

She muttered to Dolly, 'Is two weeks. Is a small sacrifice to make.'

'Woman, you know how much could happen in two weeks? In two days? People does get sick and dead in a day.' As soon as the words came out of her mouth, Shweta cringed. She cast a glance at the spot where the clay mound had been made. Rubbed slow circles over her chest, trying to calm her heart. Dolly asked, 'What if someone shoot him? What if he can't walk no more? You ready for that?'

'He gonna be a watchman, not Jesse James.' Shweta was not so much defending her husband now as she was defending her own judgement. Why did she ever say anything to Dolly? They had already made up their minds.

A knock on the door. Lata popped her head in. An old pail in her hand. 'Anything to burn?'

Shweta pointed her chin at a rice bag in the corner. 'Not the bag, Lata. Just the rice.'

Lata raised her eyebrows. 'All that rice you gon burn?'

'You could have it. It soakin in rat pee for days now,' Shweta replied. At the same time, Krishna sat up on the mattress.

'I could help,' he said.

Lata pursed her lips. 'You have to rest. You gone through enough for the day.'

'Let me light the fire,' was all he said, as he fetched the rice bag and left with Lata.

'So, you aint worried, woman? He and that Mrs Changoor up at night.'

'It aint gon be like that. He workin there for so long.'

'You know is a different story when night come.'

'What you mean?'

'A man in the day and a man in the night is two different creatures.'

'Why you say that?'

'The things that happen to a man's soul at night... Woman, I don't think we could tell.'

'I trust Hans. I aint worried.'

*

By the time Lata and Krishna were done, the pail was spilling over with pumpkin rinds, fruit peels, ripped bags and charred woodchips. They hauled it to a tall, blue oil drum behind the left and tossed the contents in. The drum stank of Niala's vomit, even while it was shut. Lata went to get the kerosene, while Krishna tamped the rubbish down with a plank.

As he did, he spotted something colourful among the mould and decomposition.

Held his breath, leaned in to get a closer look.

An unopened packet of Smarties Candy Rockets. The one Hans had bought at Salloum's and given to Shweta. He stared deeply at it, as if imprinting himself onto it. Reached into the gunk and took it out. Squeezed it in his fist. He recalled the clerk smacking his hand away from the jar. As if he never washed them. As if he were an escaped leper. Then imagined his father on his knees before the schoolmaster. Reduced to the vagabond out there, and now back here among his own family. Krishna shouldered the guilt that his mother didn't want to touch.

When Lata returned, she asked, 'Krishna? You OK?' Her face full of concern. He didn't realise he was crying until she asked him again, 'What wrong?'

'I … I …' He wasn't sure what he wanted to say. He just knew that he wanted so much more to come out of him than the sound of sobbing. Fought hard to keep it in. Took deep breaths. Blew out hard. Squeezed his wrists. His bad eye hurting from the hot salt of the tears. When he could finally speak, he said, 'Don't tell nobody bout this.'

She studied his face for a moment, brushing his hair off his bad eye. 'I aint know what it have to tell.'

'Krishna? Lata, what happen here?' It was Tarak.

'I dunno! He was normal just now. We was gettin ready to burn the rubbish—'

Krishna swallowed hard, worked hard to keep his face straight, though his eyes still watered. Fought it for a hot minute. 'Nothin to tell.'

A pause. 'You sure?' they asked in unison.

'Tarak, I goin up to the Changoor house. I have to see my pa.'

Tarak stood up straight – he was willing to do anything. 'Let's go.'

On their way there, the sky split with colour. Pink cirrus strewn across a gradient of yellow, orange and pale blue. At night, the plains became a lumbering mass of black, the coconut trees in the distance being the only landmarks to provide any sense of orientation. Night like God had snuffed a candle out over the world.

White Lady followed them on the trek, but only halfway. The dog, despite what had happened, had returned to her usual sprightliness. Animals were intriguing in that way. Death would stare them in the eyes, and they would keep moving. Most of them never cowered or cogitated about their fate. Once, when he was a child, Krishna spotted a butterfly that had fallen from a hibiscus bract. One of its wings had dislocated on a leaf. It didn't bemoan its amputated wing, wondering what life would be now only single-winged. Didn't waste time worrying about how it could now escape the toads. No, its goal remained the same. Tried its lumbering best to scale the hibiscus stalk and reach that Bethesda of nectar. It was the same with White Lady. She nearly drowned but now that she could breathe, life was back to normal.

It didn't feel that way for Krishna. He could barely open his bruised eye. His wounds still stung. Thought back to his father's words at the river. That he had to learn that some people couldn't be touched. Was that really true? Bhagran Lakhan sure touched the police. But then again – it was the last thing he touched.

Tarak asked, 'You think them police was tellin the truth?'

'Bout Rudra and Rustam?'

'Think they really kill that man from the lodge?'

While they were in holding, the turnkey officer had spoken of an incident years ago. An overseer at Lancaster Lodge, where the twins had worked as yard boys, mysteriously disappeared. He'd been building a house on the outskirts of Bell – the foundation was still there, though its freshly sawn wood skeleton had been slowly disassembled by prowlers. Until it became a frame of nothing in particular. He built this house by forcing every worker to *donate* a cut of their salary to him. One day, the twins stopped paying him and he had them flogged with a cat-o'-nine-tails. The overseer's hacked-up remains were later found spilling out of fertiliser bags down by the river, meat and tissue torn apart by vultures.

'Anybody coulda kill that man,' Krishna said with a shrug. 'They have no evidence. The police just think is them because of their pa.'

Tarak wasn't going to argue. They walked for a little while farther. Then Tarak let out, 'Is just that I think we have to be careful—'

'Even if they did kill the man, maybe he deserve it. He was stealing. If they know for sure is Rudra and Rustam, they woulda done find them and lock them up.'

Tarak nodded in agreement. The twins wouldn't be free if that were the case. 'You right. If it was up to the police, they woulda throw all of we in there. Like how they wanted to throw your ma in there today.'

Krishna stopped in his tracks. 'Don't talk bout my ma.'

Tarak hunched his shoulders, taken aback by this retort. Changed the topic, 'How long your pa gon be up at the Changoor house?'

'He gonna stay up there for two weeks. That's what he say.'

'That's a long time. How he gonna eat up there?'

Krishna shrugged. Then Tarak asked, 'Why we goin up there now?'

Krishna didn't give an answer because he didn't know exactly. At the back of his mind, the words *bastard child* kept replaying. A part of him felt like he would never see his father again. It was an ambiguous, oracular fear that not so much coursed through him, but ran a cold finger down his back. Why had Hans left in such a hurry? Why did he not bid him goodbye?

Krishna wondered if he'd been unfair to his father. He was a better father than his uncle, at least. Often, when Tarak was a boy, Mandeep got so drunk that he couldn't find the latrine. After Tarak's mother died, he said that his father got drunk, made him drink with him. Then pulled him close and squeezed his gut as if to deflate it. Talked about girlfriends he had when he was younger. No names, only features. The one with the snipe nose. The one with the riders in her gum. The one with the mile-long nipples. 'Have nobody in this world more disgusting than my pa', Tarak had said. 'But at least he give me tough skin.'

They were nearing the front gate now.

Suddenly, the sound of a blast sent a tree full of blackbirds fluttering off. From where Tarak stood, everything was shadow. The birds could have been leaves if he hadn't known better. The blast echoed long into the distance.

Tarak's eyes widened. 'The hell was that?'

Krishna gritted his teeth. He dashed over to the wire fence and craned his neck. Tarak followed and as soon as he crouched, another blast cracked through the evening air. Up ahead, two shadows stood. A man and a woman. Antumbral. He heard them laughing and the woman cried out, 'You are so *rubbish* at this!'. He recognised the distinct swing of Marlee Changoor's voice.

'The gun move every time I shoot it!' the other voice called out. Krishna immediately recognised it as belonging to his father.

They stood in the pumpkin patch, where Mr Changoor kept a Good Friday Judas as a scarecrow. The effigy draped in old soggy shreds of white. It once had a face, but the birds and the weather saw to its removal. The head was still intact. Hans stood, feet apart, pointed the gun at the scarecrow's head. Took him almost a full minute to discharge the shot. He missed by a wide margin, the bullet zooming into the brush behind it. The two laughed again. 'That was worse than the last one!' she exclaimed. 'You have to hold on tight!'

'But I am,' said Hans, his eyes solemnly drawn to his grip.

Marlee took the gun from him. She raised it, barely taking time to aim, pulled the trigger. The Judas's straw head exploded like a blast of dandelion seeds before Tarak heard the crack of the shot and her ensuing laughter. Hans standing amused in the echo.

'Krishna? What your father doin there?' whispered Tarak.

Krishna remained quiet, his expression still one of focus. Hans and Marlee kept at it, pumpkin after pumpkin, round after round.

Tarak added, 'I aint know your pa know how to use a gun. You had know that?'

Krishna wasn't sure what he knew right now.

'Come,' said Krishna. 'It gettin dark. Let's go.'

'Already?' Tarak was confused.

'Yes, already.' Krishna didn't care to stick around. The reverberating blasts agitated him, though he knew it was more than that. Something about the way Mrs Changoor was laughing frightened him more than he was willing to admit. When he finally managed to hit a pumpkin, her madcap laughter only became louder.

'We aint goin to talk to them?'

Krishna wanted to. But for the life of him, couldn't think of a single word to say now. He regretted coming. 'It gettin dark,' was all he could muster before turning around and heading back home.

13
A Small Room

At full dark, when everyone was already in their rooms, Shweta rolled up a pinch of hemp and went outside. She crawled into the wheelbarrow near the iron slagheap at the side of the barrack, struck a match and smoked until her eyes turned red. The refuse drum was burning bright just a stone's throw away. White Lady crawled out from beneath the iron and sat beside the barrow. The dog licked Shweta's hand, startling her and causing her to almost drop the cigarette.

In the darkness, in the muddle of hemp smoke, the dog's white coat made her look like a ghost. Shweta gave two swift pats to the side of the barrow, beckoned for the dog to join her. The dog hopped into the barrow, and Shweta welcomed her with open arms.

Shweta thought of her brother, who had suddenly left the barrack and moved away to Rio Claro years ago. He'd never returned, though she never expected anything different. He barely ever crossed her mind, but he did now because of something she'd observed when she was very young. Their mother had become convinced that the boy was absenting himself from the schoolhouse so that he could go bird-hunting. She asked Shweta to follow him one day. Shweta went, careful to keep a cool distance behind so her brother wouldn't notice her.

After ten minutes of walking, he met with three friends at a wooden shed, where they cornered a dog. A mangy mottled-coat pothound, abandoned by God and forgotten by time. They held the poor thing in the air, each boy grabbing onto a limb so that they all formed an X. Her brother had one of the front legs. In unison, they tugged in their respective directions, laughing as the dog cried and yelped. When they were done, they dropped the dog and continued along the road to the schoolhouse.

At this junction, Shweta stopped following. She waited until their laughing banter was out of earshot before approaching the injured dog, which now had one paw lifted limply over the others. The dog snarled at her before scampering off with a newfound hatred for humanity.

She didn't understand why her brother had done such a thing. Even now, as she slouched in the barrow, she didn't understand. She'd been fond of her brother before that day. He put on an affectionate smile. Knew how to bowl a googly, a beamer and a leg break. He'd spoken well to everyone in the barracks with never an ill word for even the curmudgeon herder who scolded him for petting the cows. Never before had she even dreamt of him performing such an act of malice. That day created a ground shift for her. Not just her opinion of her brother, but of people on the whole. At least animals were predictable, she thought. They at least let you know that they were poised to strike. They arched their backs, bared their teeth, protracted their claws. A person, on the other hand, could strike without warning – could strike after years of kinship. She knew she could never trust her brother again. Could barely think of him as her brother after that. She said goodbye to him, knowing she'd never visit.

Her thoughts rolled back to Hans earlier that evening. That he didn't eat. That he didn't seek her out before accepting Mrs Changoor's offer – why had he kept it from her for so many days, as he admitted? Still, it was a sacrifice he had made for the hope of a house in Bell Village. She should've felt happy. But there lingered the dread that he was some unfamiliar animal deep down. Just like her brother had been. She hated these feelings. His absence was like a bane. What was he doing? Was he safe? Was he thinking of her and Krishna?

Suddenly, the sun had risen. She draped her red dupatta over her head and did her morning prayer to Lakshmi before going to the yard at the first sign of light. She sat on her stool and peeled potatoes into a wicker basket. The breeze was strong that morning. A couple of tanagers struggled to balance on a barhar tree before flying away. Dew settled like sweat. Without the birds, there was only the electric buzz of morning insects. It was set to rain again, but it looked like the clouds would drift right past the barrack and send the showers over Bell Village instead.

She peered into the distance, heart buoyant at the sight of an approaching figure. But it was just a bison wobbling in front of the weepy trees. Her eyes fixed on the road while she peeled. The knife soon slipped from her hand, made a clean lick across her thumb. She sucked the blood. Beside her was a half-filled lota. She dripped water onto her thumb to wash the wound. When she was done quartering the potatoes, she dribbled some oil into a metal pan and cooked them in a crackle of garlic. She cut a plantain into thick discs and fried them to a burnt honey-brown.

In the middle of her cooking, a gruesome noise came from the barrack. A sustained grunt followed by the muffled splash of something rancid. The sound of Niala vomiting into her bucket. Shweta was ashamed to think that she'd become accustomed to it – just as easily as one becomes used to a rooster's crow.

Rookmin came out into the yard with the bucket, almost waddling as she gripped it with two hands. With one swing, she tossed its acidic contents into the refuse drum and rinsed the bucket beside the rainwater barrel.

'I have some ginger if you want,' Shweta offered.

Rookmin put the bucket down, wiped her sweaty brow. 'Ginger don't do nothin for that girl. Aint have no herb for what that girl goin through.' She twisted her mouth. 'One day is pain; the next day is more pain. What else you could do but say prayers?'

Shweta nodded.

Rookmin continued, 'I hearin talk goin round that your dream come true. That you gettin outta this place.' She smiled, but there was a sadness in her tone. 'I know you since you's a little girl, Shweta. I live my whole life in a small room. And lemme tell you, life is what you make it. Small room, big house. Life could be good and bad in both.'

A life can only be spent once, Shweta thought. There was no turning back, no changing history. The only words Shweta could muster in response were, 'Is just a hope for now.'

Rookmin picked up the bucket. 'You's a young woman. Whole life ahead of you. Still have your health. A capable husband and a child full of life. Not me. My age catch up. One child is a *mūrkha*, the other probably goin to dead. I just being honest with myself – this pregnancy might kill my daughter. Is not Niala's fault. I feel like I had to fight bad spirits my whole life. She might die with that baby inside and the next step would be making sure she don't turn into no *churel*. I can't stand to think of Niala with a pig face and tusks. You have to burn the body with mustard to stop it—'

'That aint gon happen,' Shweta cut her off, upset at the thought of the girl dying. 'She gon make it through good.' At that moment, she felt as if she were telling herself that. About Hans and Krishna. About Hema.

Rookmin's look penetrated her, knowing that Shweta didn't really believe those words. 'You get to a point where you prepare for the worst. Is only the responsible thing to carry these thoughts with you.' And with that, the old lady returned inside, the retching continuing for a few more minutes before the scene went quiet again.

A half hour went by. Another figure happened in the distance. A slow speck moving towards the barrack. This time, it was Hans. Shweta rose from the stool; she had to keep her feet pressed strong against the earth to prevent herself from dashing towards him. When his face came into view, he gave a drowsy smile before bowing his head. Greeted her with a kiss that ended as soon as it started. Her lips still puckered when he pulled away. His eyes dark ringed. She understood that he hadn't yet slept. Handed him the lota. He washed his face and rinsed his mouth.

'How it was?' she asked. 'The night?'

'Quiet. Long.'

'You probably hungry,' she said. 'So, I fry up some aloo and moko.'

'Eat later,' he said.

'It gon get cold by then.'

'Too tired to eat.' A loud yawn and headed inside.

Shweta scraped the food into a pot and placed the lid over it. Took it inside with her, Hans already asleep on the fibre mattress. Krishna as well. It was rare for her to see Hans asleep like this. He was always up before her, the only husband in the barrack to awaken before the wife.

When Krishna was five or six years old, Hans used to take him to the bisons' grazing ground, pushing him around in a wobbly wheelbarrow, the child squealing with each sharp turn. When the ride was over, Krishna piggybacked on his father, and they curveted around and around the mango tree at least a dozen times before moving on to the chenet tree with the same act. He told Krishna to pick a few while he was hoisted on his shoulders. And when the boy's hands were filled, his father let him down. Together, they pinched and snapped the chenets in two, sucked the orange flesh off the seeds. The two would be so tired from the horseplay that they'd fall asleep right before full dark, the dinner barely having gotten a chance to digest.

Seeing both of them asleep like this now took her back to those years, and a great sadness overcame her as the image of Hans and Hema came to mind. How she slept on his bare chest, clinging more tightly than she ever did to her mother's breast. Shweta rewound time back to her wedding. Pollen on the ground. Golden cloth over her plaited hair. Bamboo over them. Ixoras and hibiscus petals on a brass plate with bread. Women around her clapping and singing. Rushed mehindi flowers on their hands. Open palms stained in red henna. Then Hans beside her, cross-legged, staring ahead at a bull crossing the backdrop of the plain as the pundit chanted. The memory seemed so distant now, so foreign. It could have come from another existence. From her own imagination, even.

She rewound time even further. Her parents both dead, her brother gone. She had always liked Hans but was never sure the feeling was mutual. They'd gotten drunk at the Mayfair and kissed. She undressed for him at the river and let him take her on the bank. They married while she was pregnant with Hema. They were happy. Then Hema died. The death had propelled her out of orbit. Hans found his way back, perhaps too quickly. She didn't. Perhaps grief worked in different orders for each parent. At first, she thought of her grief as an extension of love. Now that Krishna was here, now that she had a second chance, sorrow felt selfish.

She crawled onto the mattress next to Hans, wrapping her arms around his waist and bringing him in close. He smelled different. She was so used to him smelling like the land – his musk like soil and freshly cut grass. Now he had a dusty, metallic smell of grime and oil.

She decided not to dwell on it. He was here, and that was most important. The worst must be behind now. The first night was the hardest one. Only a few more days and they'd have the money to begin anew. The flicker was now a flame, lighting the way. It was good to know that there was a path ahead. There was hope. All the other roads, all the other bridges, they would figure out as they got there.

*

An hour later, Krishna sat up on the mattress, went on all fours and crept towards the curtain. A moment of hesitation before peering in, followed by a wave of relief. His mother and father asleep, clothed, their heap of limbs rising and falling with each breath. He kept quiet as he left the room.

The cool morning wind hit him as soon as he stepped into the barrack yard. Dolly and Lata were there. White Lady asleep in the wheelbarrow. Lata sat ramrod on a stool while her mother parted her hair. She spotted Krishna peering over at them and waved. 'Krishna, come keep me company,' she said.

Before going over, he leaned over the rainwater barrel, squinting to see his reflection. His eye was darker today. Lata realised what he was doing. She said, 'That policeman aint had no right to do that to you. You aint deserve that.'

'I know,' he muttered.

'Don't worry, Krishna. The eye gon look worse before it look better,' said Dolly. She ran her fingers through her daughter's scalp. Every time she pinched a louse free, she squeezed it between her fingers until it made a soft *tssst* like a raindrop hitting a hot tava. She used a hooked twig to nip some of the eggs loose.

'*Owch!*' Lata cried out. 'You gon scrape my skin right off, ma.'

'You complain bout everything I do. You wouldn't complain if Krishna was doin it.'

Lata turned to him. 'Krishna, you want to do it?'

A shy chuckle escaped him.

'You seein, ma? I make him laugh.' Turned to Krishna. 'You look nice when you smile. You should do it more often—*Owch!*'

'I might hafta put the kerosene on it,' said Dolly, shaking her head.

Lata groaned. 'She gon set my head on fire, Krishna.'

Dolly snorted. 'This damn girl gon get me in trouble one day, you know.'

Before Lata could say anything else, her mother had already gone into the barrack. Even with her hair loose, stringy and full of lice, she could still make jokes and laugh. Even like this, she was easy on the eyes. He called back to the nights she had to sleep in his room, and how he'd gaze at her in the midnight darkness. He did wonder what her reaction would be if he had told her how he felt. Probably think of it as a joke and playfully punch him in the shoulder. She didn't feel the same way – he knew that. She only had eyes for older boys. Village boys with houses and prospects. She hoped to marry one in the future. They were her only way out, she said. Maybe then it wouldn't be so bad to move to Bell Village, now that he thought about it. In a few years, they could marry. And though the village would hold them in prejudice – at least they could face and fight that prejudice together.

Dolly returned with a rag and bottle. Tipped the bottle onto the rag. Then bundled the wet end of the rag into a ball. Lata kept focus on Krishna, her face tensed, ready to accept pain. The rag high with fumes.

Lata gave a dubious look. 'It smell like death, ma.'

'Death for the lice,' Krishna said with a small grin.

Lata bit her lip. Dolly parted her hair, dabbed the rag against the skin of her scalp. She did this five times, each prompting a grunt of *Oww ow!* from Lata.

'Leave it in there for a couple hours,' Dolly told her. 'Don't play harden and rub it out, you hear? It feelin better already, right?'

Lata's face in a grimace. 'Only burnin and pain.'

'In a couple hours you will see.' Dolly gave her a playful tap on the head. Eyed Krishna. 'Make sure she don't rub it out.'

Lata pouted. 'I hope nobody cigarette fall on my head.' She went back into the barracks, emerging with a rattan basket of clothes in her arms. 'Krishna, come help me with these clothes.'

He offered to carry the basket.

Dolly pointed at her. 'Girl, find a new spot to wash them this time, eh. Not that same river as last time.'

'Why?'

'That river nasty. You bringin back the clothes and it have all kinda muckstains on it. Have a stream not too far from here. Closer than that river that all the animals probably shittin in.'

Lata shook her head. 'The whole river not dirty.'

'Just find a clean spot then. I feel like every time you wash the clothes, I have to shake the tadpoles off—'

Lata elbowed Krishna. 'And she tellin me I's the one who like to complain.'

14
A Dirty Animal

As the river came into view, Krishna remembered the time his father had built a crab pot from old driftwood, chicken wire and a rusted barrel hoop. He set it down in the morning, as the crabs usually washed downriver, and hauled it up at noon. Looked like a box full of moving claws the first time he lugged it out of the river. He collected them in a bushel basket for Shweta to cook with boiled dasheen bush into a callaloo. The crabs turned deep red when cooked. Not red like blood but like bit tongues.

Not too long after, the crab pot started turning up empty. One morning, Hans got there early enough to find some village boys toying with it. He didn't chase them or berate them. Instead, offered to teach them how to make their own. But they cursed him and laughed at him. Took the crab pot and ran away. He didn't see the purpose of stealing the pot; he could've bet that none of them knew how to use it.

After that, he whittled down a cashew branch using a piece of stout bottle. They walked along the bank, looking for bubbles in the mud. He'd done this with his mother when he was little but had to relearn the skill. When Hans came to a spot, he jabbed the pole and twisted it. The memory of the first catch was vivid for Krishna. The sound of that deep crunch, like stomping your boot into five layers of dried leaves – and up sprouted a crab as if it were a carrot plucked from a garden. The branch would be pushed right through its belly, a white mush leaking out. His father turned to him, a glint in his eyes.

'They gon have to steal every branch from every tree to stop we now.'

Those words resonated now. Epiphanous. Every branch from every tree. His father had fought back without fists, without bruises. He didn't need to hunt those boys down. Didn't spend time on revenge. And he was still able to get crabs in his callaloo. Perhaps it wasn't always about fighting back, Krishna thought, but getting stronger.

Lata dipped the clothes into the water and scrubbed them with coconut fibre. Now Krishna did the same as he did with his father – walked along the bank looking for mud bubbles. Didn't care to catch any crabs. Just seeing them scuttle into their holes was enough for him. Scattered near some bushes were some half-buried fishbones. A couple of fishtails strewn near the bank, no doubt gobbled up by the pack of stray dogs up ahead near the water.

Lata turned in his direction, saw the dogs. 'Krishna, make sure them dogs don't come over here. Them might snatch away the clothes right outta this basket.'

'They aint look like they want to come here.'

'You aint know what animals want till they take it.'

'A man more likely to steal your clothes than them dogs.'

Lata smiled at him. 'You thinkin big bout them dogs, Krishna.'

Krishna shrugged. 'I like dogs better than people. A dog know when you feelin bad. And it don't tell you nothin for feelin bad. It just stay with you. It just know.'

'I should marry a dog then.'

'That aint gon make for a long marriage.'

'Why? How long a dog live for?'

'Fifteen years. Depend on the type of dog.'

Lata laughed. 'Fifteen years is a long time, boy. Is also a long time to be cleanin up dogshit.' She scratched her scalp until the skin broke and strands of hair got hooked in her fingernails. 'This damn kerosene aint do nothin but burn my damn scalp off.'

'Your ma say not to touch it.'

'I gon touch and scratch whatever and whenever I damn well want. Is *my* head.' Reached for another dress, started scrubbing. She said, 'My ma tell me that you might be shippin off.'

'To Bell, yeah.' A pause. 'I dunno yet.'

'Your ma say you aint want to go.' She snorted. 'Like they would ever leave your scrawny self behind.'

He felt a wave of embarrassment and wondered what else his mother had said about him. Stared at the sky as if in search of some invisible bird. 'I still hate everybody from the village.'

She laughed. 'And you love everybody here in this barrack? It gon be strange not havin you round. I gon miss you.'

'Miss me?' Part of him thought to ask her if she'd like to come live with him, though he knew that was never going to happen.

'You gettin a chance to live good. Have one life, boy. And you have a blessed one. Your pa. He is a blessed man. Plenty men in this place throw away their good money on rum and cards. Cause they aint have no plan.' In the distance, a stray dog came out of the water, shook itself off. Then immediately flopped its body into a mud puddle and rolled around until its entire torso was caked. Lata pointed to the dog. 'Like that dog over there – wash itself off and jump right back into the mud. No plan.'

'That's what dogs do. Tarak try to bathe White Lady all the time. But she always jump back into the mud.'

'Dirty animal.' She looked at the dress in her hand, the colour starting to fade. 'Seem like nothing stay clean forever. Like these clothes here. Wash, wash, wash, neverendin washing, always gettin back dirty.'

Shortly after, three boys came walking up the river. Each in short pants. One of them bareback, shaggy-haired. His beard thick, matching well with his long face. They stopped a good distance away upriver. Lata gave them a big wave, her hand moving mechanical as a metronome. A smile like she was drunk. Only the bareback boy returned the wave. The other two looked at him, shook their heads.

'Who's them?' asked Krishna, squinting at them.

Her eyes went dreamy. 'A boy who givin me the sweet eye a few weeks now. The bareback one. They come here at this time to catch sardines.'

He steepled his fingers. 'This is why you come *here* to wash clothes?'

A laugh. 'Don't tell my ma.'

Her entire body swayed as she waved at the bareback boy. Krishna's body cringed with envy.

The boy returned the wave. Laughing with the other two now. The first boy had a moustache like a big man's. The second, a broad mouth and a big jaw. They had a bushel and a small bowl of what looked like chitterlings. He ran a hand-line into the water while the other two handled the dip nets. Krishna gave him a long look, his face going pale when he realised who it was.

Krishna asked, all sincerity, 'You talk to *he*?'

Lata, taken aback by his tone, replied, 'He come up to me a few times.'

'You know who that is?' An urgency in his voice now. 'That is Dylan Badree.'

A sigh. 'I know who he is—'

'He father is the one who lock me up!' He forcefully pointed to his black eye. 'The brother, Mikey, was the one who try to drown White Lady!'

'Don't start this foolishness with me, Krishna. Dylan aint them. I aint need you sayin nothin bad bout him. I's look forward to this the whole week.'

With a grimace, 'You settin yourself up bad, Lata.'

'What you know?' She rolled her eyes in exasperation. With that, she stopped washing. Reached over, plucked a hibiscus from a bough behind her. Swung her arms with it and for a moment, looked like she would toss it into the river. Turned to Krishna. 'You think I should give him this flower?'

He folded his arms. 'Do what you want. Why you askin me? You already make up your mind.' Then mocked, '*What I know?*'

She sucked her teeth at him. 'Why you bein stubborn?'

She set the washed clothes back in the basket. Walked over to the boys. Held the flower up, twirling the corolla against her nose, blushing like she was the one receiving it. The boys were in the middle of setting up the handline now. Dylan knee-deep in the water. They stopped when they noticed her approaching. Krishna stayed within earshot.

The broad-mouthed one raised his eyebrows. The moustached one stroked his chin. Dylan made his way back to the bank. Furrowed his brow. 'That's for me?'

Lata didn't say anything, just smiled. The moustached one, 'You hafta admire the girl courage.'

Dylan took the flower, put it in his pocket, thanked her. And that was it. She came back to her spot. Grabbed a skirt with a deep mudstain that she'd been saving for last and began to rigorously scrub.

She said, 'You have to put yourself in my shoes, boy. This is what I have to hope for to get outta this place. Start lookin from early. A good one from the village. It mightn't be this one. The pundit and them say you have to wait. But the truth is you have to learn from early. Or it gon be harder later on. You have to take what good for you.'

'Trust me, Lata. Them aint no good—'

'And who good for me?' She ruffled his hair. 'You?'

She was done with the clothes and ready to go.

He told her to go ahead, that he had to pee and he'd catch up. He glanced over at the boys again. They were talking about something, looking over and snickering. Made him uncomfortable. Annoyed. And couldn't help but find out what they were smirking about. He went back to the river, creeping through the bush to get to the coppice behind the eyes. He pulled the leaves in close, within earshot. The three boys stood with the lines ready. Dylan with the hibiscus in hand.

The broad-mouthed one, 'What was that smell, Alfonse? That aint how people suppose to smell.'

Alfonse, with the moustache, 'They rub stinkbugs and cow pee on their skin, Larry. What you expect?'

Dylan shook his head. 'You aint being fair, the two of you.'

Larry shrugged. 'You see what you get for playin hotshot for them filthy barrack girls? You have licehead sendin flowers for you now.'

Alfonse raised his arms up. 'I would throw that thing in the river, eh. I wouldn't take nothin from no girls up that side.'

Dylan sucked his teeth. 'You overdoing it. She aint bad at all.'

'Probably stick that flower up she *nani* for all you know.' Larry motioned as if he were doing the same.

Alfonse yelled out, 'Black magic! *Obeah!*'

'You underestimating barrack girls,' said Dylan. 'Them is some of the best *dulahins*. Always grateful to their husbands. Waking up early to cook every day. Always there for the children. Never have to worry about them. They know how to take care of themself. Not like some of them girls in the village who feel they too good for everything. I can bet you that a barrack girl would never go behind your back for nothin.'

'The man have a point,' said Larry. 'You could have a woman on the side, bring she home and have your barrack wife cook for she. And she can't say nothin. She just grateful to have a roof over she head.'

Alfonse shook his head. 'You know every man in that barrack probably take that girl already, right?'

'Plenty experience then, Alfonse,' said Dylan in a half-mocking manner.

'She loose as a goose. How you think they get village men in the first place? That flower have some kinda Hindu hex put on it. Throw that shit in the river, Dylan.'

'If I throw it in that water, you gon shut up with your nonsense?' said Dylan.

As they went on, Krishna couldn't come to terms with how he felt. He was accustomed to being the target of such insults, but Lata being the target troubled him more. It wasn't anger that came over him but a groundswell of melancholia that snuck up from under. Felt like he was so small that it could wash him away.

He raced up the path to catch up with Lata. Glanced over at the river, now tapered to the murmur of a stream. Where the water sprayed over the rocks arose a faint rainbow. He looked behind to make sure nobody was following him. In the opposite direction, a black anvil of cloud. He spotted something strange in the water. At first, thought it to be a tilapia, but as it came closer into view, he realised what it was.

A hibiscus, surrounded by tadpoles, floating parallel to their stride.

Soon, it passed them. Lata peered in its direction, but he wasn't sure if she noticed it.

15
A Risky Move

Robinson remembered something his father had told him about people he didn't like but had to stomach. He likened the situation to a bison and its flies. While the bison grazed in the field, it would swish its tail at the gathering flies. There is rarely a moment when the bison wouldn't have to do this, and so someone seeing the bison for the first time would think it just enjoys swishing its tail. It has gotten so accustomed to this dance that its facial expression never shifts while its tail, like an automaton, bats away fly after fly. He said that people might mistake the bison's impassiveness for laziness. But such was a daily dance that eventually became part of its personality.

If Robinson was the bison, then Baig was the fly. Both lived in Bell Village. Lived on opposite sides. Baig wouldn't give him a word of greeting on the street but prattled incessantly while they worked. Mostly about race, about the differences between East Indians and Africans. Spoke as if he were a scholar on the subject. Said that Robinson was one of the few Black men who stuck around to be a father. Said he admired it but always made note that it was the exception. Asked Robinson if the notion ever came to mind for him to run away, go deep south. Work in the oilfields now that the labour riots were over. *Plenty people in this country hungry to start over!* Put fantasies in his head about it as if he were selling him the idea and expected a finder's fee. That there were many good women down south. Some of them mixed with Spanish blood. From the south coast, he could hop on a fishing boat on Erin Bay or Icacos Point and sail down the Serpent's Mouth to the mangroves in Delta Amacuro. *Venezuela is where things happenin right now.* Robinson figured that these scenarios lingered in Baig's mind because they were his own fantasies, despite Baig himself being married to a dutiful woman.

Robinson was married to a Barbadian woman much younger than himself, same as Mr and Mrs Changoor, and had a son and daughter that did well at the schoolhouse. He lived in a small house that his father built. Gave ten per cent of his salary to the church, even though it placed no real obligation on tithes. On Sundays, the congregation spilled into the street. The morning air steaming hot with people and canticles and sermons.

Baig believed that Black people should've never gone to church, and that they should've followed the old religions of Africa. Robinson did not believe in the old African religions. When he was a boy, he once went to an Orisha man's funeral and observed a ritual where the priest lifted the deceased man's toddler son and dangled him over the pinebox coffin. Passed the toddler to another man standing at the opposite end of the box. Then the man passed the child back to the priest. Passing him, left, right, left, right, until their arms formed a morbid hammock. The child bawling his lungs out. The priest laughing, saying, 'God forbid you drop that child eh!' All in the name of perplexing the dead man's spirit, so that it couldn't return to haunt his son. Robinson had nightmares about it – imagining his baby self being passed over the worm-chewed corpse of his own father. And from then on, he swore that the old African religions could never be the right path to God.

If Robinson was the bison, then the act of him swishing his tail was soliloquy. He spoke to his gardening tools, to the wood and to the metal used to construct them. Spoke to the rain clouds and asked them what time to expect the showers. Spoke to the mites in the soil, to the birds in the balata tree, to the wind over his shoulders. The habit didn't start with Baig but with men who worked with him in the machine shop. Crass men who harped on about their wives and the sahibs. Two men once debated the ways they could rape a missionary's wife and get away with it. Jested that Canadian *punani* must be as cold as a dog's nose at night. Robinson could drown out their voices with his own communing with nature. He felt at ease doing it, more in touch with God. And God would always steer him away from thoughts of sin.

But today, he was in want of gossip.

He'd thought it strange when Hans mentioned having dinner with Mrs Changoor. A full course – conch fritters, fricase de pollo, three-bean salad. Invited him inside to sit at the table. Even put on music for him. Mr Changoor never liked people inside his house. Robinson had been in careful observation of the Missus after that. Each day that passed, she wore less and less makeup. Didn't dress as stylishly. And something about her voice had changed. He couldn't tell, but something about it was off. She'd always sounded like she'd leapt straight out of the silver screen. Her inflections, the Hollywood breathiness of her voice. Now, her tone was more sing-songy. A faint meld of the Trinidadian accent emerging. She became annoyed when he asked her how Mr Changoor was going – said that she was not his mother, to know his every move.

Perhaps there was something more underhanded happening with Mr Changoor than she was letting on. He visited his memories of Baig's vulgar rumours about the Missus, sifting through his own soliloquys to recollect the words. That she was once a prostitute that the Mister had won in a card game up in Port of Spain. A prostitute since childhood, Baig had told. And that because she had so much sex as a child, her vagina became unusually wide as she matured. Could probably hold a cricket corkball firm between its walls. And that was why Mr Changoor couldn't impregnate her – it was like pouring his seed into the abyss.

Robinson had never known Mr Changoor to play cards. Or even own a deck of them. So, to him, the first fib exposed the others. But remembering it did make Robinson ponder the woman's origins. Everybody had at one point, but in the end accepted the narrative that he'd met her just as any two people met uptown. Courted her in bistros and shopping streets and guesthouses and returned here to the house with her, where they subsequently wedded. To Robinson, the simplest story was usually the one that was true.

Still, he thought himself remiss if he were to believe the Changoors were simple people with simple stories. In life, he was told that he had to have certain values. He had to be generous and honest and charitable to have success. But the truth of the world was that only the traits of the sinner – the obsessiveness, the cruelty and harshness, the ego and greed – were what brought riches such as the Changoors had.

Mrs Changoor was leaning against one of the porch pillars. Her eyes dull and smooth as planed wood. Body sleek and streamlined in a white cotton sundress and yellow mules. Her perfume water smelling of frangipanis. Even with minimal makeup, she was a damn knockout. The light clinging to her skin like she was enveloped by seraphim. And when she faced away from the light, the shadow formed a clean cleft down her profile.

She gave Robinson a slight smile.

Baig came up to Robinson around midday while he tended to the tomato crop. Took off his cap, wiped his brow. The wind carried his murmur, 'The Missus say anything about Changoor comin back?'

'She don't say much. I assume he still in Guyana.' Robinson turned to him. 'Why you ask?'

Baig scratched his chin, eyes to the porch. Mrs Changoor was gone now. 'And Hans aint say nothin?'

A sigh. 'Hans wouldn't know nothin.'

'Hans and Mrs Changoor kinda close, you aint think so? They aint seem like they could be hidin something?' Baig said. Then whispered, 'The Mister leave on the night of that rainstorm. And I read in the papers that on that night all crafts had to be grounded—'

'Oh, you read?' Robinson chuckled at his own sarcasm.

'I know you think I stupid, pardner. But I know Changoor aint no pilot. And Changoor had to be flyin that plane to Guyana heself, because no pilot in their right mind would.' Baig sounded like he was looking for validation – Robinson couldn't understand why.

'That would make him a suicide pilot then.' He jested, even though Baig had made a convincing point. The Mister had indeed left in a hurry, and it was indeed the night of the rainstorm. Still, he stuck with his belief that the simplest story was usually the true story. 'It aint we business, I suppose. We still getting pay, aint we? If it bother you so much, why you don't just quit this work? You been comin and goin as you please anyway. Put other things on your mind. It will do you some good.'

Baig put on his cap, looked at the sky. 'I think we should be watchin Hans and Mrs Changoor, is all. Something aint right with them two.'

Robinson scratched the back of his neck. A shrug.

Baig fashioned his fingers into an O and poked his index finger through it. 'You think they doin that?'

Robinson went back to the plants. 'That aint my affairs.'

'Hear his son end up in the police station,' said Baig.

'News travel fast.'

A grin. 'Is a small country.'

'They let the boy go.'

Baig looked him in the eye. 'You know why he was there?'

Robinson kept his gaze on the plants. 'Whatever boys do.'

'Beat him bad in there, I hear. Badree aint easy.'

Robinson twisted his mouth, his own children coming to mind. 'Sorry to hear.'

Without pause, 'If Hans gonna live in Bell, Badree not gonna make his life easy.'

It troubled Robinson that Baig might be right. Baig went on, 'But I wouldn't worry. Hans look like a man who could take on anything. You know he eat two buckets of mangoes a time ago? Almost two buckets. He was aimin for three. He aint somebody to worry bout.'

A faint smile escaped Robinson. 'Heard bout that. Years ago.'

'We all laugh at him that day. But I think all of we in secret wanted him to finish the three buckets. Fellas push hard for him to do it. Had him pacing up and down the yard and shoving more and more mangoes into he mouth. Another one rubbin he belly while he suckin the flesh out. Hans eat right up till he pass out.'

Robinson, still smiling. 'I remember people was laughing for days about it.'

'I hope nothin happen to the lad,' said Baig, gazing at the homestead. 'Would be a shame for somethin to happen to him here.'

Hans arrived late into the afternoon, just as Robinson and Baig were about to leave. They didn't speak. Hans gave them a nod of recognition before going towards the homestead. He looked strange, almost hypnotised. Just as he neared the homestead, music filled the house and spilled onto the porch. Baig went ahead, but Robinson took his time closing the latch on the gate. He couldn't see Hans any more once he was on the road to the hill's descent. He didn't know what else to do but offer a prayer to God for the man.

*

Krishna had the idea to gather the mangoes for his father. He felt sorry for the man. Felt guilty, especially remembering their talk down by the river. Tarak thought it was a good idea as well, that it'd be a sign of goodwill for getting them out of the holding cell.

So, in the late afternoon, they headed over to the mango tree with a crocus bag. A sort of rancid oversweet pungency wafted around the bark where a pool of black water slushed – black from a heap of fallen decomposing mangoes, where a disc of tadpoles greedily circled. White Lady left Tarak's side to sniff the water, paused, then let out a repulsed snort. A slight rain had come down earlier that morning, not fit for a flood but enough to fill the chuckholes in the compacted soil. The slightest revenant of a rainbow still lingered in the sky.

Tarak scratched his head, snapped his fingers for White Lady to stay away from the water. 'A lot of mangoes wastin down there. That's what kinda mango there, you think?'

'*Julie*, it look like.'

'That is the best kind.'

Krishna stared up at the tree like a carpenter foreman overseeing the construction of a house. 'Still have plenty good ones hanging up there. Come. Grab a stone.'

Tarak grabbed one and pelted it at the tree. Knocked a mango straight off the branch. It fell into the pool of black water. 'Shit,' Tarak said as he made a mad dash for it before the dog could get it. Dipped his hand in the water, yanked it out.

'Leave that one right there,' said Krishna.

'It still good. It just land in that rotten water. And you gon peel off the skin anyway. Put it in that bag there.'

'I aint taking that chance. Look at how that water is. Black from rot. Who know what livin in there? A crapaud could be inside that mango.'

'Is that same water the tree roots taking in.' Tarak peeled the mango, his hands yellow as the slimy skin came off. 'God say is a sin to waste.' He sank his teeth into the mango, juice dripping down his collarbone. A dozen flies came out of nowhere and started creeping all over him. He offered a piece to the dog, but she sniffed it and recoiled.

'See, even the dog scorn the crapaud mango,' said Krishna. He hurled the rock. Missed.

Tarak laughed. 'You aint know how to throw straight.' He picked up a rock, flung it at the tree. Hit the mango clean. It popped off the bough, went straight into the water.

'In the damn water again!' exclaimed Krishna in annoyance.

Tarak sucked his teeth. 'You feel I's God? I can't control how them mango fallin. Just like how you can't pelt straight.'

Krishna went up to the tree. 'Hear what. I gon hold the bag under the tree here and you pelt that stone there.'

Tarak chuckled. 'Your catchin skills better than your throwin skills?'

'Pelt the damn stone and we gon see.'

They caught close to twenty mangoes like this, much to Krishna's delight.

Krishna's shoulder hurt from having to bear the weight of the filled sack and even though Tarak offered to help with the load, he declined. Together, they made the trek up to the Changoor farm. White Lady dutifully followed them the entire way. They came up the road to the farm, but the gate was locked. Nearby, there was a break in the fence.

'You really goin in there?' asked Tarak.

Krishna furrowed his brow. 'Yeah. What the hell you think we come up all this way for?'

'We can't just go in. We goin to get shoot.'

Krishna recalled his father and Mrs Changoor shooting at pumpkins, firing shots at the Judas. Laughing like they were old friends. He shook his head. 'Mr Changoor aint there. Only pa and Mrs Marlee. They aint gon shoot we. We aint no thieves.'

Tarak was still hesitant. 'Why you don't leave the bag here? I sure they gon find it if you leave it right here.'

'I not gon leave it on the ground and let the birds and agoutis and them come and get them.' Krishna glanced at Tarak. 'You with me or not?' He felt a little annoyed having to ask that question. They were supposed to be there for each other, no matter what. Past their own reluctance. Past right and wrong. Past fear and desperation.

Tarak nodded, ordered the dog to stay. Instead, she scampered off as if she knew something that they didn't. Krishna slipped through the fence and Tarak tossed him the bag. Nearly knocked the little boy down when he moved to catch it. A web of rangoon creepers entangled some of the trees near the broken section of fence. The wind blew through a rowdy patch of rambutan trees, the red spiny fruits lying surly on the decomposing foliage. The two slogged up to the homestead. It was the first time Krishna had seen it.

Tarak said, 'That's where he livin? Lookin more fit for a mongoose than a man.'

The structure really was something ugly, Krishna thought. Everything about it warped and crooked – like toes mangled within the constriction of ill-fitted boots. The barrack at least held its own roof up. This homestead seemed to struggle under the weight of itself. Even the door hung on its hinges at a jaunty angle. He wasn't sure if it could fully close. Still, he knocked.

There was no answer. Knocked again.

No answer.

He gave the door a gentle push and it slid open with a whining creak. Set one foot inside and scanned the room. He called out, 'Pa?'

Again, no response.

He put the other foot inside too and leaned into the room, his palms holding onto the door as if expecting a great wave to come crashing into him. The mattress was moist at its base and a scud of mosquitoes and mites swivelled over it. From the inside, he could see the hole in the roof. The sun printed a circular pad of light on the floor beside some junk. He exited the room and closed the door behind him, halfway expecting it to disconnect from the hinges. He looked at Tarak and gave him a large shrug. Then shot a glance at the big house. For a moment, he considered returning home. The three windows at the front were shut, the deep purple curtains pulled tight. 'Let's knock on the door,' he finally said.

Tarak cleared his throat. 'I tellin you, we gon get shoot.' Pointed at his forehead. 'Right here. The bullet right here.'

Krishna took a few steps up to the house when he heard a crack in the air.

The gust of a gunshot.

Tarak jumped to the ground, hands on the back of his head.

Krishna was frozen in place, struck with a chilly dizziness as if he'd just moved from one world to the next. His hands went feeble, struggled to retain a sturdy grip of the bag. One of the curtains shifted, like the fluttering of an eye. As if the house had awakened.

A wild howl of laughter came from the back.

It brought Krishna back to the last time they were here, when the two were firing rounds into the Judas. He imagined himself now as the Judas. And Mrs Changoor cackling as his head exploded into a thousand threads of straw, the wind blowing the rest of him away to the darkening foothills.

'Krishna!' Tarak called out in a hushed tone.

Another shot sounded. Krishna dropped the bag.

'Krishna, get down!' Tarak called out again, his shoulders shuddering.

'They aint shootin at we,' Krishna uttered as if in a trance. 'Sound like it comin from the back.' Then started on his way around the house.

'Krishna! You gone mad? *Krishna!*'

As Krishna made his way to the back, there was another shot. Then another. To the back of the house was a shed, harrowed streaks of black running down the roof where paint had flaked off. As if the structure had been bludgeoned and bleeding from the scalp. Beside it was a small garden of dead flowers. A fence of wrought iron curlicues at the back. The door was halfway open, a snake of smoke slithering out into the air. The gunshots and laughter were coming from inside that shed. The same madcap laughter he'd heard the last time they were here.

Cautiously, he approached. His feet firm with each step. Like he had weights strapped to his feet. He held the door, peeked inside. It was dark and the gun smoke obscured everything. Mrs Changoor and his father stood side by side, silhouetted.

'Hit her eye! The left eye!' Mrs Changoor coughed in the middle of her shouting.

Hans fired a shot into the wall.

She laughed, crying out, 'You missed – you hit the poor maiden! So close to it and you still missed! Hopeless! Give me that damn thing!' She grabbed the gun from him and discharged four consecutive bullets at the wall. Krishna widened his eyes, had to clamp his mouth shut. The lady was a gunslinger.

After the smoke thinned, Krishna finally saw what they were blasting at. A large painting of what looked like a goddess and her attendants. Close to a dozen bullet holes through their bosoms and faces.

His father's jaw dropped. 'You aint need me here—!'

She turned to him. 'No, but I want you here—'

'*Krishna!*' Tarak called out in a coarse whisper, hiding behind a tree.

'Shush.' Mrs Changoor, now alert, held her hand up. 'Hans, did you hear that?'

Krishna took off. Signalled for Tarak to run as well. Both of them like mad bulls. No time to talk, no time to think. They ran past the bag of mangoes – spilled over like a dead, eviscerated body.

When they made it to the gate, Krishna glanced back.

Nobody there. Legs ready to fall off. His insides ablaze. But he didn't stop.

16
A Magic Word

Shweta was the first one awake in the barrack. She began cooking in the darkness. Picked up the pan with soaked dirt and gobar, dipped a rag into it and caressed the edges of the oven before filling it with thin sticks of firewood. She struck a match, lit the fire and threw in another stick, embers spraying out its side as it kindled. She pulled the edge of her dupatta away from the flamelets and hung a flapjack of roti from the end of a rod above the fire, watching it inflate like a Portuguese man-o'-war as it caught the rising air. Then she used a knife and incised a keyhole to deflate it. Steamed the pumpkin perfectly for the tarkari – a little too much and it would've lost its trademark moisture.

An hour later, the sun rose. She kept her eye on Krishna from time to time, his eyes moving behind the lids, the skin surrounding the bruise still darkly sore. The boy hadn't said a word that night. Didn't even crack open his magazines. Two hours after sunrise, still no sign of Hans. Then arrived the apocalyptic fear that he would never return.

She sat on the dirt ground, hugging her knees, eyes on a bale of discarded tirite straw. Pregnant Niala hacking and vomiting inside the barrack. Rookmin carrying it out in buckets. The air still cool then. From the straw emerged a scorpion, black and shiny, tail like a come-hither finger. Came right up to Shweta, just shy of her toes. Almost looked like it was in awe of her, the way one lies prostrate in worship. Suddenly, the tail went straight up like an angered cobra – like the appendage had a life of its own. An acolyte suddenly risen to betray its god.

For minutes, Shweta and the scorpion stared hard at each other. A strange feeling overcame her. If it stung her, it would be all right. If she died, it would be all right. Such feelings were treachery to the sanctity of life – it wasn't normal to feel that way. So said the pundit when he was brought to see her sister-in-law, Mandeep's wife, Tansi. Years ago, when Tarak was only a child and Krishna a gurgling baby, the woman sat in the corner of the room, running a string of japamala prayer beads through her fingers. Passed the hours like this. She stopped eating, stopped speaking. Rookmin believed that a *bhoot* had come into the barrack and stolen the woman's mouth. Even without a mouth, the woman can scream, she said. Even without a stomach, one can go hungry. And even in death, one can lust for life.

That Tansi could not move a muscle to raise her head was a disservice to the world. But Shweta remembered the start of Tansi's behaviour. Mandeep had been drunk for days and it had rained for a day and a night. Rain like death. Thunder like death. The boy had come down with illness and messed himself in his sleep. The high smell of diarrhoea pervaded the entire barrack. Ailing shit smelled much different, much more foul. Mandeep blamed Tansi for the boy's mess. Punched her in the stomach so hard that it caused her entire body to fold. The woman said nothing for the rest of the day. Lost all expression. No sadness, no regret. The next day, she was sitting in the corner with the prayer beds.

The pundit laid Tansi down in a circle of incense, dragged cocoyea stalks across her back and chanted while waving a cloth bundled with bird peppers and garlic. Soon, the malady will be lifted, said the pundit. He said a prayer, then translated, *Service in this world is the highest prayer. Loving the people around us is the greatest devotion.*

At Tansi's cremation, they tied a white sash over her eyes.

Her passing was blamed on *bhoots* and *rakshasas*, but Shweta felt like she understood the woman's condition now. It was sometimes easier to do a disservice to the world if the world had done a disservice to you. A man who held no devotion to his family was a deadbeat. A woman who held no devotion to hers was no woman at all. She realised everything that held her together was Hans's presence. All filaments connected to him. The kernel of her sanity. Hans was the shining light. He was the blessing. Divine law did not entitle everyone to everything – but it gave her Hans.

The scorpion backed down, scuttling off and disappearing into the paragrass. It was at this time Shweta decided she couldn't wait any longer. With the pot of food in hand, she made the trek to the farm.

The farm gate was open when Shweta met it, swinging in the morning wind. A man, looking as weary as a wilted vine, greeted her, introduced himself. Said, 'Ma'am, we aint ever meet in the official manner. You be Hans's spouse. My name is Robinson.' His smile made his face youthful. Warm and convivial, it was a smile to rival her husband's. He let her in, told her that her husband was fast asleep in the homestead. Pointed a callused finger at it.

The homestead was smaller than she'd anticipated. A light wave of relief broke over her at that moment. Robinson kept his eye on the small iron pot in her hand and asked, 'That there is breakfast?' She couldn't help but feel chagrin for having toted this pot all this way here.

Inside the homestead, the floor was a blur of dust. The sole light bulb in the room dangled from a curl of wire hanging from a rafter where a pair of moths refused to budge. A dankness caked the seams of the walls, making it look like the room had broken into a fever sweat. The lone window, with its ill-fitted frame, was so crusted with scum that Shweta didn't even realise it was a window at first. An old rat-nibbled couch sat in one of the dark corners. Junk flanking the walls – a stepladder, smashed crates, a broken stool, an amputated Rama murti, a deflated bicycle wheel. No bed, just a dusty mattress in the corner and a sheet that reeked of paint thinner.

Hans on his belly, one leg straight, one leg crooked. She woke him up and he rubbed his head, gave her a sleepy smile as if he thought he were in a dream. She sat beside him, set the pot down, asked if he'd eaten. He shook his head. Something about him was off. She ignored it at first, but the thought returned after they finished eating. He ate quickly but not heartily. Shweta wasn't accustomed to that; Hans usually ate like a child, sucked his fingers clean, licked the pot, made muffled groans for food he liked. He lived in the present. A man of sensations. Appreciated the afternoon breeze, the cool river on his back, the taste of water kept in a calabash, birdsong in the morning, the smell of grass on his hands, and the spicy taste of masala. All the works of God. It was strange to see her husband eat without relish.

Hans had never gotten sick. While cholera and dengue and polio and the sprue seemed to be as natural as the night wind for others, the general air of malaise had always seemed to waft over Hans's head. In fact, the only time she'd seen him in a state of utter lassitude was during the mango-eating incident years ago. But that was an extreme. He was strong, blessed by the gods. She wondered now if malady had finally penetrated him. Perhaps staying in this dust-laden shack had taken its toll on him.

He returned to the mattress, said that he had a long night and wanted to rest before the walk home. Shweta accompanied him, told him she would also rest for a spell. He closed his eyes. She put her hands on his warm skin. First, she touched the ball of his heel. His chest. The nape of his neck, which caused him to shuffle a little. At first, she couldn't elicit any reaction from him other than a sleepy groan. Little by little, she pressed every part of her against him until there was no resistance. Caressed him through his clothes. Sank into him. Finally, like a half-awakened babe, he put his mouth over her breast and thumbed the nipple of the other.

She pulled her dress over her head and lay on her back. She wasn't certain how awake he was when he climbed on top of her. But she knew that with each stroke, he came more and more into his consciousness. Felt his heartbeat in his loins. This was the closest thing they'd ever had to privacy. The door was shut. The only opening through which sound could escape was a bright hole in the roof that printed a coin of light on the floor. A feeling of pleasured giddiness came over her.

Maybe she could fool the gods this time, she thought. Her mind twisting into manifold dark tunnels. Maybe they wouldn't see her if she saw herself as another woman. Another body, another history. Maybe the wife of the man who ran the Chinese grocery. The man was stoic, always attired in an off-white cotton shirt that looked as aged as a papyrus scroll, always with a cigarette burning between his lips, seldom inhaling, letting it smoulder until it was just a nub of ash. Out of some backwater village in Shanghai or Guangdong or wherever. She gave Hans the man's body. She imagined them in a dank storeroom, shelves piled with dried goods. Mung beans, perilla seeds, crocus bags of parboiled rice. Cardboard boxes with kidney beans and dried figs and shredded coconut.

Hans struggled to maintain his erection. He got off, eyes closed as he wiggled his flaccid shaft, muttering to himself as if performing a puja for his penis. Shweta wasn't sure what to do. This had never happened before. Hans's body had always been a mechanism of fidelity to all that meant something in his life. His organs commandeering his spirit. He fiddled with his penis until it stiffened. Shifted his weight onto her body, started moving until he went soft again. Like a sponge being drained. She teased a vein on his neck with the tip of her tongue. His nostrils flared like a bull and the mechanism was chugging once more. She tried to get outside of her body again. Disguised from the gods. Aware that her mind right now was a tightly coiled spring – ready to propel her back into the true world.

In the middle of it, she opened her eyes, her gaze landing a ceramic teacup sitting on the stool. Monkeys holding hands going all the way around. The one thing pure and washed in this room. The Missus had brought tea for him, hadn't she? With cream. With sugar, spice and everything nice. Came in a slip in the middle of the night, didn't she? Watched him drink. She could picture the smile. Wrapped all the way around the woman's pretty head. Cold nipples like tiny hard outcroppings against silk.

She couldn't return to the fantasy. Everywhere she turned, the teacup was there. Monkeys all the way around. On the rice bags. On the shelves. Then floating over her like a phantom. The gods had found her. And now they were going to punish her for hiding. For having the gall to think that she could hide. Even in the cracks of the abyss, they could see her. The innermost parts of her.

The walls fell apart, her thighs now two planks of a palisade fence. Between them, a wolfdog's conical penis, crab red, moving like a vigorous hacksaw. Nightmarish pleasure. It kept going until she felt that golden orb swell in her – and immediately, she felt something tug on her. A black mass. An anchor attached to her heart.

Suddenly, she was sinking.

No, no, she pleaded. *Please let me have it. Not now.* Whisper-shouting now.

Everything else fell apart. Her mind sprung her out of the fantasy. Catapulted – her body whiplashed. Every muscle jittered. Jaw locked up. Throat constricted, chafing on itself, pain like teeth was sprouting along the gullet. Stomach and chest, a corkscrew of soggy flesh, shoulders twisting inwards like a wrung dishrag. A palimpsest of pain and punishment.

But Hans hadn't noticed; he wasn't stopping. A guillotine slicing into her now. Locked in place under the blade. An invisible crowd heckling her from below the podium. Mother Lakshmi in the middle, jeering the loudest. Shweta opened her mouth. Wider now. A scream. So loud that the herons fled the roof. So loud that it snatched Hans out of his own world. Where was he? Drinking tea with sugar and cream. Monkeys all the way around. He stopped and she rolled out from under him, drenched with sweat. The two said nothing to each other.

Her voice in short breaths now, calling his name.

'What happen now?' His voice gruff, head turned away from her.

She was taken aback by Hans's tone this time. The inflection of disrespect almost felt like he hawked a ball of spit on her. Since the visit to the police station, he had barely looked her in the eye. She was unaccustomed to his anger and wasn't sure how to assuage it. She thought of Tansi with her prayer beads, nothing in her eyes, her mind sunken into dark water. She felt like that now, helpless. Scorned for her emotion. She rubbed her chest until her heart returned to normal.

'Is not *me*, Hans. Is not me doing it.'

'OK,' he said. 'It is what it is.' As if he didn't want to hear any more. She looked at his crotch and saw that he was already soft.

'I dunno how to make it go away. I dunno how to fix it.' But she did know. If only she had the courage to utter that one word to him. *Hema*. That was all. A magic word. The one word of absolution. She thought back to the clay mound that Hans destroyed. The rice balls tossed into the mud. Rookmin had said a prayer for Hema in hope that it would make her mouth small. But a mouth sewn shut wasn't a remedy for hunger. If she and Hans could talk about her, they could figure out how to dispel the ghost. Feed it in some other way.

'Is just how things is,' said Hans.

'I want to be good.' Her eyes hot now. 'I aint been good in a long time. I want to be good for you, darling.'

He leaned over, kissed her on the cheek, his lips barely touching the skin. 'You aint need to come all this way to see me.' His voice fading.

Shweta put on her dress. Looked at him, still naked. 'You ready to head back?'

'Just want to lie down for a while. Is a long walk. You go ahead. I gon catch up. Was a long night. Next time, just wait for me. Save yourself the hassle.'

Shweta didn't know how to tell him that the real hassle was waiting for him, not making the long walk here. She composed herself, went outside. As she stepped onto the grounds, she saw Mrs Changoor. She was wearing a white dress that flapped in the wind like a crazed swan. Under the shade of an acai palm, her arms in a V meeting at the waist. The grass around her scorched brown from the sun. Shweta waved, but there was no response. Was as if they weren't part of the same world. The same plane of existence. A minute of silence passed before Mrs Changoor signalled to Robinson. Whispered something to him.

He came up to Shweta. 'I gon be heading down to Bell. Could give you a ride back if you want.'

Shweta shook her head. She wanted to walk. Robinson nodded. A dejected look, but he understood. He was the type to sense sadness. What a good man, she thought. She almost changed her mind, but it wasn't right to sit beside another man in her husband's absence, despite his innocence and goodwill. It just wasn't the right thing to do.

17
A Tiny Leaf Above Us

Wednesday morning, already past 4 a.m. *Are they going to kill Dalton tonight?* Marlee wondered. *Are they coming to kill me tonight?* She left the music on, as she had the past few nights. Glenn Miller's 'In the Mood'. She thought it best to stay beside her bedroom window and wise to stay sober this time. On this important night, it was easier to rationalise her decisions, not that she had ever believed any of them to be diabolical. She saw it as putting a trapped animal out of its misery. What was in her and Dalton's future but a series of ritualised assaults?

Dalton Changoor, the man whose trunk was brocaded with bloody scars. Looking like Prometheus, caught stealing fire from the gods. Picked apart. Picked raw, like he'd been put up for the crows. Perhaps adjured from his *mother* – God damn her painted soul. Dalton, a wretched pile of secrets. Maybe generations of secrets. He built a fortress to contain them all, filled it with pretty shades and textures. Marlee among them, as well as the heir he never had. Even with all of this, it was never enough. He didn't have everything he wanted, nor did he want everything he actually had. Always eating yet always famished.

In the end, perhaps what he needed was what every troubled man craves. Rest. Repose. She was giving it to him. Gifting it. It was a gift to herself as well. He would become free of his own plan. And she would too. Ground up by his own schemes. No more suffering or sorrow. Dreamless sleep now.

From the window, Marlee had an obscured view of the grounds and a clearer one of the homestead. Hans was also within eyeshot, shifting his weight on a stool, a slight hunch, getting up every once in a while to inspect noises coming from the dark zones around him. He reminded her of those Hollywood cowboys standing tall in the picture shows. Jawlines sharp as buffalypso horn. Voices lowered into a gritty drawl. Hummingbird hands fanning over gunmetal hammers. Eyes that gleamed with the sternness of judges. Yes, those cowboys were judges. Harbingers of judgement and justice, stamping their feet and holding onto their hats as doom came riding in.

She felt safe with him.

She went downstairs to change the record. Shuffled through the pile of vinyls like it was a deck of cards and ultimately decided on 'We'll Meet AGain'. She put the record on, closed her eyes and let Vera Lynn's voice rinse the air. In the lyrics lay the dusty remainders of her former self, shards of the past that seemed so real yet so unreal, like images captured on an old ambrotype. She as a little girl in her seaside village, using warm soot from lamps to paint moustaches and sideburns on her face. Pretending to be a sailor who cared about nothing but the seven seas. Nobody in this damned county could imagine her in that manner. That little girl was gone. That girl who strolled in the midnight tide, ankle-deep in mud, luckless and simple. Days gone now, but a part of her missed it. Maybe she, too, was like her husband. Cursed just as him. Trying to preserve a world all too willing to collapse.

A pained yell from outside cut through the music.

Marlee dropped the records, grabbed a lamp set on the table and hurried to the door. No light outside but a tubular shoot from the moon descending like a spotlight upon the grass, where something had dragged up a wake of dust. Hans was no longer at his post. All silent except for the wind. Seemed that even the crickets stopped.

Then the wind stopped.

There was something up ahead. Lying in a heap. Swallowed by the dark.

'Hans?' The name came out without thought.

She couldn't be sure unless she went forward. Nothing carried sound now. Silence takes on different forms. There is the silence that lingers and the silence that devours. It is that latter type of silence that only occurs when you know something is listening out for you. That something is out there. That type of silence has weight. Can slow things down. In the dark, everything seemed out of a nightmare. Outside of this shard of moonlight, it felt like there was no real world out there. Only nothingness. Instinctively, she began searching for any sign of life. For an owl, a bat, a mosquito.

It was as if the rest of the world had marched on, and this was just the trail of dust fading into the placid dark. She stepped towards the figure lying in the dark. A burning coldness ballooned in her gut and moved up to her chest. Was like a pane of glass was pressed against her sternum, a slow pressure building against her organs. A vice closing in. She convinced herself that this was a bad dream. That in dreams, things didn't matter. You couldn't be hurt in dreams. You could escape. You didn't have to bargain with them. In bad dreams, anything could terrify. In bad dreams, you have to search for the normal and hold onto it before you sink. But when silence has eaten everything, nothing can be normal.

As she came close enough, she saw that the figure was not Hans. Not a person at all, but a dog. German shepherd. Vishnu. On its side. Black blood down its neck. A long object stuck into its neck like a mountaineer's staff. A spading fork. Rammed straight through the ribs. Still convulsing, the life still trickling out of its nerves. Dense foam at its mouth like clabbered milk.

Something at the edge of the fork, tied to the handle. A note.

But it was too dark out here to read. She crumpled it, tucked it in her slipper. Then a loud crack pierced the air. A gunshot.

The flash of the muzzle like lightning born from the ether.

The bullet ate part of a balata tree in the distance.

She stumbled across the ground in the direction of the shot, part-hobbling, part-scampering like a soldier across trenches. Hans came into view. The gun in his hand. As he fired another shot, the gun leapt out of his grip, like a frantic fish trying to get back into water.

Up ahead, Marlee could see the target. A vanishing shadow, feet moving in strange stuttering strokes in the dark.

She rushed to the gun and aimed. Fired a clean shot at the shadow.

Then a pained grunt shot back. The shadow fell in a tumble but was back up in no time. She ran towards it, catching a glance of its head, draped in black. Eyes exposed, large as discs. A hand clamped over its leg, where the bullet must have grazed.

She fired again.

Missed.

Her hand rattled. She fell backwards onto a stubble of weeds. Everything in slow motion now. Found it hard to catch her breath after that.

Hans came running, stopped to check on her. The shadow was long gone now, merged with the darkness. Above his flustered face, a blast of stars. He helped her up, his expression one of defeat. He began, 'He come outta nowhere. I was after him. But I couldn't see him...'

'It's OK, Hans.' She gestured for him to help her up, and he hustled to do so, as if it were the one thing he could do right that night.

He was still trying to catch his breath. 'That aint no regular prowler. The dog, I never seen nothin like that, what he do to...'

'I saw what he did,' said Marlee, picking a fleck of mud off her dress. 'No creature deserves that.'

'I tell you, I aint never seen nothin like it. He take that damn fork and...'

'Next time, Hans, dear. We'll get them next time.'

'We have to call the police.'

A pause. 'I'll head down to Bell first thing in the morning. Nothing they can do right now.' She glanced over to the dead dog. 'We couldn't help what happened. You did well, Hans. I don't want you feeling bad. You're OK. And I'm OK. That's what matters for now.'

He was still shaken.

She rubbed his back. 'You were brave, Hans, darling. Like how I imagine the Lone Ranger. Guns blazing! Who knows what could've happened had you not taken chase.'

He wiped some sweat from his brow, gave her a small smile. 'Calamity Marlee,' he muttered in a mock-wistful manner, and she laughed. They took the dead dog to a small glade near the thicket of balata trees. Hans fetched the shovel and started digging. Marlee excused herself for a few minutes. She returned to the house, took off her slippers and read the note:

FRIDAY. SAME PLACE AND TIME.
SHOW UP WITH $4000
OR WE R COMMING FOR U NEXT

Another extension. And a thousand dollars more. *Goddammit* – just kill the man and get it over with! Fillet him. Feed him to the poor. She didn't care. But please God, let it be final!

She took a deep breath, frustrated and perplexed, before a thought hit her. And the thought grew into an epiphany. A thousand dollars more for what? What exactly would she be paying for? Dalton's life? His return? Were these really ransom notes or blackmail letters? It was possible that these notes had nothing to do with Dalton. In fact, these notes had nothing whatsoever. Only the knowledge that she was alone and the belief that she could be intimidated. It wasn't going to stop. This was the doing of an opportunist. No different from a snake oil salesman. With this thought came another:

If this was true and they didn't have Dalton – then where in the world was he?

She put the note in the elephant teapot along with the other two.

The stars were gone by the time Hans was finished with the hole. Marlee returned to find him stuffing the corpse into a crocus bag and then burying it. He'd cast his bloodstained shirt aside, his skin almost pear-coloured under the dimming moonlight. He looked good. She'd never had anyone besides Dalton, despite having many come onto her. Most of them clownish with cascades of flesh rolls, some even cretinous, but there were the few who could've made the day a little brighter. She denied them out of fear that Dalton would discover the affairs and she would lose this life of comfort.

She was aware of the rumours from the village – of her supposedly sybarite past. She didn't know how it started or who had started it. It was funny to people – like when the odd Hollywood starlet is discovered to have made stag films. She knew her own truth. Pleasure to her was theoretical.

It didn't have to be that way any more. She could have it all. Tonight.

It was just a thought. Lustful aspiration. But imagining it made her heart race.

Hans put his palms together, offering a prayer before shovelling the dirt back in. Marlee asked him to come inside, take a rest. He was reluctant, but she pressed him. She took him to the kitchen, sat him at the table. Pestles still in their mortars, lids on each pot, the large, charred cast iron tava still balancing against the cooking gas cylinder. On a slab of heartwood was a bowl of fruit. Mangoes, pommeracs, sucrier bananas, carambolas. Earthen crocks with more fruits.

Marlee took a mango, peeled it with her fingers and bit into the flesh. The juice dripped onto the neckline of her nightgown. Together they sat and ate the entire bowl of fruit, leaving behind a heap of banana skins, pommerac cores and mango seeds, sucked dry and velvety. When they were done, she went to the cupboard and retrieved a bottle of jamun wine. She poured two glasses and they drank. Poured another two and they drank again. She traced her finger along the rim of the glass, giving him a smile.

She urged him to take a shower upstairs. He denied her twice but again, she was persistent. Said that he smelled of sweat and dog's blood and led him upstairs by the wrist. Pointed him to the guest bedroom and told him that she'd lay a change of clothes on the bed. Dalton's old clothes should fit him, she said, though not perfectly. He didn't know how to feel about wearing her husband's clothes, but it would only be for a night, he reasoned.

She started the water for him. He stood under it until his skin pruned. Imagined himself in a light June rain. He washed his face and burned his eyes with the soap, raw and salmon-pink. As he turned the water off, a bout of dizziness rattled him. He could smell smoke on the towel. Dried himself and went to the guest bedroom. In the corner, a large rattan basket, overflowing with neglected bedsheets. A draught blew through the room, even though the door and window were closed. The room was dim, the organdy curtains filtering the waning moonlight like whey. He had never been in a room like this before. Almost felt guilty about it.

Suddenly, something shot out from under the bed.

Hans dropped his towel and vaulted into the closet, lodging himself into a cottony husk of clothes. The nubs of his elbows scraped a lane of termite-chewed sawdust from the wood. Through the slats he could see whatever it was zipping off the walls. There was more than one of them. Rebounding, hopping like ping-pong balls. Only when the creatures bounced into the moonbeam did he realise that they were froghoppers. Three of them. He noticed a crack in the wall about an arm's length from the window. The creatures must have crept in from there. The crack was quite significant. It was like the house had a mistreated gash.

Fluttering around him were nightgowns and broom skirts. He pushed his hand into them and felt a warm wave of comfort through his spine. He leaned into the clothes and took a large whiff, inhaling the faint scent of age and frangipanis and sawdust and dried perfume. Naked, he let himself fall forward into them, clasping the sleeves as if they were ropes or rappels keeping him from some fatal fall.

As he huddled against the dresses, a deep sense of shame overwhelmed him. And at the same time a sense of comfort like he had never known. He likened it to seeing the sunset come over the ocean for the first time. That same profound emotion contained in the downy texture of these fabrics in this dark dusty closet. An errant thought of how different life could be if he could stay. For five minutes, he stayed draped between the clothes, swaddled in their warmth. As if the closet itself was some kind of cocoon. Him in the midst of metamorphosis.

He emerged refreshed. Put on the clothes lain for him on the bed. They fitted strangely well. As he was done, there was a knock on the door. When he opened it, Marlee entered. She lay at a right angle on the bed, her legs dangling off the side. Beckoned for him to join. A hesitant breath. Was only then he noticed the crucifix in the room. A little inebriated, he timidly acquiesced, keeping at arm's length from her. He began in a mumble, 'So what we doin—'

She put her finger to her lips, gently shushed him. And for a while, they lay in silence. Eerily comfortable silence.

She began to reminisce, 'Before I came here, I spent most of my younger years living with many other people in this big building. Not too far from how I imagine your living conditions. We had a communal eating place, space for cooking, toilets that we had to share. It was loud and unsanitary. Most people didn't realise how bad it really was. I think people are good at making the best of a bad thing. We don't make the rain. But if there's shelter, even if it's under a tiny leaf, we'll take it. And we're so grateful for that tiny leaf above us, we don't see the bigger trees just over the hill.'

Hans took a moment to absorb her words. Then asked, 'Where you live before?'

'Where the American naval base is now,' she said. 'I barely think about it now. And I know I don't want to ever go back to living like that.'

A long silence. Hans kept his eye on the wooden Jesus, its twisted grimace bearing down at him. 'Is hard to go back to coconut fibre after lying on a bed like this.'

She put her palms to her chest. It felt good to be talking – to be really talking to somebody. 'You're the only person who knows this about me,' she said. 'Everybody else makes up their own stories.'

He shook his head. 'I aint gon tell anyone.'

She grinned and made her fingers into a gun. 'Tell and Calamity Marlee's coming for you.' At the same time, the rains came down. Instinctively, his eyes flitted about the room, searching for leaks. She reached a hand out to him. Her finger brushed his. She expected him to pull his hand away – but he let her touch him. They intertwined their little fingers.

She bit her lower lip, nervous. 'You ever thought about just throwing caution to the wind, Hans? Doing what you want in this life and not worrying what people say.'

'When I was younger,' he said. 'Before gettin married.'

'What's something that you want? Something that nobody knows.'

'Want? I dunno.' He spent a few seconds on it but came up with nothing.

'It could be anything, dear. Anything in the world.'

'To be up on an airplane,' he said, an embarrassed tone. 'See how the world look from above.'

She scooted closer to him. 'I've always wanted a horse. Not a racehorse. A nice, white mare that I could ride around the land. Dalton hates horses. Says that they drop loads everywhere. What else do you want, Hans? Don't think about it. Just say it.'

Lightning shot across the window.

'A car. Cadillac. And I gon drive it hours and hours.'

'Where would you go?'

'Anywhere. Go anywhere, be anywhere. The four points of the island.'

She smiled. Another lightning flash. 'Sounds nice. And then a boat. Sail the seven seas. I want to do that too. What else do you want—'

'Baptised! I want to be baptised! Start fresh!'

'*Baptised?*' She let out a laugh so loud that she doubled over. 'I can baptise you right now!' He laughed when he saw her laughing. She put her hands on his neck and pulled him close. Noses brushing.

They weren't sure who kissed who first. Did it matter? Rolled into each other's arms, still lip-locked. Stopped for a moment. His eyes meeting hers. Hers meeting his.

Each took a deep breath as if ready to submerge. Then kissed again, more deliberately this time. Her tongue long and soft. Every pore of his body raised. Their clothes flew to the floor. Bodies arranged across pillows. The chenille bedspread soft and welcoming under him. Like feathers lightly brushing against his skin. Their hands slid over each other in awkward impatience.

Bumping limbs and chins. Slowly, she dissolved into him, and they entwined each other. He flipped her over, licked the dimples in her hips. The arch of her back like a bridge between his body and the bedpost. She was warm, wet, flinching.

Felt like she came before he even got going.

When he did get going, she couldn't stop. He took control, manoeuvred her. She was in a constant blood rush, like it was her first time. Kicking her curled toes against the mattress. The rhythm punctuated by brief jolts of pain. Bodies like crashing waves. They begged each other for more. And outside, though it was still pouring, the sun was coming up over the range.

18

A Package Is Coming on Wednesday

'You aint good to pa,' Krishna sullenly told his mother. 'That why he aint want to be here.' The words sounded like they'd been on the tip of his tongue since he woke up. It'd been two hours after dawn, and Hans hadn't returned home.

Shweta was so taken aback by the boy's words that defence didn't come to mind. Instead, she wondered if he was right. Still, the boy had never before said anything like that to her and she couldn't help but feel a blunt pain in her stomach replaying it. She thought about asking why he would say such a thing – but was afraid to hear the response. First his father, now him. She felt like the world had turned against her.

They were sitting on the barrack floor, facing each other. Her muteness angered him further. 'You ugly,' he muttered. For a moment, she had to remind herself that this boy, this bundle of flesh and spirit garlanded with gloom, emerged from her.

'Krishna, why you say that?'

As soon as she finished the question, he flung something at her. It missed and hit the wall in a dusty poof. She turned around – it was a packet of Smarties Candy Rockets. This was why he was so upset? Over a discarded roll of pill-shaped confectioneries? Bought at a measly fraction of the price as that useless jumbo tube of silicone caulk? Hans must have known it was foolish to purchase the caulk, to carelessly waste all of that money; it was offensive to her. The thought of eating it made her sick. So, she threw it away. But that was in the past – at least, she thought it was.

'You want me to eat it?' she asked, sitting ramrod now. The ire that was in the post, finally arrived. 'Eat it and get sick and dead? That's what you want?'

Krishna pressed his palms hard against the ground. 'Pa aint want to come home because you never happy with anything—'

She pointed a stern finger at him. 'That's a lie. Krishna, shut your mouth.'

'*You* should learn to shut your mouth.'

'Boy, don't talk bout things you don't understand.' Her eyes welled up.

'I understand that you is a bitch—'

'*You aint innocent! You shitty to him too!*' she snapped at him. She took a breath, felt immediate regret for her words. Felt it even more when Krishna got up and left. Slammed the door so hard she thought it would fall off. Jolted the tears out of her. 'Krishna, I sorry! Come back!'

But the boy kept walking.

★

When Robinson had arrived that morning, he found it strange to not see Vishnu. It was quiet. Like how he imagined the world after its end. After all the false idols realised that there was no one left to worship them.

Mrs Changoor emerged from the house, fully made up. Her red shiftdress in stark contrast to the dimness of the morning. Not even royal poincianas could be so red. She fixed her earrings. Seemed distracted. Robinson figured she hadn't noticed him. She picked a twig from the ixoras and picked her teeth with it – something he had never seen her and people like her do. That was a lower-class habit. She rolled her Raleigh bicycle towards the gate.

When she finally did notice Robinson, she beamed a bright smile.

'Robinson, I need to settle some business,' she said.

'I have to tell you somethin, Mrs Changoor.'

She smiled even wider. 'Today is a busy day. I'm in a hurry.' She handed him her pocketbook as she bent down to adjust her shoes. 'Write this down for me, Robinson.'

He began to write as she dictated: *Call post office. A package is coming on Wednesday*.

Despite being in a hurry, she stared at it for a long time, studying the words, tracing her fingers over the letters. 'Where's Mr Baig?' she asked, still eyeing the note. 'He's very late.'

'That's what I have to tell you. He gone out of commission. Take a bad tumble this mornin, he say. Wife say he home in bed.'

'A tumble,' she muttered, scratching her chin.

'You need me to take you into Bell, Mrs Changoor?'

'Sweet of you to offer, but no – I need the time for myself. I need to move my legs. I've been cooped up in this house for long enough.'

Robinson nodded. 'You know, Mrs Changoor, usually that dog come runnin up to see me first thing. You see him this morn?'

'The dog. Well, ask Hans about the dog,' was all she said before riding off on her bicycle.

Hans was nowhere to be seen. Not in the homestead. Not in the field. Not down by the cherry trees. As Robinson made his way to the back, a voice called from the gate. It was Shweta. Her hair hung lank, neck drenched with sweat. She looked downtrodden, defeated by life. Couldn't even maintain eye contact. Robinson let her in, eyeing the pot in her hand. 'What's for breakfast today?' he asked with a smile.

She didn't reciprocate. 'I need to talk to my husband.' Her voice weary.

Just as he was about to tell her that he hadn't seen him, Hans made his first appearance of the day. Shweta's eyes widened when he came strolling out of the house and onto the porch. Like a sentry defending his fort. Like he'd always belonged there. At first, she didn't believe it to be him. He looked like something from an alternate life. A vision conjured by a prankish djinn. She'd never seen him in clothes like this, sahib clothes – smart rayon stripes, thinly cut, collar and cuffs – of such rustic sartorial elegance aside from his big-battered shoes, which were draped by the lower hem of the trousers that were too long for him. He was dwarfed by the clothes, nothing quite fitting how it should. His shirt loose and liberated over his body like a priest's chasuble. His sweaty collar like the hot open mouth of a dog. Hair in place like a fussy child primped for church.

Took Hans a slow minute to descend from the porch and approach her. Hesitant like a child in for a good scolding. Looked in all directions except directly at her. At first, was almost like he was pretending he hadn't seen her.

Before they could stand before each other, a morning breeze blew his fragrance in her direction. He'd been lustred with sweetness. The blunt smell of talcum. His hair in ruffles. Everything fixed into place. Tamed. When they were finally face to face, she had no comment. All words evaporated. There was something otherworldly about him.

Neither of them spoke for a long time. The scorpion came to her mind. Emerging from the bale of straw to scuttle before her, challenging her to make the first move. Was he waiting for her to make a move, or was she for him? She felt like she was always able to tell Hans everything she was thinking, no matter the weight of the words; they were like grains of sand blowing away from her hands.

She remembered her son's tirade earlier in the morning. She didn't want to be angry. To be accusatory. She just wanted him to come home.

'Where you get them clothes?' Shweta finally asked, forcing a chuckle.

Hans replied, 'Is only for today. Mine get dirty.'

Shweta took a long look in his eyes, her tone falling. 'When you coming home?'

'Have some patience,' he said. 'You have to understand that after waking through the night, is not an easy walk back. I's just need to rest a little.'

She turned to the homestead. Felt anger rising up her throat, swallowed it back. In a gentle voice. 'I cook sardines. Come and eat with me.'

Shook his head. 'Aint hungry right now.'

'I am. Let's sit down so I could eat.' She raised her skirt up a little, as if to give a hint.

He let out a heavy sigh. 'Shweta...'

Her face dropped. 'What happen?'

'That just gon lead to trouble.'

She cocked her head. 'What trouble?'

'One thing lead to another.'

'What you think I want to do?' She felt embarrassed now. 'I just want to eat.'

'No, you gonna start up...' He stopped himself. 'It aint the place, is all.'

She stepped back. Then let out a shriek. Almost fell back on her hind but caught her balance before she did. Found a tree to lean against and lifted her foot up. Robinson looking on from the distance. Hans asked, 'What the hell happen?'

With a wince. 'Something gone up my foot.'

'You step on somethin?' Barely looking at her.

Robinson came running. Grabbed the wooden stool by the homestead and brought it for her. 'Lemme see there, ma'am,' he said as she sat. Got on one knee and gestured for her to put her foot up.

Shweta usually wouldn't want another man touching her foot, but the pain was so sharp that such a thing dared not cross her mind at that moment. Hans stood behind Robinson. 'I don't see nothin,' he said.

'There it is,' Robinson said, putting his face closer, one eye shut. 'That black mark.'

'Where?' asked Hans.

'Whatever it is, it gone deep in,' said Shweta with a groan.

'If only we had a sewing pin,' Robinson mumbled. His face so close now that his nose almost touched her heel. He asked, 'You could walk?'

He put her foot down and motioned for her to stand. As she did, the pain geysered up her spine, causing her to return to the stool. Hans said again, 'I don't see nothin.'

'Maybe you should take Shweta back, Robinson,' said Hans.

There was no other choice. She couldn't walk. She gave Robinson a nod. He helped her into the passenger seat and started the engine. 'Hans, you aint comin?' she asked.

'Can't leave the premises alone like this while the Missus is out. Don't worry. I gon come as soon as the Missus return.'

As Robinson's pickup chugged down the hill, he told her about his youngest daughter. The girl had gotten a splinter in her foot when she was playing barefoot in the street. His wife cut a thin slice of potato and pasted it under the little girl's foot. Let it sit for a while before pulling it out. If that doesn't work, he said, try melting a few drops of candlewax on the spot. Let it harden and then pull it off. If all else fails, slip a mending needle slantways and try prodding at it. Imagine like picking a lock, he said.

He paused for a moment, thinking of other ways. The only other thing he had to say about it was that sometimes it went away on its own. Maybe it just comes out when you're asleep, he said. Or maybe God comes down and pulls it out for you.

*

Krishna continued up the winding ribbon of road. Part of him wanted to return to the barrack, apologise to his mother. Her words echoed, and she was right. He hadn't been good to his father either. And realised it was because he didn't want to become the compliant boy his father wanted him to be. He couldn't imagine being bossed around by store clerks and convincing himself that's just the way things are. Bowing down before people who would spit on him or call the police on him for existing. There was nothing logical or practical about going through life acting as someone's footstool. No – he would prefer to keep his black eye. He would prefer to be suspended from school. A corbeau couldn't pretend to be a peacock.

He crossed the footpath that Lata had taken to get to the river, to the spot where she washed the clothes. Curiously, he followed it. He didn't know what to expect; he had no real destination in mind. He wished Tarak was with him. Krishna had the notion that his cousin had been avoiding him since their last visit to the Changoor house. Krishna didn't blame him. It wasn't that the boy was cowardly. Tarak had already had his share of troubles in his life. He was probably off into the fields with White Lady, as if he had no need for humanity. He was probably nibbling on the end of a canestalk right now while the dog pounced on froghoppers. Nobody to mind their business.

He thought perhaps that he'd find Lata at the end of the path. He still felt ashamed of how he'd broken down in front of her at the refuse barrel. How could she see anything in him now? A boy shouldn't cry in front of a girl. The hairs on his forearm were coming out. He was too old to be acting like that. Girls didn't want a boy who looked hangdog all the time and sobbed for no reason. Then again, he didn't understand what they wanted. He thought of telling her about the things those village boys said of her but just thinking of the words made him hurt. She would call him a liar; he could foresee it. A nip of breeze rustled some wild flowers beside him. He picked a yellow one that he didn't know the name of. If he found her, he would give it to her.

When he came to the spot, he saw her. She was with someone, both figures drably shaded by a passing cloud. It was Dylan. They stooped together, smiles bright and genuine. The rattan basket of wash at his side. He helped her wring the clothes dry. Krishna hid behind some bushes, watching them. At one point, she planted an innocent kiss along the sinewy length of his jawline. Krishna squatted, stultified, imagining how he looked hiding out with the bugs in the brush. Holding some scentless wild flower as the rivers of emotion seemed to run in reverse for him.

He pictured her years ago against the peephole into her parents' room. Trying to grow up entirely too fast. Krishna felt like that now. He couldn't tear himself away. Crushed the flower in his fist as she kissed the boy on the mouth. It was brief but Krishna was convinced it was the prophecy of nightmare. Still – it didn't have to be his nightmare. There was nothing he could say to Lata now. She was a corbeau herself, convinced that she'd become a hummingbird. And soon enough, she'd find out for herself that those village boys were hawks.

He spat on the ground and made his way back.

*

As Marlee rode into Bell, a persistent wind blew a spiral of foliage across the road. A quintet of kiskadees kept eyes on her from a hog plum tree. An old woman in a shawl eating a pawpaw waited until she rode by to continue chewing. When she rode past the church, she quickly made the sign of the cross. A boy swept the front of the Western Union building with a cocoyea broom. Sleepy dogs cleared the path. A gaggle of children rolled their necks in tandem with her bicycle's spokes. Wire fences colonised by passionfruit vines. The morning was still cool. An eerie glow upon the clouds, as if the sunlight was being held captive behind them.

Marlee made sure to put on a smile for everyone looking her way. Men took off their hats for her. Even the lechers. A nervousness built up inside her, but she kept her poise. She was always wary of embarrassing herself in front of these people. Tripping on a chuckhole and getting mud on her shoes. A mangy stray dog pawing the back of her dress. Rumours or not, there was still a part of her that had gotten used to being apotheosised. You couldn't buy that in any store.

The jamun wine and lovemaking and dog-stabbing from the night before weighed heavy on her head. It was time the police knew, she figured. It would look suspicious at this point – now that blood had been shed. Albeit dog blood. She ruled out Robinson. Not that she'd suspected him in the first place. She looked at his note in the pocketbook one more time to make sure. Figured she needed to rule out one other person before going to the police.

She made her way to Baig's house. Baig, who hadn't shown up today. Baig, who had taken a tumble this morning. He lived on one of the lonelier streets, where the road was only halfway paved. Two old men sat on the corner, slapping down dominoes on a clunky round table. When they noticed her, they grinned, their teeth marked with black pits like those very dominoes. They pointed her to Baig's house. She nodded, thanked them.

Baig's house was the last on the street.

Beyond was a row of banana trees, leaves bobbing in the breeze. No gate. No plants in the front yard, only empty flowerpots and empty birdcages hanging in the front. A pyramid of chipped cinderblocks at the side of the house. It was to Marlee's knowledge that Baig had no children. His wife was a modest woman who helped regularly at the mandir when she had time.

Marlee went up to the front door, knocked twice.

Baig's wife answered, an expression of annoyance quickly shifting to surprise. Pleasant surprise. She firmed her stance and dusted off her dress, giving it a quick smoothing. Without saying anything, she stepped aside and welcomed Marlee in. The wife's hair was in a long braid down to her mid-back, a green dupatta pulled over her brow. Her right nostril pierced with a shining stud. It was a simple two-room house. The bedroom to the back and everything else to the front. The walls smeared white with kaolinite clay. A small shrine in the corner sat in devotion to Ganesha. A tiny brass idol of the elephant-headed deity rested between two iron saucers of hibiscus petals and sliced bananas. A garland of ixoras adorned its neck.

'I've come to check on your husband,' Marlee said. 'To see if he's all right.'

'Very nice of you, Mrs Changoor, very nice,' said the wife, smiling. 'That old fool is in the back, resting.' She offered to make tea, which Marlee politely refused. The wife then excused herself to check on the stove. Smelled like dal puri roti and fried bora.

'He's awake?'

'He aint leave that bed whole mornin.'

'How did he injure himself?'

'He say he was up early checking out God knows what on the roof. Then fall right off. I was still sleepin when it happen. He feel he still young, is all I have to say.'

At this moment, Marlee observed a piece of paper thumb-tacked to the food cupboard.

TUESDAY – Potatos
WENSDAY – Greens
SATERDAY – Moko, tomato, red onion, christofeen
SUNDAY – Carots, bora, colliflower, zaboka

Marlee's eyes widened. *That fucker!*

The wife noticed Marlee staring at it. 'The Mister say that too much does waste in this house,' she said. 'He tell me I cook things outta order and leave things to spoil. Friday will reach and I aint cook the bora he buy since last Sunday. So, he start writin down the days he buy vegetables. Since he start doin that, no food wastin in this house no more.' She looked pleased to say that.

'He likes to make notes,' Marlee said, trying hard to keep her voice calm.

The wife scoffed. 'All the time.'

*

Krishna hoped that seeing the twins would take his mind off everything. Lata, his parents, what he'd seen at the Changoor house. Was Marlee Changoor some sort of sorceress? Had she put his father under some spell? He wished his father had never taken that godforsaken job. He made his way along the train tracks that ran upriver.

The mud surrounding the banks pale and clammy as the flesh of a coconut. Midway through the stream, a sharp spiral of brush. Almost like a crown of thorns. Hostile, coarse. Nearby, a ruin of broken barrels, some of them bobbing with mosquito eggs. Even farther up, a palisade of bamboo sticks prodded into holes that were once filled with cow's milk. Bundled and clumsy like stag antlers. The pennants, black and red, draped limp. Where the poles struck the earth, the soil was gloopy and orange.

Rustam and Rudra spent much of their time at an abandoned shed adjacent to this river. It was empty when they found it, but they made it theirs. It was a five-minute walk off the road, secluded and obscured by bush. Nobody bothered them. In the afternoons, the boys caught catfish and at dusk roasted iguana at a fireside. Played cards. Krishna earmarked magazine articles that they liked, especially ones with pictures of pretty white women. Whenever they spoke, Rustam always spoke on behalf of them both.

Rustam had once confessed that Rudra could speak but chose not to, dedicating himself to keeping his voice limited to his mind. Speak, and your other senses begin to fail you. A whole year Rudra hadn't uttered a word, said Rustam. Believed that his brother spoke to him through his thoughts. A sort of thaumaturgy that would have never occurred without such mystical dedication. Rustam believed that his brother could do the same to those who opposed him. He could summon thunder into their heads. Or flash floods. Or solar haloes. Krishna believed that.

There are fish in the ocean that must live in the darkness, Rustam had told the cousins one evening. They remain there their whole lives. Their bodies dutiful to the darkness. As soon as the light touches them, their insides expand until they push out of their mouths. The body birthing itself. Those who dwell in the abyss must stay there. Must live, must thrive there.

Stuffed into a corner beside a torn bedsheet was Rudra's collection of animal tissues and organs. Grackle beaks, bat wing ligaments, dried tilapia gills, rabbit ears, a shoebox of severed scorpion tails. And a crocus bag full of animal bones, parts of them still creamy white.

When Krishna came to the river, he heard the sound of hammering. When he cleared the bush, he saw them. Both twins with cigarettes in their mouths. Rustam was building something out of wood and wire. Rudra sat beside on a tree stump, whittling a piece of soap. His right hand still bandaged. His collection of little soap creatures sat on a shelf inside the shack. Krishna always figured they were animals of Rudra's own invention because they didn't look like any he ever saw.

Rustam pointed at Krishna's black eye. 'You look tougher with that.'

'Not tougher than that,' Krishna pointed to Rudra's injured hand. 'How you get that? Playin with yourself?'

Rustam burst out laughing. Rudra gave them both the middle finger.

'Where Tarak?' Rustam asked, still laughing.

Krishna shrugged.

'Hope he aint still in jail.' Went back to hammering.

'What you buildin there?'

'You ever hear bout a *demon box*?' Then he explained, taking a puff, 'Is a type of box you put out in the forest to catch a demon. Like a *bacoo.* And you feed it cherries and cow milk, and it would tell you the future. Like when the rain goin to fall. Or who is the next person to dead.'

Krishna laughed. 'Stop talkin shit.'

'Yeah, I lie. Is a rabbit cage I buildin.' He wiped some sweat from his brow. 'Speakin of *cage*, how come you and Tarak manage to get outta that jail?'

'Something bout Mrs Changoor, who my pa work for. She make a call or somethin.'

The twins looked at each other. 'So, she talk to the police then?'

'I suppose.'

'What she say in the call?'

'How I suppose to know? Whatever rich people say.'

A pause. 'Your pa and Mrs Changoor have business?'

Krishna thought of her and his father firing rounds at the painting. It was too bizarre to mention, so all he said was, 'He watchmannin the place for a couple weeks or so.'

'A couple weeks.' Rustam stroked his chin. 'Your pa say why?'

'Bandits or somethin.' Krishna didn't want to talk about it.

'Them police aint shit if your pa gotta be out there bandit-huntin.' Rustam came up to Krishna, pat his shoulder. 'Shame she bail you out. We was gonna break you out, you know. Put some Glauber salts in the guard's coffee and steal the keys while he shittin himself. I say it again, them police aint shit. Anybody touch you and Tarak next time, we gettin' them good.'

Krishna chuckled. 'Yeah, yeah.'

'You want a smoke? Lemme get you a smoke.'

Krishna nodded.

'Rudra, take care of the boy.' A pause. 'Krishna, I just remember. I have somethin for you. Lemme get it.' He went inside the shack.

'All good with you?' Krishna asked Rudra as he produced a crumpled pack of du Mauriers. In it, an uneven row of half-smoked cigarettes that they'd swept off the cricket pavilion, cherries snipped, tobacco rerolled. Rudra struck a match, lit the cigarette for the boy. Then gave a thumbs up with his bandaged hand, went back to whittling.

Rustam emerged. 'Hope you aint get this one yet.' Slapped a magazine into Krishna's hand. The July issue of *Popular Mechanics*.

Krishna's jaw dropped. 'How you get this?'

'You care?'

He scoffed. No, he didn't. And as Rustam worked on his rabbit cage and Rudra worked at whittling, Krishna sat near the water where there was an ideal blend of light and shade. Nobody to tell him anything. Legs against his belly, blowing soft wisps of smoke, quietly perusing an article about microscopes. Finding a strange peace in the weevils and larvae photographed as wide as his fingers.

★

Marlee heard the voice from behind the bedroom door, 'Who that you talkin to there, woman?' It was Baig.

She thought twice about entering but quickly realised she had nothing to lose.

She knocked and opened the door. Before Baig could determine who it was, he muttered, 'Who that outside there?' When he glanced up and saw Marlee, his body sprang ramrod. She couldn't place his look. Perhaps like a little boy who had been caught in the middle of pleasuring himself. Caught not by his mother but by his bully. Two parts fear, one part shame.

Marlee closed the door behind her. 'Robinson told me about your little misadventure.'

A pause. 'Some bad luck. Couldn't make it up today.'

'Did you break anything?'

'Just a sprain. As I say, bad luck, not the end of the world,' he said quickly before giving a chuckle. 'Should be back to normal in a few days. You aint need to come all the way down...'

'I didn't,' she said, approaching him. 'But I was concerned.'

'No need to be concerned at all.'

'I don't need to be concerned?'

'No. You already...'

'Have so much on my mind. I know,' she finished his sentence with a grin.

She sat at the bedside. Lowered her voice. 'I think we all run into a bit of bad luck sometimes. That's how life is. I know that early in my life, I had my share of it. But things get better. I believe that. Don't you?'

With hesitation, 'I think things come together.'

'I see you have a shrine of Ganesha out there. Ganesha is the god of writers, you know.'

'Oh? I aint know that.'

'He is. And even Ganesha had some bad luck, right? Remind me again why he has an elephant's head.'

Baig paused as if to gather the story in his head. 'Shiva cut his head off as a lil boy. Parvati get mad at Shiva. So Shiva give Ganesha the head of the first animal he see.'

'Which was an elephant?'

'Yeah.'

'So it worked out then.'

'Yeah.'

'For Ganesha. Not so much the elephant.'

A lengthy pause between them as she looked at Baig's room. At the lone window missing a pane, at the half-closed dresser with a pair of trousers spilling out. Marlee told him, 'There are a lot of rumours that about me. They float around. I'm sure you've heard many of them. Maybe spread a few of them. Or maybe even started?' She looked at him. 'None of them are true, you know. I heard rumours that you're a low-down, pathetic, dishonest man. Are those true?'

With a nervous twang, 'I gon be back out to work in a few days. No worries.'

She gave him a long look, then shook her head. 'No, you won't.' Kept her eyes on him.

In a hesitant voice, 'What you mean?'

She got up from the bedside, smoothed the spot she had rested on. 'How do you spell *Wednesday*, Mr Baig?'

All he could do then was bite his upper lip. He knew he'd been caught.

She upturned her chin to him. 'You lost your head. And you are fucking with the wrong elephant.'

He looked surprised by her supposed clemency. 'Yes, ma'am.'

'I am curious, though. Why did you do it?'

'Just wanted money, ma'am.'

'And you thought I was stupid enough to give it to you?'

Hung his head. 'Yes, ma'am.'

'What do you need money for?'

Hung his head. 'To get started on a better life, ma'am. The bank—'

She cut him off, 'Do you still think I'm stupid, Mr Baig?'

A quick shake of the head. 'No, ma'am.'

'You come on my property again, you say a word about me and I find out – I will kill you. Is that understood?'

He swallowed hard. 'Yes, ma'am.'

'Enjoy your day, Mr Baig.'

A little while after, Marlee stood before the Bell Village Police Station. She knew the shot now. Whatever really happened to Dalton – he was most likely dead by now. Nobody had to know the letters were fake. Nobody had to know there was never a kidnapping. And nobody had to know that she ignored the ransom. She'd walk up to the front desk, straighten herself, eyes hot, take a deep breath, take the three letters out of the satchel. One by one, slam them onto the desk. Crying as any concerned wife should.

My husband has been kidnapped, maybe murdered.

Yes, I delivered the money. Yes, they kept asking for more. Yes, I was scared to talk. Yes, I should have said something earlier. Yes, I know it might be too late.

III

A Father's Sins

The man was lost for a long time. He was the tenth child of eleven. There was nothing special about him, nothing that made him stand out, nor that drew the attention of others. Animals never paid him any mind. People never remembered his name. His parents forgot to feed him. He never celebrated a birthday, never received any presents. When he bled, nobody saw. When he bawled, nobody heard. When he tried to declare his love for a girl, she didn't know who he was. Nobody tended to him when he was sick. Nobody knew when he was fed up. And nobody cared when he left.

He moved to the capital's port and found a job there. He never considered himself a stevedore, longshoreman, nothing like that. He hadn't given consideration to a title of any kind. He hadn't been scheduled to be aboard that fated day, but a coworker had taken ill. That day, the ship had been attacked by pirates in the Gulf of Paria. Hungry men who smelled of salt. They took everything that had been on board: flue-cured tobacco from Amarelinho, casks of Pampero Blanco, Winchester shotguns, boxes of AA shells. Even the engine was gone by the end of the day. Everything disassembled and splayed. All for resale. They tied up the crew, and when the skipper cursed, they cut his Achilles' heel and threw him overboard. They'd brought the disembodied leg of some large animal with them, tossed it in right after, hitting the skipper on the head. It wasn't long until the reef sharks came. They pulled the skipper under. All his dreams, under. Everything he would ever be, under. Every memory, the first woman he made love to, the first glimpse of his daughter, the schoolyard brawls he won, under.

After the skipper went over, the lost man helped the pirates throw the rest of his mates overboard. As calmly as if they were jetsam and derelict. Men he had worked with for months. Men with wives and children. Didn't matter any more. He tossed in the animal parts after them and watched them be pulled under. It was a decision he had made in only seconds. Any later and he would've been pulled under with them. He chose well – but the important thing, he realised, was that he chose his fate before somebody else could. And what was lost had finally been found. Through this act, he had convinced the pirates to take him along.

They prowled near the southwestern coast, always on the lookout for cargo ships, especially the ones that drifted right into the Serpent's Mouth. People paid passage to be taken from Cedros to the Delta Amacuro, but most ended up with the sharks. When they came across a Venezuelan cargo ship, they launched themselves aboard and put pistols to the crew's heads and told them to jump into the sea. And so they did. They took the cargo, took the fish, took the contraband. They smuggled the smugglers. Sometimes they even took the women too.

The man kept one for himself for his birthday, gave her a name and insisted she respond to it from then on. He forbade her from speaking, even to the two sons she bore for him. One eleven minutes older than the other. The man named them Rudra and Rustam. He made sure her maternal instinct remained intact. After plunging into such ugliness, she thought she'd lost the ability to remain compassionate. She surprised herself when she found room for it still. She regularly bathed and fed them, and though she and her sons had never spoken, she always cared for them with a gentleness that reminded her that she was human.

It wasn't long until the man was put in charge of the raids. He was warned about stealing from certain ships carrying wood. In those wooden planks were the vices of the world, he was told.

The pirates warned him, *Those are owned by an untouchable man by the name of Changoor. He aint dangerous but he know people who is. And he might send them people to meet you one day.* The man knew who Changoor was, knew where he lived, and once he could track his enemy's movements, he believed there was no reason to be afraid. And so the man taunted fate and knew that he was halfway relying on luck. One day, that luck would be spent.

When the day finally came, he would kill his family before his enemies could. He would do that before fleeing the country and starting over. He told himself that, no matter what, this was what he would do. This was the road, and he was going to follow it to the end. That plan went awry when his wife tried to run away. She had dreamt of herself back in Carúpano, a land bathed in golden twilight, dancers in the street, pillars of grey wood-smoke in the distance. The smell of arepas over a budare so strong that she could taste them. A long table lain with twine-bound hallacas, pastelitos and chicharron. Women singing and, her in the middle, trying her best to release her voice. But nothing would come out. A phantom in the distance called for her, told her that she could find her voice at the seashore, and so she went, kept walking until she came to where the shore rocks were as jagged and hot as a scarred malpais. Then the ground opened up and she fell into the blackness.

She found her voice in there – and woke up screaming.

The man handcuffed her to the bed, had her there for three weeks. A bark cloth rag was used to gag her mouth. He kept her naked so she could urinate and defecate easily into the fly-haloed pail positioned next to her. When he let his sons see her, she cried and begged. But they could never understand their mother's speech. The few words of English she spoke could not come together – the man had convinced her that the word for *Help* was *Cluck*. And so she clucked for her sons when he brought them to see her. He told them that this would happen to them if they ever tried to upend what is supposed to be. Wives must stay with their husbands. Sons must always love their fathers. Anything else is an affront to nature. He twisted the necks off two hens and told his sons to laugh as the headless birds scampered in circles near the rushes. The sons were ten years old then, similar in many ways. Still, to the father, there was the quiet one, Rudra, and the loud one, Rustam.

Rustam often repeated what his father imparted to him. Told him the importance of deciding what you wanted to be in this life. Some people wait for God to decide for them, he said. This isn't how it is supposed to be. No one knows how it is supposed to be, he told his sons. People are betrayed by their own intelligence. The truth is neither here nor there – it will be there one moment and disappear the next. The truth is on the tip of your nose. You can barely see it most of your life. But you look at yourself for long enough, and you will. When that moment comes, snatch it and eat it, and you will come out alive.

Their mother felt not like a mother but a presence that waxed and waned. Not so much human but a ghost that appeared in rooms, shifted things around from time to time, spoke in a language of a different realm. Of a different existence. It only occurred to them that she was corporeal at the times she was being beaten, when she bled – and they wondered why, unlike any other animal in this world, she did not defend herself.

They believed their mother had ligated and stitched moments of repose between their father's blows. Communed with the hiss of a kettle and the smell of garlic rising from metal. Lost herself in folds of cloth. Kept a glass bottle with dirt and weeds near the windowsill. For what reason, they were never sure. Something like that was hers and would now always be hers. She stared hard at the sun at twilight. Trying to remember her old name, then trying to forget it.

Rudra killed a bird one evening. A heron with a broken wing. He squeezed the neck until it stopped flapping. Cut the beak off with a rusty dagger to see what its head looked like without it. Inverted the wing like a jacket worn the wrong way. Took it apart piece by piece as if he were a watchmaker digging into tiny hairsprings and wheel jewels. Did it with pride. He'd always wanted to know how the insides of bodies looked. The beautiful spectra of tissue and organ.

Their mother was quiet in the bedroom for those three weeks. So quiet that her sons often forgot that she was in there. In the night, Rudra ventured into the room to see her, lifting her leathery eyelids to stare right into her bloodshot gaze, checking to see if she was dead. Their father would be asleep in the same room. Every night, he beat her with a rusted stove iron for trying to leave. When he untied her, she never tried to run away again. He told his sons that once you commit to something, there is nothing that can stop you. But you must commit to it fully. You must devote your entire self to it, or you become your own enemy. He told them that he knew he was going to hell – and that was all right. It was written that all kings must once behold hell. There are no certainties in life, he said, but this was something he could be certain about. He will come out alive even when he dies, even while he is on fire.

He let the boys wander the forest and the riverside but prohibited them from talking to any civilised soul who crossed their path. Brothers should be enough for each other, he said. Two halves of a whole. They were tall for their age, their young bodies wiry with sinew and scar. The brothers sometimes spoke in unison, taking turns as each other's echo. As if they drew some sort of hidden power from each other. They ate together and slept in the same bed, waking at the same time, their bladders and circadian rhythms in sync. When one became ill, the other did too. If their father beat one of them, the other asked to be beaten as well. They were never without each other. Even in dreams, they were together.

They developed an interest in animal anatomy – and so agreed to a partnership. Rustam would catch the animals, and Rudra would dissect them. Rudra clipped the wings off dead bats and examined them tendon by tendon, showing his brother which muscles relaxed as the wing unfolded. He collected iguana eggs and fish gills and bird beaks in boxes and jars, now lost to any bewildered soul that would happen across it. Even though the desire was not fully formed, the idea of walking through an endless tissue gallery was this brother's idea of a dreamscape.

One day, their father brought home a stack of plywood planks, setting them at the side of the house. He told his sons that he did not want them going near the wood. That it was not his property and, moreso, not their property. Nonetheless, by midday, the brothers disobeyed this order. Rustam had decided to play a game with one of the thinner pieces, holding one of the planks over his head, trying to balance it. Rudra giggled as the plank tilted and fell off his brother's head.

When the plank hit the ground, it exploded.

The veneer at the side blew right out. The birds on a nearby palm fluttered off. The crack of the explosion shot into the far distance. Past the lapping river. Past the hushed crunching of the bamboo.

Inside that plank was a rifle. The brothers could only surmise that within the others were rifles as well. When their father came home, he took one of the rifles and set the two boys on a long path leading to the forest.

He told them, 'Before today, there was two roads. You choose one. And now I gon set you to run on that road you choose. Not walk. Run. Because this is the road you decide you want to go down.'

He aimed the rifle at them and yelled, 'Now show me how fast you rabbits can run!'

He counted to three and began firing as they ran. The boys made a helix as they did, swerving in and out to dodge the shots. The wind cracking with each blast. Bullets nicking the earth. Clods of dust and grass sprouting with each one. They ran into the dark of the forest, climbed the tallest tree they could find and hugged each other. Stayed there for the night, being eaten alive by ants and mosquitoes. When they returned home, they had boiled yams and roasted yard fowl for dinner and slept until evening.

★

Two months later, a shadow visited the house. One usually believes that a killer waits until dark, at some strange hour, to do his bidding. But to a shadow, there was no strange hour. Every place is always the wrong place, and every time is always the wrong time. This is what the father had carried in his head since the day he threw his shipmates overboard to the reef sharks. One's fate can hide on either side of the moon. On either face of the faultless flicker of lamplight. The father had gotten accustomed to sleeping upright at the kitchen table. He knew death was always waiting. He got up, put an unlit cigarette in his mouth and went outside. Leaned against a wall and embraced the monastic silence of the land.

He went to the back of the house, where a grass path tapered towards the latrine. In that moment, a thought crossed him. A semblance of identity he had scraped for himself as a child, like a hungry dog at the back of an abandoned abattoir. He was never one to give into delusions but in that moment, he mused about a different life he could have had, still among men without having to look over his shoulder.

At least on this road he now walked, he could have some fun.

Even in this darkness, the latrine made a deep trapezoid of shadow on the grass. He pulled the Colt out of his pocket and fired six times into that shadow. A deep, loud grunt rumbled out.

Then a body slumped to the side. Fired back.

Looked like lightning coming up from the ground.

One shot connected, one grazed.

At first, the father could not tell where he'd been hit. Just knew that the metal had gone into his body. Felt the frosty shockwave through the nerves. The shadow fled towards the forest and the father gave chase. Wasn't long until he caught up. Only when he held the man down did the father see the blood dripping from his own neck. It fell onto the man's cheeks, staining them red as a circus clown's. He wasn't sure where the bullet had bit the man or whether or not it was still in there. And he still wasn't sure where the bullet had entered his own body, though every time he shifted his weight, the cold pain jostled his left side like vermin trying to chew their way out of his marrow.

He and the man tussled along a flower-strewn path that led to two jabillo trees. The spike-swathed bark that monkeys dare not to climb. The trunks and branches formed a spiny proscenium. The father picked the man up by his neck and slid his face down along the spikes of the bark. A rupture of fruiting capsules blasted from above, each raining dolphin-shaped seeds upon the two men. The sound of the heavy cracking stirring some unseen birds. The father pressed his two thumbs against the man's throat – blood still dripping from his own – until his eyes went red.

'Who send you?' the father grunted.

The man squealed one word, 'Changoor.'

When the man was dead, his body was left to the insects.

The father lit a cigarette. Then lit a candle and took it to the latrine, where he sat to inspect his body. A bullet had grazed his neck and the other had entered his left shoulder. He went back into the house for sewing thread, grooming scissors and a bottle of whiskey. Downed half the bottle and dug the bullet out with the trimmer before holding the flame to the wound. Stitched it, absorbing the pain as it came. Pain is temporary, he told himself. But vengeance is a permanent cycle. This was one shadow of many that belonged to Changoor; he was smart enough to know that. The forest can only swallow so many bones.

There was no stopping it. No turning back.

He had decided to follow through on his promise. The next day, he waited until his wife and sons were asleep, then until dawn, he sat at his favourite rickety table with a tall bottle of whiskey and a Colt already fitted with its magazine. It wasn't that he had spent those hours pondering the plan, hoping that some spirit – from the forest or from the malt – would creep into his head and yammer until he changed his mind. No, he knew what he had to do. Start fresh. A clean break. As the sun came up, the kiskadees began their call. The birds weren't his preference – he would have paid a wandering carnival to release a stampede of elephants and tigers if he could. That's how death should be, he thought. Sweaty and calamitous and booming loud.

He returned to his bedroom, shot his wife in the head. He owned her life – it was only right it end now. Then went into his sons' room. Rudra opened his eyes. Scooted forward, kicked the gun out of his father's hand. He hadn't known it was his father – he wasn't even sure that he was awake. He was running on the fuel of a nightmare, still in a reverie populated with shadows and arrhythmia, a wasp trying to sting its way out of his heart. The gun fell to the floor and fired a shot parallel, the bullet skittering like a quicksilver cockroach, slicing off a chunk of the bed leg.

Rustam woke up. The room misty with gunsmoke. He rolled to the edge of the room, grabbed the cold metal grip of the gun. When the smoke cleared, he gazed upon the face of his father, the man's unruly thatch of hair glistening as the sunlight leaked through the window like melted butter.

His father hollered at the top of his lungs, 'You forget I's your father!' before his son pulled the trigger. He wasn't sure he had actually hit the man until the boutonnière of blood bloomed from his belly.

Trembling, the boy dropped the gun. All he could recall from that point was his father picking up a pack of cigarettes from the dresser. He took his brother's hand, and they ran into their mother's room only to find her dead, skull blown open like a blooming rose of meninges and brain and bone. They ran to the river and followed the water for what seemed like hours. Ran until their limbs burned.

The father, having fainted from the gunshot wound just yards from his home, was arrested for the murder of his wife. When he recovered, they handcuffed him and put him in a cell at the Bell Village Police Station for holding until the capital's authorities could arrive. The man woke up drooling, cheek down on greasy metal, dried honeycombs of phlegm on the wall behind him.

He knew they would try to kill him right here in this cell. So, in the early morning, he pretended to be dead. When the watch-guard went to check on him, he strangled him with the chains of the cuffs, took the key, held it between his teeth and unshack-led himself.

He grabbed the watchguard's service revolver and was about to make his way out of the station when another officer shot him cold in the back. He spun around, cocked the hammer with the heel of his hand, began firing. Three bullets in the wall, one in the ceiling, two in uniforms.

Another fired back, hit him twice in the cheek. He died with a heavy thud and a bright glint in his eyes. When he hit the ground, his last breath sounded like a light snore. His last thought was the sea pulling him under before everything went dark.

*

The brothers became beggars at first. They crossed the river and set off along the Spanish Royal Road. Followed the horses north up to the capital where nobody would know them or question them. The world was bigger up there. They loitered around the moviehouse. Patrons' bicycles parked all the way down. Every once in a while, the brothers would each spring one and ride them to the scrapyard, where they sold them for a couple of dollars. When one of the previous owners accosted them – a grizzly man well into his fifties – they did feel genuine remorse and, for a month, went unseen and hungry.

They resurfaced at the fish market, begging for food. They made the mistake of asking a local textile salesman to buy a kingfish for them. The man, for whatever reason that causes people to act ugly out of the blue, had hawked a spitball into Rustam's eye. And the mistake suddenly became his. Rudra lifted a scaling knife from one of the vendors. Stabbed the man in his right buttock and ran away. After that, they returned to where they were born. Their house was still there, though destroyed, defaced and ransacked. Stray dogs had ripped the mattresses apart. The kitchen now overrun with creepers. Someone had painted HELLHOUSE large and bold on the side. The brothers lived there for a short while.

During that brief stay, Rudra had gone into the forest and found a skeleton. He looked at it for a long time as if he could commune with the dead. He didn't wonder who it was, though had assumed it was someone his father had killed. He wondered how many other skeletons were buried in the shadows of the woods. Stuccoed into muddy piles, whatever left of the cadavers stored in roots and tree trunks by now. Eventually the brothers moved on, found an abandoned shack near the river and decided to live there instead. They hunted and cooked iguana, agouti, quenk. Fished for cascadura and tilapia. Ate the meat with stolen fruits.

They soon found work in a lodge. They would live in a shed, no bigger than an outhouse, beside the barrack. Not far was the cricket field's pavilion. They earned their keep as yard boys there, weeding the grass and hosing dogshit off the walkways. Once word spread about who they were, nobody in the barrack took kindly to the brothers' presence.

The overseer especially did not like them. He was a coolie, like any of them, but believed he was a white man. Believed he could sit in their section during the football matches. Ate beef and swine like them. Once had a horse but had to put it down after its legs gave in. A steely man with a large, twirled moustache like Yama, lord of death and justice. A double-plaited ponytail like some ancient warlord. A voice tainted by a thousand cigarettes and a smell as sulphuric as the devil. He asked for a cut of the labourers' salaries. A donation. He was building a house, after all. Payments not obligatory, of course, but those who didn't pay with money would find another way to pay, he made sure.

The twins refused to pay him. The overseer had them whipped. Then had some goons hold them down while he urinated on them.

Two days later, the overseer vanished. Three days after that, his bones were found. Corbeaux took their feast of flesh, so all that was left was bone, along with a scalp, hair still attached – the man's double-plaited ponytail still apparent. It looked like the man had been chopped up, his joints and ligaments broken with a rock.

The police put them in holding. Didn't take long for the senior officers to recognise who they were – and who their father was. They denied the crime, but the police beat them for their father's sins. The following morning, they had them under interrogation, hoping that word of their father's dealings would emerge. But the father never spoke of his life outside of the house. What they had known about his crimes was hearsay. Legend. For all they knew, the bloodstains on his shirts came from chopping off fish heads.

A lawyer made them an offer of five dollars for information about buried bodies. Rustam was unapologetic, told the lawyer where he could stick those five dollars. Rudra told him to calm down. But when their mother was brought up – the truth of their mother, that she was trafficked into Trinidad, that she was not only their father's victim, but theirs as well, having been forced to bear them and bring their valueless selves into this world – Rudra spat on the lawyer's shirt and the police beat them again.

They were driven from the lodge. Driven from the village. From civilisation.

Scorned by the world itself. Like the corbeaux that feasted on that overseer.

19
A Neglected Wound

Late August

Shweta's foot was still not right. The splinter still in there, festering. Dolly helped her make poultices out of candlewax, soaked her feet in salt and even tried to use a knife to get it out, only to make the wound worse. When she suggested to Shweta that she go to the clinic, Shweta shrugged off the notion, said that Hans assured her that she was recovering. Now, days later, the soreness persisted. Dolly told Lata to help Shweta with the chores that week, especially washing and putting up the clothes. Whenever Shweta walked, she took extra care not to press on the bad heel. She was on the floor now, shelling peas into a wooden bowl, a pile of discarded pods beside her bad foot. Had a fire going for tea. Hans was on the fibre mattress, shirtless, quiet for most of the morning. Quiet for most of that week. Shweta had also kept quiet about him dressed in another man's clothes – if she didn't think about it, then perhaps it never really happened.

Mandeep came to the door. Krishna behind him. 'Big crowd at the pond,' Mandeep said. 'People and police like crazy.'

'They find anything?' asked Hans, anxious to pose the question.

'They find the truck. The pickup.' Mandeep said it like he was telling a secret.

Shweta raised her eyebrows. Krishna sat beside his father. He and Tarak had gone with Mandeep. He remembered the wrecker whirring like a metal chariot, the heavy chain angrily jangling as it pulled the Chevrolet pickup to the pond surface.

A chill came upon him to see it lain to waste like this. As soon as the bonnet had broken the crest, the rest of the chassis came up as easy as it must have sunk. Aside from a slight cummerbund of oxidation on its fenders, the separation of its front tyre and the water-thread pondweed wrapped around the steering wheel, he was surprised the rest of the pickup looked to be in good order. The bumpers were still there. The windscreen still intact and so were the leather seats.

'The Mister wasn't in it,' Mandeep added.

Hans did a doubletake. 'They aint find him?'

'Not yet. They still searchin that pond. Had a man diving up and down by the time we get outta there. That aint no small pond, Hans.'

Shweta said, 'The Missus was there?'

'That aint something to ask,' Hans said to his wife. 'She aint gon be able to stomach something like that. You could imagine comin down there to see them dredge me outta a damn pond?'

'Wouldn't like it but I woulda be there, yes,' she said with a small shrug and went back to the peas. 'What kinda wife I woulda be?'

Krishna excused himself. Shweta reminded him to be back for dinner.

'I aint think he dead,' Mandeep said. 'I think he want people to think he is. I think he leave everything here high and dry. He probably take a boat to Venezuela.'

'He wouldn't leave his wife,' said Shweta, glancing up from her peas.

'Every woman in Venezuela look like that woman, you know. He could get another one easy, easy. She is only a beauty queen here in this crusty place. Any other place, she is just another *jamette* in a pub.'

'Like you know anything bout Venezuela woman,' said Hans with a chuckle.

Mandeep shrugged. 'I see pictures.'

'And the house?' asked Shweta, checking on the tea. 'How he gonna leave that behind?'

'House?' Mandeep laughed. 'He must have money for a hundred houses.'

Hans sat up on the bed, shaking his head. 'Brother, stop this foolish talk. We can't say nothin bout the Mister's whereabouts till we hear from the police.'

Mandeep asked, 'You talk to the wife? What the wife think?'

'Why she gonna tell Hans what she thinkin?' said Shweta, suddenly annoyed by the discussion.

Mandeep was curious. 'You help she pay the ransom all them times, Hans?'

'Hans wasn't involve in that,' said Shweta. 'He aint even know what was goin on when he was there. The Missus had him completely in the dark.'

Hans's voice went low. 'The Missus was just taking precaution havin me there. And taking precaution not talkin aloud bout the Mister kidnapping. But lookin back at it now, I wish she did at least tell me what to be expectin...'

Shweta went to pour the tea into two enamel cups, one for her, one for Hans. 'Use the good cup,' he said. When he'd been relieved of his watchman duties, he brought home a souvenir – the teacup. The same white ceramic teacup Shweta had seen on that day she and Hans were in the homestead. He placed it among the shelf that held all the religious effects. So there it sat pretty, flanked by a picture of Hanuman and a kalasha topped with a coronet of mango leaves. Every time it caught her eye, it was as if the monkeys painted on it were all dancing in a circle, taunting her.

She didn't mention the teacup to Dolly or anyone else. She already knew what her response would've been, *What kinda woman would give another woman's husband a gift?* She wasn't in the mood to have her decisions criticised again or to be judged. Tried her best to bury the thoughts, focused on her relief of Hans being back home. She reluctantly poured the tea. Remembering her son's harsh but perhaps true words, it seemed silly to kick up fuss over a teacup.

'That aint lookin too good,' Mandeep said, pointing his chin at Shweta's foot. 'You aint think you should go up to the clinic, girl?'

'No clinic,' Hans said, after some hesitation.

Mandeep raised his eyebrows. 'It look infected.'

Shweta smiled faintly at Mandeep. 'It gettin better.'

'Better than what?'

Hans turned his body to his brother. 'We see worse than that, Mandeep. Remember when we was small and we was all runnin bout that train station. We aint have no workboots then. Get all kinda twigs and metal all up in we feet. And it had that boy with we. Firaz Ali. Remember Firaz?'

'Yeah, he get the rubella.'

'He get that from the clinic. Because his mother take him every time he get the smallest cut. They never used to wipe down the table good. See, you can't go to the clinic for every small thing. Your body would forget how to heal itself.'

Mandeep held his palms up, backed away. 'You know more than me, brother. You's never wrong.'

'It gettin better,' Shweta repeated, gathering the empty pea pods, her voice trailing off.

Mandeep asked, 'When you two gettin ready to make the move?'

Shweta turned to Hans. 'Just a few more papers and it done, right?'

He pursed his lips. 'It in the works.' He quickly finished his tea and got up. 'I should go down there now. We was suppose to straighten out some things.'

'The man aint gon think you harassin him? Is the third day in a row you going to see this man.'

'You want the place or not?' He slung a shirtjack on, left it unbuttoned.

She kept quiet after that.

*

The twins were supposed to accompany them to the pond earlier that day but hadn't shown. After Krishna washed himself at the rainwater barrels, he fetched Tarak, and they trekked to the shed. Rustam was nodding off under a bergamot tree while Rudra sharpened a knife against a grindstone. The four sat around a charred bundle of sticks that held up a rusty metal pan.

Tarak started, 'They lift that pickup out of that river like it was nothin. I think everybody was expecting to find Changoor in it still. But he wasn't. The man just vanish.'

Krishna nodded. 'That diver was goin up and down, up and down, lookin for him.'

Rustam asked, 'They say who find the pickup?'

'Some man living up that hill,' said Tarak. 'A mason.'

'Make you wonder what other things it have underwater,' said Rustam. 'Or underground.'

Tarak nodded. 'Must have a whole other world sink down.'

Rudra nodded, pressing the edge of the knife against a callus on his thumb. Rustam had nothing else to say.

'What you two thought bout Mr Changoor?' Krishna asked the twins to break the silence.

Rustam looked down. 'We aint have no business with him.'

'I never think he was a bad man,' said Krishna, leaning forward.

Tarak had his eye on Rustam still. 'How come you wasn't at the pond today?' he asked, realising it hadn't been brought up. 'You was suppose to meet we there.' His tone more curious than accusatory, but the question made the twins go silent again.

'We aint want no business with Dalton Changoor, is all,' said Rustam.

'Why?' asked Krishna.

Tarak was curious as well.

Rudra gave Rustam a nod, as if giving him permission to tell the story. Rustam pursed his lips, almost forcing the words out, 'Remember when he was lettin everybody into his place to play cricket?'

'I gone twice,' said Tarak.

'Only once for me,' Krishna added. 'He was too strange.'

Rustam said, 'Me and Rudra was there one day. We just turn up. And he look at we for a long time. Then gon into the house and come back out with a gun and start shootin—'

Tarak's eyebrows shot up. Krishna as well. 'That was *you*?' they said, almost in unison.

Rustam paused his story, licking his lips.

Tarak went on, more surprised than anything, 'You's the ones who start that?'

'*Start?*' Rustam scoffed.

Krishna was also in disbelief, his eyes wide. 'You all aint never say nothin bout this before.'

A hint of nervousness creeping into his voice, Tarak asked, 'You steal from him?'

'Steal? We aint never do nothin to the man,' said Rustam. 'Is like the man just went mad when he see we. Say the devil come to take him. We aint gone down to the pond today because we aint want nobody sayin we had anything to do with it. As I say, we aint have no business with Dalton Changoor.'

Rudra nodded.

Tarak stroked his chin, looking as if he expected more from the story.

Krishna felt obliged to say, 'Now that they find the pickup, I aint think my pa need to be up there no more.'

Rustam shook his head 'Aint true. I see your pa yesterday evenin, goin up to the Changoor house.'

'Nah,' Krishna replied. 'Nah, he was in Bell yesterday. He aint gone to work this whole week.'

'He don't have to be workin to be goin up there.'

'Why he would go up there then?' asked Krishna, oblivious.

Rudra raised his eyebrows.

Rustam shrugged. 'How I gon know? But we aint goin up there to find out. And that is final.'

Tarak bit his lip. 'Must have somethin we don't know.'

Rustam gazed at the sky. 'It have a whole world we aint know. A whole world underwater. Aint that so, Tarak?'

Tarak furrowed his brow, disliked being put on the spot.

Rustam continued, 'I think we could get all agree on what I just say. We aint gon get involve in nothin with the Changoors, you hear? That go for all of we. And that is final.'

Krishna pursed his lips. 'But if my pa was up there—'

Rustam widened his eyes. '*Final.*'

Rudra nodded. Tarak as well. Krishna was the only one holding out. Looked like he wanted to say something but knew there was nothing else he could say.

'Final,' Krishna gave in with an annoyed shrug.

Rustam clapped, got up, went into the shed. He returned with a burlap bag, opened it for Krishna and Tarak to see. It was full of orange mushrooms. 'You know what this is?'

Krishna and Tarak shook their heads. 'This gon give you the *blood power*. It gon help you see your soul. See every ghost and jumbie floatin across this land. You will find your soul when you eat this. You will see it, smell it, eat it, shit it out and then eat it again.'

Rudra let out a wide grin.

'Where you get it?' Krishna with a nervous smile.

'Me and Rudra dig for hours through horseshit to get this.'

'And you goin to *eat* that?' asked Tarak, twisting his mouth.

'*We* goin to eat it. The four of we,' said Rustam. He closed the bag. 'Not yet. When the time right.' He took the bag back into the shed.

Tarak shuddered. 'Hope you fellas know I aint eatin nothin that was in horseshit.'

Rustam eyed Tarak. 'You know everything grow from shit and return to shit, right? Even you. You aint no better than that same horseshit you scornin.'

20

A Goddess on Fire

Shweta cleaned the lota. Then fetched an old piece of barkcloth to wipe the purulence off. As she did, she felt a nasty heat escaping from the pus. Still, she was set on believing her husband when he said that it was getting a little better each day. She didn't want to protest or complain.

Even Rookmin didn't seem to believe any of it. She picked fever grass for her, told her to bandage the wound with it. A blessed body will always accept the healing properties of the earth, she said. Rookmin had her own worries, however. Niala's condition had worsened, said she no longer had feeling in her legs. She now had to drag herself to the vomit bucket by her elbows, pulling the dead weight of the limbs behind her. Cried, asked God to cut the child out of her before it cut itself out. Like a mantis-head creature with razor pincers, tearing out of her uterus, leaky with yellow lochia, ready to gnaw her head off. Rookmin ground scorpion peppers using a mortar and pestle, rubbed it over her daughter's knees with a warmed rag. Then poured gallon after gallon of water down the girl's throat until she was peeing clean and clear as a mountain stream.

The old woman warned Hans that something was growing inside of his wife. Hans shrugged it off, telling her to mind her own business. Krishna would have agreed with his father at any other time – but seeing his mother deteriorate before his very eyes made him question the man.

On that afternoon, Hans said that he was going to Bell Village. Shweta gave him a disconsolate nod, bundled her ingredients and went to the yard to start cooking. She tied a miracle leaf around the sore and sat on a short wooden stool, keeping her good foot flat and her bad one on tiptoes, the rank sore off the dusty ground. Beside her was a queue of bowls: diced tomatoes, onions, bell peppers and chives chopped fine as confetti for the rest of the buljol. Krishna pulled up a crate, kept an eye on her as she prepared to panfry strips of saltfish. The boy hadn't much spoken to her since their spat about the candy. It hurt her – but she knew that he would come around. He was a sensible boy.

She gave him a concerned glance. 'You good?'

Krishna shook his head. 'I good.'

'Nah,' she said, leaning over to put a gentle hand on his shoulder. 'You aint good.' She flipped the cod with her free hand. 'Krishna, I goin to tell you how you was different from other children. I remember when Lata was a baby, that girl couldn't stop cryin. Was like jumbies was comin for she every night. Dolly tell me that it was so much noise that she wanted to leave the girl by the river, that she coulda barely take it no more. Your cousin, Tarak – he always had gas. Belly always givin him pain. Always crying and farting, especially in the night. Used to wake everybody up.'

She laughed as she said the last line, and Krishna cracked a wide smile. This brought a vivacious shine to her eyes, something that had been absent since Hans's return. She rubbed his shoulder and continued, 'But you was different. You stop cryin from early. Instead, you used to stand the pain. We never know when anything was wrong with you.' She paused to toss the other ingredients into the pan. The onions fell into the sizzle, quickly browning. The greens and reds of the other vegetables made the dish look like a wild overgrown garden in the charred pan.

She turned to her son again, a solemn look in her eyes. 'I only know somethin was wrong when you get quiet. And now you always quiet.'

He bowed his head. 'Sorry, ma.' He really was. Since her injury, he'd felt guilty about the fight.

She gave him a warm smile.

At the same time, Hans stepped out of the barrack.

'I nearly finish cook,' she said to him, giving the buljol a stir.

'Will eat when I come back,' he said, gazing out at the mountain. Took a deep whiff. 'Smellin good. Make sure you and Krishna save some for me.'

Shweta gave it another stir. 'Buljol don't taste good cold.'

But he had already left.

Shweta pursed her lips, took the pan off the fire and set it on a flat stone. Looked at Krishna and brushed some hair off his face. 'I suppose is better you remain a quiet boy. Than pretendin to smile through your problems.' Her mind went back to Hans greeting everyone with smiles during Hema's wake.

She put her arms around him. He reciprocated, feeling a swell in his throat but all he could do was nod. 'Sorry for callin you ugly, ma.'

'Good.' She ruffled his hair. 'Cause I aint.'

She looked back out at the road as Hans's silhouette was now just his shadow. The fresco of the dusk coming over the mountain. Together, the two ate in the yard. Krishna's fingers nimbly pinching every last shred of cod. Shweta was only halfway through her plate by the time he was done. Her fingers soppy with oil still. He told her that he was going to take a walk down to the guava trees. She gave him a nod, then pointed to a line of swifts taking off from a tree behind them, a single bird at the rear trying hard to keep up. She didn't need to explain that that meant rain would be coming tonight.

⋆

The pathway leading up to the Changoor farm was flanked by a peristyle of power lines on one side and a patch of wild banana plants on the other. The sun was going down faster than usual, evoking the brooding nature of the lonely road. The trees gilded with golden shadow. The shadows stretching farther than they should have, as if desperately trying to veil a hideous secret.

A moment's examination of the sky made the rain clouds apparent to Krishna. He should be turning around now, he thought. He had no lantern, no flashlight, and already had enough difficulty seeing in the dark. But he kept on forward, even when the banana patch beside him had begun to lose its shape, slowly turning into a black amorphous wall, and the distant wind took the sound of incoherent whispers. That wind swept an unpleasant heat his way.

Up ahead, past the Changoor gate, was a bright light. Near the end of the road. A bonfire.

He was pulled towards it. A haze of embers like fireflies. In the blaze were mostly boxes, newspapers. However, one item stood out – the large Chinese painting he had seen earlier. Trapped within, a goddess on fire. Her countenance indifferent, unbothered as the canvas crinkled around her. Her maidens at each side, their features now as if panicked in the flame, warping and contorting. As if absorbing the pain for their deity. Forever bound by duty.

The gate to the farm had been left open, slowly shifting in the evening breeze as if beckoning him to enter. Upon his first step inside, the image of Mr Changoor's pickup being lifted from the pond fell upon him. Water pouring from all its joints as if it were a giant perforated bucket. He thought of the people gathered to see the spectacle. Eager to see a body. Dejected when none turned up.

He trod carefully towards the house, kept in the shadows, half expecting a ghoulish Dalton Changoor to appear behind him, grab him by the shoulder. The man's eyes chewed out by catfish and herons. Tadpoles swimming figure-eights in and out of the orbits. His voice in gurgles, begging for life.

Even though death crossed Krishna's mind from time to time, he'd heard very little talk of the afterlife. His father rarely spoke of death – the man's face going spasmodic upon the very mention of the word. His mother had once explained to him that death was the passage of the soul from one body to another. The body like a caterpillar's cocoon. The soul emerging, sprouting butterfly wings, fluttering into another body. Krishna had asked his mother, 'Why it don't just fly away? Why fly into another body?' And his mother's response, 'One day. When the wings come out big enough.'

He recalled the detached look in her eyes as she'd said those words and how quiet she had gone for the rest of the day. As if she had difficulty believing the truth she so claimed. If it were true, however, Krishna wondered if Mr Changoor were indeed dead. And if he were, what had his soul flown into? Would it come to reclaim the house? It was difficult to believe that a man who owned so much on this Earth would leave it behind so easily.

Krishna stood before the house now, completely enveloped in its shadow. It lit up like a moon descended from the sky. Each of its many windows and alcoves a crater on the surface. The quiet of the evening broken by the music blaring from inside. A symphony of brass and crooning. Rising into an energetic jig and then nosediving into a solo vocal.

He took a breath, went up to the house, peeked through a window. A slit in the organdy curtain. He immediately recognised it as the children's toy room. He'd only seen it the one time but could already place the chests and floor pillows and pop guns and the radio rambling loud of *The Green Hornet* with that distinct American twang.

That room was mostly empty now. The toys and pillows still there but stacked in a forgotten corner. Along the base of the wall, a cluster of liquor bottles, some upright, some toppled, one broken in half. All uncorked and drunk dry. An open space in the middle, Mrs Changoor in a white nightslip dancing madly in it. At least, it looked like dancing. But not any type of dance a high society woman would be doing. He couldn't take his eyes off her, kept trying to focus on her face to make sure it was really her. She danced like the Madrasi. Women with jasmine in their hair, vibhuti smeared on their forehead and their minds banished to Naraka. Women that bit. They would ride a man at his own wake. Take pleasure from pain. Sear their own skin and laugh while doing it. He'd only heard of women being so unguarded, until now. Each turn of Mrs Changoor's heel making it look like she would keel over. Her legs going one way, her body another. She was many animals at once. A chimera of chimeras.

As she danced, a strap of her slip fell to the side. She did not stop to fix it and the more she moved, the more it shifted to reveal her cleavage. Even when her breast was fully bare, she didn't notice. Didn't care. Danced in her own tiny vortex that sucked in every responsibility in the world. Anything that held accountability.

She reached her arm to the other side of the room.

She wasn't alone, Krishna quickly noticed. His father was there. He took the bottle from her.

Krishna couldn't see his face, but he was certain of the fact. He was doing the opposite of the woman. While her body swayed in disarray, he remained seated on a leather chair, as attentive as the teacher's pet during roll call. His father's presence compounded the madness even further. Positioned within this snapshot of symphonic anarchy.

Mrs Changoor sang, 'Ding dong! The witch is dead! Which witch? The wicked witch!'

Whatever was happening here – it made Krishna sick with guilt and anger and anguish. He felt simultaneously terrified and betrayed. Powerless to this derangement. He had the urge to pelt a stone and break the window.

Instead, he bent forward, released a heavy gloop of vomit on some overgrown bougainvillea. He wiped his mouth, started on his way back. Pieces of the burning goddess fluttering downhill. A black cloud hid the moon. The moonlight teased out the shape of the land, though in only dark shades of blue and grey. But it was enough for Krishna to find his way home. The drizzle came down before he could get back to the barrack yard. And when he got there, his mother was waiting for him, the firewood still alight. She took him inside and dried him off.

'I wonder when your father comin home,' she said.

21

A Better Offer

Hans was drenched. He stole across the hallway after midnight and skulked into the room, sopping wet. Krishna had been asleep on the fibre mattress and woke up to see his father drain each boot, the water dripping onto a pile of straw in the corner. He flung them towards the shelf, nearly knocking over an aarti oil lamp. Took off his soaked shirt, flung that too.

'That rain come outta nowhere.' He sat on the edge of the fibre mattress that Shweta was lying on, taking a moment to catch his breath. She put her palm on his back and rubbed in gentle circles, momentarily pausing as if trying to feel for his heartbeat through his spine.

They stayed like that for a half minute before she told him, 'Your skin cold. I gon make some tea to warm you up.' She took her time getting off the bed, flinching as her weight pressed on the dark sore of her heel.

Krishna kept a cobra's stare at his father as he got up from the mattress to take the ceramic teacup from the shelf. Set it on the brass plate with the other cups. Shweta put up a small pot to boil while she minced ginger with a pestle. Added a bay leaf and a pod of star anise. The rain continued pouring outside while the air inside remained sticky and stagnated. She ignored the water from the roof dripping onto her nose and into the pot.

A sharp crack of thunder shook the earth. Even their shadows vibrated with the sound. Despite the clamour of the rain, she could hear Dolly and Lata in the adjacent room, feigning fright at the thunder before laughing at it. As if taunting nature to try harder. The thunder came again.

'People tryin to sleep here!' Mandeep yelled out from the other side of the barrack. Dolly and Lata giggled, playfully shushing each other like schoolgirls up to secret mischief. The next peal of thunder was met with another jovial scream.

Shweta finished with the tea.

'The good cup,' Hans reminded her.

For a moment, Shweta lost herself gazing at the monkeys on the ceramic. 'Drink so you don't catch the *ammonia*,' she murmured, pouring the tea.

Hans took a sip and for a moment his face reshaped to its old companionable configuration. The warm, pollened energy in his eyes. Like he'd been shuttled back to some golden memory. His skin flushed. He closed his eyes and for that moment stepped out of his skin. Shweta had noticed the shift. The man who sat on the bed was his old self once more, at least for that minute. She thought back to Hans's irascible appearance before that moment. His gaze of cold intent. Small, acerbic mouth. Each breath of hot air a disinclined nicker. The countenance of a stranger, a mimic.

A cold spray of water suddenly came from the wall behind them, a single drop falling onto Hans's forehead. And his expression shifted right back. The affable look, the warmth in the eyes, the flush of the skin – all extinguished and summarily replaced by the features of the stranger once again. He set the teacup on the floor and went to the tiny spout in the wall. 'What is the point?' he muttered and then exhaled, shaking his head. 'Piece of shit!'

Shweta bit her tongue. Krishna watched on.

Hans turned to his wife. 'We aint getting the lot. They make a better offer.'

She crinkled her brow. 'What you mean? Who?'

'Somebody else offer more for the lot in Bell. I offer everything we have. Them offer more. I lie and say I have even more to offer. And yet them offer even more than that. So they have the lot now.'

'That ... is how it work?' Shweta asked, trying hard to hide her disappointment. Krishna, on the other hand, couldn't conceal his miserable frown.

'A waste.'

Shweta remained quiet. There'll be other plots, she tried to console herself. Other opportunities. And they still had the money. Another could go on sale soon. Maybe even for a better one. Still, something in the back of her mind couldn't help thinking that Hans had botched the deal. Why did he mislead her – tell her that the deal was going fine?

Hans returned to the mattress.

Shweta accidentally scraped her sore against a sliver of charred wood. The pain shot right up to her eyes. She imagined each vein filling with hot cigarette ash. But she held in the whimper. Picked at the sore like she was trying to undo a button and removed the tiny black woodchip.

Krishna, quiet this whole time, said, 'Ma, make sure to wash it.' He dipped a torn strip of fabric into a water pail and handed it to her. She wiped the wound, her eyes rolling back from how tender it'd gotten. A thick glob of dark blood seeped out.

Maybe she should get it stitched, she thought. But the very thought of taking a needle to the sore made her squirm. As she turned, she accidentally pressed down on the raw spot. Swallowed hard, bit her gum to keep from crying out. Felt the anger rise up. Turned to her husband, 'Hans, you been goin to that man every day. You tell him a brick fall through the roof and nearly kill your son?'

He sipped. 'It done, Shweta. I aint want to talk.'

She stooped before him. Face to face. 'You tell him bout how everybody here have to share a latrine? You tell him bout the rat piss in the rice? Bout how we could hear everybody business through the walls? You tell him about our dead d—' She had to still her tongue. *Hema* at the tip of it, ready to roll out with the spurt of venom. *No*, she told herself. She wouldn't desecrate her daughter's name in that way. For her memory to become part and parcel of a domestic dispute. It would've been the first time her name had surfaced the dark waters in years – and no, no, no, it wasn't going to be in this tone. She fought it, swallowed it, sent it back under.

'No.' His eyes simmered as they met hers. 'I aint lookin for pity.'

Another waterspout materialised. A sprinkle of cold. Hans turned around, his back to Krishna and Shweta. Thunder boomed again, and the two next door screamed and giggled. Shweta remained hunched over, staring into the hole in her heel. The sound of the rain in oscillations. Niala groaning and crudely retching. If nobody had known of her affliction, they could've been forgiven for thinking it to be the yowling of hellspawn. Rookmin cantillating a mantra in Hindi, conjuring forces and spirits and powers from under the skin. White Lady scratching the barrack door to come inside. Mandeep's voice admonishing, '*Tarak, don't open that door. She gon pee and smell up the whole inside!*' Thunder again. Screaming again. Laughter again. This time, Sachin had joined in. '*Ha ha ha!*' Teeluck and Kalawatie periodically banging the wall, the sexual sough of their voices like wind sucking and swelling through a hollowed tree. Their feet ritually knocking against something metal, maybe an altar plate. Rookmin's mantra rising to an ululation.

Hans angrily hit the wall three times, as if the force could stop such a coterie of clamours. Krishna held his head. The motley crew of sounds having a sort of crushing gravity of their own in his mind. Orbiting him like accusatory insects. Shweta reduced to murmuring something about the wound, speaking to no one in particular. Her voice, so weightless and immaterial among the din. Hans remained with his back to them both. Krishna had not known it, but since his return home that evening, his mind was being slowly colonised by rage. His eyes set glowing iron hot. Perhaps he, too, felt as insignificant as his mother. Lost in noise. And he wanted to say something that would be heard.

In the midst of the cacophony, the boy blurted out, 'Pa is lyin. He wasn't at the village this evenin.'

Hans shifted on the mattress a bit before turning his neck to look at the boy.

Shweta's mouth curled into a curious frown. 'What?'

Hans gave the boy a peculiar look as if he wanted to believe he had misheard. Krishna repeated himself, 'You wasn't at the village this evenin.'

'I wasn't?' asked Hans, his entire body turned now.

Krishna sat up straight. 'You was at the Changoor house.'

He had expected his father to follow up by asking how come he knew that, but instead, the man took his time to sit up on the edge of the mattress. Shweta leaned against the wall, trembling a little. She loathed suspecting the affair, tried to push it out of her mind every time it reared its head.

'This is true, Hans?' She held onto a gossamer of hope.

'You know why I was there to see the Missus?' said Hans, scratching his chin. 'With Mr Changoor missin in action, the Missus say she still need to have a person to watchman the house at nights for a little while. And she gon pay me for it. So I went to say I would take the job.'

Shweta's entire face changed at that point. Her jaw and cheeks at rakish angles. Eyes round as a wary owl's. 'You never talk to me bout this,' she said. Shifted her body towards him. 'When you was goin to say something?'

Krishna began, 'You lyin, pa—'

Shweta cut in, 'I thought we was done with all this.' Rose up, her bad foot on tiptoes. Lightning and thunder outside. 'You aint taking that job, Hansraj.'

'LOOK AT THE WALL!' Hans exploded. 'Water comin out of the fuckin wall!'

Shweta balled up her hands. 'What you cussin for? Cussin aint gon do nothin to stop the damn water.'

Thunder boomed again. But this time, no scream, no laughter.

'He never went into the village,' Krishna repeated to deaf ears.

'Marlee is going to help we find another lot as soon as—'

'*Marlee?*' Shweta came closer to Hans. 'I's your wife and I tellin you – you have no more business at that house. It aint right for you to be there. Not in the night. Is like we aint even exist when you over there. You become a total stranger—'

'Woman, what the *fuck* you want from me?' Hans said, rubbing his palm over his face. 'You want money – so I gone out in them canefields, hours in the hot sun, breakin my back for small change, comin home with my arm halfway out the socket. I gone out there and get the money. You say is not enough. You want more. The boy too skinny, you say. So I start workin at the farm. The Mister treat me good. The Missus treat me good. I come home with more money. Then you say the boy nearly dead so you want a house in Bell. I take on more work, to wake day and night for a week straight. I work and I slave. Now you say I livin two lives—'

'I tellin you not to take the job!' Shweta was adamant. 'I forbid you!'

Hans wiped his face again. 'You feel you better than everyone else in here. But you aint. Which wife talk to she husband this way? You aint never had manners. Never was brought up right.'

'I aint brought up right?' Shweta bit her lip. Thunder again. No screams, no laughter. The dog still scratching the door. No moans, no retches, no recitations for the gods. 'I don't take care of you? You aint eat here in a week, but I still cookin for you. You aint hardly say a word to me since you come back...'

'I aint have nothin to say.'

Her eyes burned now. 'A crow could peck out your eye, and you wouldn't have nothin to say!'

Hans spoke through his teeth, 'If I was any other kinda man, I woulda knock you down already.'

Shweta threw her arms up, inched closer. 'So what kinda man is you then? Who is you really, Hans?'

He sucked his teeth. 'What the hell you mean, *who I is*?'

'You aint never know what you want, Hans. You always all over the place lookin for it. It aint in me and it aint in Krishna. It aint in this family. So you out there lookin all over for God knows *what*. Now you lookin in other people house for it. Lookin for who you is. Let we know when you find it!'

He turned his head away. 'You feel you deserve more than what you have. But you have way more than you deserve. I's so fed up of you, woman. You's an ungrateful wife, is what you is.'

'*Deserve?*' Shweta sat on the ground, gazing at her feet. Her voice in a low pensive tone now, 'You say them bold words to me like you is God. I have news for you. You aint God, Hansraj Saroop. Who's *you* to tell *me* what I deserve in this life?'

'You *always* have it too good, is what. Look at how you talkin to me.'

'And what you think *you* deserve, Hansraj?'

'Not this shit you givin me.'

'What shit?'

He waved his arms. 'All this *shit*!'

Shweta shook her head. 'I thought you was a better man.'

'And I thought I coulda have a wife I could fuck—'

Shweta spun him around, slapped him hard. Her eyes immediately pooling with fear and regret.

He slapped her back with such force that it was like an ocean wave had flipped her over.

At the same time, Krishna lunged headfirst into him. Started pummelling. In that moment, the boy was nothing but veins and knuckles and bone. The pain hissed through his hands as if his nerves were loosed pressure valves. Skin curled off in small bloody ribbons.

Hans lifted the boy, threw him against the wall. His back knocking bowls and saucers over. The picture of Hanuman fell facedown on the ground.

Krishna fell like a beaten rag doll, contorted, unable to sturdy any part of himself. They both doubled over, heaving.

Hans muttered, 'Krishna, I sorry—'

The ceramic teacup hit his head before he could finish. Fell to the floor and shattered hard.

Shweta had cast it with all her might. All rage zipping across the room. Krishna, still on the ground, looked at his father, stunned. A trickle of blood ran down the man's forehead, the rest of his body upright and unfazed.

It took Hans a few moments to realise what had transpired. And when he saw the ceramic shards on the floor, he reduced himself to the stance of a little boy about to receive a caning from a schoolmaster. About to receive blows from his own father. Clung to the wall, slumped to the floor like a great failure had come upon him. Krishna remained in the corner; his face buried into the crook of his elbow. Wishing he had never brought anything up.

'We aint even married, me and you,' Hans mumbled as if disoriented.

Shweta stood on tiptoes, bellowing at her husband as if to conjure the thunder outside, '*GET OUT! DON'T COME BACK!*'

A grave expression came over Hans's face as he realised that what was done was done. He opened his mouth as if to apologise – but it was easier to just walk away. The others trickled into the hallway. Rookmin clasping the front of her sari. Dolly and Lata with their palms to their mouths. Kalawatie, with only an oily sheet covering her sweaty breasts, peeking out with eyebrows raised.

The thunder came again.

Hans opened the barrack door. As he did, White Lady walked in, shook herself dry. Again, Hans hesitated – did a regretful half turn back to the hallway. But then ran off, disappearing into the heavy rain.

22
A Vision of Truth

A rustling riverside fire separated the cousins from the twins. The boys sat on large rocks lain on opposite ends, a parabola of ants going from one to the other. Tarak scratching the back of his neck. Krishna with his chin up, more determined than ever. The river's calm laminar flow oblivious to the tempest in Krishna's mind. One of his molars had loosened during the fracas; he had been tonguing it the entire day. His mind sullied and resullied by images of his mother doubled over in pain, and the teacup splintering against his father's head.

While Rudra washed the orange mushrooms in the river, Rustam used a knife to open a tin of condensed milk. With a crafty smile, he told Tarak and Krishna that the milk's sweetness wasn't enough to take away the bitter taste of the mushrooms, but it would keep them from vomiting their organs out. Tarak had great reservations but vowed that Krishna wouldn't take the mushrooms alone. Krishna was ready to enter the dark portal – escape this mad world for a night, as the twins had put it. Dive into their own blood. In blood, there could only be the vision of truth. In blood was a brand of buried omniscience, as blood held the past, the present and the future.

Krishna knew it was too late to back out as he eyed a vintage of moths dipping into the fire before him. He'd often wondered what was it that drew moths into flames. Some of them made spirals over the cinders that weaved out of the wood, disappearing as white wisps into the night wind. The ones that smouldered became part of the fire, their peppered white deepening slightly to the hue of cigarette ash. It was his father who had told him that the moths never did this with intent. Moths see light and fly to it, he said. Always searching for the border between deep darkness and the billows of the moon. The moonlight to them is hope. But to a moth, there are many things that resemble moonlight – that they can only hope is moonlight. It is that hope that turns on them and gets them killed. When one is that small in this world, the perspective warps to see aspects of the mundane utterly illuminated. A speck of lint as a burden on the back. A yawning mouth as an eternal wind tunnel. The moon as pale fire in the endless black sky.

Krishna wondered, if moths could think, what would be their last thought before the fire swallowed them? There were so many things in this life that were like this. Everyone searching for that long, cool, curling comber of moonlight.

Hans, the moth. And Marlee, the flame.

Krishna began to well up at the notion that the man he'd known his whole life had changed. Or worse – had always been this way. Like every other wastrel out there.

His mother had tended to his bruises like a dog licking another's wound clean. They fell asleep together. He, with memories of her pinning his trousers, dousing his hair with coconut oil. The rim of his nostrils brushing against her ear so that she could feel and hear his cooing breaths.

Rustam handed Tarak and Krishna the mushrooms. They dipped them in the condensed milk and ate them. Then they sat on the ground, looking up at the night sky. Up there, a boneyard populated with skulls with gold shillings planted in the sockets. All staring back with fixed grins.

And in this vastness, Krishna felt simultaneously magnified and diminished. Stars falling through their hands like sand. Pinged as they fell into the black echo. Shadows gyrating in the trees. Demons howling from the mountain. In the sky was the infinite. At first, unnecessarily spacious and arbitrary and disorganised, eating itself and getting fatter and fatter like a tumour. Too big for itself. Too big for God, even. But in the black echo, it made sense.

He looked at his hand. There was fire in his fingers.

Did not burn him, could not burn him.

Fluttered like a hummingbird at first. Then it went inside his hand. Glowed. Pale light in him now. And he knew he had to take the fire to the mountain.

Told this to Rustam, whose laughter was on loop.

Then Rudra, whose face folded in like timarie leaves.

Tarak remained frozen in time, his breathing loud and stertorous.

'You seein them scorpions?' he asked.

Rustam laughed again but the sound came out like a cicada. Krishna turned to the mountains, the dark autochthonous rocks moving like wings.

Raised up. The Corbeau. Bigger than God.

No. This *was* God. God was bigger than God.

Krishna had awakened that morning to find his mother beside the clotheslines, a heavy wind whipping the fabrics around her. Just standing there, staring ahead at nothing. She was there with him now. The clothes turned into severed bird wings. And even though they were ahead of him, he could feel the pinions brush against his skin. That morning, when Krishna crossed his mother's line of sight, her dim expression remained unaltered. Just as it was now. He called out to her, but the wind blew his voice away. Tugged on her dress, still no response. Memory blurred with the present. Her, still staring straight ahead. The wind beating the clothes against his face. Called to her one last time. She slowly turned to him, no break or snap in the expression except for a faint flush of warmth in the cheeks.

'Come inside,' she said. 'Pray with me.'

As she turned on her bad heel, she winced, nearly lost her balance. Krishna held onto her, worried now. The meat of her heel had turned a darkish green, like the skin of a spoiled avocado. A pungent odour seeping out. The heel split open and swallowed her body whole.

She was gone.

Krishna screamed at the bird-mountain. When it moved, the whole land screamed back. Rustam still laughing like a cicada. Krishna looked all over for his mother. Where had she gone?

He asked Tarak. 'Where she gone?'

Tarak on the ground, kicking at the dark.

Krishna on him, punching him in the chest with his fiery fist to get him to stop. The bird-mountain was watching. 'Where she gone? Where she gone?'

He felt like something was filling him. A gas. A blackness. Felt like he could squat and expel a neverending anaconda of shit into the river. Filled him until he could remember no more.

When they awoke, Rustam told them that they had seen their true selves. Said the dead brain was like hard, dried clay. In life, the brain has the consistency of curdled butter. Soft, wobbly, easily penetrated. Always changing inside. But that there was something underneath. What they saw was that something.

Krishna screamed at the mountain with Tarak now. He screamed until the world fell apart, and he found himself back in the barrack. His mother was on the floor, writhing in pain. Mouth open like a snake about to disgorge a tapir's bones. But nothing came out but a guttural gag. She tried to pull herself up, lost her balance.

She fell, helpless as a tortoise flipped on its back. Tried to pull her body up by grabbing onto the shelf, kneecaps grazing the floor with each tug. Limbs slow like they were gliding through water. Jaw snapped shut like a bear trap. Couldn't pry itself open again. Krishna felt like the ground was opening beneath his feet. A deep gurgle rumbling below, miles into the Earth, like the gravelly call of a dozen toads. But the sound was coming out of his mother's seized throat. Her arms twisted inwards, hands curled into cups as if preparing to accept an offering of panchamrita during prayer. Krishna stared with wide eyes. Shweta's body shuddering like a prolonged death rattle.

The angels all flew away. The devil had taken his mother and she was about to die.

But he could not do anything but close his eyes. Maybe if he went to sleep in the dream, it would be over. Maybe the bird-mountain would come back and carry him there. While his mother twisted into a dozen different shapes, he went back to sleep.

He didn't wake until hours later.

Sachin was kneeling beside him, crying. 'Krishna, Krishna,' he said, barely able to catch his breath. 'They pick she up and take she away, Krishna.' Was only then that Krishna shuffled out of the shambles of his mind and realised that the dream – was no dream at all.

23
A Time to Speak

Robinson sat in his pickup, debating whether or not he should drive down to the county hospital. On one hand, he felt it wrong to visit a woman who was not his wife, not his blood. On the other, his curiosity had taken hold of him – just as it had when he'd discovered that Hans had moved into the big house. Mrs Changoor had taken him in, washed him, soaped him, perfumed him, trimmed his hair, cut his nails, shaved his whiskers, dressed him in a pinstriped shirt and loafers. She put Hans to work, but he remained within the realm of the house. Worked on repairing cupboard doors, applying sealant to the deck, checking for cracked caulking around the windows. She put on music and cooked lunch for him. Robinson was fairly sure of the moments they would fornicate. They always put on a fresh record before doing it and finished before the crank resetted.

He was unsure if it were meant to be secret or not – but knew better than to question either of them about it. She hadn't yet hired a replacement for Baig and she had ceased giving Robinson directives for any real work. His job had been reduced to grocery and hardware errands, which he lamented. He had loved the land more than he realised. He didn't remark on his feelings, though felt the need to put his hat on. Draped it over his eyes.

He had once mentioned to his wife his suspicions concerning Hans and Mrs Changoor. About the firing of Mr Baig. And the killing of the dogs. She grated cocoa for him in boiled milk and reminded him that he ought not comment on the dalliance to anybody. Wasn't becoming of a man like him. And that if he were unhappy with his new tasks, he should leave.

There was nothing to be done about Hans and Mrs Changoor. It was what it was, Robinson accepted. Hans had never spoken much of Shweta, but Robinson sensed a kindred spirit upon meeting her that day she had injured her foot. He'd always figured barrack women to be crass, vulgar, lifting their skirts to any stranger who came within two steps of them. Women who believed in talking animals and bones and dark magic. Then he overheard Hans talking to Mrs Changoor about how Shweta had to be taken to the hospital. Usually, the hospital was reserved for certain companies and estates – employees and their immediate families – so a woman named Dolly, who'd lived in the same barrack and worked in the canefield as a water carrier, had convinced the people there that Shweta was her sister. This, he overheard as well.

At the day's end, Robinson wanted to ask about her status. But Hans and Mrs Changoor had already gone inside. Put on a fresh record. They were in bed, he was certain. He couldn't wait for them to be done. So, on that afternoon, he drove his pickup down to the hospital.

The last time he'd been there was for the birth of his second child about a decade ago, and he was thankful that he had such little familiarity with the place. Outside, the building looked like a weatherworn stack of yellow crates, sitting on porticos and speckled all around with tilted louvres. Inside, the walls were pickled white, and the air smelled of pine. His gaze swivelled to an empty gurney and then to the woman at the front desk. Her hair was tied into a puffy ball behind her nurse's cap. He had recognised her from church – and from the familiar look she gave him, he knew she had recognised him as well.

'You have a Shweta Saroop warded in here?' he asked.

Not hesitating, she checked her logbook. As she skimmed the names, he felt compelled to add, 'Wife of a coworker. Hear she was sick. I know I aint family, but I thought I would come to pay a kind word.'

The woman gestured for another nurse and relayed the room number to him. The nurse led Robinson down a hall that smelled more and more of bleach.

She told him, 'Poor woman can't say a word to help herself, I tell you. Probably a good thing. Because if I had a husband like hers, I woulda have more than a few words...'

A squeaky wheelchair made it from one room to another.

'What you mean?'

'Aint made a peep yet,' she whispered.

'That aint right. You sure?'

She led him into a room with six hospital beds, all occupied. At least two patients he could see were paying the price for being old beyond their natural lifespan. Shweta's bed was situated nearest to a window, where white sunlight crept in through the mint-green curtains.

Instinctively, he put his hand on the metal railing. As cold as a quick swipe of antiseptic. He took off his hat, held it against his chest. He found it hard to keep his eyes on Shweta. Faded cotton dress over her body and a beige orhni over her dark hair. Body stiff on the bed, flat as unleavened bread. A small remnant of masking tape on the ball of her nose, probably to hold a nasogastric tube in place. Left foot swathed in bloody gauze. She was awake, eyes open but could barely angle her neck to look at anything but the polystyrene tiles.

'Mrs Saroop, ma'am,' he said. 'All the angels are with you.'

The nurse excused herself. Robinson pulled a stool close to the bedside, sat hunched over with his fingers steepled. On a clipboard beside her bed was scribbled, 'S. SAROOP. TETANUS GRADE 2. LOCKJAW, CANNOT SPEAK. DEBRIDEMENT OF LEFT FOOT DONE. PENICILLIN IN IV.'

Robinson began, 'Even kings get ill. In the Bible, I come across the story of a king struck down by disease. Was told to set his house straight in case the worst happened. I remember how the verse describe it. Said he was like a shepherd taking up his tent. Like his work was done. Was a feeling worse than no other. That there was nothing else left to do but wait.' A pause. 'I imagine part of you probably feel like that, Mrs Saroop. Maybe waiting for your husband to show up. It's a shame he aint had the good sense to do so yet.'

Shweta let out a soft grunt, shook her head slightly.

Robinson continued, 'I will pray for you, and I will pray Hans to regain his good sense. I believe God loves all of His people. Let the Lord be your refuge and strength in this time. For He keepeth the bones of all good people—'

'Who the hell are you?' A voice from behind him called out.

Robinson rose from the stool, looked over. A boy. Dressed in a shirt stitched from flour bags and a pair of old trousers cut off at the knee. No shoes. The staid expression of a weary accountant. But in him, Robinson could sense a mounting might, same as any animal that came across another trampling their turf. 'You are Hans's boy?' he said. Then, before the boy could repeat the question, he added, 'Name's Robinson. I work with your father.'

The boy sat on the stool, looked at his mother. 'He send you here?'

Robinson suddenly in chagrin, playing with his fingers like a schoolboy trying to justify being tardy. 'Send myself here, sir. Met your ma a couple times and figure it aint right to let time go by and I aint pay a visit.'

'Pa come with you?'

Robinson removed his hat, held it to his chest. 'No,' he said, hanging his head low. 'There's some things on this Earth I don't understand. And one of them is your pa's conduct right now. I know your pa to be a good man. One of the best.'

'OK,' was all the boy said.

Shweta's hand twitched.

The boy turned to him. 'You went to school when you was young, Mr Robinson?'

'For a little while,' he said, after a pause. 'Learn myself to read, write, do sums.'

'I can already do all of that.' The boy looked at his mother again. 'Tell pa I aint going to school in September. I have to stay home and take care of ma.'

'Perhaps that is best then,' Robinson admitted, though surprised at the boy's haste.

The boy raised his eyebrows, as if he hadn't expected such a reply. He let out a quiet sigh and his shoulders dropped a little as if a weight had been lifted. Still, he felt the further need to explain, 'Pa think the schoolhouse good for me but nobody in that schoolhouse gon miss me.'

Robinson realised he was not speaking to an ordinary child about any ordinary thing. Even his own children had never taken such sombre tones with him. He muttered under his breath. 'Boy, you listenin to me?'

The boy nodded.

'Forgive your pa when the time come.'

'That's it?'

'Yeah. If not for his sake, then for yours.'

He returned his gaze to his mother. A half minute passed before his reply. 'OK.'

When Robinson returned home that day, his wife had stewed fish with coriander and thyme. His son was playing with his daughter's toy piano. His daughter was out under the Governor plum tree, gathering some in the dip of her dress. Never ate fruit before washing them. He sat at the table, musing of what he had told the boy. To forgive his father. It seemed hypocritical now – as he was finding it hard to forgive Hans himself.

He woke early the following morning. He drove to work. Hans was on the porch. He handed him the spare gate key. 'What you givin me this for?' asked Hans.

'I gonna miss this place,' Robinson said with a tiny smile. He took his hat off, held it against his chest. 'Give the Missus my regards.'

Hans stared at the key in his hand, swallowing hard as if a sudden sadness had come over him. 'You really leavin? What you gon do?'

'There's always things to do. Don't worry bout me.' A long pause. He was hesitant to speak but at the same time, wanted to get the words out before Mrs Changoor could come out. 'Go see your wife, Hans.'

Hans cast his gaze skyward. 'Yeah.'

'Your boy is contemplating not goin back to school. Said he has to take care of his mother.' Robinson couldn't pretend that what he was saying was normal. 'Damn you, Hans, I dunno what you doin, but it aint right.'

Hans took a deep breath. 'I gon make it right.'

'You will? How?' Robinson had to ask, 'You in love with the Missus, Hans?'

'Yes,' Hans said after some hesitation, his eyes meeting the old man's. 'And Shweta too.'

'No, no, no, you can't split something like this in half. There come a time when you have to make a decision.' A quiet anger in him emerged the more he spoke. 'You playin with fire here.'

Hans folded his arms. 'Just mind your own business, Robinson. I gon figure out the right way to do this.'

Robinson couldn't help but feel heartbroken. He put his hat on. 'No servant can serve two masters. You can only be devoted to one. You gon end up despising the other. Or losing everything.'

Robinson spent the rest of the day at home helping his wife prepare lunch and dinner. He made sure his children's books and stationery was in order for the start of the new academic year. Had a quiet dinner of smoked herring with his family. When night came, he knelt before the foot of his bed and prayed for everyone in his life.

IV

A Clean Break

She woke her two sons that morning. It was still dark. Told them, 'Is time to go.'

'Now?' asked the older son.

'Yes, now now. All them crabs all wash downriver.'

'But the sun aint out yet,' said the younger one.

'The sun will scare the crabs. Come. Be good boys.'

The younger one said, 'All right but I hafta pee.'

'No time for that. We hafta be there before the sun come up.'

Their father was sleeping in the cot beside them. The older one asked, 'What bout pa?'

'No, no. Let him sleep. You know how he gon get if we wake him up.'

Birds in the sky. Fish in the river. Crickets in the night. God put them there and they never have to worry about trying to be anything else in this world. That's where God put them and they stay there and do well with it. And if they do well with it, God will put them in a better place in the next life. That's what their mother had always told her boys. That's what the woman told herself. The brothers were born one year apart. They were strong, beautiful boys. After the first one came into the world, the woman planted flowers in a barrel trough. Flowers were perpetual offerings to the gods. The perfume-weighted air of petals will keep the land warded from evil, she knew.

She was a tired woman, malnourished, skin like bitumen. Barely spoke but showed her kindness through quiet gestures and brief smiles that exposed two supernumerary teeth. Her father had sold her to her husband for ten dollars. Not long after she moved in with him to the barrack, she learnt that he believed the Kali Yuga was upon them – the slow apocalypse of the world.

Before meeting him, she had never before conceived of such a thing. The end of the world? To her, the Earth had still seemed so new and vibrant. There was an inherent peace, even among all the quarrels that people had. The world always seemed bigger than the boisterous people in it. The hum of the mountain louder than any rowdy cuss. The whispers of the water more forceful than the insults of a drunk.

At the river, she sat, her eyes halfway closed now. Her leg covered in black pockmarks, cigarette burns among the insect bites. The land warming under the coming dawn, the shadows of everything contorting and bending. In her sight, the older son picked up a shard of driftwood and punctured the mud to scare some crabs out, but none emerged.

The younger brother shouted, 'Ma, aint no crab down here!'

'Check by that pommerac tree there.' She pointed in the far distance.

The older one asked, 'Where you gon be lookin, ma?'

She didn't reply. Her mouth moved and out came a quiet prayer that she had never before rehearsed. The rhoticity of the words like the smooth rolling of the plains. The language of the earth and time gushing out of her like a dam in her had been destroyed. When the prayer concluded, she opened her eyes, gazed into the water. Looking out for some sign from Goddess Kali. Her tiger skin, black tongue, glowing cinders for eyes. A finger to point her in the right direction. A way out of this life of pain.

She'd been told that every woman bawls out to God when they push babies out of them. If God meant life to be painless, then shouldn't your coming into the world be so? But it wasn't so. Never had been. God made the canal the circumference of a shilling for a reason – all humans had to know pain. Dealing it and taking it. A mother must endure hell for her sons to be kings, she'd been told. But was that really true?

She had heard a story about a worker's brother – that his wife had just left her husband and children behind. Five children. Made a clean break. But everybody wanted to know – where to? She worked in the fields and had no other prospects. Out there, she was nothing but a woman expired. Maybe she just got on the Spanish Royal Road and started walking. Maybe hitched a ride on a donkey-cart to the capital and never returned. Or maybe her husband was lying, and she was dead in the ground somewhere. Still, the idea had been planted. And, over time, germinated. Felt like a great forest growing inside of her. The leaves spiralled inside her throat, ready to burst from her mouth, in search of the daylight. In search of fruition.

She turned to her sons and a sudden feeling of regret overcame her. Why did she bother to wake them? Were they to come with her? If they went missing, their father would look ten times as hard for them – and her. It couldn't be this way, she knew. They would eventually forget about her. Soon, the sun would rise and set the same without her. The tides would go in and out still. The morning birds' song would not falter.

They stood before her. 'Aint nothin here,' the older one said.

The wind brought a haze of pollen with it.

'Go ahead downriver,' she instructed. 'Far far down.'

She stood up, pointed, far, far away. To a stretch of gully sprawled messy with jhandi flags and gomphrenas and deadfall and broken clay pots that were believed to hold *atman*, the breath of life. All lain in dedication to the cremation of bodies. Where the river was full of ghosts.

'So far?' The younger brother stood akimbo.

'Listen to your ma. Go!'

The sons followed the river, poking the mud to no avail. They didn't spend more than three minutes there. When they returned, their mother was gone. Usually, the crackle of leaves would electrify the air, pushing against sycamore zephyrs in waves of soft sizzles.

But now the sound was absent. The wind lay dormant.

Though, from time to time, it gave the illusion that it was there – like a cowering child peeping its head through a door before going into hiding once more. That was what it felt like – everything was in hiding. The rainflies didn't buzz, the cicadas didn't click, the grass sat as still as plastic.

The boys looked at each other, puzzled. 'Ma?'

Their eyes searched silently for any sign of life, waiting for some flock of egrets to slingshot out from the bushes, waiting for a single mulletfish to brush the river's crest, even hoping for a distant whiff of cow dung. Even shit has life in it, after all. Slowly the feeling that everything was in hiding was replaced by a feeling that everything had moved on. The realisation that time had left them behind. The world like an overexposed photograph that had been burnt by leaks of light. It had marched on and all that was left was this trail of dust fading into the windless morning.

They were not only alone but abandoned.

'Ma! Ma! Ma! Ma!' The older son called out in all directions.

The brothers split up. The younger one ran upriver. The older one towards the bridge. Ran until he was out of breath. Ran until his head hurt and the light looked like careless smudges. Nearly keeled over. Suddenly, he felt a hand reach out to his shoulder. He looked up. It was her – it looked like her. In the sense that it was someone wearing a suit shaped like her. Her eyes bulbous and red from crying.

All she said was, 'My handsome Hansraj.' Then she walked to the riverbank. Pulled her dress over her head and stood bare-breasted. Raised her arms over her head like she was greeting a new day. She waded into the river, washed her skin, washed her hair. The water like cold metal against her skin.

The boy couldn't help but watch. Washed herself as if nobody were watching, her lips thin, eyes open to the world. Nipples going hard like bits of volcanic rock.

They returned to the barrack. She set up a cooking pan in the yard with a bowl of shredded cod, onions and tomatoes. Went into a crinkling sizzle as soon as the oil made contact.

Struck a match and lit a crag of padoux wood beside her. The tips black with ash. Reached into a basket beside her feet for a large breadfruit and set it in the middle, its mouth to the flame to suck up the steam. She stoked the flames under the breadfruit, the wind sweeping the smoke towards the plain. Squatted at the clay chulha, bent over to smell the cooked tomatoes, bundled like eggs in a nest, each roasted to a red wrinkle.

Two days later, her husband beat her with the blunt side of a cutlass for spilling the rice bag.

The next morning, she made her clean break. Drank a bottle of paraquat.

At her cremation, her husband only had three words: 'She was weak.'

24
A Big Stone

Late September

Dolly and Lata toted their clothes upriver, stopping at a point where it curled into the shape of a kidney. The gentle water was matched by the languid brush of breeze through the bamboo. Both were now warmed by dawnlight. On their way there, they passed a group of young boys from Bell, pants rolled up to their knees, spreading a large white blanket almost end to end where the stream narrowed. The blanket released a soft gleam as it caught the light. The boys laughed as a rush of sardines surged into it. There was a fat one, no older than twelve, no doubt the young king of the group, who took notice of Lata. Opened his mouth at her and stuck out his tongue as if to drink rain. Then flicked his tongue like it was a nervous fish. Dolly hadn't noticed the boy. Despite the physical revulsion she felt, Lata's only response was a series of protracted blinks as she walked on.

They set their baskets on the bank and began scrubbing. Dolly in a joking manner, 'If I had more childrens, I coulda have them do this for me.'

'Well, you only have me. Is me and me alone,' Lata said. A small smile.

'I never did want plenty childrens, eh. Some women out there with seven, eight childrens. How you could love all them the same? You want to do so much for so much childrens, you end up doing very little. Was me and your father making a dollar together so we aint bad off now. We aint have no house but we have a roof, and we have food in we mouth.'

'You never wonder what is like to have a house, ma?'

'If you thinkin bout house, then you better find a good boy.'

'That seem like the thing to do.'

'That is how it is. You see a woman lookin good, smellin good – is only because she find sheself a good man.'

'Like Marlee Changoor?'

Dolly pursed her lips. 'Like that one, yeah.'

'I see Mrs Changoor yesterday,' said Lata. 'She look pretty. Prettier since Mr Changoor dead and gone.'

'That is makeup and money have she lookin like that every day.' A pause, pointing at Lata. 'And don't go runnin your mouth how the man dead. We aint know that. They aint never find no body. For all you know, he run away to Venezuela. To America. Runnin away from the devil still.'

'That is why Mr Hans there now?' said Lata with a chuckle.

Dolly was unamused. She wrung a dress dry, saying, 'Hans is a damn dog in heat. I use to think of Shweta as a lucky woman. She gone through hard times as any woman, but she had Hans by she side, at least. But look what happen to she now. I try to warn she so she can't say nobody lay the cards down for she to see.'

'Is tomorrow she gettin out that hospital?'

'Yes, tomorrow.' Dolly dipped another dress.

'Ma, you wish you did marry somebody other than Umesh?' Lata tried to make it sound like small talk.

A steely look that quickly turned to sadness. 'No. Your pa was always here.' Turned to her daughter. 'And have respect for your pa name.'

'He used to beat you so much.'

'Don't talk like that. You forgettin you come from him.'

'That aint change the fact.'

'Lemme tell you somethin. If your pa was alive and somethin ever happen to me or you, bet your bottom dollar that he goin for them with a grass knife in hand.'

'Still aint change the fact.'

A heavy sigh. 'Your pa cause pain in this life, but that is cause all he know is pain. When he dead, it leave a big hole in me. I try to fill that hole with you. But still have pieces missin. Marriage is a different kinda thing. It have things you want to do and things you don't want to do. But you have to do all of it. That is the first thing the pundit will tell you bout marriage.'

'That aint soundin like the right thing.'

'You think I wanted to wipe your shit, girl? No, but I do it. When you devoted to somebody, you have to do these things.'

Lata found it hard to accept her mother's words. 'So you love pa this whole time? Even when he *buss* your eye with a belt buckle?'

Dolly spoke slowly, knowing that these ideas were difficult to accept. 'You will learn that you could love somebody who hurt you. Once they takin care of you and doin right by you.'

Lata shook her head. 'Not me.'

A scoff. 'Don't think it so easy. I rather a man like your pa, who beat me but still do right by me and you. I rather that than a man like Hans. Mash Shweta up into little pieces and leave she high and dry to pick them up while she could barely move a muscle in that hospital. And now poor Krishna have to take care of she. It aint right. What Hans dunno is that this whoring Mrs Changoor aint want no husband. You think she gon keep Hans around for long? Is only one thing she want before she move on to the next one. What Hans could give she except a good ride? He aint have no money. He aint know nobody important.' Looked Lata in the eye. 'Hans floatin through *maya*.'

'*Maya?*'

'Mistaking dreams for the real world. Hans right now in a dream. A dream where he have no wife and child. A dream where he belong to a big house instead of the life that God give him.'

'You could wake from a dream like that?'

'He will wake up. Mark my words. He and Shweta Saroop – the two of them bound by God. Every bend in the road don't bound to bring happiness.'

'That is what you think it is? A bend in the road?'

'That is what the Gita say.'

'He aint believe in no Hindu book no more. I sure he aint believe in no *maya* either.' Lata looked at her mother. 'Now that he baptise.'

Dolly stopped scrubbing again. 'Baptise?'

'He a Christian now.'

Dolly pursed her lips in confusion.

Lata went on, 'They pelt the Hindu right outta him.'

Dolly shook her head. 'Lata, Lata, what the hell you talkin bout, girl? How you know this?'

A serious pause. 'A boy tell me. He live in Bell.' And in the same breath, 'That boy, he want me to come to the Ramlila next week.'

Dolly couldn't help but feel flabbergasted. First the baptism, now this boy who's come out of nowhere. 'Lata, what the hell you talkin bout? What boy you talkin bout?'

'Dylan. That's he name. I already tell him yes.'

'Dylan?' Dolly, still taken aback.

'Yes.'

'And you want to go to the Ramlila? With this Dylan?'

'That is what I say, ma.'

A pause. 'Near Cheddi Settlement? The *big* Ramlila?'

'Yeah.'

'OK.' Dolly's voice trailed off with her gaze over the river. Sounded like it ebbed away with the water. 'And he from Bell Village?'

'Yeah.'

'I already tell you what I have to tell you bout them boys from the village—'

'I know, ma.'

'This boy, you have to make sure he is a real—'

'I like him, ma. I aint stupid.'

A tiny smile and a sigh. 'I know I aint make no stupid child. But it have plenty stupid people out there. That is what I sayin. To make sure you know that—'

'I know that, ma.'

'You still young—'

'And gettin older by the day.'

'Lata, if you aint careful—'

'I gon be careful.'

Dolly stared at her reflection in the water. 'Anything happen, you turn round and walk right back here. Any bad sign you get, listen to God. You understand? As soon as a bottle of rum come out...'

'I aint gon be stupid, ma.'

'Sometimes it aint bout being stupid, Lata. Sometimes you just in a strange place at a strange time with strange people.'

'They aint strange people.'

'You know if something happen, no man gon want you after that. You know that? Look at Niala—'

'I know.'

'You think any man gon want Niala now? I aint Rookmin, you know. I can't take on somethin like that happenin to you.'

'I know,' was all Lata could say. 'But no boy gon want me if I just stay here and get a hunchback from scrubbin clothes and shellin peas.'

'God aint give we much, Lata. But what we was given, we have to protect.' A long pause. 'How old is this boy?'

'Bout two or three years older.'

'He have a schooling?'

'Yeah. He father have a big job. But he dunno what he want to do yet.'

'He do anything he could get lock up for?' Dolly started scrubbing.

Lata laughed at the idea. 'I doubt he ever gettin lock up.'

She leaned over, kissed her daughter's temple. 'You have to dress nice. I have an old sari tuck away somewhere in a box. I gon dust it off and wash it later this week. If you did tell me before we come here, we coulda be washin it right now. You aint need no jewellery or nothin. Just the sari alone would look nice.'

Lata gave a confident nod, a great smile emerging.

'You ever went to the Ramlila, ma?'

Dolly nodded. 'Once and never again. Went with your father. Right before you was borned. We went with some fellas from the canefield. Your father was countin down the days, I remember. He wanted to see the Ravana. Big like a house. And they shoot a flaming arrow into it. And everybody watch it burn. After, your father went in the back of some bushes sober and come back out drunk. Coulda barely walk. Fallin down all over heself on the way back. I had a mind to leave him lyin right there on the road and let them throw him in holding till he piss the rum out.'

'How it look? The Ravana?'

A nod. 'Is somethin everybody should see once but that aint the point. Is bout bringing back order to things. To the whole world. Ravana, the king of demons. King of Lanka. Take away Rama's wife from him. And Rama bring a whole army for him. Cause if Ravana feel he coulda take a next man's wife, what else you feel he coulda take? But people don't go to the Ramlila for none of that. They just go to drink rum and piss themself. Just like your father when he went. When you see that Ravana burnin, take everything bad round you and throw it in that fire too.'

'That's what you do?'

'I try.'

'And what happen?'

'I dream you that night. Before you was even in this world. We was up on a mountain and I remember seeing a fire. You was that fire. And a year later, you come.'

*

The boys sat at the riverside, splitting pomegranates with their thumbs, flicking the rinds into the water. Twilight was upon them and the scarlet ibises were settling onto the mangroves in the distant marsh. Together, they sat on the logs and Krishna talked about his mother – that she was getting out of the hospital the following day. That he was nervous about taking care of her.

'Why must the chick care for the mother bird?' asked Rustam.

Tarak pursed his lips, thought of his own mother staring at the wall, staring at the water, nothing else in her world but the prayer beads. Her eyes vapid and how she bled through them as she died.

Krishna's gaze lingered at the setting sun. 'Pa never come to see her.'

'He think he see another world,' Rustam said, spitting a line of pomegranate seeds into the dirt. 'No matter how much the world turn, no world but this one.'

'Is that Marlee Changoor,' Krishna murmured. 'She like a worm in his head.'

'So what you want to do bout that?' asked Rustam.

Krishna looked him straight in the eye. 'Give them a good scare. Go up there and put scorpions in the bedroom.'

'Scorpions?' Rustam and Rudra looked at each other. 'What the hell that gonna do? We have no business with that house. And you shouldn't neither.'

Krishna was surprised with their response. 'What you mean, "I shouldn't have business?" I now tell you why I have business with it.'

The twins exchanged a glance. Then Rustam pointed at a large rock laying at the side of the river. 'Look over there. What you see?'

'A big stone,' said Krishna.

'Tarak, what you see?'

'Same thing.'

'Yes, that there is a big stone. Imagine that this evening, you leave this river, and you suddenly think about that stone. That stone would be in your head or out of your head?'

Tarak answered as if asking a question, 'The stone is both in and out of my head?'

Krishna thought hard about it. Looked at the stone, then turned away. 'If I thinkin bout the stone, then is in my head.'

Rudra snorted. Rustam said, 'How come your head don't fall off then? If you want to carry all them stones in there?' He put his arm around Krishna. 'Your pa aint here. He choose to be in another place. But you choose to carry him in your mind anyhow. And you bring him all the way here to the river. A little boy carrying a big nonsense man and a big sick woman. How you expect to walk proper?'

'It getting late, Krishna,' said Tarak, looking at the setting sun.

Krishna turned to the twins, frustrated. 'Who gon carry my ma, if not me?'

'Your ma will carry sheself. Goin down to that Changoor house aint gonna do nothin,' said Rustam, taking another bite of the pomegranate. 'Not for you and not for nobody.'

'Let's go,' Tarak said, tugging at Krishna's arm.

Krishna pulled away. 'I think you two scared of the Changoor house, is what.'

'Don't start a quarrel.' Tarak gave up his attempts to drag his cousin off.

'Changoor is trouble, Krishna,' said Rustam. 'I warnin you.'

Krishna finally made to leave with Tarak, this time of his own accord. Before they walked off, Rustam warned him again, 'You two better stay away from that house.'

Or else what? Krishna thought.

As the two cousins made their way across the field, Krishna beckoned for them to stop at a guava tree, fixed his gaze on the ground, at the upturned earth where the birds had been pecking for worms. Some of the worms still stuck in the huddle of patties, dried out by the afternoon sun, almost like flakes of rock folded into the shapes of question marks. A section of wooden fencing led up to the road, its construction abandoned before it could finish, perhaps a remnant of something greater. He imagined his father putting these very posts down, digging the holes, pouring the gravel and tamping it level.

Beside the fence was something distinct and bleached. The split skull of an agouti, perhaps, all the teeth intact on the jawbone. Krishna picked it up.

'What you doin with that?' asked Tarak, scooting beside him.

'Who the hell that woman think she is?' Krishna blurted out.

Tarak shook his head. 'You aint need to get yourself in no trouble now. Your ma still in that hospital—'

'How come he could just forget bout we, Tarak?' Krishna scraped up some pebbles and angrily threw them into the wind. He held the agouti jawbone in his hand like it was some weapon.

Tarak had no words for it.

Krishna answered his own question, 'That woman. That is why.'

'Rudra and Rustam...'

'Forget them.' Krishna spat on a guava root. 'Them's cowards.' Turned to Tarak, his eyes hot. 'We gonna go down to that damn house right now.'

Tarak held his arms over his head. 'Krishna, what the *hell*—'

'If you aint goin, I goin by myself.'

When they got to the farm, it was already dark. Tarak fidgeted the entire way. When they made their way over the fence, Krishna noted that the avocado trees had become bare.

Tarak told him, 'Since all them up in them other settlements hear that Mr Changoor gone missing, they comin every night to steal crop. Is like a free for all out here, I hear.' A nervous pause. 'They might mistake we for them – we should turn round and head back.'

Krishna didn't listen, kept on going until he came to the house. He stood before it, arms to his hips like a gunslinger. Tarak hid behind a rambutan tree. All of the lights were off. The house in hibernation. He wondered, where was Mr Changoor? What if he were to come home right now – this very night? Would things change? The more he thought about it, the more he realised how terrifying it was to disappear. Neither dead nor alive. Just missing. To be gobbled up by the world.

Krishna hadn't spoken about what he had planned to do – if there were any plan at all. Tarak remembered that there was music the last time he was here. There were only the crickets and the toads now.

Krishna turned to Tarak. 'What you think happenin in there? What you think they doin?'

Tarak bit his lip. 'Krishna, we have to go.'

'You think he on top?' he said, as if in a daze. 'Or she on top?'

'Stop!'

Krishna marched towards the porch.

Tarak gritted his teeth. 'Come back here!' he called out. 'You crazy? What you doin, boy?'

Krishna set the agouti jawbone on the rattan mini-table and walked back to the same spot he'd been standing. As he returned, Tarak scolded him, 'Why you put that damn skull there? Go and take it off that table right now!'

'Give them a scare.'

'Scare? What that gon do? You gon scare them into shootin you, is what. You givin *me* a damn scare now.'

Krishna almost in a trance now, his words slowly dripping out, 'Before my pa work here, I used to wish I could live here. You never used to wish that?'

'It aint never cross my mind,' Tarak reluctantly answered.

'That is a damn lie.'

'It aint.'

'It cross everybody mind.'

Tarak shook his head. 'The only wish I have is that we could leave here. I hate this house.'

A long pause from Krishna as he squatted. 'I hate it too,' he said, picking up a rock and, with all of his strength, pelting it towards an upstairs window.

It missed, ricocheting off the wall with a loud clatter. The light came on.

Tarak clenched his fists. Someone was coming. He could hear them. Footfalls on the staircase. More lights coming on. Krishna wasn't budging. Was as if he wanted to be caught. '*Boy, damn you!*' Tarak hissed, hoping he would snap out of whatever insanity had taken hold of him.

As soon as the door came open, the two boys fled.

Just before they did, Tarak could make out the silhouette. It was Marlee Changoor. And though he couldn't be sure – it looked like she had a gun in her hand.

25
A Snake in the Grass

Shweta was discharged from the hospital after she regained the ability to swallow. They advised that she keep to simple foods and fluids for a week or two. Rice and pigeon peas mashed with a pestle, hot ginger tea, coconut water, bananas and meatless sancoche, if the ingredients could be sourced. Ambulation was to be kept to a minimum as a quarter of her heel had been trimmed off with curettes and surgical scissors. It would be a few months until she would make a full recovery – but it was the plan, they guaranteed, so long as she kept her wound clean.

Mandeep had asked an associate at the estate to borrow a donkey-cart to transport Shweta from the hospital. Krishna and Tarak went with him to assist. The orderlies stifled a laugh when they saw the donkey defecating near the driveway before realising they might be the ones to shovel it up. They brought Shweta out onto a wheelchair and helped her onto the tray of the cart. She sat with her back against the rim of the tray, her bad foot elevated on Tarak's knee. Held her son's hand the entire way, gazing up at the sky, which had never looked more blue. Closed her eyes as the mid-morning breeze came over her hair.

They rode past the missionary school on the way. Children outside, mulling about, recess time. Others tossing a cricket ball back and forth. Near the fence, girls playing with each other's hair. The infants in circles around the flagpole. Others playing hopscotch, jump-rope. *Good riddance*, Krishna thought.

Dolly and Kalawatie were waiting in the barrack yard to help carry Shweta to her room. Rookmin sitting near the rainwater barrels, smoking a neat roll of kush. Shweta was flanked by the two waiting women, hoisted by her shoulders, as if she were levitating into the barrack. Rookmin got up, followed the women's lead. Mandeep opened the door and the women set her down on the fibre mattress. As soon as Shweta had a moment to settle, Rookmin knelt beside the woman, blew smoke into her face. Told her to breathe it in, let the sweetness into her body.

'Lord Vishnu is with this one,' she said with a grin as Shweta took a whiff.

'No doubt,' said Dolly, adjusting Shweta's legs. 'She lucky.'

Krishna said, 'Careful with the foot.'

Dolly gently set the bandaged foot on the mattress.

Rookmin said before leaving, 'I have fever grass. Lemme put it to boil.'

Though Shweta could speak again, all she had said was a word of thanks to those who helped get her home. Now she was impatient for them to leave. She wanted a moment alone in her room. She had missed the warmth of the air within the barrack. The organic feel of the wooden walls, even the misaligned planks that had fretted loose over time. The light knifing through the faults of the ceiling. No longer did she have to endure the sounds of creaking beds and midnight groans and patients squealing as tubes went in and out of their faces. The stark whiteness of the lights and uniforms. The dread fear that lurked at night when death came to visit patients in other rooms. She'd already seen the mental paralysis in some patients' faces. Perhaps a hint of it had filtered into hers.

For the next few days, everybody tried to help. Mandeep scaled coconut trees and drained the water into spent rum bottles. Dolly and Kalawatie took turns making food. Was not much, just what they could afford to spare. Was never enough to fill a stomach, but it made do. Murali put up some shillings for fresh gauze and masking tape, which Tarak fetched from the pharmacy at the village. Krishna kept his mother's wound clean, washing it with the lota and replacing the gauze. Tied sohari leaves to her feet with twine whenever she had to use the latrine. On afternoons, Tarak and Lata went out to pick guavas, bananas and sapodillas. Kept them in a crocus bag. It was a collective effort, though both Krishna and Shweta kept aware that such goodwill was temporary. Everybody had their lives to carry on with. You can only pity a person for so long, Shweta knew.

She found herself reaching out to Krishna the entire afternoon. Wanted to hold him. Perhaps because there was so little else to hold onto.

*

Dolly dug through a crate in search of the old sari. She hadn't opened it in a while and found herself in curious delight at some of the articles inside. Lining the box were dried lily petals that she had kept as a little girl. A single bangle that she had discovered at the riverside and brought home against her mother's wishes. Some of Umesh's old shirts, which he only wore when he was out in the canefield. And his trousers with the leather belt still intact.

The same belt Lata had mentioned. He had nearly taken her eye out with it. A month later, he caught the sprue. He couldn't keep any food down. He'd lost so much weight that his skin looked like it was molten candlewax. Hans managed to get him to the hospital. One night, Dolly dreamt that Umesh had died, and he was dead the following morning.

She found the sari near the bottom of the crate, held it up for the light to catch its black fabric. A band of dust had gathered at the ends of the transparent pallu, falling to the floor like light brown snow. She had a dark burgundy blouse that would pair well with it but knew that it would have to be adjusted. Lata was a small girl, and the loose blouse would make her body look outmoded. When Dolly had worn it those years ago, it was the opposite – so tight that it lumped up her back fat. She laid the articles of clothing on the mattress, assessing how she would make them complement Lata's body.

A squabble came from the yard.

Dolly went to see. Out there, Hans and Rookmin. Hans, hunched and sweaty and stumbling over his own feet. Rookmin, sitting on a crate, cool with a kush cigarette in her mouth. Dolly didn't recognise the man at first. He was attired like some census taker from the town, in a utility blazer that unflatteringly flapped in the breeze and trousers that he couldn't quite keep hitched to his waist. He bent his knees inward as if holding in a perpetual pee.

'You aint comin in here,' Rookmin told him flat. 'Let your wife rest.'

He pointed an unsteady finger at the old woman. 'I have something important to tell them.'

'You come here to cause mischief. Your wife aint need none of this. And I aint havin it neither.'

Rookmin blew some smoke.

'What the hell you want, Hans?' asked Dolly, stepping into the yard and making her presence known.

Hans turned to her. 'Listen to me...'

'You's a snake,' said Rookmin, smoke in her mouth. 'A snake in the grass.' She threw her cigarette on the dirt, extinguished it with her bare heel.

Dolly turned to the door and saw that Krishna was there – how long he had been there, she wasn't sure. Krishna looked as if he was forcing himself to stand as upright as he could. He looked at his father for a long time, trying not to act surprised by his strange, bureaucratic appearance. 'Ma sleepin,' he said.

'Don't cause no trouble with the boy, Hans,' said Rookmin, returning inside. Niala had just begun retching again.

'I have good news,' Hans said, approaching his son, smiling too widely. When Krishna said nothing, he put out his arms halfway as if to beckon for a hug. The boy stood his ground, folded his arms. He continued, 'Mrs Changoor gon help me find a house. For you and your ma!'

Krishna stood, perplexed. He was afraid to ask but did it anyway, 'And what bout you?'

Hans swallowed hard. 'How your ma doin?'

'She doin good without you,' Dolly said sternly. 'Answer the boy question.'

'The house is for you and your ma. I gon come see you every day.' The words caused the boy's entire body to wilt. When Hans saw this, he added, 'Mrs Changoor goin to buy a horse. If you come visit, I could learn you how to ride round on it.'

Krishna wondered if his father had gone mad. He looked down, couldn't find the words. Dolly took the boy's hand and led him inside, whispered to him, 'You aint need to listen to no more of this.' Turned to his father. 'Hans, you hurtin this boy.'

He pointed at the door. 'The boy is big enough to make his own decisions. All I tryin to do is a good thing and—' At the same time, Niala began to cough, hack loudly from inside.

'You aint come to do the right thing,' said Dolly. 'You just tryin to make yourself feel better.' Niala retching in the background. 'Now aint the time for that. OK, Hans?'

Hans shouted, '*Krishna!*'

Rookmin came back out. 'Hans, you cause enough trouble here. That Changoor woman chain you up bad, you hear? What if she don't help you buy no land? What if she aint give you no money? What if the Mister aint dead? What if he come home? What the hell you gon do then? Where the hell you gonna go?'

'Leave me alone, woman,' Hans muttered. '*Krishna!*'

Rookmin came up to his face. 'You leave that boy alone. And leave Shweta alone.'

'Old woman, my whole life, you aint never like me.'

'I like you even less now.'

He looked her straight in the eye. 'Don't say another word to me.'

She did the same. 'You have demons in you.'

Dolly called out, 'Rookmin, just let him be.'

Hans cleared his throat. 'Rookmin, I gonna—'

'You no good! Weak! Just like your father!'

Hans grabbed the old lady's arm, spun her counter-clockwise. She yanked her arm back, landed on the dirt with great thud, accompanied by a violent pop. Her face twisted, each wrinkle showing. Held onto her shoulder as she writhed on the ground.

'*Hans, stop!*' exclaimed Dolly. She ran into her room, grabbed the belt.

Ran up to Hans, began whipping him with it. Whipping like she had eight arms.

'I aint—!' he cried out, holding his arm up.

Then another joined in the frenzy. White Lady came scampering out from the slagheap, bit Hans on the calf. Bit to draw blood. Her snarl made her mouth edge up to her nose. All teeth bared.

Hans kicked the dog off him before running into the field. As Hans fled, Rookmin raced over to a rock that was lying in the yard. With her good hand, she flung it at him, but it landed just beyond the man's feet. Then she sat on the crate, working to catch her breath. Dolly fetched some daru for the old woman, reminding her to sit still. Rookmin took a long swig before Dolly offered her the belt. The old woman bit down hard on the leather and closed her eyes. She barely winced as Dolly snapped the shoulder back into place.

26
A Testament to Life

October

It was twilight when Shweta asked Rookmin to take her for a walk. Two weeks had passed, and her legs had begun to regain their strength. Rookmin was hesitant at first but decided that a short stroll would do them both good. She took Shweta down to the bison pond, just five minutes from the barrack. The wind had picked up and the sugarcane arrows swayed like heraldic banderoles beneath the sunset. An old samaan overlooked the pond, silently eyeing the two as they paced a slow circle around it. When they were done, they settled onto the grass. A lone bison lowed behind them as if annoyed by their presence.

'The baby name is Ananda,' Rookmin told her. 'It was Murali who name him. Truly, it shoulda be Niala to name the child. But the nurses ask him for a name, and he give them one.' A pause. 'Ananda is a good name. He and Niala still in the hospital. They just want to make sure everything OK with them. But it lookin good.'

Shweta said, 'I always know your daughter woulda pull through.' She hadn't believed it but was now happy to be wrong.

'He have skin light as cream. And green eyes, they say. Green as a green fig.' Pride swelled in Rookmin's voice. 'He is blessed. A testament to life. Better be, after what what my daughter gone through.'

'Cleanin up all that vomit every day,' Shweta said, nodding.

'Is more than that,' said Rookmin. 'Murali tell me a story long time ago when he come down with a bad fever. He say his pa take him down to Tully Settlement, to a goat farm. His pa say that a rakshasa had gone in him, was killin him dead. The sadhu tell them they needed to go down to the goat farm.'

'Why a goat farm?'

'For a goat.'

'To do what?'

'Kill it and drink the blood.' Rookmin looked up at the sky. 'Murali say he aint want to do it. He say is different from when you kill a fowl. Fowls is stupid creatures, he say. Goats is just stubborn. So he say he just stand there with the knife in his hand for a long time. But his pa run outta patience and take his arm and guide the knife cross the goat scruff. They had a bowl ready to collect the blood. His pa drink some and then give the bowl to Murali.'

Shweta imagined the situation, her own tongue contracting at the thought. She could imagine the bowl in the boy's hand, feeling like a great weight, his bones suddenly gone brittle. She didn't have to ask if Murali drank the blood. Rookmin went on, 'He get better and better as the days went by. The goat blood drive that rakshasa right out. He aint have to believe in the blood for it to work. So I thought bout it with Niala. She aint believe in nothin.'

The old woman kept her eyes in the sky as if waiting for it to fall. She said, 'Have a sense of duty that we all bound to.' The woman's eyes came upon Shweta. It was getting dark now.

'That's true,' was all Shweta could say to that.

Rookmin pulled out some prayer beads that were tucked to the side of her sari. Began fiddling with them. 'That goat farm still there today. I walk all the way there. Leave home before dawn and get there round sunrise. Crooked red building, look like they paint it in blood.'

'When you went?'

'About two days back. The man in charge – he say he always start early in the mornin. Had goat and sheep and cattle in there. He say he would say prayers for them and kill them with this bolt gun. Had blood on his beard. He bring a bull and he shoot a bolt into he head. It aint gone all the way through. So his bull start to trample, eyes bleedin out. He shoot it again and it fall flat. I aint lyin, girl – I aint frighten of nothin and it frighten me to see it. I ask him how he could do it. He tell me that everything he kill return to God. That he wish he could offer up a thousand goats to God a day if he coulda afford it. Everything, heart, muscle, guts, gullet in the name of God.' She tucked the prayer beads back into her sari and looked in Shweta's eyes.

Shweta found herself on the verge of tears hearing about the bull. The act of killing was never supposed to be a sane thing. But nobody doing something for years would believe they're doing the wrong thing. Everyone tries to find a way to justify their existence. 'The goat gone down with a single bolt. And I get the blood and bring it back for Niala and...'

'The baby borned good.'

'Yes.' Rookmin nodded. 'Bless Niala and bless that child. Fair skin, green eyes.' A pause. 'Is best that it happen this way. Last year, Murali was out and about in that village tryin to get a good man for she. But every time he come back, he say Bell Village have no good men. None of them was no good. One of them lie bout havin a job. One wife dead and wanted Niala to change she name to the dead wife name. Another one, they say beat a woman to death.'

Shweta thought about her own husband. Living in a big house up on a hill, now filled with withering trees and conspiracies. Rookmin had never said who Niala's baby's father was and nobody ever asked. Rookmin continued, 'I say Niala aint need no husband. I say she could raise that child sheself. He gon be happy enough. He gon have some fun in this world, I will make sure as long as my heart beatin. I say forget man. Man will destroy you.'

A sudden wave of melancholy came over Shweta. She grabbed onto the old lady and burst into tears. Grabbed onto her torso like the earth would suddenly give way and devour her. Moved her hands down to a thin ring of exposed skin at the old woman's bodice. The skin was hardened, but not hard. Hans's body had been lined with calluses. Lumps like ruined seeds tucked into the flesh. The old woman held her back. Frogs croaked softly from behind the bushes.

It quickly turned full dark. A black ridge of clouds moved above them, clearing the way for the moon. Swifts flew overhead, followed by a tinkle of cold rain. Both women remained as they were, unmoving as figurines in a diorama. The aftertone of thunder high above.

Rookmin motioned for them to get up. 'Come, girl,' she said. 'The rain comin down soon.'

She grabbed onto Shweta's arm, but Shweta pulled away, shook her head. Rookmin leaned against her. 'You wan stay in this rain?'

Yes, Shweta thought, still crying. She wanted to stay and let sickness befall her.

'I aint strong enough to lift you up,' said Rookmin, getting up. The drizzle had started. 'But I gon make some tea for you when you reach inside. If I stay out here, I gon catch cold. I want to live to see my grandson grow up.' With that, she was gone.

As the rain came down, Shweta walked to the shallow end of the pond and into the water. Seated herself so that the armada of water lilies ebbed around her elbows. The steely-blue of the plains seemed so far away. Everything losing its outline in the blur of the rain. She submerged herself, let the water take her. Her body now floating carefree as driftwood. Her mouth underwater, she let out a long scream. Screamed until she felt like her head would explode.

27
A Feast for Demons, A Feast for Gods

The plan was for Lata to meet Dylan and his friends at the railway station at 5.30 p.m., sit at the kerb, take their first drink there. Then slowly continue drinking all the way on the forty-minute trek up to the Cheddi Settlement grounds to see the Ramlila celebrations. Aimed to get there after sundown, aimed to get peak drunk as the effigy of Ravana burned. Then somehow, in their midnight incoherence, make their way back on the dark road with only a flambeau and their wits.

Alfonse bought the rum around noon from a pub outside of the village. He, Larry and Dylan pooled up money for three bottles, which they packed into brown paper bags. None of them were of drinking age, but Alfonse's moustache was bushy enough to fool the clerk. They wouldn't dare purchase the alcohol from a pub in Bell because Dylan's father knew all the owners well. None of them were going to risk agitating the man who carried the title DSP.

Lata had arrived a half hour early. The October days were shorter, so the sun was already halfway down, leaving the sky strewn with fiery cirrus. Everywhere bathed in golden light. The railway station at evening time was well lit and fairly populated. Was like a magnetic force pulled the youths there by the twilight. Like evening birds to the trees. She only knew stories, descriptions. Impromptu wrestling rounds. Top-spinning matches. Drumming and rhythm and singing. Girls and gossip and gambling. That evening, there were only a few people mulling around, not one of them paying her any mind. She sat on the kerb by herself, waiting, looking out at the road for Dylan and his friends. She wrapped her pallu around her neck as the breeze picked up. Her mother had adjusted the blouse to go with her black sari.

Five-thirty came and still no Dylan.

She began to fear that no one was coming. Or perhaps they had all gone ahead without her. She wondered if to start on the road by herself. Her mother's warning shot to mind – anything odd happens, turn right around and return to the barrack. She kept optimistic as the minutes stretched longer and longer.

*

What was most shocking to Krishna was that the rabbit was alive just ten breaths ago. Now it was not only dead but dismembered. Vivisected. The rabbit's head, looking flatter than it really was, lay at Rustam's feet while Rudra tore off the limbs with his bare hands. Did it with utmost poise and self-assurance. His tugging steadfast, determined like a bellringer's hands. Dutiful, habituated. They did this over the fire that they built beside their riverside shack. Krishna in a humid delirium while the twins remained focused as apothecaries. White Lady sat up to watch, her ears pinned back, wagging her tail, the glow of the vermilion flame in her eyes. Tarak sat a close distance away, near to the river, watching the moonlight zigzag in the water.

The rabbit's head took two final gulps of air after it came off its body. Three other live rabbits stayed crouched in a cage, looking on as if nothing of significance had just taken place. So lay the nature of things.

Using the blade, Rudra made a longitudinal cut through the abdomen, clean and graceful like the glide of a sarangi's bow. The pelt came off easily. As if it were not part of the rabbit's body, but a rabbit's uniform. He pulled the fur off the feet like one would remove socks. Undressed the rabbit until it was only gummy membrane. The torso came open with the jiggle of a young woman's breast.

Unexpectedly to Krishna, the insides yielded no smell. The innards reminded him of the sweet smorgasbord one would find at a Diwali celebration. The dark brown of the liver a bulb of gulab jamun. The beating red of cardiac muscle as rose rasmalai. The colon as a bright spiral of jelabi. The rest of the pale squishy parts like prasada. A feast for gods. All delight inside, all to be consumed.

Krishna felt vulgar looking on as the pieces were plucked. It wasn't vulgar like spying behind the curtain. Or watching through a peephole. There was nakedness and then there was *this*. The clockwork of an animal. All the humours and viscera and rugae and protoplasms. There was more than just blood and flesh to this body. All that had been wound so tight coming undone as Rudra's blade cut deeper and deeper. Bones snapping and crunching like stalks of sugarcane. Tendons fibrous like a sucked orange's vesicles. Blood gushing as if the rabbit were still alive. Gushing even as Rudra ripped out its organs and deposited them into a metal bowl. Like the body refused to surrender to death.

Rustam, noticing Krishna's anxious expression, said to him, 'You lookin at this meat like you want to eat it raw.'

The boy shook his head. 'I's just lookin.'

'What bout you, Tarak?' asked Rustam.

Tarak was still at the river. 'Raw meat aint no interest to me.'

A sharklike smile from Rudra. Rustam said, 'You's raw meat. A pile of raw meat.'

'I think I's more than raw meat,' said Tarak, looking at the other caged rabbits. 'Have more to a person than that.' Turned to the dead rabbit. Its tongue had begun to slither out of its decapitated head.

Rustam nodded. 'Don't have no right and wrong no more, not since we share blood with you. It only have the Corbeau. Nothin now but the *blood power*.'

Rudra prepared a coal pot with water, set it on the fire. Threw the rabbit parts in.

★

Six p.m. The sun was nearly down.

They finally arrived. Dylan, Larry, Alfonse and someone else. As they came into view, she realised it was Mikey. Mikey the Mosquito. That was Dylan's nickname for his little brother. Buzzing in their ears. Telling secrets that nobody cared about.

Mikey sat on the edge of the kerb, peering out at the yard where a few others mulled around. She already knew why. Dylan's one vice was that he couldn't hold his liquor. Their father initially did not mind Dylan sitting at the plastered kerbs at the station to have a beer or two. But he had to promise that he wouldn't drink the hard stuff – no rum, no whiskey and certainly none of that Chinese baiju. A promise kept for two weeks. Maybe one. One taste opened the floodgates. Dylan would end up on the railway lawn that he himself helped tend, splayed like a boxer knocked out by a haymaker. It was an embarrassment for the deputy superintendent to see his son like this. Like a vagrant. The worst type of drunk. The type that pissed themselves in public like a baby.

So now Dylan wasn't allowed to go anywhere without Mikey.

The three older boys were passing around a bottle of rum, taking long swigs. Mikey stood by himself, far from the others. Larry pointed to Lata's feet, said to Dylan with a laugh, 'These barrack girls have a different kinda style. You see what happenin here? She wearing two different sandals. You seein that?'

Lata didn't have to look. Her left sandal was a banana colour and the right was a dark-russet brown. 'I couldn't find the other side to my good sandals,' she said, her chin up.

'Why you aint wear two of the same kind then?' Dylan asked with a chuckle.

'Cause *this one*,' and she wiggled the russet brown one, 'don't hurt my foot. But it missing the other side. The other one hurt my foot. But I rather one foot hurt than both hurt. Is a long walk.'

Brought a tiny smile out of Mikey.

Dylan shook his head, also smiling. 'That's somethin else.'

Lata nodded. 'Make the most sense to me. I walk all the way up to this station and my foot aint hurtin yet. I gon get some blisters after today but at least it would only be on one foot.' A pause. 'You like my sari?' A brief twirl. 'This my ma own. She fix it up for me.'

Dylan took another swig from the bottle. 'It look good. Nothin wrong with it.'

He handed her the bottle. She took a drink of the rum.

They started on the road. On the way there, she drank. The more she did, the more she felt the need to talk about anything and everything. Anything that her gaze fell upon was met with a comment. The eastbound birds, the unnatural tilt of a coconut tree, the rosy fingers of the crepuscular clouds, the old houses up on the hills. The sandflies moving in a slow circle, the cows on their way home, the way they reminded her of her mother. As they came closer to Cheddi Settlement, Dylan related a story his father had told him.

Cheddi Settlement was notorious for men who brewed and sold bush rum. Sold it for cheap, by keg and by bottle. Pretended to be livestock farmers and bought large amounts of molasses and cane rinds. Brewed it on the foothills of the range, called it *mountain dew.* Came down armed with cutlasses in case a competitor tried to break one of their donkey's legs. The way to Cheddi Settlement wasn't treacherous but it was flanked with elements that could be. On the path, squatters put up shacks on the hillocks. In some of those shacks were thieves, rapists, con men.

'You gon protect me?' she asked, already drunk.

'I was dependin on you to protect we,' Dylan said, prompting a laugh from his friends.

'What make you think I could protect you?'

Larry said, 'You have more gods than we, is why.'

Lata reached for the bottle. 'You should convert to a Hindu then.'

'I just aint believe in that. Hindu shit aint make sense.'

'Same here,' Alfonse threw in.

Lata asked, 'You know the Ramlila is a religious Hindu festival?'

'Religious?' Dylan took the bottle from her. 'Not if we gon be there.'

*

Tarak was the only one who didn't eat the boiled rabbit. White Lady ate the bones. When they were done, Rustam said to Krishna, 'You have things on your mind.'

He couldn't shake his father's image in his new clothes – shifting from side to side as if the fabric made him itch. It enraged him – but at the same time, made him shamefully curious of the man's new lifestyle. It couldn't last. Hans looked so desperate and stupid dressed like he was, Krishna thought. Like a bird garbed in another's plumes. He then pictured Lata in her mother's old sari and mismatched sandals, eager to impress a crowd similarly eager to insult her. He'd warned her – there was nothing else he could do. His mind catapulted to Niala before the pregnancy. Before she lay on the ground for nine months, curled like a dead centipede, an insect in the dirt ground. He replaced Lata in her position. Vomiting buckets of excreta. No control over pee, over shit, every slop, every discharge. Before the pregnancy, she had a bright soul, just like Lata. Bit of a tomboy, to her mother's chagrin. Took her brother on expeditions through the mud to pick guavas. In her good dress, napped under the samaan tree. Played with the donkeys and bison near the loading station, dilating her nostrils to mimic them. All of that had been destroyed, Krishna thought. It was hard to imagine that she once had prospects.

He didn't want to bring it up. Didn't want to think about it again. Felt wretched and jealous and pathetic thinking about it. What was the point anyway? She only liked boys who could get her out of the barrack. Drug her and dress her up in dreams. No different from his father. Nothing mattered to these people except themselves.

Nevertheless, there was a small part of him that wondered if he was wrong. That there was a way to transcend bodies, to hop into another life and live it to its fullest. Perhaps there was more to his father's chameleonic move. That he was fed up of being berated and mistreated by the world. Kneeling before schoolmasters and desk sergeants. Waking up filthy in a world that equated cleanliness to godliness. That it was something that had added up over time, greater than the sum of its parts. Or perhaps it had been spontaneous. Still, there was that small notion, nettling Krishna like a boil in his cheek, that he was underestimating his father.

*

When Lata crossed into Cheddi Settlement, she could already hear the music. She and the others followed the tune, made their way to the grounds. There in the moonlight stood the demon king Ravana.

The biggest one yet. The structure was more meticulous than any other in the village. It was at least triple the height of the tallest man. Bamboo had been split and peeled to make the wicker for the skeleton. Chicken wire as the ligaments that held it together. Old bedsheets painted and pasted with gum onto bamboo. The main head hand-painted with the sharp owl-like pupils and the grimace of a rabid bat. The protruding moustache made from cocoyea branches slicked and dipped in black paint. The other nine heads, oval cuts of wood strapped to a plank that pierced the central head like a spear.

The spectacle was the centrepiece of Ramlila. Plays and costumes and colours and songs. It was where friends converged, husbands met wives and enemies were forced into eye contact. A transaction of recipes and gardening tips and gossip. Where one learnt that nani's curry gave everyone diarrhoea. Or that beti's Muslim son secretly ate swine or tantie's eldest daughter was frigid. In the background, two tabla players fiddled with a rhythm. Then the tune-up of a harmonium.

The only lights now were the moonlight and several clay deyas surrounding the stage to the front. The jaws of the mountain black in the far reaches. The rum had turned Lata into an octopus, made her grow several arms. She couldn't stop wrapping them around Dylan. But each time she tried to keep a grip, he became very slippery. She as well. She slid right off him like he was a mossy rock. Fell on the grass, laughing.

Mikey shook his head and walked off.

Alfonse said, 'Look how this girl acting. She aint never drink a drop in she life.' He and Larry then turned to head into the darkness towards some trees. They took the rum with them.

Larry asked, 'You stayin with the girl?'

'You go ahead.'

'Where them going?' Lata asked Dylan.

'To drink. Can't drink with these pundits watchin.'

'Where your brother gone?' she asked, noticing that Mikey had strayed.

'Who cares?'

They sat at the back, far from the stage. Everyone was on a black tarpaulin stretched over the grass. An old pundit in his eggshell dhoti took centre stage before the audience. Seemed as old as the Sanskrit chaupai he was reciting. The moonlight reflected off a large cyst on his forehead. Two old women in front of them argued about the amount of ghee needed to prepare prasada. The mothers forced their children to sit at the front, thinking they would extract some sort of meaning from the pundit's poem.

'Look at all these people here,' Lata said as if she'd just now noticed them. 'You think all these people from here? Or you think them come from all over – like we?'

Dylan said, 'They come from the other settlements, I sure.'

'You know anybody here?'

Shook his head. 'Nah.'

Lata's attention drifted to the large effigy of Ravana. 'I want to see them burn that thing down,' she said. 'That look like it take weeks to put up. It bigger than any house here. Imagine them build that whole big thing just to burn it down.'

*

Tarak glanced over at Krishna, who slumped his shoulders. 'Krishna, you know your ma aint doin good. Let's head back.'

Krishna kept his eyes fixed on a heap of wood beside them. A single leaf caught in a spiderweb there. 'I want the mushrooms. I want the blood power.'

Tarak let out a sigh. 'I aint think that's a good idea, Krishna.'

Rustam eyed him. 'You denyin the boy?'

'I aint,' Tarak said, jerking his shoulder. 'I's just lookin out for my cousin.' He turned to Krishna. 'You take that shit, you gon do somethin stupid. You gon go back up to that Changoor house again.'

Rudra shot a look at his brother. Rustam asked, '*Again?* What you mean, *again*?'

Krishna would've preferred it not be known. But now that it had been said, he had no regrets. They were supposed to have an oath, weren't they? Their souls criss-crossing. They were supposed to have the same blood. If his blood boiled, so should theirs. What rippled through him should ripple through them. What happened to that? It felt more like he and Tarak were the twins' subordinates. He hated feeling so powerless.

Rustam came up to Krishna, so close that their noses almost touched. 'What the hell you was doin at that house? You stupid? We agree it was final – that we have no business—'

'Who's you to call me stupid?' Krishna stepped back, folded his arms.

Rustam pointed at Krishna's eye, still slightly purple. 'You want the police to black up the other eye? If they aint gonna do it, I will.'

'Calm down,' Tarak sighed. Rudra held up his hand, showing the same sentiment.

'Don't tell me what to do,' Krishna grunted. 'I gon burn that house down if I want to.'

Tarak got up, tried to separate the two boys. 'Krishna, shut your mouth.'

'You better be jokin, boy!' said Rustam, laughing.

'*IS JUST A WOMAN!*' Krishna stomped the ground. 'Is not God livin there! Is just a woman and a man!' Some scattered leaves swept up as he stamped his feet. The dust like fine white ash in the night. The guttering fire reflecting off his hot, sweaty face.

Rudra raised his eyebrows. White Lady lifted her head.

Tarak got up to calm Krishna down. Went behind him, patting his elbows, trying his best to get him to sit. The rabbits huddled into a corner of their cage, the tips of their ears silver in the moonlight. Krishna did not budge, stubborn as a man seeking revenge for a life unlived.

'You watch yourself,' Rustam's unflustered tone slowly evaporating, leaving behind something cold at its core. His voice trying hard to regain its coolly rational timbre. 'You think you strong but you can't even take down some nancyboy schoolboys by yourself.'

Krishna gnashed his teeth. 'Say I gon down there and break all the windows. What you gon do?'

'You give him them damn mushrooms, he might really do it.' Tarak was serious.

*

When the pundit was done, two men began the music. They were cross-legged on a stage of pallet boards lined with old brocade sheets. Fingers fluttered over the tabla and sarangi. Dylan couldn't sit still. Lata noticed his eyes kept straying to the dark trees. She asked, 'They still down there drinkin?'

'Yeah.'

'You want to go with them?'

'I good here for now.'

She lit up a little until he added, 'I might check them just now.'

Her gaze fell on a little bareback boy at the front dressed as Lord Shiva, body patted down with sky-blue makeup and the front of his hair tied in a bun. A smear of scarlet sindoor on his forehead. Two bead necklaces, too large for him, draped his neck. Dylan was getting more and more impatient.

'Their hand aint getting tired?' He nodded at the tabla players. 'I aint think they burnin this ugly thing now.'

'You want to take a walk?'

'OK.'

They began a slow circle around the grounds, staying close enough where they could still hear the music. 'You aint worryin bout your brother?' she asked.

'He probably on his way back home to tell my pa bout the drinkin,' he said, folding his arms as if a wind chill hit him. 'That is the kind of person Mikey is. You aint have no brothers?'

'Nah, is just me.' In the same breath, 'I feel like if I had a bigger brother, life woulda be a little easier.'

'Why you say that?'

She pursed her lips, feeling glad to tell him the truth. Though she wasn't sure if it was her or the alcohol drawing the words out. 'I think he woulda pull my pa off my ma when he use to beat she. Pa dead now. But it aint easy with just me and ma.'

He looked at her. 'Your pa beat your ma? Like bad?'

She slinked in closer to him. 'Yeah. I aint know what to do. I couldn't do nothin...'

He gave her a soft nudge, moved back. 'You hate him?' His tone direct.

Lata stopped in her path. 'I try not to. I aint want hate in my heart. I know I wanted to leave and never come back. But I aint want to carry the hate with me. My ma tell me that a room – like where we live – is one of the smallest places in the world. And we's just small people living in that room. So she aint have room for that kinda hate.'

He turned to the Ravana, still standing high. 'When you think they gon stop singing and burn that piece of shit?'

For a second, Lata was taken aback that he had nothing to say to her response. But she didn't dwell on it. 'They hafta do it before them old ladies fall asleep.' She paused, 'You seem sour.'

'I aint sour.'

'Sure?'

'Yeah, just bored. And fed up of all this music.'

She came closer again, put her hand on his cheek. Moved in for a kiss.

And so they did. Ended as soon as it started. She moved in again, but the kiss couldn't sustain itself. 'You taste so bad,' he said.

She hugged herself as a cold breeze blew by. 'What you wanna do now?'

'Find Larry and Alfonse.' They headed down to the trees, where it was darker than anywhere else. She couldn't see anyone's face, but it was apparent there were many men down there. Everyone just a black blob. Larry passed the bottle to Lata, who took several long gulps. The bottle passed around but by the time it got to Dylan, it was empty.

'Open the next bottle,' he said.

Larry slurred, laughing, 'The rum done, Dylan, boy. We drink it out.'

Alfonse added, 'We? Is *you*! You and your girlfriend!'

Lata got on her knees, began to retch.

'So what we gon do now?' Dylan asked.

'You aint gon see bout your girlfriend?'

'Mind your business.'

Lata opened her mouth to vomit but nothing emerged.

Larry suggested, 'I know a fella living a lil ways from here. He have so much *mountain dew*, it flowing out of he ears. We aint doin nothin here anyway. We could head over there.'

Lata suddenly felt very tired. Wanted nothing more than to sleep. 'I wan stay right here,' she said, the words bumbling out. 'Not no house.'

'I vote for the mountain dew,' said Alfonse.

They started on their way back to the grounds.

Lata trailed behind. 'Dylan, you… leavin me here?' But they were already gone.

The darkness closed in quickly. 'Dylan… ?'

*

Krishna and Rustam locked eyes and for that moment, Tarak wasn't sure what was going to happen. White Lady's tail stood up. Tarak motioned for her to keep still. Rudra kept his eyes on the fire.

Suddenly, Krishna rushed over to the rabbit cage. Knocked it down. Stood over it as if he didn't expect it to topple. An unnecessary display of power that he immediately regretted. The cage door flung open, the three rabbits pushing out.

Rudra stood up now, his expression like a mother annoyed by her baby's cries.

For a few seconds, Tarak remained in his braced position, eyes shut. When he reopened them, he saw the three blanched shapes limping away from the fire, melting into the dark. White Lady took off after them, disappeared as well. Tarak whistled for her to come back but to no avail. Rustam calmly walked over to Krishna, and they stood face to face, dwarfed by the bamboo.

Not even Tarak saw when Rustam raised his fist to Krishna. It happened in an instant, was like time had skipped. Krishna lay on the dirt, spitting out a rope of blood. Looking up, he released a howl at the twins. Tarak rushed over to get him, but he could not keep hold of any part of his body. Krishna kicked on the ground like an inconsolable griever at a pyre.

'Krishna, BEHAVE!' Tarak finally cried out.

Krishna morphed into a whirlwind of limbs, rising up to meet Rustam, their grunts in a vehement tremolo. Tarak fought with all his might to stop the scrap as it edged closer to the fireside. He could at least dance around them, lead them towards the river instead. His eyes fell upon an old iron pail beside the logs, filled with the stench of aged animal flesh. Thought of dipping it into the chilly river and splashing the two as if they were stray dogs battling in the barrack yard.

Rudra went into the shed. Rustam raised his hand as if to stop him but quickly changed his mind. When Rudra came back, he returned with something in hand. A knife. The flickering glow of firelight reflected in the steel. He held it up over Krishna.

'Rudra, stop!' Tarak cried out.

With all his might, Rudra plunged the knife into a tree stump beside the squabble. Krishna shrieked, scooting and scuttling away. His foot nearly brushed against the firewood. A silence came upon the group. The wind winnowed through the bamboo again, tiny currents of dust coming up from the ground as if the world had long mouldered.

Rudra strolled over to the knife, picked it up. Held it with two hands, arms upraised to the moon. The fire wavering behind him. 'Changoor try to kill we with this,' Rudra spoke, his voice almost exactly like his brother's. He took the blade back to the shed.

'Changoor?' Tarak said, turning to Rustam, his hand to his still-racing heart. '*Dalton* Changoor?'

Krishna was breathing too hard to say anything.

Rustam said flatly, 'We aint kill him.'

Tarak looked at him in disbelief. Krishna was still trying to catch his breath. Both of them, no words whatsoever. Nothing but crickets and the light slush of water. Something dense and sour in their throats, the cousins and the brothers wary of each other now. Some scheme cunningly maintained. A wind picked up, rustled the bamboo. The four returned to the fireside, the cousins and then the brothers. From where they sat, the brothers cast longer shadows. Their unyielding expressions showed no misgivings.

Rudra sat before the fire once again, motioning for the boys to do the same. 'He come to we. Few months back. It was rainin like death.'

Tarak squinted. '*He* come to you?'

'Yes. Right here, he come.' Rudra pointed at the ground. 'This very river...'

'Why the hell he would come here?'

'Just listen,' said Rustam.

Rudra tossed a piece of wood into the fire. 'Remember when we tell you how he shoot at us that day? He thought we come for his life. Somethin bout how our pa send we to kill him. Kill the wife too.'

'We aint know nothin bout that,' Rustam threw in.

Rudra added, 'Whatever business pa had with Changoor aint known to us.'

'But he had business with we now, firing that gun at we.' Rustam made a fist.

'We couldn't let him get away with that. So we come back one night. All we was gonna do was slash the tyres of that truck.'

'I suppose we was too slow.' Rustam sounded ashamed to say the words. 'He see we comin up from the back. Then he run inside the house – probably to get his car keys. But we was already gone.'

Rudra continued, 'So we come back here. The rain come down by then. We aint never think a man like that woulda find we here, but he find we. He drive his pickup off the road and come runnin down to this river. That night, the rain was comin down like God angry with the world. Loud. The thunder, loud. We was in the shack there. He was sneaky. I remember when I first see him. All I see was the eyes. He stab me. Right in the hand.' Rudra pointed to his hand that had been bandaged this whole time. 'With that dagger I just show you.'

Rustam added, 'An inch closer and the thumb woulda come right off. You could imagine life is like without a thumb?' He snapped his fingers twice. 'Can't do that. Can't hold your prick to piss. Can't even wipe your ass proper.'

Rudra picked up, 'After that, he crack a shot out at me. Then crack one out at Rustam.'

'He had a gun?' asked Krishna, similarly enthralled and perplexed. 'What happen to the knife?'

Rudra said, 'The knife was in my skin.'

Rustam added, 'If he come out with the gun first, both of we woulda be the dead ones.'

'But if you aint kill him,' said Krishna, 'how come he dead?'

The twins looked at each other. Rudra turned to the shack and came back out with a silver revolver. Tarak stared at it as if it were something otherworldly. Even just the sight of it sent a chill down his spine. Rudra handed it to Rustam, who held it by the barrel end. Without a word, Rudra took the pail, scooped up water from the river and doused the fire. There was only moonlight and shadow now, each of the boys just a dark, wispy outline. The shrubs and the bamboo susurrating around them.

'We get the hell out,' Rustam finally began. 'We run through the bamboo there till we see some lights. Was the pickup. He leave the engine runnin. The driver door was open. We jump inside and lock all the doors. Not the smartest thing cause he coulda just shoot we through the glass. But he aint do that. He run up to the doors, bangin on it. We couldn't even see him, the rain was comin down so hard. But we coulda see the gun. He was holdin it like this.' Still holding the barrel of the revolver, Rustam moved his hand in slow, tapping motions. 'Trying to break the windscreen with the grip.'

'And then it gone off,' Rudra concluded.

'It gone off?' asked Krishna, on the edge of his seat.

Rudra pointed to his neck.

'He dead like an ass. It gone off and *right through*,' said Rustam, pointing to his neck as well. 'So I tell you, we aint kill the man. But who gon to believe that?'

'So you understand now? If you cause trouble at that Changoor house tonight, tomorrow, any day of the year,' Rudra said, 'then is not only jail. They will take we to hang.'

Krishna was a little relieved to see that the barricade around the Lakhan brothers was more fragile than they had impressed upon the land. That perhaps when they surveyed the darkness, they were witness to the same gaps of nothingness as everyone else. Victims of the same divine violence. An owl mourned from the west. The stars awaiting approbation from their weary minds.

'So where you put the body?' asked Tarak, steepling his fingers.

'Where nobody would find it,' was all Rustam was willing to say.

'And you drive that car into that pond,' Tarak muttered, piecing it all together.

Rustam nodded. 'Was still rainin like crazy and we didn't know what else to do. So we drive it to the pond, let it roll into the water. When it went in that water, lemme tell you, we thought it woulda never go under.'

'But it come back up,' Tarak asked. 'What bout the body? What if they find that?'

'I tell you already, nobody goin to find it.' Rustam moved his arms as if he were flapping giant wings. 'It all over the land and sky by now.'

Krishna remembered the rumour of the overseer – torn apart by vultures.

'Tonight aint bout Dalton Changoor,' said Rudra, going into the shack. He came out with a burlap bag. Handed an orange mushroom to Krishna and one to Tarak. They sat facing each other. There was no condensed milk this time.

Krishna popped the mushroom into his mouth.

Damn you, Krishna, Tarak thought, doing the same.

The boys lay on the ground, waiting for the blood power to take hold. As it did, Krishna rose from the dirt like the reanimated dead. Covered his eyes as if a blinding light had manifested before them, held his head as if it had ignited like a wild brazier. He spotted White Lady. Wagging her tail. She entered a thicket and he followed.

She appeared as a white smear in the inky dark. Like bright mist from afar, almost. She sat on the dirt, her wagging tail a distortion of the shadows around her. Her mouth smudged with blood. The yellow handkerchief around her neck had flecks of red. Two mangled rabbits behind the dog, halfway eaten.

The river was lonely, yet he could hear voices, laughter. The aggregate knowledge of the people lost in mud and shale. Millennia of land fading into the night. Somewhere out there, he remembered, a demon was on fire.

*

Lata groaned. It was difficult to place anything when she started coming to her senses. Struggling to find the truth. The truth was that she had been drinking. All of them had. The truth was that they left the station sober, arrived drunk. The truth was that Dylan and his friends left to get more rum. And she put her head down on the grass. Blacked out. The truth stopped at the moment she woke up into this darkness. She didn't know what happened to the truth or what she and God did with it.

She felt like she was being levitated. Carried somewhere.

'Dylan? Dylan?' Moving her lips to say the name, at least. Or trying to. The pallu had been stuffed into her mouth. But the voices that returned to her didn't belong to Dylan or his friends. They didn't seem to speak to her, only to each other. Only instructions. *Hold here, hold there. Grab that part, this part. Quiet, quiet. Make sure, make sure, make sure.* She didn't know how many of them there were, where they came from, or who they were.

She couldn't scream. Didn't understand why. The harder she dug to find her voice, the more she hollowed herself. Her heart racing, the rapid beats blending together like hot air hissing through her chest. Her entire face red and sweaty as her body began to shudder. One held her arms down as what felt like waves of bright heat pulsed deep into her flesh, bones, humours, ligaments.

She fell on the grass. Then a body fell on her. Hands and lips. Even though her body could feel everything, the pressure, the weight, everything felt false. A divorce of skin and spirit. A series of rogue impulses and misfirings. Perhaps everything that was to be felt couldn't come out all at once. Was like musical perforations being registered onto a player piano. One chord at a time. Sensations must all have boundaries.

Her sari ripped. Skin goosepimpled. Blood in flushes of hot and cold.

Above her, the moon. Growing arms out of it. Pinching, then groping her sides. Raising her waist up. Two pairs? Three pairs? She couldn't see. It could be an entire crowd. There could be no repercussion if everyone took part. There could be no remorse if everyone was guilty. And there could be no madness if everyone was mad.

She turned her head to the side. She couldn't see the faces beside her, but she could see the stage. She could see the Ravana. The beat continued, tabla and sarangi. Kathak dancers came to the front. She stepped outside of her body and joined them. Bangles on their ankles and crescent-moon spangles on their noses, red turmeric bindis between their eyes. The dancers raised their heads to the dark rainbow of kurtas and saris in the audience.

Were there angels above? Should she call for them? Sometimes calling out for an angel brings the wolves instead. Sometimes you just lie in wait, fighting just enough to keep alive, hoping you come out in one piece.

In the night, it was easy to see visions of her childhood vice in the night sky. Her parents as pale sexual revenants among the constellations. She had seen her mother shake in similar ways through the peephole. From the sky, it felt like God was murmuring to her, telling her to be strong, be calm until it was over.

But she knew it couldn't be God.

God would tell her to save herself. Tell her to scream. Kick them. Bite them. One of them licked her face. She felt nothing. Wondered if she were dead now, nested in a corpse. Rigor mortis setting in. A great inertia. A body hollowed by all the things it couldn't do. Couldn't scream. Couldn't cry. Couldn't feel.

Applause and music spilled over her cocoon of hot shadow. She felt like she was underwater, listening to the terrestrial world. Her body like the meat under a torn toenail. Her mind still scrambling to put everything together. Boyish laughter now. And the constant weight on top of her. Was so heavy that it didn't feel like a human at first. Not a person. A donkey, maybe. A donkey trampling. Crushing her ribs. For that same moment, she felt like that was all she was – a ribcage with a heart and lungs glowing inside it. Her hands somewhere else. Her feet, up in the black trees. Everything else seized, scattered.

She felt the wind blew right through her. She was invisible. But not gone. Not yet.

It wasn't too late. They weren't in her yet. She was still intact, her body still connected by strings. She just had to pull herself together, collect the parts. Collect herself. First, she found her voice. A whimper escaped. And then the first second of a screech. Felt a hand clamp her mouth. That moment, she found her teeth. Bit down hard. Found her limbs. Shoved and kicked. Found a fire locked in her chest. Lit her body on fire so that they couldn't touch her. Bit, scratched, put knees to groins.

This bitch crazy! And they vanished. All of them.

She got up, bones shuffling, put her palm to her ripped blouse. No timeline she could lay out. It started and then it ended. Except it didn't really end. What happened in between had nothing to do with the mind, she slowly began to realise. This was a betrayal of the body – why was she wet? Like some reprobate organ had suddenly been stitched in with the others, making her feel pleasure when there was supposed to be pain. Pumping chemicals through her, toxic and sweet, turning her into something else. Making her fluent in a language she did not realise existed. Such a thing could never come from God, she knew.

She shambled towards the crowd, trying to keep her sari from disassembling any further. A man stepped forth towards the effigy. An archer. The tiny flame breathed life into the rag wrapped around the arrowhead. On the stage, the pundit held the yellowed pages of the chaupai, scrunched in his nervous palms. Dropped the pages and they flew away like a vintage of moths into the dark. The dancers like beating hearts in the back. The archer let loose the burning arrow. It flew to the Ravana's chest, cloth and bamboo and rushes and reeds whirling in a fiery tornado.

The Ravana burned hungrily in the background. Its pained face like a devil laughing in the flames. A sun in the dark night. A wind came upon the field, blew the heat towards the trees. The archer was still poised with his feet apart, one knee bent, the other straight, toes pressing hard against the dirt. The pose was so perfect that it must've taken weeks to rehearse this very moment. Women with their hands clamped together like they had just finished clapping. The sizzle of flaming cloths beating angrily before them. The burning scents of camphor and pitch pine. Music filled the air again.

'You see that?' said a child, pointing at the burning effigy. 'That was like somethin straight out of a storybook!'

The effigy keeled over, fell onto the grass, still burning.

The crowd bawled, a mix of shock and delight. The demon king's pained rictus still scowling at its onlookers. The boy dressed as Shiva went close to his mother, as if he wanted to cry. His mother held him tight, stroked his hair and laughed. While everyone else was looking at Ravana burning, Lata was fixed on the sight of that boy. There stood the God of Destruction, like a schoolboy after a caning. There stood the God of Destruction, trembling with fear.

She lumbered across the grounds, struggling against her own weight. Her body still felt foreign. Like it had to reteach itself how to breathe. Made her way back to the main road. Stayed on the road, tried her best to. But the alcohol was still in her, still like a ball rolling back and forth inside her brain. Every few minutes, she stopped to catch her breath, making sure she still had her arms, her legs. Making sure her eyes still worked. Sometimes she felt like she was only seeing what her mind wanted her to see – like in that margin between waking and dreaming, where one can see through their eyelids.

As she walked, the road didn't seem like the road. The trees didn't seem like trees. The stars didn't seem like stars. They were all shapes. That's what everything was. Circles and rectangles and triangles. And shapes were just lines, straight and crooked. Lines that bent and snapped into corners. The moon was a circle. Like the iris was a circle.

Her head ached. She didn't know if this was the alcohol any more. And didn't know what direction she was walking. She tried to keep on the road – but what was the purpose of keeping on the road? Where was the road going? She gazed at the mountains. Black triangles. They brewed rum on those triangles. That's what Dylan had said. Like there were rivers of rum up there. Like whiskey bottles grew on trees. South was the dark abscissa of ricefields. She held her head, tried to steady herself.

Then noticed that a shadow had been following her. Getting closer.

She panicked, veered off the road. Picked up the pace. Continued until she came to the river. Passed more shapes on the way. Turned around. The shadow still behind her. She picked up a rock, big as her palm. Turned around, held it up. Said to the shadow, 'Come closer and you dead!'

The shadow spoke, 'My brother—'

And she screamed.

'Stop screamin! I was just lookin for my brother—' But she wasn't listening.

Threw the rock, hit him square in the head. Knocked him out cold and kept running.

28
A Death Wish

Lata kept along the river. It would take her home – that's what she believed. She passed more shapes on the way. Kept walking until she saw light. A fire. Took a few steps closer. A fire by the riverside. Four shadows around it. At first, thought it to be the same group from the grounds. Shadows were just shapes, after all. There was no other substance to a shadow.

A white blur came scampering up to her. Started barking. Took the shape of a dog. Then filled out white. She'd never before been so glad to see this damn hound. White Lady went quiet, came up to her. Sniffed her crotch. Sat as still as a monk as if offering herself to Lata. The shadows became longer as they stood up. Their faces came into view as they came closer. Faces that made sense this time. The faces to the front were Krishna and Tarak. To the back, the twins.

Krishna was the first by her side. Tarak was more cautious, came up to her but kept an arm's length away. Krishna said her name. 'Lata? That's you?' It was at that moment she remembered she had a name. He noticed her torn sari. 'What the hell happen?'

He carried her to the fire, sat her down. Rustam opened a goatskin canteen, told her to drink. She sipped, then drank the whole thing. Tarak carried her to the river to wash her face. Krishna went too. Asked her once again what had happened, but she wasn't ready to answer. He splashed water in her face one more time. She waved her hands, told him no more.

She returned to the fire with White Lady. The dog rested at her feet, and they were all quiet for a long time. Finally, she said, 'Thank you.'

Krishna asked, 'Lata, what happen?'

Kept her eyes on the fire. Didn't say anything.

Tarak told her, 'You smellin like rum.'

Krishna asked, 'Who do this? Dylan Badree do this?'

The dog went up to Lata, sat with her tail curled like a pepper leaf. Shook her head again. 'Aint have nothin here for you,' Lata told the dog.

'She aint want nothin,' said Tarak. 'She could sense when somethin is wrong. She smart like that.'

Lata gently stroked the dog's head.

'The girl don't want to say nothin,' said Rustam, 'cause she don't want to spoil how you think bout her. So if you care bout this girl, you wouldn't ask if somethin happen.'

Lata fixed her eyes on Krishna's. The flicker of the flame in his iris. The iris was a circle, just like the moon was a circle. She entered the fire in his eyes, rewound time to the moment the Ravana was set ablaze. All of her emotions, her uncertainty, confusion, pain lined up one after the other, streamlined. All points meeting like a knife's tip. God would want her to save herself, she thought. In the dark, if God puts fire in your hand, you don't put it out. You carry it all the way to the mountain. She began to shake again. Her throat jerking. She grabbed the end of her ripped sari tight and wrung it like she had just finished scrubbing it over the river. The knife she forged in her mind stabbed her over and over.

'I aint want to go to jail,' she said, rubbing her head.

'Jail?' Tarak asked. 'Why you talkin bout jail?'

She thought of the rock in her hand. How she brought it on that boy's head. Terror and sadness and anger and confusion. All of it bundled into a ball of pain that filled inside her. She started coughing, hacking, like she had a hairball in her throat. Ran to the river, and the hacking turned to retching. Krishna went by her side, rubbed her back.

She turned to him. 'I hit somebody. A boy. With a stone. He was followin me. I—'

'Where?' Krishna asked.

Her eyes grew hot. 'Somewhere upriver. A distance away. I dunno.' She wanted to vomit again. 'What if he dead?'

'We should leave,' Tarak said.

She heaped her torn sari up. She didn't know how she was going to face her mother. 'What if he see me?' said Lata. 'What if he come for me?'

'Is too dark to see anything,' Tarak said.

'Get her home,' Rustam told Krishna. 'Me, Rudra and Tarak – we gon go out there and look for the boy. Make sure he aint see nothin.'

'Me?' Tarak bit his knuckle. White Lady got up, as if keen to join. 'And what if he dead? What then?'

'Then he aint see nothin,' Rustam said, laughing. 'Let's go.'

And the twins went out in search, Tarak and the dog behind them.

When they were gone, Lata got up, went to the river, found a patch of grass near the bank, laid her head down. 'Give me a minute,' she said to Krishna. He sat on the embankment beside her. A cold breeze lapped softly against the water, and he could feel it on his tongue. A rusted metallic taste.

Lata opened her eyes, spoke, 'I not gonna talk to you again if you tell my ma anything.' Her voice like a ghost.

'Your ma gon find out. Look at your sari.'

She took a while to ask, afraid to know the answer, 'You think I stupid, Krishna?'

With a heavy sigh, 'No.'

'My ma aint never gon think the same for me. She gon say I ask for it.'

'You aint need to ask scorpions to sting, Lata.' He noticed Dalton Changoor's dagger still embedded in the tree stump. Plucked it out. Felt like he saw the man's ghost in the sheen. 'But you livin still,' he said, trying to read the foreign words etched into the blade.

She sat up on the grass, hugged her knees. 'Nothin happen. I want you to know that. I use all my strength. I fight them. I aint let them take anything from me. I still have everything.'

Krishna nodded, happy to believe her. 'You was dancing and step on a dog foot. And it get angry and rip the sari. I see it myself. And we scare it away together. How that sound?'

'Step on a dog foot. OK.' She got up, ready to head back.

*

The three boys stood over the still-unconscious boy, brushing the night insects away from their faces. In the air, the deep drone of wind through the sycamores. The river beside them, lapping over stones smooth as lozenges. White Lady had spotted the boy first, splayed across a pocket of shadow beside some bamboo. Nobody said a word when they realised who it was. The crumpled skin beside the eye. It was Mikey Badree. Still breathing.

They couldn't believe it. Here he was, bleeding from the forehead, bested by a barrack girl.

Rustam muttered, 'So we find the little nightstalker.'

Tarak had no words.

Rudra asked the other two, 'What you think we should do?'

'I think we friend here have a death wish. We should stick a branch up his ass,' Rustam said, laughing. 'Think he gon report that to the police?'

Tarak didn't find it funny – mostly because he couldn't tell if Rustam was joking. 'We see him. He breathin,' he said. 'Don't need to do nothin else.'

Rudra asked, 'Your friend gon be OK?'

'Lata will live.'

'No. Your other friend.' Rudra pointed at White Lady, who had been growling so softly that the sound fused with the water. She arched her back as if ready to pounce.

Tarak snapped his fingers at the dog. 'Ease up!' But the dog kept on, wouldn't listen.

'Think she remember him?' Rustam asked. 'Smart dog. I aint blame she.'

Tarak called out, 'White Lady! Behave!'

Then the dog pounced on Mikey. Bit him right in the crotch. The boy's eyes flew open, bawling, gasping so hard that he started coughing. His entire body bucked. Flipped over. Hands clenching the dirt. Jaw agape. Eyes watering. Was like a hundred bees had stung him at once.

Tarak ran up to the dog to pull her off.

Mikey pushed his feet back, kicking the dog in her snout. She retaliated, biting deep down into the ankle.

The twins urged Tarak, 'Leave them! Let's go!'

Tarak felt like his intestines were unspooling, watching Mikey kick his dog. With all his might, tried to pull the dog off. Pulled until he couldn't catch his breath. Until his eyes were bloodshot, ready to plop right out the sockets. The twins jumped in as well, one of them tugging at Tarak's shoulder, the other at his torso. Limbs knotted over each other.

'Leave the dog!' they urged again.

Mikey scooped up some pebbles in his hand. Flung it at the dog. Gravel in her eyes now. Released a high-pitched yelp, began to writhe. He glared up at Tarak and the twins, all the rage in the world.

'*You dead!*' Mikey said through his teeth. Pointed at Tarak. '*Dead!*' Then at the twins. '*Dead!*' Then at the dog, still pawing her face, wincing. '*Dead! Dead! Dead!*'

Tarak wanted to explain – but there was nothing to explain. Before anything could be said, Mikey ran off. Vanished in the darkness. Rustam's face was still. Rudra's eyes hollow. A cold wind blew, and the chirping of the crickets slowed. It worried Tarak that the twins had gone quiet. Had they made a terrible mistake coming here? He sat on the dirt beside the dog, eyes shut tight, her tongue lolling out long and red like a lobster's tail.

Rudra pulled on his sleeve. 'We have to get outta here.'

'We gon be ready for him,' Rustam said. Tarak didn't understand what he meant by that. Wasn't sure he wanted to understand.

'Pick up that damn dog, we have to go,' Rudra urged Tarak one more time.

29
A Heap of Meat

Shweta spent much of the morning in her room. Her hair loose, her warm clothes bundled up to her bodice. The caulk along the walls had begun to break off, tearing off slivers of wood with it. Tiny peepholes where the rain could enter once again. The room was dim, the only light being the scattered streams of diffused light from the roof. Everything blurry like dispersed steam. Four moths stood static, camouflaged against the curtain. Every once in a while, when Hans came to mind, her heart raced. Panged. She held her hand to her chest like she was pledging her allegiance – but for what? Rubbed her palms in circles over her sternum.

She had no words for Krishna, whose eyelashes were thatched with dust. He slept in his own parallelogram of shadow in the corner. Barely left the room, barely ate. She put her dupatta on and asked him to pray with her. Afterwards, he and Lata had gone for a walk.

She went outside to the barrack yard, where Niala was pacing with baby Ananda in hand. Niala hadn't spoken much since the baby was born, though she seemed happy to be walking again. Walked barefoot on the hot pebbled ground, the baby held close to her, muttering to him the names of each object, creature and plant. Rookmin had berated her for wandering too far. Niala had made it to the immortelles close to the river and picked a fallen flower for the baby to smell. Shweta had overheard her expressing the fear to Rookmin that she felt he didn't have much time on this world – maybe if the world could know him, it would decide to keep him around a little longer.

The paranoid fear brought Hema to mind – she knew the feeling.

When Sachin overheard the conversation, it made him similarly sad to know that his nephew might be gone soon. He was just born – it was not fair that God would take his children so soon. So during the day, he went out in search of things his nephew had never seen. The past few evenings, he had brought back a caterpillar, a dead wasp, a wedge of bracket fungus, an oriole feather and a heliconia. Shweta had taken notice.

'You goin down to the river today?' she asked Sachin.

Sachin lit up. 'Yes, Ms Shweta. Today I gon get some bamboo. Big piece of river bamboo.'

'I can come with you?'

'Yes, Ms Shweta, yes. You gon get bamboo too?'

'No, no.'

'Then what you gon get?'

She thought about it for a while. Then with a small smile, 'Maybe a snail.'

She didn't tell anyone else she was going. Rookmin had been tracing her every step, as if she had taken on the role of some surrogate mother. Honestly, Shweta was tired of being treated like an injured child. When she got to the river, she sat on a tuft of weeds on the bank, a low patch of ginger lilies behind her. Watched the frogs, shiny as the rocks they perched on. Their attention on the insects overhead. Hyacinths hovered in clumps beside a bend in the river.

Sachin pointed at the rocks, 'Snails stick to them rocks, Ms Shweta.'

Shweta approached the rocks, and the frogs jumped into the water. 'I aint want to get my foot wet,' she tell him. 'Aint snails crawl on bamboo too? Maybe if we find the bamboo first, we gon get the snail at the same time.'

'Snail crawl on bamboo!'

They walked along the riverbank until they came to a palisade of bamboo stalks. Sachin rushed between them, combing and parting them for snails. As he did that, something strange caught Shweta's eye. At first, it looked like a rock, much too large to be in the river. As she got closer to it, she saw that it was a bag.

Large, white crocus bag, brown and heavy at the bottom. Washed up along the bank.

Flies had enhaloed the bag.

She prodded it with her foot – half expecting some creature to leap out of it. The bag wasn't tied. The mouth of it lay limp in the dirt. Shweta felt a great dread to look inside. She remembered something she'd heard a pundit say. That people only like to see pretty things. They don't like to see ugliness and rot and death. But those things are part of life as well. People are frightened of things because they serve as reminders of how much pain there is to this life, to this body they inhabit. Everything that is dead will one day melt away into the air. The wind and the heat will eat it all. And everything witness to the air will breathe it in and have it in them. For the same things that make up one creature make up all creatures. The same things in the bull and the manure and the deadfall of the earth make up the same sweet ingredients of mittai, the same sweetness of the banana and the jamun. The body is but a heap of meat, destined for death. Death lying like an unbloomed flower. All shall breathe in death and breathe out death onto everybody they meet.

She opened the bag.

Then closed it immediately.

Teeth and ears and fur and blood. It was only when she saw the yellow handkerchief that she put the broken shapes together. The same yellow kerchief that White Lady kept around her neck. She bit her knuckles, went to the river and kept her eye on Sachin, zipping along the bamboo, still in search of the snail. Peered at the river. The water still flowing when it should have stopped.

She returned to the bag, held her breath and stuck her hand in to retrieve the yellow kerchief. Washed it in the cool water and wrung it clean. The blood had sopped all the way through, giving it a more orange hue now. She clutched her heart, finding it hard to breathe. She called out, 'Sachin!'

He raced over to her. 'Find the snail?'

When she showed him the bag, he took a long look inside. Much longer than she could ever stomach. His face dropped. 'Who do this?'

Her heart still racing. 'I dunno.' In the same breath, 'We shouldn't leave her here.'

Sachin slung the crocus bag over his shoulder and lumbered all the way back to the barrack.

When they arrived, he set the bag in the middle of the yard beside some old coal pots. Rookmin sat on a crate beside the barrack entrance, smoking kush.

'What that you bring there?' she asked.

Shweta asked, 'Tarak here?'

'Why?' Rookmin said, getting up.

'TARAK!' Sachin yelled out.

Tarak emerged from behind Rookmin, his face haggard, awakened from slumber. Shweta was at a loss for words when she saw the boy and for a moment, regretted returning to the yard with the bag. Rookmin took another pull of her cigarette.

Shweta approached the boy, handed him the blood-soaked kerchief and then pointed to the bag. 'Tarak, I aint know what to say.'

Rookmin scrunched her brow, confused. But Tarak seemed to immediately piece things together. In a quiet voice, 'Where?'

'By the river,' said Shweta.

Sachin asked, 'Who do this, Tarak?'

Tarak fell to his knees and for a half minute, just stared at the bag. He dropped the kerchief and the wind carried it into the plain. It wiggled down the macadam road. Rookmin asked, 'Shweta, what the hell goin on?'

Shweta didn't want to speak.

Rookmin turned to her son. 'What's that in that bag there, Sachin?'

'Is White Lady, ma.'

'Somebody kill that dog and throw it in that bag. That is what you sayin to me, boy?'

'I aint know, ma.'

Soon after, Kalawatie came out. 'What goin on here?'

'Somebody kill the dog,' said Rookmin, pointing to the bag. 'Stuff it in that bag there.'

Kalawatie turned to Shweta. 'Why the hell them do that?'

Shweta hugged herself, a sudden dizziness coming over her. 'I dunno.'

'Nasty people in this world,' said Kalawatie, shaking her head. 'What that dog ever do anybody?'

'She never do nobody nothin,' Tarak muttered. He wiped some snot from his nose.

Shweta went up to Tarak, still kneeling on the ground. 'You should take that bag down somewhere in the field and give the dog a proper burial.'

Tarak got up. 'Have nothin proper about this.'

She added, 'Don't open the bag. Just bury the bag.'

Sachin threw in, 'I could tell you what it look like in the bag if you aint gon look and see. She look like—'

'Shut your mouth!' said Tarak, gritting his teeth.

'Don't talk to him so, boy,' warned Rookmin, getting up. 'That kinda rough talk aint gon bring that dog back.'

Tarak walked to the end of the yard to the iron slagheap where White Lady used to sleep. Sat on a patch of fissured soil, craned forward, holding his head like he was surrounded by clangorous noise. Rookmin signalled for Sachin to come to her, and he obeyed. Niala came out of the barrack to see what all the ruckus was about. Kalawatie maintained that somebody should give the dog a burial and maybe even sing a song. Tarak wanted none of it. The sooner he was away from people, the better. Flies had begun to settle on the bag. The earth always had an appetite for the dead. Didn't matter if it was a king or a caterpillar – when the earth smelled meat, it salivated.

Kalawatie was about to go back inside. 'You goin to bury that dog, Tarak?'

Tarak grabbed a shovel near to the slagheap and went to get the bag. A sense of duty placated something ugly in him before he could pick it up.

'I could come, Tarak?' asked Sachin.

'He should go by himself,' said Shweta.

'Yes, leave that boy alone,' said Rookmin, taking another pull of the kush. 'You do enough for the day, you hear?'

Tarak headed in the direction of the range, the shovel in one hand and the bag in the other. 'Bring back that shovel when you done, you hear?' he heard Rookmin call out from behind him.

*

When Krishna heard about White Lady, his stomach burned as if he'd swallowed fire. Inhabited the last painful moment the dog must have endured. Trapped in the crocus bag. Through the blackness, a lobed moon entering her senses. Behind the grunting, the shriek of insects, the water. Behind the pain, the papery texture of the material gripping her convulsing body. The ragged metallic taste of blood. Nothing but black bound to black. And when the final blow came upon her and there were no senses left to study.

Pictured Mikey Badree delivering that final blow. He knew it was him.

This was beyond Glauber salts, dogshit in shoes and scorpions in a latrine. Beyond throwing stones and words. Ultimately, common sense and humanity was superseded by the desire to prove oneself worthy of demons. This had gone far – too far. And Krishna would have been fooling himself if he didn't admit that he was scared. The fear deepened when Tarak hadn't returned that evening. He'd gone out to bury the dog. It was nearing nightfall and there was no sign of him. There was nobody Krishna could go to for help – nobody that could be bothered. He wasn't even sure of the twins any more. Even Mandeep didn't seem to care – the man was asleep, dead drunk, in his room. Krishna felt helpless. Tarak, with admirable control, had been with him all the way on the battered trails he decided to take. It was then Krishna realised that his cousin was the only loyal person in this giant obscenity of a world.

He couldn't just stay at the barrack and do nothing – he couldn't underestimate what could happen to Tarak. He tucked

Changoor's dagger into his pants. His mother was in the yard, cooking. He avoided her, making his way out back. There, he found Lata at the refuse barrel. Just about to set it on fire.

'You aint seen Tarak?' he asked.

She shook her head. Looked him straight in the eye. 'Krishna, we in trouble?'

'No.' He hoped he sounded convincing. 'But Tarak shoulda be back by now. I need to go out and look for him.'

She lit the barrel on fire. Put her hand on his shoulder, speaking low, 'He gon come back. Stay here. I aint want you goin out there.'

Krishna pulled away. 'I have to find him. He out there alone.'

Tears were coming out now. 'I cause this trouble, Krishna. It was me.'

Seeing her cry made his eyes heavy. 'Is not you. Them is the ones who start it.'

She put her arms around his neck, still crying. 'Please stay here.'

The heat from the blaze radiated onto them. His shoulders slumped, resigned. Looked at her for a long time. Her hair straggly from sweat. She held onto him tighter, a remora to a shark. The distant din of thunder sounded. He remembered when they were younger, around this time of the year when the rains came every few days. The sky electrified and pounding with thunder. And his mother had told him that the thunder came because God was angry. And when he told this to Lata, they would try to figure out who God was angry with. Searching each person in this barrack who must have done something to offend God. Or if God simply hated all of them.

Right now, Lata must have thought it was her. The thunder was her fault. Her affection now was not reciprocation of his, but guilt. She moved in to kiss him – but the kiss felt as if it were one for forgiveness. There was nothing romantic about it. It was his first. He kissed her back – didn't feel right. At this moment, it wasn't real. But perhaps it could be later on.

He was too worried about Tarak. He had to find him.

★

Tarak stayed off the road, instead keeping his feet on the rugged land. Initially thought of burying the dog within the canefield since that was where she spent a great deal of her time, but ultimately decided on a discreet place farther up, beside an old mango tree. A light wind swept over the plain. He stared ahead at some storm clouds over the mountains.

It was approaching evening by the time he had finished digging. Half a dozen times, his hands went numb as he wrestled with thoughts of revenge. He thought back to White Lady biting Mikey Badree – and had no doubt that this was his doing. Thought of all the things that had led to this point. If only one thing had been different, if only there had been one turn in the road, it might not have led to this.

A caravan of ants shuffled from the tree roots along the mound of the bag. He picked it up and tossed it in the hole. Spared no time in refilling. Kiskadees in birdsong above him.

He squatted beside the grave for a few minutes, his mind reeling with so many thoughts that he couldn't settle on any in particular. The land oblivious to his surly state. The howling of dogs, aligned on some tableau fixed into his mind. He fantasised that, far from earshot, the bell in the Presbyterian church was tolling for his dog. Though he knew a dead dog was of little consequence to the world. But he loved her – and she had kept hate out of his heart. Still did. He couldn't say the same for anyone else, not even his cousin any more.

Suddenly, he shuddered as if cold water had been splashed on his skin. The sensation came as fast as it went. He decided to take a walk and so went towards the mountains until he came to a section of the highway. In the distance was a figure travelling from the east. He sat on the asphalt, waiting for it to approach. A marvellous roan horse, drawing a carriage into town. Neither the horse nor the driver paid him any mind.

When the horse was gone, Tarak stepped in the middle of the wide road and looked around. To the west was the capital. Salesmen and umbrellas and carriages and white jackets and boats and stuccoed buildings with big windows. To the east were the fishing villages. Coconut trees and sargassum and dinghies and shrimp stalls and seines bursting with fish.

He laid the shovel against the trunk of the mango tree, beside White Lady's grave. He made the decision right then and there. To live here was to live with hate. And to live with hate was to slowly rot. But right now, his heart was beating, and his legs were strong. There was another world out there. He could find it – the same way the dog had found him. And there must be something out there that he could love – and could love him in return.

He closed his eyes and spun in a circle. Stopped, reopened them.

Began walking in the direction he was facing, without hesitation.

He didn't know what else to do but walk. Didn't matter the direction. He would know his destination when he arrived. And he reckoned that he'd figure out the next step when he got there.

30
A Way Forward

The night air was cold, and in the distance garbage fires dotted the landscape like beacons sending messages of doom. The land uncaring and apathetic. The eutrophic patina of the pond looking like rust under the dusk. Krishna didn't see the boys when they struck. Didn't see their faces. Didn't even know that they'd been watching him the whole time. Mikey was one, he was sure. He didn't recognise the others.

They prodded something foul against his mouth. Only when it was close enough did Krishna realise it was dogshit.

'*Eat it*,' a voice commanded him. '*Eat it and swallow it!*'

He shut his mouth tight, wriggled to free himself. One of them clamped his nostrils together. He would've rather suffocated than open his mouth to breathe. But his body gave way. As he gasped, they put it in his mouth and clamped his jaw shut, the might of a lobster's claw. He struggled, eyes rolling back into his head. He refused to swallow, every string of muscle taut. A palm moved up to his mouth, firm as a tick ready to suck blood.

'*Chew it!*'

He finally squeezed out of their grasp. Immediately ejecting it from his mouth. Bit one of them in the cheekbone and another on the wrist. He couldn't get a count of how many there were. All he saw was hands and fists. They sent him tumbling into the pondwater. Tried to swim to the other side. When he emerged, they were there. They were everywhere. Grabbed onto him and wailed on him. The knuckle marks impressed on his cheeks like fingerprints on modelling clay.

He managed to squirm out. He grabbed the dagger, gripped it tight. They kept their distance but didn't retreat. Krishna ran into the field. Ran like hell. Didn't matter where.

Ended up in the forest depths, where he lost them.

After full dark, Krishna realised that he wouldn't be able to last the night in the forest. He sat on a fallen log, his body weak with hunger. In the daytime, the moussara and crabwood and icaque and acajou formed an overhead sieve, where the light could still creep in. At night, it formed a cage. Darkness all around, pressing on him from all sides. A sound of scuffling made him raise his hand as if to parry a blow. The air thick and stale. Some creature hissing a fathomless distance away.

If he could find a stream, he could find the river. And find the twins along that river. But he discarded the thought. It was too far. Too dangerous. Nightmares of White Lady swished in and out of his mind's eye, superimposing themselves against rocks, against the spur of Joseph's coats before him, against the single coin of moonlight to his side. His mind freewheeled through the schoolhouse, to the fat face of the headmaster scolding him, to the boys running circles around him – it all seemed like wonderful simplicity compared to now.

He thought of heading back, but the barrack could not protect him. Neither the building nor the status of it. His mother, as much as she provided for him, was powerless. He clutched the dagger against his chest. He was safer here in the darkness than back there.

His mind reeled back to when he was six years old and had taken his father's work boots without permission. Toted them to that same bison pond, where he put them on, each boot like a large casket that slid up past his kneecaps. He wandered among the water hyacinths, craning to see the guppies and tadpoles and snails and the dragonflies dipping their tails between the lilies. When he was done, he came out of the pond and set the boots beside the samaan tree as he went to play with the bison. When he returned, the boots were gone.

He spent an hour searching for them, not believing that they could've been stolen.

When evening had come and Hans was searching for the boots in the barrack, a gloomy guilt overcame the boy like never before. Hans had asked everyone in the barrack if they'd seen his boots before coming to Krishna. And when he did, the boy's head hung like a scarf of lead was wrapped around his neck. Krishna didn't understand how his father had immediately known his involvement and thought him to have some special power. Still, Hans's eyes remained patient and warm when he told the boy that all he had to do was admit the truth and life would find a way forward from there. Krishna broke down in tears as he described every detail of what had happened. At the end, his father held him close.

Perhaps it was time to admit the truth now, thought Krishna. That he needed his father more than ever. Him and Mrs Changoor. They had gotten him out of that jail cell. They could get him out of this now. One phone call and it could be over. They would show him the way forward. They owed him that. There was nowhere else to go to now, nothing to look forward to if he remained in the barrack, forever hiding from his former classmates. No sanctuary, no place to rest his head. The Changoor house, as much as he hated to admit it, was now his beam of hope. There was no more place for sanctimony and judgement. Only the flimsy belief that his father still loved him enough to save him. The notion that forgiveness was in order.

His arms had been ravaged with mosquito bites by the time he was out of the forest. A wave of intense relief caught him as the half moon came into view and he was out of the gullet of the woods. Still, he kept a steady grip on the dagger. The rains suddenly swept down, but he kept on the road until he came to the slope up to the Changoor farm, passing the banana trees and the power lines. His body held a type of renewed energy that guided his feet through the lucifugous path. When he came to the gate, it was locked, and so he scaled it, his feet landing on a mat of foliage and morass on the other side. The house was up ahead, a single window electrified. Swollen with music. Along the path to the house were stone troughs filled with zinnias, dying and flattened. Behind the troughs were bougainvilleas gone limp.

For a flicker, as if God made him see out of his father's eyes, he realised a life in the Changoor house. Where the rooms were ventilated and cool. Where Marlee Changoor pretended to be a mother and he pretended to be a son. His stomach filled with foreign flavours. The dress and aroma of a sahib's son tattooed onto his skin. And privilege as both a shield and a sword that could be used against his enemies. A life where problems evaporate in the sound of his voice, in a stare. Where revenge could be carried out in the swish of a signature. Where he would eventually ascend and own this house. Territory and earthly delights. He could have Lata, and Lata could have him – somebody greater than some village boy, some flunky deputy's son. And all his sons and daughters, free from danger and disease. Life could be like the photographs in the magazines. Life could finally be lived.

It was only a flicker of a daydream – but in it, he saw the promise of another world. For that moment, he held adoration for another life.

And you couldn't live in two worlds. You had to choose one.

He knocked on the door, but the music and the rain were too loud.

Then reached deep into his lungs and shouted out, '*Pa!*' The crack of his voice bouncing off the walls, ricocheting into the dark. There was no response.

He shouted it once more – again, no response. The word like a large iron ball in his lungs.

Impatient now, he did as he'd done before, as if muscle memory had taken over. He picked up a rock with his free hand and aimed it at the single lit window.

It missed, hitting the wall instead. He did it again, this time connecting with the glass. The pane rattled and the rock bounced off. He saw the curtains move behind it. Waited a half minute but nothing happened.

He picked up another rock, wound up his arm and made as if he were pitching a corkball. Launched with so much force that his entire body rocked forward. Still holding the dagger tight. He flinched, knowing that the rock would break the window. Heard the glass break before it actually happened. A loud scream.

Then the music stopped.

He still had the dagger in his hand when the door opened – and that was that.

*

Shweta did not cook that evening, did not eat. When night fell, she lit a flambeau and sat cross-legged on the grass at the end of the barrack yard, peering out at the road. The wind had abated, though a muted swoop of leaves still blew by the post. The moon sat bright, a cynosure among the festival of stars. First, Tarak was gone. And then Krishna. They had their ways of dealing with the dog's death, she reckoned.

If she had to wait out here for the entire night for her son, she would. She didn't know what she would say to him upon his return. She thumbed the wound on her heel, which had scabbed and hardened into an itchy black nucleus, the skin around it tightening to seal the hole that was once there. Couldn't risk going out there and undoing weeks of healing. She wished Hans was here and felt simultaneous gloom and disgust for wishing such a thing. She missed him – but couldn't forgive him. She hated talking about it – didn't need anyone's pity. Constantly rewound time in her head, revisiting memories, both good and bad. She remembered a joke a pundit had made about family at their wedding. That women needed to be protected against their own best interests, and that men needed to be protected against their own desires. She didn't understand it at first, but she felt like her situation now thrust her right into the punchline.

She thought back to Hans as a little boy, only ten years old, long before she had held any romantic interest in him. He had a posse back then. Four other boys from other settlements. They glided through time, through the long hours of childhood tedium. The night meant nothing to them, even at that age. They caused mischief, but no one regarded them as unpleasant. They stole, but no one regarded them as thieves. Wandered into women's kitchens in the village and took jam right off the shelves. Kept the bottles and milked other farmer's cows. If there was bread left to cool, it would be gone. They were hardly ever reported so long as they never harmed or destroyed.

Shweta sneered at them, until she realised that those boys were all he had. Hans's father was a terror, both public and private. She had feared the predicted effect of having a child with Hans – that he would become his father. When Hema was born, she thought of him like a wild horse tamed. At first, he dealt with the things other men in her life wouldn't have dared to. He bathed her, sang her to sleep, cleaned her shit. If he had breasts, he would have fed her. But after the first two months, he tired of such things. Was as if he had expected the baby to take care of herself after a few months had passed. When she'd developed a rash on her leg, he told Shweta that it would go away on its own. During her bout of colic, he said the same thing. And when she died, she now wondered if some veiled part of him basked in relief.

She fell asleep in the barrack yard, in her same sitting position. She awoke at dawn, realising that Krishna still hadn't returned home. She didn't know if her foot would hold up on the walk, but she was so worried now that she had to try. The ground and the air were still cool from the night. The sky now a pale violet. The birds gathered in the trees. She stayed on the road, keeping an eye out for the ruts. Went very slowly when the road started to slope.

She made it to the gate of the Changoor house. It was locked. In the distance were the rambutan trees. Many had fallen to the roots and rotted. The shrill sound of cicadas in the balata trees. The house visible in the backdrop as if it were in meditation, in a forest glade. Beside them was a single lime tree, each of its fruits diseased and invaginated. Some brown as tobacco. A row of anthuriums beside the trees were dying, some already desiccated. The sun coming up behind her, giving the land colour.

When she called out for Hans, the winds carried her voice towards the house. She kept her eyes on the windows for even the slightest movement.

She didn't see the creature approach. A white mare sidled along the other side of the fence, stood before the gate. It had sad eyes, like a forlorn lover in farewell. Stood as tall as Shweta. The wind ruffling its mane. Shweta reached her fingers through the iron to touch its face. Before she could, it made a half turn and wandered away as if she were never there. Shweta waited for five minutes before she saw the door open. A white robe. It was Mrs Changoor.

She came up the track, kept far enough away so that Shweta could not properly see her face. The dawning sun cut it in half, only the mouth and chin illuminated. The woman folded her arms, her slippers buried in the muddy foliage.

Shweta took a deep breath. 'I come to see my husband,' she said.

'He is asleep,' said Mrs Changoor.

'Asleep? You sure?'

'I am.'

'Wake him up,' she said. 'His son ... Our son gone missing.'

'Missing? Since when?'

'Last night. He gone out and never come home.'

'Where did he go?'

Shweta was ashamed to say that she didn't know. 'Nobody see him. Hans should know, we need to go out and look for him.'

Mrs Changoor shook her head. 'Give it a little time. I bet he'll turn up.' Mrs Changoor turned around as if to go back inside.

'Let me talk to Hans,' Shweta said impatiently. 'If he really sleepin, wake him up.'

Mrs Changoor was similarly impatient. 'It's very early in the morning.'

'Late, early, that don't make no difference. Krishna is missing. Hans might not want to see me. But bet your bottom dollar, he aint gon take it easy when he find out Krishna is missing and you aint say nothin. I live with Hans for years. He is always awake before dawn, before the roosters. Go get him.'

'He's a boy. Boys wander. It's a fact of life.'

'What you tellin me?'

'He'll turn up. Please go home.' Something doleful in her voice.

Shweta felt her eyes getting hot. She was going in circle with this woman. She grabbed onto the iron bars of the gate. 'It aint right what you doing right now, Mrs Changoor. You take away my husband. But don't take him away as a father to Krishna. God watchin. It aint right.'

'This gate remains locked at night. Even if he wanted to get in, he couldn't.'

A pause, and then it hit Shweta. 'I never say I thought Krishna come to this house, Mrs Changoor. What you talkin bout?'

An astonished pause, then a nervous laugh. 'When Hans wakes up, I'll tell him about Krishna. And he'll decide what he wants to do. In the meantime, please go home.'

Shweta wiped her eyes. 'Just let me talk to my husband, you witch.'

After a long pause, Mrs Changoor answered, voice laced in venom, 'He isn't your husband, ma'am.'

Shweta's face fell. Released her grip of the gate. 'What you mean?'

'You didn't marry in the church.'

A pause. 'So what?'

'So you're not really his wife. Not under Trinidadian law.' Mrs Changoor didn't seem to take delight in telling her this. 'The sooner you understand this, the better.'

Shweta turned her eyes to a crusty trail of leaf litter covering the track. Ants streeled a crumpled spider. A row of flamingo flowers beside the trees were dying, some already desiccated. Twigs and deadfall strewn without restraint. The sun was so hot that the plains in the distance seemed to tremble. It was the counterpoint of anything godly and good. If Hans chose to stay here out of his own volition, then she felt sorry for him. He was truly lost now.

Rookmin's conversation about Niala came to mind: *Forget man. Man will destroy you.*

'He aint the best man. You goin to get tired of him after a few years,' Shweta said, putting her chin up. The tears stopped. She couldn't cry for him any more. 'And then you goin to throw him away. When that time come, Marlee Changoor, you better tell him he have nowhere else to be in this life.'

Mrs Changoor's face fell a little – as if some unspoken reality had hit her. 'Time will tell.'

'You's not the one who have to worry. Is him. You's his only hope now. Without you, he have nothin. No place in the world.'

'Go home, ma'am,' Mrs Changoor said, before turning to go back inside. 'I'll let Hans know that you came by.'

V

Deadwater

'Shweta ... Get up. Shweta, get up.'

'Shweta, oh God.'

'Girl, how to say this?'

'Some boys was playing near a river ...'

'We real sorry. We dunno what happen.'

'We really dunno how this coulda happen, who coulda do this ...'

'Between some rocks ...'

'Oh God.'

'How Krishna end up there, we dunno.'

'Oh God, girl.'

'Who coulda want to kill this boy? Oh God!'

'Some boys near a river find him ...'

'Murali done gone out to buy bread and biscuits. I will make coffee.'

'Shweta, say something nah, girl. Oh God.'

'Give she some rum. Give me some too. Today aint a good day.'

31
A Wake

The barrack yard was already crowded. As instructed, Lata had placed a flambeau every six steps around the perimeter of the yard and was now setting each alight. Then she did the same with some deyas on the macadam road leading up to the entrance. It was early evening, the sky troubled and fragmentary with claws of carnelian cirrus. The clouds fissured with lightning even though there was no sign of rain to come.

She placed the last flambeau and continued towards the ricefields. Walked for ten minutes, no destination in mind. Walked to feel the breeze. A stirring came upon her soul as a pale mantle of herons made an axis along the plain. Suddenly, the birds rose like a great noisy mountain coming up from the earth's salt. Hundreds of birds scattering and rocketing skyward. For a moment, she thought they would fall back to the earth.

She squinted, two figures in the distance. Two boys kicking the water.

Returned to the barrack yard where the slurring chatter rinsed over the sombreness of the evening. People old and young were still arriving from all over. Devotees from the mandir; a reserved retinue from the church; tatterdemalions from Tully Settlement, from the fringes of the village. People from all the nooks. For miles, news had spread about the killing. There was nothing like the wake of a child to pull people out the woodwork. Distant relatives. Gamblers. Old friends. The uninvited.

The unknown. Come for food, come for drink, come for any chance of a bacchanal.

There weren't enough chairs and stools but some made do on flour bags and rice bags. Others on upturned pails and pine crates. A cauldron of coffee and sugar bubbled in the corner, the fire growing angrier as the night winds built. The smell hot and dull and deep. Two men huddled behind a bush, peeing with a vengeance. Mandeep on the dirt, his back against one of the barrack yard pillars, trying to will the last drop of daru onto his tongue. Looked into the mouth of the bottle as it finally trickled out into his eye. Meandering past him was Kalawatie with a saucer of salted biscuits. Her eyes dark, resigned. Four men used a large crate as a table, shuffling cards, dealing, cussing, biscuit crumbs falling out of their mouths. Shillings passed here and there. The wind shifting the draw and discard piles together. Deadwood falling on the grass. Three little boys pretending to be trains, up and down, up and down. More cussing, more biscuits. Banging the crate. Candle lights going in and out. Flames going left and right. Calls for matches. Calls for ice. More coffee. More biscuits. The light went out again.

Three older women stood around the coffee, talking of the boy who was dead before he could live. Thirteen years old, found in a river with a bloody hole in his belly. The boy regained a pulse two hours after they brought him to the hospital, one claimed. He sat up on the gurney, causing two nurses to faint. Looked at the orderly with big eyes before falling again. And he was gone once more. They spent thirty-five minutes trying to revive him. The doctors had recorded two times of death.

That is bullshit, Lata thought as she walked past.

She thought back to when they brought the body back to the barracks, submerged him in a large basin, rubbed his limp body with wet sponges. A sash tied around the hole in his belly. Shweta face to face with her dead son. Held him up, his arms bending back almost in a crabback pose. She remained quiet. The other women bawled for her.

Spectators had gathered around the rummy players now, laughing as they flung cards and cussed. Kalawatie made the rounds again with the biscuits. Not even halfway through and all were gone. A woman from the church brought bread, said that it was baked in an oven bigger than this yard. Behind the barrack, Dolly was frying eggs and making sandwiches for the barrack residents. Lata sat down, watching on. Felt disconnected from everything. With all these irregulars here, she felt like she couldn't recognise anything as she knew it. The roof of the shed was blacker with soot than it had ever been. Rumours and conversations crisscrossed the yard.

You have to be a real demon to kill a child.
I aint believe everybody have to dead. You could live forever in this body.
You gon dead either way. It comin one way or the other.
Even god's does dead.
The boy body inside?
He on a bed inside there somewhere.
I think they waitin for Pundit Narine.
They will be waitin till tomorrow for that man.

Lata went to check on her mother at the back to see if the sandwiches were done. Shweta hadn't eaten for the entire day. All she'd done was drink. Rookmin gave her rum. Kalawatie gave her rum. Teeluck gave her rum. Dolly handed Lata the sandwiches stacked on a plate and told her to get them to Shweta. Lata didn't want to go inside – especially not into that room. It was difficult seeing Krishna like that. Her mother told her that some things must be done, as hard as they may seem. As Lata moved past the rummy table, one of the players called out, '*Dahlin, dahlin! Bring the ting here, bring the ting here!*'

Lata ignored them, kept moving. The door to the barrack was open. A stream of people were looping in and out. She didn't know any of these people. Freeloaders. Like patrons of a freakshow. She squeezed in, moved past the line towards the end room of the barrack. Two of the other room doors were open, stacked with biscuit tins and flambeau bottles. Niala sat in one of the rooms, facing the wall, breastfeeding her baby. At the end of the line, people looked in, pirouetted and came back out.

Lata squeezed in. It was so compact that the people around the bed seemed to form one large chimera of necks and arms.

Krishna's pale shell, dressed in trousers and a white square-neck shirt. Half-rolled in a white blanket. His body had been turned so that his head could face the south. Tulsi leaves set beneath his feet. A sohari leaf with a dollop of rice on the floor. Flies astir in helical movements, up and down, up and down. Three deyas burning in a brass saucer. Shweta doubled over like a devotee in a mosque during solemn prayer, her rear cocked upward.

Lata set the sandwiches down, trying her best to keep the boy out of her periphery. Just being in the room was like a great weight pressing on her head. She crouched beside Shweta, 'Ma make this for you. You have to eat.'

The voices of half-drunk women filled the room.

Give she space. Give she space.
She body aint able to digest no food right now. Too much sadness in she.
Gon get some more rum for she, you hear, girlie?

Rookmin said, 'She gon eat later, Lata.'

When Lata glanced at the plate, one of the sandwiches was already gone.

A man put his hand on Shweta's shoulder. 'Mrs Saroop. Shweta,' was all he could say. She recognised Robinson's deep voice among all the clamour and confusion around her. Talk of bright red energy in her sacrum. Or fire burning inside her, like an oven ready for strong mangrove wood. Of busybodies and newsmongers who walked miles to salivate over a dead child. Of soothsayers who claimed to know her future child would be fair of skin. It was nice to hear her own name spoken so gently in the middle of it. She put her hand on his, stroked his wedding band with her thumb before letting go. He said nothing else, exiting the room as silently as he came.

Lata left the room, returned to the yard. Stepped beside the rainwater barrels to wash her face when she noticed tiny bubbles of foam against the scrubbing board placed there. Piss. Cupped some water in her palm and threw it on the board. She peered into each barrel, half expecting to see spirals of vomit marbling in the water. Washed her face again. From where she stood, she could see the planks that covered the peephole to her boarding room. That particular nook of the world swathed in dark, tucked away from everything. Wondering now why she was ever so curious about what was happening on the other side, and why she had to keep returning. To see something more? Something different? This night, she felt like she was drifting from peephole to peephole.

Two young women, a tall one and a short one, were sitting beneath the jackfruit tree. Lata stood a comfortable distance from them, the wind carrying their voices.

The tall woman said that she heard it was a police officer who shot Krishna. That they found him walking down by the river and mistook him for a goat thief, didn't even ask who he was before they pulled the trigger. The short woman sucked her teeth, told her that she didn't know what she was talking about – that an officer wouldn't just pull out a gun and shoot a child. The tall woman remarked that the goat thief was a short man, could be mistaken for a child. At this point, the two women shot a look in Lata's direction.

Lata left, returned to the front. A pickup truck pulled close to the yard, knocking over two flambeau bottles. Tied to the tray were two boxes. Four men helped bring the first pinebox to the centre of the yard. The sounds of stools and buckets shifting and people clearing the way. A tall man in a black shirt came up to the box and motioned for the men to bring it over. The murmuring rose as they set it down. The box was open, lined with hay and cheap cloth. The bottom was padded with ice and long past waterlogged. It was drooling from the base.

Undertaker, this casket soaked! You reach so damn late, all the ice melt!

Look it have a hole in the bottom. That wood rottin. All that water gone spill out, eh.

That is deadwater in there? You could work a good obeah with that.

A child deadwater, to boot. Careful with that.

Undertaker, sell me a bottle to cook my mother-in-law food in. Maybe she gon go deaf and dumb!
Gimme two bottles, undertaker!

'That aint my line of business,' said the undertaker. 'You want to put a proper hex on somebody, make friends with an Englishman.'

Lata showed the undertaker to the barrack. A minute later, Rookmin emerged with Krishna's corpse, holding him against the crook of her shoulder as if he were a sleeping baby. The undertaker helped her put him in the box. His hands looked strong and veiny, but he placed the boy with the same tenderness as if he were his own son. As soon as the boy was in the box, a deep groaning came from all the women gathered around, like rumblings of a distant storm that drizzled pulings before bursting into a torrent. *Oh God! The boy dead! Oh God look at how he dead! Why God take this boy oh God! God why you take him from this world oh God!*

A sole nervous chuckle escaped from the crowd. *But the small man was lyin down dead inside all this time, same way. Allyuh woman doin like the small man now dead.*

Nostrils flared with mucus as a seizure of grief swept from one end of the crowd to the other. Bumbling like a bat in a locked room, clattering madly against the windows. One woman wrapped her arms around herself as if she were strung up in an asylum waistcoat. Another grabbed her great big breasts and dipped them into the box, bawling.

The only quiet woman was Rookmin. A mammoth amongst the mewlings, she stood resolute like a primordial rock against the crashing waves of mourning. A low wreckage of weeping faces in a semicircle around the dead child. Rookmin stood with her arms in a V. Even if the death god Yama came dancing up from this boy's cadaver, she would look him straight in the eye and let him know she stood her ground.

An old woman came up to the box, her face shrivelled when she peered into it. Her lip rose all the way up to her nostrils. Exposed her toothless mouth when she spoke to Rookmin,

'What a sweet child. I sorry he dead. What a pity. So young. You taking this real good, mama.'

Rookmin shook her head. 'I aint the mother. The mother inside.'

The undertaker turned to Lata. 'You know this boy well. I could tell.'

Lata froze, her eyes stuck to the sky, quickly turning dark now. The undertaker took a deep breath. 'You could kiss the forehead if you want, girl. If you feel it would help.' The man returned to his truck, sat at the rear wheel and dreamily smoked a cigarette.

It didn't feel real, looking at Krishna's body. Wasn't the first time Lata had seen a corpse. Her father was lain before her too, probably right at this spot. Didn't have much of a wake. A few labourers had shown up, paid their respects and left. Looked at the mass of grey lumpy flesh in the pinebox and nodded, not doing much else. Came and went, but at least they knew him. He died suddenly – but at least he was dying and then dead. Krishna was just dead. A dried-up gulch. She couldn't accept that this was him in that box. Stared at him long enough to believe that it wasn't. His face looked too long. Eyes too wide. Mouth too small. And all these people gathered around him, teetering with grief for a child whose name was still lost to their minds. Found love in a stopped heart. Same with her mother. Her father nearly took her eye out with a belt buckle and yet she loved him more in death than she ever would in life. The living deferential to the sins of the dead. As if love was a flightless bird in life – and only truly soared when it sprouted angel wings upon death.

An old lady went to the field and picked some allamandas, ripped the petals and sprinkled them on the boy's torso. Brought fistfuls of yellow lupine, portulaca and butterfly vine. Threw them in the box. Went to the sapodilla tree, snapped a coralita vine and tossed it in there too. Now the inside of the box was host to a budding botanical garden, interstitial with cloth. She returned with two handfuls of cow gobar and smeared it on the side of the box.

Rookmin pushed the woman away. 'Aint your place to do that,' she said sternly.

The woman stuck her tongue out and walked away.

Just then Dolly brought Shweta out to the yard, walking her slowly to the coffin. As soon as Dolly saw the box, her throat began to jerk as if she were going to vomit. Shweta didn't stand over the box when she got to it. Instead went on the ground in a foetal position and closed her eyes. The men at the rummy table were calling for more coffee and biscuits.

Once again, Lata drifted away, walked to the east end of the yard. An old, bearded man was talking loudly. Spoke about a civilised India existing when *all them white man was still in trees*, that Indian people just allow anything to happen to them. They will join the white man's army and eat the sacred cow for him. Put their mouth on the bullet casings and bite the cowfat off it to fight for the white man.

She wanted to scream at these people. None of them knew Krishna!

Walked away again, towards two shadows leaning against the jackfruit tree.

The twins. Removed from everyone else. She suddenly found herself wading through the haze of that blighted night she met them at the river and began to shudder, almost uncontrollably. The twins didn't move. They might as well had been two mannequins placed to stand in the dark. Two decoys.

'Who do it?' one finally asked.

Lata didn't say anything at first. Had no answers. She shook her head, eyes getting hot. 'You think it was that boy I hit...'

'We will find out,' the boy said. 'If is him, we gonna burn his house down.'

A part of her wanted to tell them not to do that – that it would make things worse. But how could it be worse than this? She couldn't yet process his absence. Though she'd repeatedly told herself that she had no part to play in his – no bigger than the Demon Lord Ravana had – she knew that there was nothing she could do now. Revenge wouldn't bring him back. It was too late. And there was nothing worse than too late.

She asked, 'Tarak come with you?' The entire evening, she had scanned the crowd for Tarak. Still suspended was the notion that he'd return. Every time her eyes caught the iron slagheap in the yard, she looked out for the twirl of White Lady's tail.

'Maybe we should expect a postcard,' was all the twin said.

Lata felt like Tarak had abandoned her. Beneath that feeling, however, was an odd admiration for the boy. A hint of jealousy as well. And she wondered how she would fare in the big, hungry world out there if she were to one day decide to leave the barrack. Her head began to throb.

The boy asked, 'Krishna say anything bout where he was goin? Where this coulda happen?'

Lata thought about it. 'He say was goin to look for Tarak.'

'He aint say where?'

A few more tears escaped, despite how hard she was fighting them. 'I shoulda stop him. I shoulda hold him down and stop him.'

The twins nodded. 'He was unstoppable.'

Lata let out a laugh between the tears. 'He was, yes. They say he was like his pa.'

A pause. Then one of the twins asked, 'Where is he?'

'Who?'

'Krishna's father. He aint here.'

'He aint been round.'

A longer pause. 'He know what happen?'

Lata shrugged. 'Krishna's ma went to the house earlier and say he and Mrs Changoor could care less about Krishna. But that was before ...'

Before she could finish her sentence, they had walked off. Vanished. She wondered if she had been hallucinating and for a moment wished that she had been. That the entire week was some scrambled fever dream. The dread had not been fully realised – she knew this. It hung onto her chest like some parasite burrowing its way into her. The hole would become bigger and bigger, swallowing everything in her.

Sachin ran up to Lata, pointing at a blur in the field. 'That's him, I tell you! Krishna come back to life. You see that! That's Krishna! That's Krishna!'

Lata patted his shoulders. 'Sachin, calm down.'

'Krishna turn into a white horse! Ridin through the dark there. It growin, it bigger now!'

She turned to look. It wasn't growing, whatever it was – it was coming closer. Probably a mule that got loose from the canefields.

'Have somethin else out there.' He peered out, eyes widening. 'A light! A jumbie spirit, it is! The horse breathe out that bright light!'

As the light drew closer, the man who was carrying it came into view. As if the darkness chipped and flaked away around him. She couldn't yet see his face but knew his urgency from his determined gait. His tawny hamburg hat seemed to float in mid-air. Wore a navy-blue flannel button-up too big for him, pants high and secured by a leather belt that glimmered under the moon. At first, Lata thought he was one of the sardars at the canefield but quickly placed his face when it came into view – it was Hansraj Saroop. She cautioned herself against saying anything and hoped that he hadn't noticed her.

Sachin hurried towards the crowd in a staggering trot, towards his mother, shouting, 'Mr Hans come! Mr Hans come!'

Hans clicked off the torchlight in his hand and stuffed it into his oversized trouser pocket. Took off his hat, held it against his chest. His face wet and gaunt, eyes growing bigger and bigger. As soon as he saw Lata, he burst into tears. Could barely walk now. Lata had never seen the man like that. He hugged her, squeezing until she felt strangled.

He shuffled through the crowd and towards the box in the barrack yard. Sweat still dripping from his brow, thatched with beads of it. His gaze shifted from his wife curled on the cold ground to his son in the box to the darkness that blanketed the landscape. Then back to the horde of people around him, a hundred mutterings at once like moths in his hair.

That's the father?
This man look like he come outta hellfire.
Where he was this whole time?

Hans couldn't bring himself to look at the box again and so the image of his long-dead daughter in transcendence stayed with him, a broken doll cast out of a workshop.

'He dead, Mr Hans!' Sachin said, getting close to the body. Put his head in the box like an animal sniffing bait. 'Krishna dead! He dead and gone!'

Hans turned his gaze to his wife on the ground. Her gnarled toes and blank stare. Then to Rookmin.

'You finally wake up, Hans,' Rookmin said.

Murali sat sombre on a pail. He put his head down, the frizz of his beard glistening with sweat. Hans was too shaken to speak. He lay on the ground, curled up in the same position as his wife and let out a long loud groan. At the back of the crowd, he swore he spotted Robinson, hands in his pockets, his head above the others. When he blinked, he was gone.

A momentary silence fell upon the yard.

The twins came closer, burning this image of Hans's anguish into their minds. They'd never before seen such grief from a man, almost theatrical, and wondered if it was indeed a performance. It was like someone had stabbed the man in his gut. Perhaps this was the sound of pent-up regret. The wailing of what could have been. But something about his behaviour seemed off, rehearsed.

Rookmin approached him, prodded his shoulder with her foot. 'Get your ass together,' she said. 'The boy dead. Shweta tell we you couldn't even care to come off your bed to look for him when he was missin. Show some decency and strength for him now. You owe the boy that, at least.'

The statement raised more than a few eyebrows. Even the men at the rummy table had stopped their game to observe. Rustam and Rudra looked at each other. They didn't say anything, but each knew what the other was thinking; they cracked their knuckles and wandered to a distant corner of the crowd.

'Is the white horse! The white horse!' Sachin cried out.

The crowd turned to the field, where a horse stood, still as a toy. In the shadow, its coat looked as grey as a wasp's nest. A pale diamond on its forehead. Sitting atop was Marlee Changoor in a billowing white nightgown, burrs caught along the hem, seraphic, almost druidical. She didn't look like herself in the night. A shaded duplication of herself – of the image she hewed from bright colours and expensive foundation. The crowd fell into a steepened silence – only the uncushioned sounds of insects and wind churning.

Shweta raised her head to the woman, strands of hair pendulous over her worn eyes.

Marlee descended from the horse, walked towards Hans, her body gliding with magnificent grace. The smallest babble of voices was emerging, but the woman's stare cut it right back down to deep silence. Her eyes were a broadsword slashing the throats of degenerates.

She came up to the box, gave a side glance to the boy inside. Turned to the crowd, 'A carriage is on its way for the body. The body will be taken to the church and will be buried in the yard there. Please clear the way when it arrives.'

The statement caused the sea of faces to warp with confusion but not a word, not even a drunken one, was said. The crowd stood before her stiff-legged and quiet like scolded children. Shweta started quivering. Clenching and unclenching her fist slowly – the idea flickering in and out of her head. Lips parched. Her body on the verge of inverting itself. She held her fist in readiness. The world closed in as Shweta muttered to the woman, 'You have no place here.'

'I've come to support Hans,' Marlee said, her lips trembling, well aware of the truth to Shweta's statement. 'I'm sorry for—'

'Stay out of this. He aint your child.'

Marlee, hanging her head, told her, 'Hans and I talked about it. It's only right for Krishna to have something civilised.'

'This morning, you aint want nothin to do with him. You aint make sense, woman.'

Marlee blinked several times, as if she had pebbles in her eyes. Her pale knuckles twitched a little; she tried to still them, but she couldn't hold on for long. Her body was giving way. 'I'm sorry,' she said, her eyes downcast. 'Hans doesn't want what his daughter got. He doesn't want to burn another body down by the river.'

Shweta got up from the ground, her body rocking like a strong wind could knock her over. Blood boiled and foamed. She turned to Hans, still curled up and sobbing. Felt like she could throw herself down dead on top of him.

'You... You...' The words emerged in breaths. 'You... You tell this woman about our...'

A gentle hand came on her shoulder. Hans's breathing now like snorts, like the sound a night animal would make as it feeds on something unknown in the blackness of a jungle.

'Hema?' Marlee said, a bit mystified. 'Yes, he—'

Shweta swung at Marlee, her entire body thrusting forth with the punch.

The crowd shifted back like an eldritch mass as Marlee went down. She fell backwards against the casket, her head hitting the scar of the wood. Krishna's body sat stable.

The casket's waterlogged base, however, tore right open.

A gush of cold water rushed over her head and down her collar. She discharged a scream. The wind carried the scream to the sky and there it met God. She shrunk, now dwarf-like beneath Shweta. Both women panting loud as if they held tempests inside them. Hans got to his feet, looked down at Marlee.

She reached out her palm for Hans to help her up. He wiped his face, shook his head, slowly stepping back from the commotion.

'Hans, help me up,' she said, a hint of disbelief emerging.

He put his hands on his head, held his temples so tightly that he dug his nails into them.

'Help me!' A large bead of blood between her teeth.

He walked towards the field, disappearing into the darkness.

Marlee rose to her feet, the front of her nightgown soaked and stained with dirt and deadwater. She stood there, in that lingering moment, half hoping that she was in a dream. Kept her head down to the growing puddle at her feet, her hair still dripping, jaw slightly juddering, too afraid to meet the expressions before her. The carbuncled crowd of winced eyes and gritted teeth, slowly imprinting in their minds this ruined image of her. And the slow realisation that Marlee Changoor was now a cursed woman – or perhaps she always was.

A single titter came from the yard. Marlee muttered to the crowd, voice filling with rage, 'Don't laugh at me. You have no *right* to laugh at me.' As the tittering went on, she hissed, 'I can have your house bulldozed by morning – don't you dare laugh at me!'

The titter blew up into a fit of laughter. Only then had she realised it was coming from a man in the crowd. Sachin pointed to Marlee and exclaimed, 'She get the deadwater on she! Deadwater!' He began to jump up and down, still hollering, 'She get the deadwater! DEADWATER LADY! DEADWATER LADY!'

Shweta upturned her eyes to the stars and laughed like she had never laughed. Laughed until she coughed and spat gobs of mucus on the floor. The others slowly joined in on the laughter. Some children and drunkards ringing in with Sachin, *DEADWATER LADY! DEADWATER LADY!*

Lata shouted it as well.

Old ladies got on their knees and prayed.

Shweta was on the ground now, rolling with laughter.

Hans was gone. So was the horse.

Marlee ran into the barrack, the stench of death and vomit immediately hitting her.

She called out to Hans but there was no answer. Searched each room for him. No sign.

The sole occupant was the young mother breastfeeding her child. The laughing incessant, conflagrant in the background like a fire cracking the overstory of the world. An inferno that would engulf all of the long night. She burst out of the barrack and ran into the night. Quickly lost herself in the dark. Standing in the middle of the moonlit pasture, the sounds of crickets and owls and spirits could not drown the laughter from her mind.

The clouds swallowed the moon. She kept going forward, calling out to Hans, the only reply was the laughter that always seemed to be one step behind. As if darkness itself could follow in her footsteps, as if darkness itself could laugh. Sat on the grass, whistled for her horse. It would come trotting any time now, she thought. And when it did, it was the only thing she could see. The animal nuzzled her hair, the rheum in its eyes like it had been crying. When she hopped on, she couldn't tell which direction was which in the moonless darkness. But the horse trotted anyway. It knew its way home, she believed. And so did Hans.

32
An Admission

Hans woke up, screaming. It was still night. Darkness all around. He could hear the sound of running water nearby. Could feel the clayey loam at his heels. The thick memory of condensed milk on his tongue mixed with the aftertaste of something noxious and irreligious. A vaporous mist hung over the moon, seemed to form gossamers all the way down to the earth. He didn't realise he was shackled until he tried to get to his feet. Hit his chin on the dirt. Remained quiet. Didn't call for help. He could see the mountains way in the distance, moving in the same way a boa's length would. Peristaltic. He couldn't see her at this moment, but he knew Marlee was looking for him. Her white horse riding luminously across his mind.

The twins appeared before him in an instant. As if they had been spirited there. Sitting cross-legged before him, their eyes dark and narrow as buttonholes. The river behind them. The matrix of starlight above, blurred and radial in his drowsiness. Hans knew who they were, though they were only shadows to him, their features eaten by the night. One held a cutlass while the other had a gutting knife. They asked Hans about his dream, what could've awakened him with such a fright. Hans was silent at first – knowing that it was hardly a dream. But he had never before spoken of it. Not to Shweta, and not to Marlee.

He'd been young. Couldn't remember the exact age right now. Hans remained in quiet deliberation for a moment, shuffling again in the dirt. As he spoke, he recalled when his mother woke him and his brother to catch crabs at the river, relinquished her grip on his little fingers. He couldn't describe the look in his mother's face then. Was a forlorn blend of fear and confusion and doomlike sadness. That strange moment of denial upon learning of a close death, the realisation that nothing will ever again be as it was. That the whole world had shifted gear. Then for a moment, she disappeared. He believed that for that moment that she had left. Left him and his brother behind. But she changed her mind.

She returned, took their hands, and told them that they should head back to the barrack before their father woke up and found them gone. When they got there, the man was asleep on his belly. What would have happened if his mother had continued running? If she had taken him and his brother away to the other side of the island. But instead, she stayed. Then killed herself.

How different life could have turned out.

The twins asked him if it made sense pondering that kind of thing now. Hans thought about it for a moment. Said he wasn't sure. Said he wished he could fix everything, wished he could bring his son back.

At that moment he glanced over at the mountain. It was moving again. He saw a fire moving through it; Marlee, searching for him. The twins pressed on. Asked him which life he preferred. To Hans, it had all seemed like another life, another world. Life was simpler before he slept on a good bed. Before he could eat until he was full. Before he could finish inside of a beautiful, civilised woman. An obscene guilt so deep in him now that it caused physical revulsion. His voice became softer and softer the more he spoke, realising the twins' blades were drifting closer and closer to his neck.

Having a cutlass drawn meant something. The blade not just a weapon but an extension of the raging soul. Swallowing hard, nervous of the nature of the answer, he asked them what the knives were for. One's answer was to scrape the metal against his temple; the other claimed that there would be no use for them if he told them what happened to Krishna. A rush of goosepimples ran down his arms. The world, the wind now as understated as a cat's purr.

His voice cracking, he asked them if they were going to kill him. They told him that the truth would save him – that they believed he knew what happened to Krishna. He paused for a long time, deliberating. Perhaps hoping for rescue. But the twins were keen on the sound of footfalls in the night. There was nobody coming for him. There was no further need for bloodshed, so he closed his eyes, pleaded with the boys, addressed them as the sons of Bhagran Lakhan. Told them that they were born into bloodshed – and that if blood were to be shed now, let it be his. He said that last part with his lips quivering and teeth chattering.

He kept a firm eye on the sky, holding himself steady. He spoke slowly now. Started with the shadows on the farm that manifested after Dalton Changoor's pickup was found. The trees that those shadows uprooted and made off with. Like a slow dark tide making its way towards the house. And it was only a matter of time before the waves came crashing through the window. He paused again, breathing hard.

Said he came out the front door and fired the shot without thinking, without looking.

That it was an accident. That he did not mean to kill his own son.

Accident. The twins recalled Dalton Changoor coming for them, the bullet lodging into his own head. An accident. A mishap. Misfortune. A bullet misflown. A misfire. They had no word for this – but they knew it wasn't that. An accident could only be blamed on God.

Hans felt the blade press against his neck, breaking the skin. All sound was absent at that point. Rasped right out of the atmosphere. The wind died. Though, from time to time, it gave the illusion that it was there – like a cowering child peeping its head through a door before going into hiding once more. That was what it felt like – as though everything was in hiding. The toads and the crickets, the grass sat as still as stones.

Marlee had come out to see, Hans explained. She told him the boy was still alive. Put him on the horse and intended to take him to the hospital. And that he died along the way. He shut his eyes tight, shaking now, barely able to contain himself. Had to bundle the words a few times before he could say the last part: that she took his body to the river and dumped it there, no, left it there, no, *laid* it there.

But if he was alive when she left, the twins were curious to know – *why didn't you go with her?*

Hans couldn't say. They gave him two minutes, but through his erratic breathing, the words never came. They knew he was lying. Gave him another chance to tell the truth. That it was Marlee with the gun. And Hans on the horse on the way to the hospital.

After a long minute, Hans said that Marlee was a beautiful, innocent soul.

They told him to close his eyes, talk to God. Because only God could forgive him now.

Hans grovelled, mumbling a prayer until he went quiet. The mushrooms had now fully worked their way into his system. They loosened his bindings and stood over his slumbering body, looking at each other.

And so, the question came: what were they to do with Hans?

And though neither spoke a word, the answer came to both at once. Simultaneously, they sheathed their blades. It would not be right to kill in Krishna's name. Not for their friend, one of the only people in this world who believed their blood wasn't laced with venom. No, he did not deserve to have his memory sullied like that.

Killing Hans would only make people feel sorry for him.

Let that bastard finish himself off instead.

33
A Reflection

Hans sat in the darkness. The crackle of leaves electrified the air, pushing against sugarcane zephyrs in waves of soft sizzles. It wasn't morning yet, but the night was coming to a close, a tarpaulin being pulled away from the land. He held the hope that he had been released from the nightmare, but when he cast his eyes on his undone bindings, he knew that the terrible fate had been real. A blunt pain radiated from his shoulders up to his eyes. The knife wound on his neck still stung to the touch. His legs rigid as old rocks. Still, he tried to stand, stiff in the early wind. The dawnlight appeared as a single painted fingernail hoisting itself over the mountain range, glowing hot and focused as a soldering iron. The few shadowless clouds like cowlicks in the sky.

He walked in circles at first. Headed east and then west. Down one road and back up again. The sound of the kiskadees rising. Even with the land springing to life now, he couldn't enjoy any of it. He thought about the agoutis, the picoplats, the water nymphs. Dalton Changoor's German shepherd hanging from its leash, drowned in the rising river. This land was their home. And all creatures came from the land and returned to the land.

He started on his way to the No. 11 bridge. Walked along the trainline, putting his feet from sleeper to sleeper. Past the mangrove coppice and the battered banks that lay mottled with camouflaged caimans. Continued to the section of river that he had considered sacrosanct for so many years. Stood in the middle of the bamboo arch and looked at the water. A palisade of sycamores printed coins of shadow on the water's crest. Sat down on the bank, his body halfway tilted towards his reflection. The ditch frogs popped up in observation.

He imagined how it would be to become part of the river. He would take off his shirt, enter the cool water. It is in every living thing to want to survive. Even if the mind becomes wretched with visions of death, the body always tries to pull itself out. Pull itself to the crest and breathe. He imagined how the water would become colder as the last seconds went by. And how a man once regarded to be moulded in the image of the war god Subrahmanya would look when the river carried him away. Dismantled and discarded by all the lives he wanted to live, tried to live. Nowhere left to go now but down, down, downstream.

34
An Offertory

Picture that weird and wonderful transition from night to day. Simultaneously slow and sudden. The Orphic moment where the early morning resembles dusk. The way dew-dropped spiderwebs hang undisturbed under the shade of snapdragon pods. The little trenches of compressed grass the red-rumped agoutis leave behind as they scurry. Froghoppers leaping off tiny platforms of olera. Greenflies on thyme. Stray dogs trotting up the empty highway. A sprauchling of kingfishers washing themselves downriver. Crabs bundled in traps. The wisdom of the earth held in marl and argillite. Each bird to its bough. Each fungus to its bark. Each bison to its turf. Things sprouting and things decomposing. The natural order of things, all things in position, trying their best to sort out their place in the world as the sun creeps slowly westward. Some parts of the land still curtained in night.

In the barrack yard, the remnants of babble and bustle had quickly faded with the morning breeze. The odd playing card scattered on the ground. Two jacks, an ace, a joker. The smell of burnt coffee and spilled alcohol. The pinebox at the centre no longer holding the dead boy. Inside the barrack, five rooms. In one of them, two mothers quietly slumbering. Shweta with young Niala's son nestled in her bosom, as if maternity could be leased – as if love could be borrowed, returned and borrowed again. In the neighbouring room was the girl, Lata, who agreed to stand watch in that quiet hour when the dead boy was carried off, knowing it was what he would have wanted. To the west, where the dawnlight was yet to arrive, among some toppled bamboo poles and muddied jhandi flags was a pile of fronds and branches set ablaze. Within that fire was the bones and the ashes of the boy. An offertory of black smoke billowing up to God.

Past the opposite bank, quietly sitting atop a knoll, were the twins. Rustam and Rudra. Rudra and Rustam. Overlooking the burning body, eyes bloodshot from lack of sleep. The peaceful day ahead of them. They scooted closer to each other, with nothing but each other's company, watching the fire but focusing on all that lay beyond. A thought occurred to move east until the roads curled behind the Northern Range. Somewhere remote, behind God's back, where they couldn't be bothered. Where sins were easily forgiven. Where the past could be prologue. They weren't sure yet if such a place existed. But reckoned when they found it, it would be waiting for them. When they got there, they would know.

Acknowledgements

My gratitude goes to the following people: the late, great Angelo Bissessarsingh; my late grandfather, Jagroop Sookhoo; my parents, Ashraff and Merle; my wife and kindred spirit, Portia; my in-laws, David and Brenda; the elders of La Paille Village, 'Brother Tate' and Indal Singh; and to all others I consulted (and eavesdropped on) over the years; for giving me the foundation and materials to build and layer the sociocultural landscape and ecology of this novel. To Zanifa Mohammed and Renelle Wilson, for doing more than I asked when I needed feedback. To my agent, Chris Wellbelove, and his assistant, Monica MacSwan, who both understood this story and these characters to their very core; and to my editors, Alexis Kirschbaum and Gabriella Doob, and their respective teams at Bloomsbury and Ecco – the final product would not be what it is without their passion and dedication.